Dear Reader,

One of the things ~~please~~ keep them ~~coming~~ from you all!) is how much you enjoy the variety of *Scarlet* characters and storylines. That's why choosing the month's books is always such an exciting challenge for me. Will readers prefer the ups and downs of married life to a story about a single woman finding happiness? What about books featuring children?

This month all of these themes appear. The heroines of Clare Benedict's *A Bitter Inheritance* and Margaret Callaghan's *Wilde Affair* are both, in their very different ways, prepared to make sacrifices for the sake of a child's happiness. *The Second Wife*, by Angela Arney, highlights the problems involved when two single parents fall in love and decide to combine family forces. In *Harte's Gold*, by Jane Toombs, the no-nonsense single heroine faces a different sort of family problem: how to protect her susceptible grandmother from being conned when a film company rents their ranch and she has her doubts about the attractive leading man.

Whatever your taste in romantic reading I hope that you enjoy this month's *Scarlet* selections.

Till next month,

Sally Cooper

**SALLY COOPER,
Editor-in-Chief – *Scarlet***

About the Author

Angela Arney has been a published romance author since 1984. She's had a varied career, which has included working as a verbatim shorthand writer, cabaret singer, a teacher, hospital administrator, caterer and finally a full-time writer.

Angela is interested in the theatre – she writes for and directs local amateur companies. And she and her husband love travelling – time allowing. Last year she went to France, Greece, the Czech Republic and New England, USA.

Her other main interest is the farmhouse in Brittany which she and her husband have almost finished restoring. As the author says, 'We love France, the French language and French food.'

ANGELA ARNEY

THE SECOND WIFE

Enquiries to:
Robinson Publishing Ltd
7 Kensington Church Court
London W8 4SP

First published in the UK by Scarlet, 1997

A copy of the British Library Cataloguing in
Publication data is available from the British Library

ISBN 1-85487-998-7

Printed and bound in the EC

10 9 8 7 6 5 4 3 2 1

CHAPTER 1

I ought to be happy. Ecstatic! All the things a woman is supposed to be when the man she loves has just asked her to marry him and she's said yes.

Somewhere lurking at the back of her mind, but, alas, just out of reach, Felicity was sure that was how she really *did* feel. But if only it were at the front of my mind, then I'd *know*, she thought moodily. Instead I have this gloomy apprehension looming over me, blotting out all the euphoria. Oh, families! she thought crossly, at the same time feeling an illogical surge of love. That was the trouble really: in families, emotions were always in a permanent state of flux. At least, in her family it seemed to be.

A vision of her mother and her daughter flitted through her mind. She knew she ought to have told them long ago, months, in fact, that she and Tony were seriously considering marriage. But as usual, along with all the other things she didn't like doing, she'd put it off, and now the day had arrived when it could be delayed no longer. They would have to be told, both of them. She was going to marry again.

Realizing guiltily that she was being paid for her worrying daydream, Felicity fiddled with the frayed edges of a dog-eared manuscript and tried to concentrate and read. But her thoughts insisted on trudging dolefully from one thing to another, round and round in a circle so that she ended up where she'd started, only more depressed and confused than before she'd started. There was no point in thinking about it, she told herself firmly. It was time to *do* something.

'Not working late tonight, surely?' Oliver Dickens popped his head through the half-open door of her office. He was her boss and the managing director of Dickens Books, and Felicity was very fond of him.

'Just for a while.'

Oliver came in and perched on the edge of her desk, pushing the manuscript out of the way in the process. He looked at her fondly; Felicity was the daughter he'd never had. She was of medium height, plump in a feminine way – he liked that in a woman – had short, dark, wavy hair and enormous cornflower-blue eyes. All in all a very attractive young woman. He was glad she was getting married again at last; she deserved some happiness with a good man. 'Where's the happy girl we all popped champagne corks with at lunchtime?' he asked. 'Not having second thoughts about remarriage, are you?'

'Of course not.' That was the truth. It wasn't marrying Tony that bothered her, it was the knock-on effect it would have on everyone else that perturbed her.

Oliver leaned across the desk. 'Go home,' he said

firmly, 'and tell your mother and daughter the good news. They'll leap about with joy. I'd place a bet on it. Be over the moon.'

Felicity slowly put her pens into a desk drawer. 'There will probably be a bit of leaping about,' she said, 'but I have my doubts that it will be with joy.'

Oliver's round face creased into a reassuring smile. 'Stop worrying,' he ordered. 'So? They've got used to having you to themselves all these years. But given time they'll get used to sharing you as well. So off you go. And for goodness' sake remember to tell that daughter of yours first. She's likely to be more difficult than your mother.'

Felicity rubbed her eyes wearily and Oliver became a blur. 'Why Annabel particularly?' she asked, yawning. She took the manuscript and added it to the pile above the radiator. No point in reading it now; she'd never give the author the attention he deserved.

Oliver nodded approvingly at the pile of typescript. 'Sensible girl,' he said.

'You were going to tell me why you thought Annabel might be difficult,' reminded Felicity.

'Because she's a teenager and they usually are. My two daughters were *always* difficult, usually about nothing. Thank heavens they've both grown up now.' He bent down, rummaging about on the floor, wheezing a little as he did so.

Felicity watched him and worried. 'You ought to lose weight, Oliver,' she said. 'Take care of your heart. Isn't that what the doctor said?'

'Yes, yes, I know. And I *will* diet. Next week.'

Felicity grinned at Oliver's familiar reply, although Oliver didn't notice; he was still too busy rummaging. 'And you've got to look after yourself as well,' he puffed. 'Find the courage to go home and tell your mother and daughter *now* that you have plans for your own future for once. And when you play your trump card – the fact that you'll be living in the country – even Annabel will be won over. Anyone with any sense wants to move out of London.' He stood up. 'Here, take this with you. A bottle of champagne. That should help oil the proceedings.'

'Oh, Oliver! You shouldn't have.'

'Why is it people always say that?' demanded Oliver. 'When they should be saying, wonderful, thank you!'

'Wonderful, thank you!' Felicity leaned across the desk and planted a kiss on his leathery cheek. A thought flickered briefly: I wonder if Tony's cheek will feel like this when he's old. It was a nice idea knowing that she'd be there to find out. Then she said, 'I said you shouldn't, because you shouldn't. But I am grateful, truly I am.' Oliver beamed and backed out of the door.

Felicity's spirits suddenly lifted. What was she worrying about? This was the 1990s. Other women changed their husbands more often than she changed her hat (she only had one, which she hated) and this would only be the second husband in the whole of her so far fairly uneventful life. It would be all right. Of course it would. After all, she was only thirty-five; she had a right to a life of her own. Neither her mother nor her daughter could expect her to remain a widow for ever.

* * *

4

But it seemed Annabel did expect just that. And what was more, she left Felicity in no doubt about it.

'I don't *want* a new father.' Annabel's voice was high pitched and squeaky with rage. 'I like my dead one. He's no trouble. He never interferes.'

Now is the time, murmured her subconscious, and Felicity plunged on, playing what Oliver had said would be her trump card. 'But darling, just think. We shall be living in the country.'

Annabel's expression spoke volumes. Unfortunately the wrong volumes. She appeared to view living in the country as a fate worse than death. 'I don't want to live there,' she said sulkily. 'It's full of grass and trees, and insects which bite. And even worse, there are no decent shops.'

'Of course there are more trees than London, and even more where we shall be living because it's in the New Forest,' Felicity said, carefully choosing the least contentious of her daughter's statements. 'But there are towns nearby, and the shops there are just as good as London.' Blanching before Annabel's unremittingly frosty glower, she added hastily, 'Well, nearly as good.' She supplemented another sweetener. 'And you'll have your own bedroom, which you can decorate exactly as you like. Tony has said so.'

Nothing, however, was going to placate Annabel. 'I'm not going to the country,' she said stubbornly, adding, 'and anyway you're only marrying him because of *sex*! I think you're disgusting.'

'But sex is . . .' Felicity had been about to say that it was a beautiful thing between two people who loved

5

each other, but Annabel had conflicting and very positive views.

'We've just done sex at school *in detail* so I know everything about it,' she said with all the authority of a precocious thirteen-year-old. 'We had to watch a video and I can tell you, it was absolutely revolting. Naked bodies rolling about. It's bad enough watching two young people do it, but you are both so *old*! I can just imagine Tony with no clothes on. Ugh! Ugh! Ugh!'

Felicity stared at her daughter aghast. She had just assumed, wrongly it now seemed, that because she seemed so grown-up, Annabel had known all about sex for ages. In all the magazines she left lying around, articles on sex were the most numerous. How could Annabel have got her facts so wrong? And what kind of video was it she'd seen at school? She made a mental note to speak to her daughter's class teacher at the next parents' evening. But for now she had to manage Annabel's hostility. 'Married people do it all the time,' she said briskly, reasoning that a matter-of-fact tone was best.

'Ugh!'

Felicity ploughed on, determined not to be intimidated by Annabel's antagonism and ignorance. 'Married people have sex – I mean, make love. And it's the love part that's important; the sex is a by-product.' She felt quite pleased with herself. An inspirational couple of sentences of explanation. She exhaled a sigh of relief. That should do the trick. But as soon as Annabel spoke she knew she hadn't succeeded, and reflected that just

6

lately her daughter had perfected the knack of making her feel a very inadequate mother.

'I shall *never* get married, or have sex.' Annabel slumped down in her chair, a heap of seething resentment.

'Well, I *am* getting married,' said Felicity. 'And I am not asking your permission. And you, young lady, are coming to live with me and Tony in Oakford, and that is that.' Bludgeoning Annabel into submission was not the best form of psychology, but by now Felicity was despairing of the gentle touch.

'Then I shall take Tigger with me.'

'You can't. You know that cat belongs to Gran. But you can have a kitten later on, when we've settled.' Annabel opened her mouth, no doubt to object, but Felicity got in first. 'Now, go on up to your room and do your homework, Annabel. I *am* getting married, just get that into your head, and this is the end of the conversation.'

'All right.' Annabel literally hurled herself out of the room. 'But just don't ask *me* to be bridesmaid!'

Tigger sauntered past the hurtling Annabel. Rumbling like a motorbike at full throttle, he wound himself around Felicity's legs. She bent down to pull at one of his tattered ears. Tigger had been a fighter all his life, although lately he'd become more mellow, sensing that the new, younger neighbourhood cats could probably beat him at his game. 'Oh, Tigger,' she cried, 'why does life have to be so complicated.'

But, as life wasn't in the slightest bit complicated for him, Tigger rumbled on happily, while Felicity took a deep breath and prepared to tell her mother. At least, she consoled herself, she can't be as bad as Annabel.

'Well, my dear, I do hope that you are going to buy a new bed, *and* have the bedroom completely redecorated.'

Has life played a nasty trick on just me, or do all mothers and daughters misunderstand each other? Felicity wondered. After thirty-five years as a daughter she was no nearer to understanding her mother now than the day she'd been born.

'Mum,' she said trying to keep the impatience from her voice, 'here I am telling you that I am going to get married – something, I might remind you, that you've been nagging on about for years – and all you can do is ask if we're going to get a new bed.'

Her mother's train of thought was not to be deflected. 'Well, are you?' she demanded.

Felicity began to feel increasingly irritable. Oliver's champagne was still chilling in the fridge. Fat lot of good there would be in opening that; nothing would oil the wheels in this house. 'I haven't discussed such a thing with Tony,' she said. Then added, 'And to tell you the truth I haven't even thought about it.'

Irene Hobbit took a genteel sip from her schooner of sherry, pushed several wisps of straying grey hair back into the bun at the nape of her neck, and smiled sweetly at her daughter. 'It's the first thing *I'd* have thought about,' she said.

Felicity took a deep breath, gritted her teeth, counted to ten, then went across to the sideboard and poured herself a large glass of red wine. 'Why can't you be like anyone else, and just say congratulations?' she asked. 'Don't you want me to be happy?'

'Of course I do, darling. Don't drink too much wine, you'll pickle your liver.' Felicity opened her mouth, about to say that judging by the daily amount of sherry her mother consumed, *her* liver must be well and truly pickled by now. But she closed it again as her mother carried on talking without pausing for breath. 'That's why I'm pointing out all these snags to you.'

Felicity found difficulty in following her mother's train of thought. 'A bed isn't a snag.'

Her mother ignored her and, waving her sherry glass theatrically, brought it to a halt just in front of her left breast. Felicity thought, not for the first time, that her mother was wasted. She had the ability to make a drama out of the most mundane happening. She should have been on the stage. 'I know what it's like being a widow,' intoned Irene in a voice which would have reached the back stalls of any theatre. She paused, sighed deeply, then added in sepulchral tones. 'Believe me, I know.'

'Yes, but . . .'

'One gets lonely. Terribly lonely in an empty bed. But that's no reason to go rushing into marriage without thinking about it very, very carefully.'

She had to pause for breath and Felicity took the opportunity to put her point of view. 'Mother! I'm thirty-five years old. I've been a widow for nine years. I've now met someone I want to marry. After nine years you can hardly call that rushing.'

'Ah! But you've only known Tony for four months. I

9

don't trust men. He probably wants someone to wash his pants and socks.'

'He has a machine for that! And, for your information, the last four months have been the best months of my life. We're not teenagers. At our age four months is quite long enough. What do you expect us to do? Wait until we're drawing our pensions before we get married?' In spite of her good resolution, Felicity forgot to count to ten and began to lose her temper again, this time with her mother.

'No need to raise your voice, darling,' her mother replied smoothly. 'I'm only trying to help. Trying to clear your mind.'

'Going off at a tangent about beds does not help clear my mind,' Felicity said, infuriated by her mother's serene expression. Of all the traits her mother possessed, switching on to her 'I'm a very reasonable, long-suffering woman' was the worst. 'We've lived together too long, you and I,' she snapped, tossing back her wine and refilling the glass.

Irene Hobbit raised her eyebrows, squinting ominously at the wine bottle in Felicity's hand, her half-moon glasses sparkling in the subdued light of a nearby table-lamp giving her a professorial appearance. 'Why do you always say that whenever we're having a serious mother-and-daughter talk?'

'Because it's true,' Felicity said. 'I should have taken Annabel and moved out years ago.'

'Where to?' enquired her mother mildly.

'Anywhere.'

'You've never earned enough money. All you've ever

had is that rotten job as a commissioning editor for Dickens. You've never been well paid, and always spent your time struggling to surface through a pile of scruffy manuscripts.'

It was true, she never had earned enough money to live in the manner she enjoyed. If she had stayed on her own, she could never have afforded to live in Primrose Hill. Not for the first time Felicity cursed herself for setting her own trap and then promptly falling straight into it. But despite of her mother's poor opinion of it, and the equally poor salary, she loved the work. And although it was a vain hope that her mother would ever understand, she still tried to explain. 'As I've told you before, it's all I've ever wanted to do. And I am grateful to you for letting me and Annabel live here all these years, but . . .'

But her mother, now in full flood, was on to one of her favourite topics. 'Why on earth you've never moved to another, bigger publishing house I'll never know.'

'I like Oliver Dickens. He's one of the few publishers left with any scruples.'

'Exactly! Which is why Dickens Books don't make much of a profit. He'll go under soon, you mark my words.'

That was another great difference between them. Irene Hobbit looked like a sweet, gentle, grey-haired sixty-five-year-old. But those who did business with her knew that she was sharp and shrewd, and as hard as steel. She could sniff out a bargain, buy it, sell it, and bank the profit while others were still thinking about it. Her trade was bric-à-brac, *Hobbit's – Fair Prices Given*

11

and Fair Prices Charged, and she ran more than a dozen stalls throughout London's street markets. Three in Camden Lock, near to the tiny Primrose Hill mews house she shared with Felicity and Annabel. 'Of course –' Irene paused, took another sip of sherry, which emptied the glass, and sighed heavily '– you've never had a head for business. Take after your father. Maybe Annabel will be better. She could take on Hobbit's when she's older. Never be short of a penny or two if she does that.'

'I don't want her to be a street trader.'

Irene jerked her head back sharply. 'There's nothing wrong with honest trade. You've not done too badly out of it. But of course, now that you are marrying a doctor . . .'

That was tactless. 'Mum, I don't mean there's anything wrong with it. But I hope that Annabel will go to university and then, well, after that, we'll just have to see.'

'She still might decide to become a street trader, as you call me!'

'She might. She can make up her own mind later.'

'Very gracious of you,' Irene sniffed.

'However,' Felicity rushed on, determined to get the message home once and for all, 'in the immediate future she'll be living with me in the country.'

'What about her ballet? She's doing so well with the grades at Miss Leonora's Academy.'

'There will be ballet classes at Oakford.'

'It's a village,' her mother said dismissively. 'You said so yourself.'

'Well, if not in Oakford then definitely at Westhamp-

12

ton. That's only ten miles away and is an enormous town.'

'It might be big, but it's in Hampshire, and that's still the country. Annabel will hate it.' Irene Hobbit thought anything beyond outer London was suspect. She'd been evacuated to a farm in Sussex during the war, and stayed, very reluctantly, for a week. That week had been enough to convince her for life that the country was a nasty, unhygienic place full of wild animals and very peculiar people.

'She'll love it down in Hampshire,' said Felicity, firmly squashing all her own doubts. 'And anyway, once we're there she'll probably go right off ballet and become horse-mad. There's a pony at Cherry Trees called Cotton-Socks, and a large dog, a Labrador I think, called Prudence.'

'You're afraid of dogs. Always have been,' scoffed her mother.

'I am *not*,' said Felicity, the accusation rankling because it was the truth. 'You put me off them, so I'm just not used to them.' She tried to steer the conversation back on track. 'Anyway, I've already told Annabel that I'm marrying Tony, and . . .'

'What did she say?'

Felicity had no intention of repeating the painful scene she'd recently had with Annabel.

'Well?' her mother repeated. 'What did she say?'

'She wanted to take Tigger with her.'

'Over my dead body!'

Felicity couldn't help smiling at her mother's vehemence. The battle-scarred old tom-cat was the apple of her eye. 'Of course I told her she couldn't because he belongs to you.'

'She can visit him.'

'I've told her she can have a kitten to go with the dog.'

'They'll fight,' said Irene pessimistically.

Felicity was determined to remain positive. 'And I told her that she can decorate her own bedroom just as she wishes. That was Tony's idea. He said it would help her to bond with the place.'

Irene set her empty glass down with a bang. 'Huh! She can bond, but *you* have to make do with what his ex-wife chose!'

They were back to square one. Felicity lost her temper. '*You* are just being bloody-minded, Mum. Sometimes I get the feeling that you want me tied to your apron strings for the rest of my life.'

There was a long, uncomfortable silence while Felicity regretted her impetuosity and Irene fiddled with the stem of the empty sherry glass. Neither looked at each other.

Then Irene suddenly looked up, and with one of her mercurial changes of mood was all smiles. 'Perhaps you're right,' she said. 'Maybe I am a selfish old woman. I've got used to you and Annabel being here. I suppose, if I'm honest, I'd begun to think you always would be. I shall miss you, but I shall manage. All I want is for you to be happy.' She held out her glass. 'Pour me another sherry, darling.'

'What about *your* liver?'

'Damn my liver!' Felicity obediently sloshed sherry into the glass, passed it to Irene who took a huge gulp.

14

'It's not just the fact that you'll be leaving that bothers me. It's . . . oh, well, never mind. Least said, soonest mended, as they say.'

'It's never least said with you, Mum,' Felicity said, wondering what was coming next. 'You'll tell me sooner or later anyway, so you might as well spit it out now.'

'Well,' Irene hesitated, then said, 'it's not easy being a second wife.'

Felicity smiled. 'A very profound remark. But what on earth makes you say it? You've never been one.'

'No, but I've plenty of women friends who have, and they've all found it difficult. It doesn't seem to matter much whether the first wife is dead or an ex and alive; the ghost of her always lingers.'

Felicity laughed outright at the idea. 'That's ridiculous. I had a husband once, so what about him? Or other people's ex or dead husbands? Are you trying to tell me that they linger on as well?'

'Of course not,' said her mother firmly. 'Once they've gone, they've gone. Men just don't have the staying power.'

CHAPTER 2

Tony wore glasses. That was how they'd met. He'd been up in London for a conference, and on the Tube had taken them off to polish them, only to have them knocked out of his hand by Felicity. She'd been reading and, suddenly realizing that the train was about to leave the station she wanted, had leapt up, cannoned into Tony, knocked the glasses flying and then trodden on them.

'So sorry.' About to push through the sliding doors, Felicity had seen that the lenses had parted company with the frames, and the broken ear-pieces were now only suitable for someone whose ears grew two inches from their eyes. After doing all that damage Felicity felt she couldn't possibly abandon him and leave. Bending down, she began to retrieve the scattered parts of the spectacles. The doors hissed shut, and the train drew out of the station.

'Oh, don't worry. It's all right.' Tony smiled, and groped about short-sightedly for his glasses.

Minus his glasses it was possible to see that he was absolutely gorgeous. He had enormous tawny brown eyes fringed by long, long dark lashes, and slightly tousled hair streaked blond by the sun. He was so attractive that Felicity forgot about her missed stop. It's not fair, she thought, looking at his amiable, smiling face – a man shouldn't be allowed to have lashes like that, or be let loose to smile at women in that way. It was a long time since she'd flirted with anyone, so long she'd almost forgotten how to do it. A second later, however, she realized that she would be wasting her time even if she did as it soon became obvious that he couldn't see a thing. 'Here, let me,' she said, and, scooping together the remains of his glasses, put them in his hand.

'Oh, dear!' He fingered the jagged remains.

'I'm afraid they're beyond redemption,' said Felicity feeling guilty. 'Do you have a spare pair?'

'Oh, yes, of course. I'm as blind as a bat without them.'

'You'd better put the spares on, then,' said Felicity, 'so that you can see me, and know who it is you're going to sue for breaking your glasses.'

He shook his head and grinned engagingly. A blond lock of hair fell across his forehead, giving him an even more attractive boyish look. Felicity felt herself becoming more and more enamoured. 'Don't worry,' he said reassuringly. 'I won't sue; no need. I'm insured.'

The train rattled on through the blackened tunnels and Felicity sat down beside him. 'That's a relief,' she said, 'because I'm not sure I could afford to replace those at the moment. They look terribly expensive, and my finances are in a parlous state, as usual.'

'I'm sorry,' he said, and sounded genuinely sorry. He wrapped the broken glasses in a clean handkerchief and put the resulting package in his pocket. 'Will you tell me when we get to Piccadilly?' he said. 'I need to change there for the Bakerloo line.'

'Where are your other glasses?' asked Felicity. She also felt responsible for his welfare. It wasn't fair to leave him blundering about short-sightedly on the Underground. At least that was what she told herself, it had nothing to do with the fact that she didn't want to leave this attractive man.

He turned towards her, gave a bone-melting smile and a philosophical shrug. 'That's the problem. They're at home. And I live in Hampshire.'

So that was how Felicity and Tony came to spend the evening together in a bar just off Piccadilly Circus. Before going to the bar Felicity went into the chemist's on the Circus and bought two rolls of sticking plaster. Then spent half an hour assembling and taping pieces of plastic to the lenses until the heap once more resembled spectacles – more or less. While she did this, Tony told her his life-story. Or part of it. The important part. The fact that he was divorced, unattached and free.

'Here.' She finally handed him the spectacles.

Tony took them, put them on, peered at her and said, 'Why, you're beautiful,' then looked in the mirror and roared with laughter. 'Hell! I looked as if I've just come out of the local hospital's emergency room. And a low-tech one at that.'

'It's the best I can do.' Felicity looked doubtfully at the spectacles. They did look a bit of a mess.

But Tony was happy. 'They'll do fine. I can see, that's the important thing.'

Their friendship flourished from that moment on, and it took Felicity a whole week to remember why it was she had originally wanted to get off at Tottenham Court Road. It was to buy a book, which in the end she never did buy.

When she told her mother how they had met, far from thinking it romantic, her mother said, 'You don't want to go getting yourself mixed up with a blind man. It would be a terrible liability.'

Felicity waltzed around the kitchen in Primrose Hill, clasping an imaginary Tony in her arms. He was so tall, so muscular and beautifully solid. Everything a man should be. 'Don't exaggerate, Mum. He's not blind. Just short-sighted. And I think I'm in love.'

'It will wear off in a week,' said her mother. Her tone sounded hopeful, or so Felicity thought, and the set of her grey bun registered disapproval.

But the feeling hadn't worn off. Their relationship had gone from strength to strength until they'd finally made the decision to marry.

The weekend after Felicity broke the news to her daughter and mother, she went down to Cherry Trees to be with Tony. She loved the weekends at his house. Just the two of them. Even the housework was fun.

Not that she did much of it. Tony always said, 'Oh, let's leave all that. Time enough for a routine when we're together permanently.' Always added, 'And anyway, Mrs Balfour comes in tomorrow.'

And as her mother had always taken charge of the

kitchen and house and Felicity's domestic skills were practically non-existent, she happily complied and did leave it all. Besides, Mrs Balfour, who Felicity had never met, always left the house so frighteningly clean that she was sure that germs would never dare to poke their heads out of wherever they lurked. Most weekends they ate out at country pubs, returning to Cherry Trees to make love. It was an idyllic existence.

Now, she lay in the crook of Tony's arm, her head resting on his shoulder. They had just made love, very thoroughly, and very, very satisfactorily. Felicity had forgotten how it was to feel erotically sated and knew that in spite of what her mother said about it being difficult being a second wife, there was no way she wanted to go back to the uneventful celibate life she'd lived for the past nine years. She'd never even thought much about it before, and on the few occasions when she had, always assumed that her hormones were dormant or that she must be sexually retarded because she hadn't met a single man who had really turned her on. But one glance from Tony's soulful brown eyes and she'd been hooked. There was no doubt now that her hormones were in perfect working order, and her sex drive, once put into gear by Tony, was happily steaming full drive ahead.

Now, basking in the soporific afterglow of sex, they lay close together watching the slowly deepening dusk settle over the countryside outside the bedroom window of Cherry Trees. Tony called it a cottage, but the house was huge and rambling, with an enormous garden, a paddock and numerous outbuildings. Honeysuckle grew all around it, the fronds trailing along the open window ledge sending its delicate perfume drifting into the room.

Tony gently manoeuvred her into a more comfortable position. 'Happy, darling?'

'Blissfully.'

'Not long now before you make an honest man out of me. All this illicit sex is worrying me.' Felicity giggled. That was another nice thing about Tony. He said the most ridiculous things, and made her laugh. He kissed her, then said, 'Have you told Annabel and your mother?'

Felicity puckered her face, remembering with distaste the scene with Annabel and the difficult conversation with her mother. Not that she was going to bother Tony with any of those details. They were her problems, not his. 'I told them both yesterday that we were getting married in a fortnight's time.'

'I bet your mother's first thought was that you've not given her enough time to buy a new hat. Most women seem to think of things like that.'

Felicity hesitated. Now she thought about it, her mother hadn't given the actual wedding day a single thought. All she'd been obsessed about was the new bed. She eventually said, 'My mother is not most women.'

Tony chuckled. 'You can certainly say that. She's a real character. What *did* she say?'

'Oh . . . um,' Felicity prevaricated and tried to think up a suitably plausible lie but was finally reduced to saying, 'she gave me all sorts of good advice.'

Tony kissed her again. 'I thought you knew all about the birds and the bees.'

Felicity grinned. 'Not that kind of advice, silly.'

'What kind, then.'

'Oh, you know. The usual. About not rushing into things, etcetera. But I told her that we were old enough to know our own minds, and pointed out that I've been on my own for nine years.'

'And I've been on my own for nine months. Well, nearly nine months.'

Felicity raised herself on one elbow and peered down at Tony. He was lying flat on his back, eyes closed, looking satisfied. Nine months! That wasn't long. It was something she'd never asked about, but had somehow mistakenly assumed that he'd been alone for much longer. She said so. 'I thought it was longer.'

'Long enough. I need a woman in the house.'

Suddenly her mother's words echoed uncomfortably through her head. *He needs someone to wash his pants and socks.* 'What for?' she asked, suddenly struck with suspicion.

Tony began tracing an erotic wiggling line with one finger down her stomach. 'Have a guess,' he said.

But an uncomfortable seed of doubt had been sown. His ex-wife had been here in this very bedroom less than a year ago. Ignoring his invitingly lecherous tone of voice, Felicity removed his hand and, propping herself up on both elbows, looked around the bedroom. Strange, she thought. Why have I never noticed before how very feminine it is, and how aggressively English Country Cottage. Everything pink and frilled.

Not my cup of tea at all. 'Tony,' she said slowly, 'I don't like the decor of this room.'

All Tony did was to laugh and pull her back down into the crook of his arm so that he could kiss her. 'We've never spent much time looking at the decor since we've known each other,' he said. 'There has always been something much better to do.' Then, rolling her over on to her back, he began kissing her again in earnest.

But Felicity's mind was otherwise occupied, and she struggled free. She should have given her mother more credit for common sense. This *was* another woman's room, not hers. And she didn't like it. 'Tony, let's be serious for a moment.'

'Why?' Tony's expression was far from serious.

'Because we can't make love all the time,' said Felicity far more sharply than she had intended, and then felt mean when she saw his happy expression change to one of puzzled anxiety. 'Once I'm married to you there will be other things to do.'

'Such as?' asked Tony warily.

'Ordinary things like living a normal life, doing housework. Then I won't be able to miss the decor. I shall see it all the time. Did you choose it?.'

Recognizing defeat when it stared him in the face, and obviously not liking it, Tony flopped bad-temperedly back on to his own side of the bed and said in a distinctly grumpy voice, 'Of course not. Do I look like a pink frilled type of man? No, Samantha chose it. Every damned flounced frill, the carpet, the pictures. Everything.'

He didn't like it either by the sound of it. So there should be no problem in changing it. But Felicity wanted to make certain that every last vestige of Samantha would be eradicated and was determined to leave nothing to chance. 'Everything?' she repeated.

'Everything. Even the bed.'

Felicity sat bolt upright. That was another thing; she'd never thought about it before, but now she *did* think about it, she felt, well . . . she tried to think of a word, and 'sleazy' was the one which came to mind. There was something immoral about sleeping in another woman's bed. Then a comforting thought struck. Maybe Tony had bought a new mattress; after all, that was what *she* would have done. Of course he would have . . . but even so, she had to ask. 'Is this the original bed? The one you made love on when you were married?'

'Of course.' Tony was looking more and more puzzled. 'Although Samantha and I . . . well . . . our sexual activity tailed off noticeably towards the end of our marriage.'

So he *hadn't* changed the mattress! 'I'm glad to hear it,' said Felicity, beginning to feel and sound distinctly frosty.

'What is all this leading up to?' Tony by now was not only looking puzzled, he sounded it as well.

'Well, for starters we need a new bed,' said Felicity.

Now she had Tony's attention. He sat bolt upright too. 'A new bed!' From the horrified tone of his voice Felicity figured she might as well have said a new house. 'But,' he spluttered, 'this one cost a fortune. It's good for at least another ten years.'

'Not with me in it, it isn't,' said Felicity firmly. She could almost see her mother standing on the other side of the room, cheering her on, and slopping sherry all over the ghastly pale pink carpet in the process. Start as you mean to go on, that was what her mother would have said, and that was what she was doing. 'We need a new bed and bedroom. Surely you must see that I can't start off married life as your second wife by sleeping in the first wife's bed.'

Tony groped about on the bedside table, found his glasses and put them on. 'It's never bothered you before,' he said, sounding incredulous. 'We've made love in it often enough over the past four months.'

'That is different. I'm not married to you yet. When I am it will be different again.'

'Heaven preserve me.' Tony's voice began to rise a shade louder. 'I do not understand you.'

That makes two of us, thought Felicity, by now feeling angry and hard done by, and wondering at Tony's obtuse attitude. 'And I don't understand why you can't understand the need for a new bed. How can you be so insensitive?'

Tony gritted his teeth. Felicity knew he was doing that, because he had what she thought rather nice long lines either side of his mouth, and now the muscles either side of the lines were rippling. He was annoyed. His next words confirmed his annoyance. 'Why do women always rant on about men being insensitive when they can't get their own way?'

We're having a row. Our first row. Felicity quailed at the thought. She didn't want to argue, but neither could she let the matter drop. 'You *are* being insensitive. Why can't you see the point?'

'That's just it,' said Tony. 'I *do* see the point, and the point is, why throw good money down the drain? Heaven knows we're not going to be that well off once we're married. I'll have you and Annabel to support, plus Hilary, Philip and Peter. Children don't come cheap, you know.'

'You should have thought of that before you had so many.' It was a bitchy thing to say, but it popped out before she could stop it. 'Anyway,' she added, feeling slightly self-righteous, 'I can keep myself and my daughter. I shall carry on working. Oliver Dickens has already agreed that I can have all the new manuscripts sent to me in Hampshire. So I don't want your money.'

'Oh, darling.' Tony put his arms around her. 'Don't let's quarrel. I don't want you to work. Besides, once we're married, my money will be your money.'

But Felicity, although hating their first quarrel, wasn't quite ready to be won over yet. 'How can you say that your money will be mine? Most of it seems to be earmarked for your tribe of children.'

'Three isn't a tribe, darling. And anyway, the first ones turned out to be twins, so that doesn't really count. Just think, you could have twins, then all of a sudden you'd be the mother of three.' Tony gave her a hug. 'Think about that.'

Felicity did think, and the prospect horrified her. 'I don't want any more children,' she said firmly, hoping that Tony felt the same. Now she thought of it that was something else they'd never discussed. Suddenly she panicked, and felt she had to ask. 'Why do you say that? Do you want more?'

'Good heavens, no,' said Tony. 'As I said before, we're not going to be that well off. A divorce is expensive. I'm still paying out and it's still crippling me. I certainly can't afford any more children.'

'Good,' said Felicity and then started worrying all over again. She'd always thought doctors were very well paid. They always seemed to have enormous houses, and Range Rovers, boats and horses, all the material possessions most people only ever dreamed about. So why was Tony different, and why was he still paying out for the divorce? 'Tony,' she said carefully, 'we've never talked about money before. I thought all the financial things in your life were sorted out: you were divorced, and Samantha got the children and everything was done and finished with, apart from the children's visits here during the school holidays.' An event which she was dreading, although she'd not mentioned it to anyone, always telling herself that she loved Tony therefore she was sure to love his children, because, after all, they were an extension of him. But in spite of all this reasonable logic, all thoughts of their impending visits caused her to break out in a hot sweat of irrational and nameless fear. A fear exacerbated by the fact that she had yet to meet them.

'I *am* divorced,' said Tony, 'and Samantha *has* got the children. But nothing is ever completely done and finished with, especially not when there are children involved. My first family is an ongoing commitment. I still have their school fees to pay, and that's quite a chunk out of my income, plus the fact that I've had to take out a second mortgage on this house to pay Samantha her share.'

'Oh,' said Felicity. Of course it all made sense. She'd just been too blinded by love to take it into consideration.

'Yes,' Tony took of his glasses, and laid back on the pillow as if even thinking about it exhausted him. 'At the rate I'm going, I shall be pushing up the daisies long before this house is paid off.'

'Oh,' said Felicity again. Second mortgage! School fees! Shortage of money! A niggling but potent flicker of doubt settled over her. Perhaps my mother was right, she thought. Four months isn't very long. Maybe I don't know him well enough to marry him. Maybe if I do want to marry again I should find myself an unencumbered male – although most of the unattached attractive males in the right age group always turned out to be gay. Suddenly the future, instead of being painted in delicate hues of rose-pink, looked grim. She looked around the bedroom, Samantha's bedroom. *That* was pink. 'If it's all so difficult,' she said carefully, 'why on earth did you ask me to marry you?'

Tony reached up and pulled her towards him. 'Because I love you, darling,' he said earnestly. 'Truly I do. I shouldn't have painted such a bleak picture. It's a bit difficult at the moment, but it will all work out. I'm doing an extra locum session at the General Hospital in

Westhampton to help pay off the second mortgage so there's no need to worry about that.'

Felicity felt herself weakening. There was nothing to worry about. If Tony said it would be all right, then it was bound to be. She wanted to believe him. She *did* believe him. And besides, there was her money as well. 'My piffling fifteen thousand a year would come in useful, then.'

'Well, if you are determined to carry on working, yes, it would,' Tony admitted.

There was one more thing to settle. 'I still want a new bed and new bedroom decorations.'

To her delight Tony relented. 'Of course, darling,' he said, and kissed her.

She kissed him back. 'When?'

'Just as soon as we can possibly get it done.'

That, Felicity knew, was like saying how long is a piece of string? But it was better nothing and she decided not to push her luck. Besides Tony's fingertips were marching tantalizingly up and down her stomach. She relaxed and snuggled back up against him, and was just preparing to give herself up to a burst of pure carnal pleasure when the door exploded open and a large, golden brown, furry form leapt on the bed and firmly wedged itself between them.

'Oh,' groaned Tony. 'I must have forgotten to put the latch on the kitchen door. Prudence loves sharing the bed with me. I'm afraid I let her up here when you're not here.'

'Well, I'm here now,' grunted Felicity, trying, ineffectively, to push Prudence off the bed.

'Yes, but remember, she was my only friend long before I met you,' Tony said.

'This dog is too possessive,' Felicity gave up pushing. The furry lump settled in, effectively keeping them miles apart. She sat up and glowered at Prudence, who opened one brown eye, which unsettlingly reminded Felicity of Tony's eyes. 'This is ridiculous,' she said. 'I'm not having my love-life ruined by a dog. She has got to learn that I take priority up here.'

But Prudence wriggled her bulk further down into the bed, and Tony roared with laughter.

CHAPTER 3

Tony was not a coward. At least he did not consider himself to be a moral coward, and was hurt when Felicity called him one the following morning at breakfast.

'It's just that I hate scenes,' he'd said. 'In fact I'd do anything to avoid one.'

'Well I'm glad you can at least admit your failings,' Felicity said, briskly stirring the coffee in the cafetière and at the same time plopping sliced bread into the toaster.

'I wouldn't call opting for the quiet life a failing.' He took off his glasses and polished them. The sun streaming in through the kitchen windows showed up all the dusty specks and smears. 'Can't see a damned thing, even with these on,' he said, peering at Felicity.

'It *is* a failing when you're putting off doing something that you know you have to do,' said Felicity firmly, determined not to be put off by his appealing expression. Much as she loved him, she was determined that he had to face up to reality in the same way that she had. And now that she had found out that he was

31

dragging his feet, she was pushing him into action. Not something to be relished, but something which had to be done.

'I know.' Tony sighed, feeling guilty. It was the truth. He *was* putting it off, and Felicity's unexpected aversion to Samantha's style of decor the previous night had rattled him so badly that now he wanted to put it off more than ever. It was unlike her to get heated about anything. Since their first meeting they had sailed along smoothly, on their own little sea of love, as he called it. Tony was a true romantic at heart, if not very original when it came to expressing his feelings. Although Felicity teased him about it, saying they were a dull couple, until last night there had never been a ripple on the surface of their relationship, and Tony relished every moment they spent together. Now, still unsettled from the argument of the previous night, he wasn't sure he could face another one today, although he had serious doubts that Felicity would be at all sympathetic to that line of argument.

'You know that I've told my family,' continued Felicity. 'Now you must tell yours. You really cannot leave it any longer. There isn't much time before the wedding.'

Tony poured himself a cup of black coffee, and stirred it thoughtfully, wondering how he could get out of ruining his day, at the same time acknowledging that he was being cowardly but unable to help it. He hit upon a brainwave to postpone the moment. 'I think I'll pop down in the week. They've broken up from school. That way you and I can spend most of today together instead of splitting up and going in different directions.'

'Procrastination is the thief of time,' quoted Felicity, thinking at the same time, heavens! I sound like my own mother! Seeing the dismayed expression on his face, she relented a little. 'Tell you what. I'll come up to London with you and meet them. Then I'll get back home. I've got to get back early anyway. I brought some work home with me which has to be done by Monday before I go back into the office.'

'Oh, no,' said Tony quickly. 'Telling them is one thing, but for them to meet you on the same day would be too much.' He fervently wished, not for the first time, that he'd had the courage to tell them about Felicity earlier. What on earth was going to be their reaction?

'For heaven's sake! Why would it be too much? I haven't got two heads. They must be wondering what I look like by now. They're bound to be wondering about their father's new girlfriend.' Felicity thought he was making a rather large mountain out of a molehill.

Tony drew a deep breath. There was no escape. He'd have to tell her. 'They aren't curious, because they don't even know of your existence,' he said despondently.

The toast flew out of the toaster, pop! pop! as if to underline the magnitude of his omission.

Felicity sat down, automatically buttering the toast and passing a slice to Tony while she digested this information. The kitchen, washed in the clear fresh light of early morning, was peaceful and tranquil; the only sound, apart from the tick of the old clock on the wall, was from outside, a high-pitched clink, clink, clink of a blackbird establishing his territory somewhere in the garden. And yet she sensed turbulence. Into this sunlit haven their respective families were intruding, drawing up battle-lines, pushing them apart. For a second, but it *was* only a second, she wished that they were both totally free of other people. But that was being selfish, and anyway, if they were, neither of them would be the people they were today, and they probably wouldn't have fallen in love.

'Oh, Tony,' she said gently, suddenly realizing that he too was fearing an intrusion into the little world of their own which they'd managed to create in the last few months. She reached across the table and clasped his hand.

Embarrassed at being found wanting and yet at the same time glad that she knew, Tony held on to her hand gratefully. 'You are right,' he said. 'I *am* a coward, but I will rectify it. Today. I promise.'

'It won't be nearly as bad as you think,' said Felicity, hoping that it wouldn't be, and making her voice sound positive. 'You wait and see.' Crossing her fingers, she said a little prayer that Tony's children would be more receptive to the idea than Annabel had been.

Tony cheered up. Of course Felicity was right. It couldn't possibly be bad enough to warrant putting it off any longer. He got up purposefully. If he was going to do something, now was the time to start. 'I'll fax them a letter this minute, telling them all about you *and* the wedding, and say that I'm coming up later today.

Then I'll go up to London and make arrangements for them to come to our nuptials.'

Felicity had her doubts about the wisdom of sending the children the news in a fax, but stayed silent. Tony must know his own children. What they could, or would accept. All the same, she felt she had to sound a warning note. 'They might not want to come to the wedding.' Felicity thought of Annabel.

'Of course they will. I *am* their father.' Obscurely Tony felt that this solved everything. Father, children, they belonged together, divorce or no divorce. The fact that they were no longer with him all the time was not the crucial point. They were bound to want to be present when he was doing something important, like getting married again. It was common sense. If Felicity had asked him why he felt this, he couldn't have explained, but the thought cheered him nevertheless.

'Yes,' said Felicity, thinking that his being their father was most likely to be the greatest obstacle, but wisely keeping her own counsel. Tony would have to cope with his offspring as she had coped with hers. Only let him do it better, she prayed fervently.

Tony stood in a defensive position, his back to the closed door, and gazed at his three children, his previous optimism evaporating now before their combined glowers. He couldn't decide who looked the fiercest: Hilary, or the twins, Philip and Peter. They were in Hilary's bedroom, the boys slumped in white wicker-work chairs, and Hilary sprawling on the bed. All three had packets of crisps which they were crunching noisily with their mouths open. Tony gritted his teeth. He knew they were doing it to annoy him and was determined not to give in to them by rising to the bait.

Hilary's room was elegant. It was painted white with subtle touches of green here and there, the green reinforced by a large trailing plant in a snow-white ceramic pot, placed strategically on the window sill so that its curving lines provided a direct counterpoint with the geometric lines of the wide sill. It was a perfect room, nothing out of place, and everything matching. But Hilary hated it. To her it had an unreal quality, and only served to remind her every day of the way their lives had become equally unreal during the last year. She hated the room and hated her life now, and often thought about her old room at Cherry Trees which had cabbage roses on the walls, and was full of prized possessions. A one-eyed rocking horse, old boxes of Lego, comics, books, and one whole wall reserved exclusively for the rosettes she'd won at pony club competitions.

'Junk,' her mother had said emphatically when she'd whisked them away from their father to live in London. 'I've never really liked your room, and Piers absolutely loathes it. He says that everything in Cherry Trees is the epitome of bad taste.'

Hilary had looked up the word 'epitome' but was none the wiser for her diligence. Archetype, embodiment, quintessence, it was all those things and more. But the only thing she *did* know for certain was that Piers, her mother's partner as he was called, didn't approve, and because of that neither did her mother.

Although there had once been a time when she could remember her mother being enthusiastic about the roses on her wallpaper in their old house, and helping her pin up the rosettes, saying how pretty they looked. But that was a lifetime ago. A different lifetime. Life before Piers.

Piers was the editor of a *very, very* glossy magazine all about homes and gardens. He was always talking to people on his mobile phone, sometimes barking orders at unseen people, and at other times putting on what Philip called a 'smarmy' voice and calling people 'darling' and 'love'. And now their mother had a mobile phone too, and agreed with everything Piers said and was even writing articles for his magazine. She had once used Hilary's bedroom to illustrate an article called 'The Perfect Bedroom for a Town Child'.

'But I'm not a town child,' Hilary had said resentfully when her mother showed her the article.

'You are now,' had been the tart reply.

And now her father had come to reinforce that fact. She *was* a town child. Life at Cherry Trees was vanishing for ever because he was about to marry someone else. Someone called Felicity who had a daughter called Annabel. Hilary decided from the moment she knew of their existence that she hated them both.

She and the twins fought most of the time, but they were unanimous on one subject. Their parents. By hook or by crook they were determined that they were going to get them back together. Philip, the elder of the twins by ten minutes, was the prime mover in their plan, which until now had seemed simple and fool-proof.

'It's just a question of waiting,' he'd always said. 'Although they are divorced, neither is going to marry anyone else.'

Hilary had always been a little doubtful. 'I think that Mummy and Piers are bound to get married. After all they are living in the same house and have the same bedroom.' Hilary attached great importance to this fact.

'No, they won't.' Philip was confident. 'Piers won't marry Mummy. I know that because I overheard him telling her that marriage was for mundane people, and not for them. He said that theirs was an open partnership, and that they didn't need a piece of paper to tie them together.'

'What did she say?' Peter was curious. He disliked Piers as much as the others, but privately would have preferred his mother to marry him rather than live in sin. Like Hilary, he too attached great importance to the fact that they shared a bedroom. Sharing a bedroom if you were not married was living in sin. He knew that, and it bothered him. Brother Tom had always said that living with someone you weren't married to was living in sin, and that was wrong. God didn't like it. And Brother Tom knew about these things.

'Oh, Mummy muttered something about Piers being absolutely right, and that she'd had enough of being ordinary,' said Philip bitterly. 'Sometimes I think she'd agree that the moon was made of blue cheese if that horrible man said so.'

'I like being ordinary,' announced Hilary. 'I hate this poncy house and all the poncy people who come here. Of course they're all ordinary really; it's just that they pretend not to be.'

'Well, Dad is ordinary and doesn't ever try to be anything else,' Philip had said then, which comforted them all when they thought about it. 'And he hasn't even got a girlfriend or anything. And Mummy is bound to get fed up with this Piers bloke sooner or later. After all, it's only lust.'

Hilary said nothing, afraid to admit that she had no idea what lust meant, and wished she were as clever as Philip and Peter who seemed to know so much more than her. But she did have better luck when she looked that up. 'Pleasure, delight, a longing for something . . .' She hadn't bothered to read on. That was enough. Although why on earth her mother found Piers a pleasure and delight she couldn't imagine. Perhaps it was because he was always calling her *precious* and *darling*. She couldn't remember their father doing that. And Piers was always telling her she was the thinnest and most glamorous woman he knew, which made Hilary doubly depressed because she'd put on a lot of weight since they'd moved to London. Only yesterday one of the girls in her class, at the Woolston Day School for Girls in St John's Wood, had called her fat.

'It's better than being anorexic,' Hilary had shouted back, before hitting her. This had resulted in her being reprimanded and kept in by the form teacher for shouting and fighting, and having to say

39

in front of the whole class, 'I will not behave in an unladylike fashion.' Then to crown it all she'd been given homework for the Easter holidays. Woolston Day School was private, and had a reputation for turning girls into intelligent, desirable young ladies, unlike Hilary's previous school, the Westhampton School, which had the dubious reputation of having a high number of girls in the top form who were teenage mothers. Westhampton girls left school with a wide range of mixed abilities, some to be check-out girls at the huge hypermarket in the out-of-town shopping complex, a few to university, and the vast majority with no idea of what they wanted to do except have babies. That was by far the most popular ambition. Hilary had liked Westhampton. It was undemanding and suited her.

'Brother Tom,' said Peter darkly, 'says that lust is the work of the devil and should be resisted.' The twins went to a Catholic boys' boarding school, not because they were Catholics, but because Tony thought it had a good academic record, and they, unlike Hilary, were both very bright. Samantha also preferred them to be away from home because life was much quieter and the house stayed tidy. The school, St Boniface Boys' Independent Grammar, was staffed mainly by brothers who wore long old-fashioned habits, and had old-fashioned ideas to go with their garb.

'Have you told Mummy that?' asked Hilary hopefully. 'About lust and the devil, I mean?'

'Don't be ridiculous.' Philip was scathing. 'If she'd

resisted the lust bit in the first place, we wouldn't have been dragged away from Hampshire to live in bloody London. Pity though,' he said, turning to Peter, 'that you didn't mention it to the judge, because if you had then he might have given us to Dad instead of Mummy. I don't know why he had to palm us off on her. She doesn't care two bloody hoots what we do or where we are these days.'

'She used to.' Hilary was still loyal even though her mother paid her scant attention these days.

'Brother Tom says it is sinful to swear.' Peter again.

'Damn Brother Tom,' said Philip. Hilary noticed that he was swearing a lot these days. 'He's a silly old man who thinks if he prays and lights enough candles he'll change the world.'

'I like him, and I *do* believe in the power of prayer.' Peter was very fond of Brother Tom. He had been a great comfort to him since the break-up of their parents' marriage. Peter could tell Brother Tom anything. All his awful nightmares, all his fears, all the things he could never, ever tell Philip or Hilary, and particularly not his mother or father. 'I pray every night,' he said, 'that a miracle will happen and that Piers will disappear and Mummy will love Daddy again.'

'So much for your prayers,' Philip had said this morning in a choked voice, throwing down the fax Tony had written telling them of his impending marriage and his intention to visit them. 'He's bloody well going to get married, and he's coming here this afternoon to try and persuade us to go. What a nerve!'

41

'I'm not going,' said Hilary, and burst into tears.

'Neither am I,' said Peter, and ran out of the room and up three flights of stairs to the tiny attic room which Piers had very graciously said he could have as his own private room. Peter knew what his mother and Piers thought, and Philip and Hilary as well. They thought he had his CD player and video up there, and played silly war games on the video. He did have them there, but they were rarely used. Peter's room had another purpose, one which he kept secret because he knew everyone else would think him crackers. In the middle of the room stood a table draped with a white cloth, and standing in the centre of the table was a small wooden crucifix. School, and the brothers' serene and strong religious faith, had deeply affected Peter. When Tony and Samantha had parted and it became obvious that his ordered world was falling to pieces, Peter had turned to Brother Tom more frequently. And now, since their forced removal to London, Peter had created his own private sanctuary to retreat to. He spent hours on his knees in front of the makeshift altar praying that everything would come right in the end. Sometimes he thought that if he hadn't had boarding school, Brother Tom, and his own little chapel in London, he would have gone mad. But now a letter from his father had spoiled even that. Destroyed what he'd been praying for so earnestly. With one violent movement he tore the cloth from the table, sending the crucifix tumbling to the floor. 'So much for the power of prayer,' he shouted, echoing Philip's words.

* * *

Now, he sat in his chair by the side of Philip, munching his crisps as loudly as he could with his mouth open, because he knew that would annoy his father. But let him be annoyed, he thought rebelliously. He agreed with Philip. Their father had a nerve even daring to come and see them.

Philip had said, after they had all calmed down a little and re-read Tony's fax, 'Between them they've mucked up our lives, and now Dad is finishing it off for good. He should be punished.'

'I'm not going to the damned wedding,' Hilary said. If Philip could swear, she reasoned, so could she.

'We none of us will go,' agreed Philip. 'And I'll tell him so when he comes.'

'Right.' Peter and Hilary agreed that Philip should be the spokesman. He was much better at dealing with grown-ups than either of them. Besides, as Philip pointed out, he was the eldest, by all of ten minutes.

'We're not coming to your wedding. We've all agreed.' Philip stared at his father then turned his icy blue stare towards his brother and sister. 'Haven't we?' The fierce expression in his eyes brooked no dissent or weakening.

Hilary knew that without Philip she would have weakened. She was not strong-willed like him. Lying on her bed, she shifted about uncomfortably. Now that her father was actually standing before them, his brown eyes looking so worried behind his horn-rimmed spectacles, she felt sorry for him. Perhaps they should go. A wedding was important. Even a second one. And after all, it wasn't really his fault that their mother had fallen out of love with him and in love with Piers. *He* hadn't changed. It was their mother who had suddenly changed into a different creature. He was still the same. Suddenly Hilary longed to throw her arms around him and say, 'I love you. I've always loved you.' But she dared not. Philip had decided he should be sent to Coventry, and Philip was the boss.

The waistband of her jeans cut into her flesh, reminding her of all the weight she'd put on since leaving Cherry Trees. Sticking one thumb into the waistband, she tried to ease the pressure but that only made it tighter and in turn that made her more depressed. Unhappily she crammed another heaped handful of crisps into her mouth.

The action was not missed by Tony. The children's continual crunching was driving him mad. 'I don't think you ought to eat so many crisps,' he said sharply, then immediately realized that this was *not* the way to make friends and influence his children.

'Why not?' Philip stuck out his chin aggressively.

As he'd already said it, Tony thought he might as well go the whole hog and explain why not. 'Because they aren't nutritious. Crisps are full of unhealthy calories. You don't need them. I notice you've all put on weight, and it's probably because of those crisps. You never had them at home.'

'You sound like a bloody doctor,' said Philip, hoping to tempt him into really losing his temper.

They all saw him wince at the word 'bloody' and waited.

Tony counted to ten, then counted to ten again, and succeeded in quashing the roar of disapproval it would have generated in the old days. His anger petered out, it just didn't materialize; because while he was counting Tony watched and his heart bled for the three children. They might be teenagers, but they were still children, *his* children, and none of this was their fault. Shouting would do no good. So he merely said, 'I sound like one because I *am* a doctor, and that's why I'm fussy about health. Besides, and much more importantly, I love you and care about what you do. As I said, you didn't eat them at home. So why now?'

'This is our home now,' said Hilary in a muffled voice, because she was trying hard not to cry, 'and we can eat what we like. Nobody says anything. Nobody really cares. Besides, there's nothing much else to do in London except watch TV and eat.'

Tony took a deep breath. 'Your mother does care,' he said quietly. He was always careful never to belittle Samantha before them, no matter what he thought. 'Besides, you could come down to Cherry Trees more often. I'd come and get you, you know that. You'd get plenty of exercise there. Old Cotton-Socks is plodding around the paddock just longing for you to come and ride him. And Prudence misses her walks as well.'

At the mention of Cotton-Socks and Prudence a tear did squeeze its way out and trickle down her cheek. But Hilary wiped it away quickly before Philip could see. Philip would be furious. She couldn't show that she cared. She dared not. After all, they had all agreed that the only way to try and do something, *anything*, to make their parents come to their senses before it was too late, was to be as distant and awkward as possible.

'There is a reason we don't come often,' said Philip in a voice which suddenly shocked Tony. He hadn't heard it like that before and it hit him like a shower of cold pebbles. Philip's voice was distant and hard. It reminded him of Samantha, and made him feel even more uncomfortable. It was the way Samantha's voice had been when she knew she was wrong but was determined to get her own way. 'The reason,' continued Philip, 'is that Cherry Trees is a holiday home. It's not a *proper* home. When you and Mummy split up everything, you split us up as well, as if we were part of the furniture. Now we live here. This is our home, with Mummy and Piers. Cherry Trees is just a place we're supposed to visit.'

'I had no choice,' Tony mumbled unhappily. How wrong Felicity had been. It won't be that bad, she'd said. Not that bad! This was ghastly. Much worse than he'd ever foreseen.

'You did.' Philip, the spokesman, continued in the same hard, voice. 'You had the choice of not divorcing. You and Mummy could have lived apart for a bit, then given it another go.'

There was a long silence while Tony tried to work out what to say. Finally he started. 'I know when we split up everything took you by surprise, and you couldn't believe that our life, your mother's and mine, was so bad that we couldn't continue. But it all began to go wrong a long time before she met

46

Piers. Life isn't simple. I wish it were, but it isn't. It's very difficult, and as your mother made it absolutely plain to me that she would never give it another go, as you put it, I decided to divorce her. Staying married without a wife is living in limbo, and I couldn't do that for ever.'

'All right. But surely you don't have to marry this, this . . .' Peter spoke up, but then courage failed him and his voice tapered off into silence.

'This other woman,' said Philip nastily, managing, Tony thought wryly, to make Felicity sound like a whore and a witch of the first order. 'We don't want a stepmother.'

'We don't *need* a stepmother,' cried Hilary, and turning away buried her face in the pillow.

'You'll like Felicity, I promise you. Prudence likes her, and you know animals are a good judge of character.' That was not *quite* true. Prudence was jealous of Felicity and had lately taken to trying to sit on his lap when she arrived at the house. However, by now Tony was desperate enough to lie, even though he suspected that the children knew it wasn't the truth. But he didn't care. Pride flew out of the window. He *had* to have his children's approval.

But his plea was ignored. 'We aren't coming to the wedding,' said Philip icily. 'And you can't make us.'

That of course was absolutely true. Short of dragging them there by the scruff of their necks, Tony knew he couldn't make them do anything. He waited a moment, hoping against hope that perhaps Hilary or Peter might relent. Then he said, 'I'll tell Felicity that you're not

47

coming. She'll be very sad. She was looking forward to meeting you.' This, of course, was not strictly true. She hadn't exactly said she did *not* want to meet them, but Tony was able to recognize anxious apprehension when he saw it. But by now he was clutching at straws in the wind; they *had* to think Felicity was panting to meet them.

'And you can tell her something else,' Philip shouted, 'tell her that we hate her.' His clear young voice rang around the sparsely furnished bedroom.

'Yes.' Peter, gathering courage, joined in. 'We shall hate her for ever and ever.'

'Amen!' said Philip.

There was nothing more he could do or say. A woman would probably have burst into tears, but men, thought Tony with an increasing sense of desolation, can't do that. Suddenly he realized that he'd never really thought enough about the effect of the divorce on the children. Because they had not said a lot, or made a terrible fuss, but had gone with their mother when told to do so, he had assumed that they had taken everything in their stride. 'Children are so resilient.' He could remember saying that to friends. But had he really believed it? Or had it been an easy way out? An excuse, giving him more time to brood on his own problems? Only now did he see that the hurt he and Samantha had inflicted had scarred them deeply.

He turned to leave. There was nothing to say. Not at this particular moment. Perhaps later there'd be a way to repair some of the damage. But not now. He left the room, closing the door so quietly that it was almost as if he had never been there at all.

'There! That's told him,' said Philip furiously.

Hilary sat up and looked at him. To her astonishment Philip's fierce blue eyes were glistening with unshed tears.

CHAPTER 4

'Oh, darling, I'm so sorry,' Felicity said. Tony had turned up on the doorstep of the house in Primrose Hill to tell her of his children's reaction. He looked so dejected that she longed to throw her arms around him, but, aware of her mother's eagle eye over her shoulder, restrained herself.

'Not altogether surprised, are you?' said Irene waving him through the passageway into the kitchen. 'Like a drink?'

'No, thanks, I'm driving. And yes, I was surprised,' Tony admitted. 'I thought they would want me to be happy. Be glad, but . . .'

'But what?' Irene prompted.

'Mum!' Felicity cursed her insensitivity, and signalled frantically with her eyebrows that she should leave them alone together.

Irene ignored the signal and, pouring herself a gin and tonic, waved the tonic bottle at Tony.

'Yes,' said Tony to the tonic bottle. He turned to Felicity. 'I hadn't reckoned on such a savage reaction. My own fault, of course, because I hadn't even thought about their hurt. The fact that I'm marrying again is an unpleasant reminder that life as it used to be is well and truly over.'

Felicity put an arm around him. Mixed in with her genuine regret was an overwhelming feeling of relief knowing that she wouldn't have to meet them yet, and a sense of guilt because she too was a coward. 'Give them time,' she said. 'It isn't long since the whole world as they knew it skidded off the rails and ground to a halt. Divorce must be traumatic for kids. They don't want to lose you, and I suppose they think I might take you away.'

Tony suddenly wondered. 'How did Annabel react?'

Felicity pulled a rueful face but before she could answer, Annabel, who'd been listening outside the door, burst into the kitchen. 'If you must know, I'm not exactly ecstatic about the news either.'

Tony began to feel slightly annoyed. First his own children, who did have a good reason – they'd been hurt – and then Annabel. But Annabel had never known her father. Why should she object? 'Why on earth not?' he demanded.

'Because I like things as they are. I don't need you.' Annabel poured herself a gin.

'But your mother does, and that's important to me.' He took the gin glass out of her hand. 'And you are much too young to be drinking spirits.'

'Oh, God! He's started playing the heavy-handed father already,' Annabel shrieked, and snatched the glass back.

Felicity pushed in between them, and, taking the gin from Annabel, poured it down the sink.

'What a scandalous waste of good gin,' she could hear her mother muttering.

'Go to your room, Annabel,' she said quietly, 'but please apologize to Tony before you go.'

'What for?' Annabel was defiant.

'For being rude.'

For a moment Tony thought Annabel was going to spit straight in his eye, then she muttered ungraciously, 'Sorry,' and slunk out of the room before he could say anything.

He looked at Felicity and raised his eyebrows. 'Are you going to tell me that *she* doesn't want to lose you either?'

'Exactly,' said Irene.

Tony began to despair of children in general. 'But she's coming to live with us.'

'Of course, and she isn't going to lose me. I've explained all that to her. So do shut up, Mum.' Felicity glared at her mother, who finally took the hint, and after refilling her glass left the kitchen. She turned back to Tony. 'And yours aren't going to lose you either. They'll all come around to the idea eventually. They'll have to.'

Tony began to look a little more cheerful, then he grinned, and, catching hold of Felicity, spun her around and held her by the shoulders. 'No wonder you were so careful not to elaborate the other day,' he said. 'You must have had quite a scene with Annabel. One which you decided to keep quiet about! Talk about being crafty.'

Felicity decided to ignore that. 'We'll persuade them

to meet me after the wedding,' she promised. 'They won't want to stay away from you for ever.'

Thinking back, Tony was not quite so sure, remembering the truculent, hostile expressions of the three of them, but said, 'I've told Samantha that if they change their minds she is to let them come. And she's agreed. I hope that's OK with you.'

'Of course, darling,' said Felicity, leaning forward to kiss him. But she took the precaution of crossing her fingers behind her back, and although feeling black with guilt, nevertheless said a little prayer that there would be no changing of minds. In her considered opinion it would be much better all round if she met up with the children once they were well and truly married.

Felicity wanted a quiet wedding, and had said so on more than one occasion. She had said it loudly. In fact, *very* loudly to her mother.

Irene Hobbit, on the other hand, had definitive, and completely different ideas, and Felicity lost the battle on the Wednesday evening ten days prior to the wedding. She was up in the room which all three of them at the Primrose Hill house referred to as 'Antiques Attic'. It was where Irene did her pricing for the stalls, and was stacked from floor to ceiling with bargains she'd acquired from house sales or other stallholders who were too ignorant to know the true value of what they were selling. A veritable Aladdin's cave. On that Wednesday night Felicity was helping her tie price tags on an assortment of silver apostle spoons. She ought really have been reading the manuscript Oliver Dickens had pressed into her reluctant hands as she'd left the office that night.

'This author is such a nice, unassuming young man,' he'd said, passing her the tatty brown paper parcel. 'Give it a good going over and see if we can do anything with it.'

Oliver never read any manuscripts himself, at least not at first. He relied on what he called his gut feeling about people, not a terribly reliable indicator, as Felicity knew only too well, and left the difficult task of deciding whether or not something was publishable to Felicity. One glance at this particular piece, however, and she'd known it hadn't a hope in hell of making it into print. It didn't need a good going over, it needed tearing up. So she'd ended up pricing apostle spoons, and arguing with her motsher.

'Let's keep the whole thing very low-key,' she said once again.

'It's not every day I launch my only daughter out into the sea of matrimony.' Irene huffed on to the back of a spoon before polishing it vigorously; no tarnished silver on *her* stalls to pull prices down.

Felicity had a momentary vision of herself gliding, like the QE2, down a slipway, streamers and balloons floating and billowing behind her, tied on to her backside. 'I was launched, as you put it, fourteen years ago when I married Tim.'

Irene paused a moment, apostle spoon poised mid air, then she sighed. 'Ah yes, Tim. You know, I've almost forgotten about him.'

'So have I,' Felicity admitted. She too paused and thought back. Tim and her; it all seemed a long time ago now. 'We had such a short time together. The memory is hazy, but all my recollections are of the good times, nothing bad. My life with Tim has faded like a sepia-tinted photograph. When I do think of him, which is not often, all that I can conjure up now is a faint, warm glow. My main memory is of his brilliance at physics. He would have been a world-renowned professor had he lived.'

'*My* main memory is of his obsession with mountains. Bloody things.' Tim had died in a climbing accident, and Felicity always had a sneaking feeling that her mother thought he'd done it on purpose. Suddenly Irene raised her head, and, staring at Felicity, said sharply, 'Tony doesn't climb, does he?'

'No, thank heavens.' She grinned mischievously. 'Not with his eyesight!'

Irene digested this bit of information then turned her mind back to the imminent wedding. 'Anyway, one could hardly call your first marriage being launched. More like dipping a toe in the water. You were both at university, not a penny between you, and your father, God rest his soul, hadn't exactly left me with a fortune so I couldn't help then.' She sighed again, and peered closely at the hallmark on the stem of the spoon she'd been polishing, then muttered, 'Fifteen pounds.' She tied and marked the label. 'Not bad really,' she held up the spoon, 'considering I only paid twenty pence for the whole boxfull.'

'Not bad!' Felicity laughed. 'I'd call it daylight robbery. So much for Hobbit's' fair prices!'

Her mother gave a wickedly unrepentant chuckle. 'That's why I can afford to give you a good send-off this time. I've seen a lovely dress in Laura Ashley. Pink with little green sprigs on it. Lovely for Annabel. She's sure to want to be a bridesmaid once she's got used to the idea of a wedding.'

Felicity gave a little shriek of slightly hysterical laughter at the mere thought. 'Surely you must know that Annabel would throw herself under the 74 bus rather than be a bridesmaid.'

Irene's attention had been caught by another blackened spoon. 'A St Peter circa 1900,' she muttered triumphantly, polishing it with all her sight, adding vaguely, 'Is there a number 74, dear?'

'It's the one she catches to school every day. And you know how she hates dressing up. She would never agree to wear a dress, especially not a frilly one. Apart from wearing her leotard for ballet, the only other thing she'll consent to wear at the moment is a man's black suit and Doc Marten boots.'

Her mother sighed heavily. 'Ah, well, in that case I suppose I'd better forget that idea,' she said in a disappointed voice, adding wistfully, 'It is *so* pretty though.'

'Do me a favour, Mum,' pleaded Felicity. 'Forget all the rest of your ideas as well.'

'Nonsense,' said Irene energetically. 'I've already had a word with Tony. He's very enthusiastic and happy for me to arrange things. What's more, he's bringing fifty guests.'

'Enthusiastic! Happy! Fifty guests!' squeaked Felicity in dismay. 'But he never mentioned anything to me. I thought he agreed about a quiet wedding. Even his own children aren't coming, I'm going to meet them later.' Her mother looked down quickly and rummaged in her box for another spoon, but not before Felicity had caught a glimpse of the wicked glint in her eye. 'You've put him up to it,' she accused. 'I suppose any moment now you'll be telling me that his family are coming too.'

'Oh, no, I don't *think* they're coming,' her mother said quickly. 'But he *is* keen. His exact words to me were, "I want a knees-up, not the stuffy affair I had the last time." Apparently his parents arranged it, and as they've both passed on, God rest their souls,' a momentary pious expression flickered across her face, 'they can't be offended. He's told me to go ahead and make all the arrangements. So as you've done nothing yet, I have. Of course, the Brompton Oratory would have been wonderful, but . . .'

'We're not Catholics, and Tony is divorced, so thank heavens that's out,' breathed Felicity.

'Or St Margaret's, Westminster,' mused Irene. Then she looked up and gave a mischievous smile. 'But eventually I've been realistic and come to terms with the Camden Register Office.'

'Which I *had* booked anyway,' Felicity pointed out, heaving a sigh of relief.

'However,' Irene said exultantly, 'I *have* persuaded the vicar of St Matthew's to give a blessing – ' Felicity groaned ' – and let us use the vicarage garden for the reception. If it rains we can use the church hall, but I'm praying hard that it won't. And I booked Butter Fingers to do the catering.'

'Butter who?'

'Butter Fingers,' said her mother. 'Those two MPs' wives who do a lot of catering for the Houses of Parliament. There's been loads written about them in the newspapers recently.'

Felicity grinned, remembering the articles, and raised her eyebrows. 'I'm surprised they don't call themselves Banana Skins,' she said.

'No need to be sarcastic, dear. The important thing is their menu. They do wonderful old-fashioned things, like shepherd's pie, and bread and butter pudding. They suggested that we have a shepherd's pie and champagne reception.'

Felicity groaned again. 'It sounds as if I'm marrying Jeffrey Archer.'

'Pity you're not. He's awfully rich, and seems to be able to knock up a best-seller in the twinkling of an eye. Can't think why Dickens Books didn't get in there and snap him up.'

The last apostle spoon was tied and priced with a flourish. 'Let's get back to the nitty-gritty, darling,' said Irene seriously. 'There is one small point worrying me, and that is the fact that we shall have to rustle up at least another twenty guests for our side, otherwise we'll be hopelessly outnumbered.'

Aha! thought Felicity, feeling pleased. Now here is an easy way to keep the numbers down. 'We haven't got that many relations,' she pointed out. 'And there's nothing we can do about that.'

Nothing, however, was going to deter her mother.

'Nonsense, of course we can. You've got lots of business contacts, and so have I. They can come as friends, and we'll invite even our most distant relatives. Uncle Harold and Auntie Edna from Yorkshire can come.'

Felicity shuddered. She'd only met them a few times but the meetings were printed indelibly on her mind. 'Must we? He drinks like a fish and she swears like a trooper.'

'They only do that because they're married, dear. They get on each other's nerves,' said her mother serenely. 'But as I've always said, it might very well pay you to keep in with them. They've got a tidy nest-egg stashed away. Keep on the right side of them and they might leave it to you.'

'And pigs might fly,' said Felicity.

'Trust in God and keep your gunpowder dry. Cromwell said that,' her mother remarked enigmatically.

Felicity couldn't follow the complicated machinations of her mother's mind and was too tired to try. The wedding day was bearing down on her like a huge black mushroom cloud, its edges curling down, crushing and extinguishing all life-forms, including her own.

'I don't know about being launched. I've got a

horrible feeling that I'm about to be sunk,' she said pessimistically.

The wedding day dawned bright and beautiful, and to her surprise Felicity felt cheerful. The tiny patch of garden at the back of her mother's house had suddenly come alive as if to say, 'spring has arrived!' the brambles, which rampaged everywhere – neither Felicity nor her mother were keen gardeners – were covered in small fresh leaves. Brilliant green bunting for my wedding day, thought Felicity. And a clump of celandines in the damp patch at the far end of the garden had exploded into bright, shiny yellow stars. She gazed dreamily out of the window. I could write a book today, she thought wistfully, if only I had the time. Then the telephone rang, reminding her that she certainly did not have time. Not today, anyway.

It was Tony. 'I love you. I love you,' he said, then burst into a rousing chorus of, 'Oh, what a beautiful morning.'

Irene erupted into the room and snatched the phone. 'Stop talking, and hurry up,' she screeched, 'otherwise you'll be late for your own wedding.'

'Irene,' hissed Tony. 'Can Felicity hear?'

'No.' She turned her back on Felicity and walked away from the window.

'I think Samantha and the kids are coming to the wedding after all. Do you think that will be all right? Should I tell Felicity?'

'Yes, and no,' said Irene.

'Do you mean they can come?' whispered Tony.

'Yes,' said Irene.

'But not to tell Felicity.'

'Exactly,' said Irene. 'It's much too late in the day for you to do it. I'll do it. Now hurry up and get yourself ready, otherwise you'll be late.'

'I love you,' said Tony.

'What were you on about?' asked Felicity, struggling into her new dark blue summer suit. Once zipped up she looked at herself in the mirror. Not bad, in fact quite good. Lunching on a carrot and an apple for the past fortnight had paid off. She'd lost weight and it really showed. Strange how the loss of a few pounds gave one added confidence.

Her mother came and stood beside her. 'The blue suits you, darling,' she said. 'Brings out the colour of your eyes. You should wear it more often. Now hurry up and finish dressing, time is galloping past.'

Felicity sat on the end of the bed, beside a pair of very high-heeled navy blue shoes. They were very elegant, but she just knew that by the end of the day she wouldn't be able to wait to kick them off. Still, as her mother had said when they'd bought them, she didn't get married every day. 'You didn't tell me what it was you and Tony were talking about,' said Felicity, unwrapping a new pair of tights.

'Oh, last-minute arrangements,' prevaricated Irene hastily, then said, 'I hope Tony hasn't been drinking already. He's just told me that he loves me.'

'Full of general *bonhomie*,' said Felicity with a happy giggle, as she carefully wiggled her toes down into the new tights.

'Which is more than can be said for your daughter,' said her mother. 'She is downstairs. Dressed in black from head to toe. What's more, she's made up her face with ghastly pale make-up, half a ton of mascara on her eyes and she's got dark purple lips. She's either off to a funeral or about to audition for the Wicked Witch of the West. Certainly not off to a wedding.'

Felicity giggled. Nothing, not even Annabel, could dampen her spirits at the moment. 'Take no notice of her. She's going through a difficult stage.'

'At thirteen!' said Irene sharply. 'You'd better knock that on the head, my girl, and straight away. If she's difficult now, what on earth is she going to be like at sixteen?'

At the time Felicity didn't dare stop and think about it. Partly because all the magazine articles she'd read on modern parenting advised a warm, laid-back approach, and partly because she found Annabel so annoying that quite often her own natural tendencies teetered on the psychotic. Strangulation had often fleetingly crossed her mind. But silence, she'd decided, was best, when the only thing she could think of to say was, 'I could kill you!'

But later, at the shepherd's pie and champagne reception, which judging by the rate both were disappearing down the assembled company's throats was a great success, she did pause to reflect on her own daughter's behaviour. A state of affairs brought about by the circumstance of meeting Tony's own thirteen-year-old daughter. If Annabel was difficult, Felicity decided, then Hilary was verging on the delinquent.

It had all started with *The Hat*. The moment she and Tony had been ushered into the vicarage garden through a cloud of confetti thrown by well-wishers, much to the outrage of the church hall caretaker who was rushing around vainly trying to sweep it up with a dustpan and brush, Felicity had noticed first *The Hat*, then the woman beneath it. She was tall, and so slender that she made Felicity feel that she ought to enrol with Weight Watchers that very moment, and her pale lemon outfit shrieked designer label.

'Who on earth is that woman?' she whispered to Tony. 'She certainly isn't one of *my* guests.'

Her guests were all very ordinary, except Uncle Harold who was well away on the champagne and had a generous dollop of shepherd's pie on his tie. Auntie Edna's language had been fairly moderate, so far, although her hat, which almost certainly would have won a prize at the Chelsea Flower Show, was beginning to tilt balefully over one eye. An ominous sign.

Tony turned in the direction she was pointing and went bright crimson. He prayed that Irene had told Felicity about Samantha, but, already beginning to have a faint inkling of how his new mother-in-law did things, doubted it. He coughed, swallowed, and said in a rush and as nonchalantly as was possible in the circumstances, 'Her? Oh, that's Samantha.'

Felicity gasped, confirming Tony's suspicions. 'Your ex?' she asked icily.

'Yes,' said Tony, desperately trying to sound calm and matter-of-fact. 'I did mention it to . . .'

Felicity didn't let him finish. 'You've asked your ex-wife to *our* wedding, and you didn't even have the courage to tell me? What a cheek!'

'Hear, hear,' shouted Uncle Harold, who'd always had an uncanny ability to sniff out a row. 'Nothing like a really good row for getting a good wedding party going, that's what I always say.'

Luckily hardly anyone heard him. They were all too busy eating, drinking, or talking loudly in order to be heard above the music, which for some reason was playing a rousing chorus of 'There'll Always Be An England' at that particular moment. The church care-taker was doing the music and, from the selection he'd played so far, appeared only to possess tapes of wartime records.

But Irene heard him. Marching smartly across the lawn, she pushed Harold back down in his chair and refilled his glass. 'Shut up, Harold,' she hissed, 'or you'll be going back to Yorkshire sooner than you thought.'

Miss Shrimpton, Oliver Dickens's secretary of thirty years, also heard him, and nudged her boss sharply in the ribs. 'I do think, Oliver,' she said disapprovingly, 'that the man over there is inebriated.'

'Very likely, Joan. People often are at weddings.' Oliver smiled indulgently. It had taken a great deal of persuasion to get Joan Shrimpton to the wedding. In the end she'd come because he'd said that as a widower he needed a respectable lady to accompany him, and that he wouldn't go on his own. She'd come for his sake, but she didn't really approve because Tony was divorced, and also because there was to be champagne. She herself was drinking mineral water. *Still* mineral water. As far as she was concerned, Aqua Libra was positively decadent. The pastor at the Evangelical Mission Church she attended had assured her of her place in heaven, and she had no intention of jeopardizing that place by taking one step out of the virtuous line she had trodden all her life. It was, after all, the only thing she had to look forward to at the end of her old age.

Having firmly squashed Uncle Harold, Irene then strode over to Felicity and Tony. 'Do keep your voice down, Felicity, dear. This is a wedding.'

'I know. *Mine!*' said Felicity angrily. 'And Tony's ex-wife is here.'

Irene patted a worried Tony's arm. 'It's all right. I'll explain.'

Felicity scowled. 'Ten days ago you were trying to put me off Tony; now you're defending him.'

'Trying to put her off me! Is this true?' asked Tony.

Irene ignored him. 'Tony didn't ask her,' she said. 'He asked his children, and as you know they refused. But this morning they said they would come, but only if their mother brought them. So what else could I do? I invited her, and her partner, Piers Berkeley-Holmes, plus the children of course.'

'*You* invited her!' Felicity was incredulous.

'Yes, dear.' Irene looked suitably penitent.

'But why didn't anyone tell me?' She turned to Tony, who was shuffling his feet and looking extremely uncomfortable. 'Why didn't *you* tell me?'

'Because I'm a moral coward,' he said. 'You said so yourself. Darling, can you forgive me?'

'I, oh . . . well,' Felicity felt herself weakening and it occurred to her that she always did when he appealed to her better nature. 'I suppose so, damn you!'

Tony hugged her, and planted a kiss on her temple. 'Thank you, darling,' he whispered.

'Anyway,' said Irene, slightly belligerently because she didn't see why Tony should get all the absolution, 'they have a perfect right to be here. Your own daughter is. Samantha is only here to hold their hands.'

Felicity looked at Tony. His face registered a mixture of emotions. Humour, nervousness, hopefulness but most of all love. Love for me, she reminded herself. *Me*, not Samantha, who is an ex. What a mountain I'm making out of a molehill. Samantha poses no threat. She looked across at Piers Berkeley-Holmes, who had the eerie appearance of having stepped straight from the pages of *Tatler*. Samantha and Piers went well together. Just as she and Tony did.

'Come on,' she said to Tony. 'You'd better introduce me to your children, and your ex,' she added.

Halfway across the lawn they were waylaid by a large woman wearing a loudly patterned floral dress.

'My dear,' said the woman. 'I must congratulate you. A wonderful wedding, and so different! Champagne and shepherd's pie, a terrific combination. I shall tell the vicar of Oakford. We could have it at the June fundraising for the church roof, although I fear fizzy cider will need to be substituted for the champagne. I look forward to meeting you –' she fixed Felicity with a beady eye '– on one, or perhaps several, of Oakford's committees. There are so many good causes needing your support. Samantha always graced us with her presence, and we shall be very pleased to welcome Tony's new wife.'

Felicity opened her mouth about to say that she doubted that she would have time, but the woman had already zoomed off at great speed to pinion someone else in a corner. 'I have no intention of being on committees, any of them, especially not those previously *graced* by Samantha,' she told Tony. 'Who was that woman?'

'Alice Appleby, the senior partner's wife,' said Tony. 'Good-hearted woman, in her own way. All right in small doses.'

But Felicity had already lost interest. She was much more concerned about Tony's children. 'Why didn't they want to meet me?' she asked nodding in the direction of the three children standing close to Samantha.

'Well . . . they, I mean the children aren't . . .' Tony knew he was making a hash of it and started again. No point in beating about the bush; he might as well tell the truth. 'The problem is this. They didn't want me to remarry because Samantha and Piers aren't married and don't intend to be. They are all harbouring a forlorn hope that one day we'll get back together again.'

'It would help all of us, then, if Piers and Samantha got married,' observed Felicity. 'Because then they would know it was finished for good.'

'I gather Piers refuses to entertain the thought of marriage.' Tony shrugged. 'Perhaps he thinks he may want to dump her later. I feel sorry for her.'

Sorry for her! So he still felt something. Felicity looked at the gold band so recently placed on her finger by Tony, and felt a whole lot less secure than she had five minutes previously. Supposing Piers did dump that gorgeous creature and she came and pleaded with Tony to take her back? What chance would she, Felicity, have? It would be like putting Beauty and the Beast side by side and saying, 'Choose.' Not that she could exactly be called a beast. But Felicity was realistic and knew she was definitely not a raving beauty. She was reasonably attractive, but ordinary. Whereas Samantha was extraordinarily beautiful. Suddenly she felt worse than ordinary. She felt frumpish in her dark blue summer suit, and matching leather shoes and handbag. And suddenly the pounds she'd shed were not enough; beside Samantha she felt fat. She longed, passionately, to be coathanger-thin and elegant, and felt bad-tempered because she wasn't.

'They'll be all right eventually,' said Tony, still talking about his children. 'You know what kids are like. They never want things to change.'

Felicity pulled herself together. Of course he'd never leave her for Samantha, and it was true what he'd said about the children. She remembered Annabel's objections and felt guilty that she'd never mentioned how much she'd objected to Tony. 'Of course they'll be all right. Just give them time. We agreed the other day, didn't we, that your divorce must have traumatized them badly?' she said. 'Time, that's all they need.'

Tony sighed. 'I'm afraid they were traumatized from the day they were born. I knew it, although I never wanted to admit it, not even to myself. In fact, this is the first time I *have* admitted it to anyone.'

Felicity was puzzled. 'Knew what? Admitted what? Admitted what?'

'That Samantha hated being a mother. She just wasn't cut out for it.'

By now Felicity was even more puzzled. 'But if that's the case, why did she fight you for custody?'

Tony gave a lopsided grin. The divorce case was something he had no wish to dwell on. He'd never stopped wishing he'd got to Pillson's first. Pillson's was the London firm of solicitors Samantha had engaged. Too late Tony had seen their discreet advertisement – 'Divorce – Sensitively but Strenuously Handled'. Strenuous had been right; he wasn't so sure about the sensitive bit. It was entirely their doing that Samantha had got the children by playing the heavily loaded mother-bonding card.

'They had the choice,' he said sadly. 'The children, I mean. So I suppose they must love her more than me. I've decided that there's no such thing as logic when it comes to emotions. Especially emotions between mothers and their children. They are the most difficult of all to suss out.'

Felicity thought of her own turbulent relationship with her mother and daughter. 'No,' she said slowly. 'I suppose you're right. Logic doesn't enter into it.

The bond is there whether you like it or not. Even Samantha, although you tell me she isn't a natural mother, obviously has that special bond.'

'I suppose that's what it is,' said Tony. But he sounded unconvinced.

CHAPTER 5

Felicity's initial burst of sympathy for Tony's poor traumatized children rapidly evaporated when faced with the onslaught of their unadulterated hostility. Hilary was introduced to her first. She was a large girl, much larger than Annabel, although the same age. Felicity wondered briefly whose idea it had been to cram her ungainly shape into a pink, silk, over-frilled dress, the belt of which cut her in half so that she looked twice as large. The poor thing looked as if she had escaped from a birthday party and grown, and grown, and grown, like a character out of *Alice in Wonderland*, and then come to the wedding before anyone could catch her and change the dress for something more suitable.

Hilary stood before Felicity, a smouldering pink blancmange of a girl. 'I hate you,' she said eventually, extending a fat, food-smothered hand. Felicity noticed that she only proffered the hand after an ostentatious nudge to do so from her mother. 'You've stolen my father,' she added venomously.

'I'm pleased to meet you, Hilary,' Felicity said,

baring her teeth in what she prayed would pass for a genuinely caring stepmother-type smile. Were there any genuinely caring stepmothers about? She was beginning to doubt it, and surely not if they were faced with a stepdaughter like this. But she soldiered on. 'I think you should know, Hilary, that I didn't even meet your father until after your mother had divorced him. So you see, I didn't steal him.'

'As good as,' mumbled Hilary, retrieving her hand and fleeing back to her mother's side. 'And I shall always hate you.'

Samantha's face was completely hidden by the hat, so Felicity didn't have the satisfaction of seeing even a flicker of expression. The black brim of the hat moved slightly, but *that* gave absolutely nothing away. She turned to Hilary again and smiled once more. 'Well,' she said as warmly as possible in the circumstances, '*I* don't hate *you*, Hilary, and I never will. And I hope that in time we shall learn to be good friends. I know this isn't easy for you; it isn't easy for any of us.'

'You didn't have to make it worse by marrying my father.' For good measure Hilary stuck out her tongue. Felicity noted that it was the same unpleasant shade of pink as the dress.

'Hilary!' snapped Tony. 'Behave yourself.' Hilary stuck out her tongue again, and crossed her eyes for good measure. Not much evidence of parental control there, thought Felicity, her heart sinking. Surely Tony wasn't one of those weak fathers who delegated all the discipline to the mother? 'She's at a very awkward age

72

at the moment,' he whispered. A slightly plaintive whisper, Felicity thought, and felt irritated.

She was about to snap right back that it was no excuse for such behaviour, but then remembered Annabel. Tactics dictated that it might be unwise to criticise at the moment. After all, Tony would be *living* with her awkward daughter, whereas she only had to meet his offspring occasionally. That was, at least, something to be thankful about.

And where was Annabel? Felicity looked around just in time to see her daughter down a whole glass of champagne in one gulp. She was sitting with Uncle Harold and Auntie Edna. All three were roaring with laughter. Annabel was lounging back in her chair in a most unladylike way, her long, thin black legs with the clumsy Doc Marten boots on the end sticking out, very nearly tripping a waitress as she scurried by carrying a tray of glasses.

Aunt Edna's Chelsea Flower Show hat had slipped as low as a Guardsman's bearskin, but that didn't prevent the glass from unerringly finding her mouth. Felicity could see Samantha's partner, Piers, looking across at them distastefully, and wrinkling his long nose slightly as if they were a very unpleasant smell.

Aunt Edna was shouting and swearing, her words carrying like a clarion call across the green velvet of the vicarage lawn. 'And I bloody well told 'im. "'Ere, I said. What do you take me for? A daft bugger? Well, that's where you've made a big mistake," I said. So you can bloody well bugger off.'

Annabel shrieked with raucous laughter.

Felicity cringed, fervently wishing a black hole would open up in the lawn and swallow all three. She glanced across at Hilary and Samantha. Was it her imagination, or was Hilary looking enviously at her black-clad shrieking daughter and drunken relatives?

She turned to Hilary once more. Why didn't Samantha say something to help things along? Keeping one anxious eye on Annabel, she tried to smile again, but her face was aching with all the artificial smiling it had done so far, plus the fact she was attempting to keep track of Annabel's antics, and the smile wouldn't materialize. She gave up, and said, 'Hilary, my dear, I have no intention of quarrelling with you. Especially not today of all days.'

'I am *not* your dear,' said Hilary loudly, looking her straight in the eye with bone chilling dislike. 'And you are not to call me that.'

There was a long awkward silence. Then two rather podgy boys were pushed forward. 'This is Philip and Peter, and they are both fourteen,' said Tony, leaping into the gap. He attempted a laugh to lighten the atmosphere, but failed miserably, and wished he had followed his instinct in the morning and put Samantha and the children off. I should never have asked them in the first place, he thought wretchedly, and Samantha shouldn't have brought them. Somehow, putting some of the blame on to Samantha, if only in his own mind, did lighten the load a little. He smiled encouragingly at the boys. 'Although they're twins,' he said, 'they're not completely identical. Philip has blue eyes and Peter has brown ones.'

The twins edged slowly forward towards Felicity, and she felt a sense of hopeful relief. They did seem just the teeniest bit more approachable than their sister. Not so openly hostile; more dejected than unfriendly. 'Hello.' Her smile was met with a stony stare from both and she quickly realized that she had misjudged them. Neither would look straight at her; both stared at something apparently totally fascinating just above her left shoulder. It was immensely irritating, but Felicity continued in the same friendly tone of voice. 'I can see that I shall have to be careful when I'm am with you, otherwise I shall be getting muddled up.'

'Dad already has,' said one in a loud, disinterested voice. 'He always gets our eyes wrong.'

Ah! So that's Peter, who has blue eyes not brown, thought Felicity mentally making a note. She turned to Tony. 'How can you . . .?'

'But there's no need to worry,' said a rather anxious voice. It was the boy with brown eyes, which were softer, rather like Tony's. Felicity smiled. Now this must be Philip. He certainly looked much more promising, almost teetering on the verge of being pleasant.

'There's no need to worry because you won't be with us to get into a muddle.' The other boy's blue eyes were hard and unflinching. 'We're not coming back down to Oakford until after you've gone. We've all made up our minds about that.'

Tony closed his eyes. Samantha might have warned him, instead of letting him assume that because they'd changed their minds they'd had a change of heart. The boys were being even worse, if that was possible, than Hilary.

'Don't be so stupid,' he said. 'Felicity isn't going anywhere. She's going to be with me at Oakford for good. And you *will* be seeing her because you are coming down in the school holidays. Your mother and I have agreed on that. So you might as well get used to it.'

Surveying the bad-tempered looking trio standing before them, Felicity decided that she'd be heartily relieved if they *never* came down to Cherry Trees. As far as she was concerned this one meeting was one too many.

Tony turned towards her, saw the dislike sparkling in her blue eyes and panicked. Everything was rapidly spiralling out of control. He put his hand on her arm. 'Take no notice of them, darling. I haven't got them muddled. Philip is the blue-eyed one and Peter has brown eyes. They're just trying to confuse you.'

'With great success,' said Felicity in a frozen voice, jettisoning any faintly lingering ideas of playing the saintly stepmother. The halo was strangling her. 'Just remember,' she said in her most glacial tones and looking straight at the children, 'that when you do come down to Oakford, don't try playing silly games with me. I shall be fair and helpful, and I shall expect the same treatment from you. If we get this fact straight right from the beginning then I'm sure we shall all get along just fine.'

With one accord the two boys turned tail and fled back to their mother, clinging to her lemon-clad arms as if their lives depended on it. Then all four turned and began to walk away.

Wretches, the lot of them, thought Felicity, including Samantha, and feeling vicious.

'Oh, damn! I'm not sure that was the best thing to say. You've upset them, Felicity.' Too late he realized that perhaps he should have been more tactful. 'Oh, Felicity!' He groaned. 'Sorry, but they do seem very upset.'

Felicity ignored the apology. She was feeling too angry to be won over by a sorry! 'Not nearly as upset as I am,' she snapped.

Caught between the devil and the deep blue sea, Tony had to make a decision. He decided that Felicity was likely to be much easier to placate than his children. He'd sort them out first, if possible, and make it up to her later. 'I'll have to go and make the peace,' he said. 'Excuse me, darling.' Then, leaving Felicity standing beside her mother, he followed the quartet across the lawn.

'Why is it men always panic at the slightest sign of trouble?' murmured Irene.

Felicity, torn between bursting into undignified tears or shrieking at Tony to come back, which would have been equally undignified, stood in silence and seethed. Then she turned to her mother. 'Anyone would think that I'd said that I was going to put them up against a wall and shoot the lot of them.'

'Not such a bad idea,' said her mother with an uncharitably malicious chuckle.

'Don't you laugh!' Felicity glared at her. 'You invited them.'

'I know, darling. But how was I to know that they were going to turn out to be so ghastly? However, just remember this. No one is perfect. Not even you!'

'Spare me the homespun homily, *please*,' snapped Felicity, wearily helping herself to another glass of champagne from a passing waitress. Might as well get sloshed, she thought moodily, it's the only way the rest of today is going to be bearable. Of course, her mother was right, no one *was* perfect. And common sense told her that Tony's children were probably being evil because they'd been hurt by their parents. She realized too, that she and Tony should have talked about them more, foreseen possible problems so that they could be met halfway. And she should have made an effort to meet them instead of keeping Tony all to herself. But too late now, the damage had been done. Marriage was a compromise, and she'd have to get over her animosity and compromise with Tony's family. Compromise, compromise! What a depressing thought. During nine years of widowhood, the only real compromising she'd ever had to do was for Annabel. And that hadn't been a hundred per cent successful. Was she ready for long-term comprises? She wasn't at all sure. And now, after meeting Tony's children, she wasn't sure that she could ever *begin* to like them.

'Mum,' she said miserably, 'my first attempt at playing happy families has been a hopeless failure, and I honestly don't see that . . .'

'Not hopeless,' interrupted her mother, 'but not an

unqualified success either. And don't start thinking that you'll never be able to get along with them, because you've *got* to.'

'Don't remind me!' said Felicity.

'Darling, I did warn you that being a second wife wouldn't be easy.'

Felicity looked across the lawn to where Tony was standing with his family. Samantha, or at least The Hat, was bobbing up and down animatedly, and Tony looked as if he was pleading. Damn him! thought Felicity, feeling horribly shut out. That little clan has made up its mind, they're *never* going to let me in. 'But you didn't warn me that I had to go straight into battle on my wedding day,' she said wearily.

'Gird your loins,' said her mother enigmatically, 'and start as you mean to go on.'

'Gird my loins! The way those wretched children looked at me, I think I may need to invest in a suit of armour.'

Irene chuckled mischievously. 'I might just be able to help you there. I've got one on the Camden High Street stall. Bought it in auction at Hendlesham Hall recently.'

In spite of everything Felicity had to laugh at her mother's expression. 'Oh, Mum,' she said ruefully. 'What have I done?'

'You've married the man you love,' said her mother firmly. 'And now it's up to you to make a go of it. Don't leave it up to him. Men are hopeless at these sort of things. Let him fix the car or clean out the drains; when he's not doctoring I dare say he'll be able to manage that. But when it comes to emotions, especially the maelstrom of family emotions, men are hopeless.'

'A maelstrom!' said Felicity. 'Oh, but you make it sound difficult.'

'Just keep your sense of humour,' said Irene, skilfully swopping her empty glass for a full one from another passing tray, 'and you'll be all right.'

'It's all right for you to be so matter-of-fact and detached,' grumbled Felicity. 'You're not moving to Hampshire and inheriting a ready-made family. Although, thank God, they'll only be there for the school holidays, and not even all of those.'

'Quite right, dear,' said Irene contentedly. 'I'm staying put, right here in Primrose Hill. I've never been keen on lots of children, and if you take my advice you won't be going all broody and starting to have more babies.'

'Certainly not,' said Felicity with absolute conviction. This was one thing she *was* sure about. 'A baby is the last thing I need. Anyway, at thirty-five I'm too old. But, Mum, you will come down to Hampshire sometimes, won't you? Just to visit. The fresh air will do you good, and it's so quiet and peaceful there.'

Irene snorted. 'I prefer the bustle of the crowds, the cars and the pollution to fresh air any day.' Then she relented and gave a wicked grin. 'But I'll come and liven you up from time to time.'

Tony came back. 'That's settled,' he said. 'I gave them all a good telling-off.'

'I thought you were going to appease them,' Irene remarked wryly.

'Oh!' muttered Tony vaguely. 'I did that first, then I told them off.'

'What was Samantha nodding at?' asked Felicity. 'I could see her hat going up and down like a yo-yo.'

'Nodding at the children, I expect. I hardly exchanged a word with her. Not that we ever did exchange many words.' He put an arm around Felicity, and squeezed her hard. 'Don't look so worried, darling. I promise my children will behave like absolute angels in future.'

I'll believe *that* when it happens, thought Felicity, but, remembering what her mother had said about *having* to get on with them, wisely kept her mouth shut.

'And now, darling,' continued Tony, 'don't you think we ought to be going? We've only got a week to ourselves, and I want to make the most of you.'

From the gleam in his brown eyes Felicity had a good idea of what he wanted to make the most of, but she didn't feel as enthusiastic as usual. The episode with his family had left her feeling strangely exhausted and depressed. She just *couldn't* have a headache on her wedding night! Could she? She caught a glimpse of her mother's warning expression, drew a deep breath and said gaily, 'Come on, darling. I can't *wait* to leave.'

At least that's the truth, she thought dispiritedly, and realized that she'd started compromising already. She was a wife.

CHAPTER 6

'*The bed was a snap buy back in the sixties for £5 and after a good polish and a new mattress it was transformed to fit into the elegant Victorian-style bedroom you see in the photograph. This is where the story ends. After years of hard work, the run-down terrace house in Holland Park has been transformed into an idyllic London townhouse.*'

Samantha tapped out the last word of her article, read it through, then sat back with a self-satisfied sigh. Yes, she had managed to strike just the right note, practical and yet at the same time making the overall elegant effect seem easy to achieve. Not, of course, that this was true. But that was the secret. To make the readers keep turning the pages, to think that they could do it too. Piers would be pleased.

The alarm on the small clock on the desk rang, a persistent buzz until Samantha turned it off. She sighed again. The alarm intruded, reminding her of duties she would rather forget but couldn't. Venetia was expecting her. Venetia relied on her visits to brighten her life. Or at least, Samantha supposed she did. She paused for a moment and stared out of the window of the small room which was her office in the St John's Wood house. It looked out into the side passageway in which the bricks had been painted white and fitted with manger baskets. Pansies had recently been planted in the baskets and the passageway was a riot of dark blue and yellow. Very tasteful and elegant, quite different from the Notting Hill house where she'd been brought up by Venetia, her maternal grandmother, after her own mother's early death. She sighed again. Yes, she must go. Even although it would swallow up the whole afternoon and probably make her late back, something which would make Piers look at her with disapproval. He hated her visiting the Notting Hill house, said it was not the *right* area to be seen in. Piers had very fixed ideas about some things. What other people thought, or might think, was important to him. He couldn't bear to be tainted by anything he called lower class. And although most of Notting Hill was both trendy and hugely expensive, the high prices hadn't reached the small pocket where Venetia lived, which was still definitely lower class.

But in this instance, surprising even herself, Samantha had put her foot down where Venetia was concerned. She *was* her grandmother and she owed her something. Although most of the time she wasn't quite sure what that something was, nevertheless she wasn't prepared to desert Venetia entirely. So, leaving her office, she rang for a taxi and prepared herself for her monthly visit.

The taxi lurched and weaved in and out of the traffic, on its way to Notting Hill and Venetia, and with nothing else to do Samantha sat mulling over her life. As it had been, how it was, and where it was going. Self-absorbed, she didn't notice when the taxi passed the maze of streets just off the market, or notice that Irene Hobbit was there working on her stall, haggling with a tourist over the price of a piece of French faience. Since meeting Irene, both she and Venetia regarded her with disapproving admiration. Disapproving, because running market stalls was such a common, working class thing to do, and admiration because she was successful at making money. Venetia, she knew, particularly envied Irene this ability, and, despite her disapproval, had taken to sidling past Hobbit's stall trying to pick up a few hints on how she managed it. But today Samantha didn't notice Irene; because for the first time since leaving and divorcing Tony she began to wonder just exactly where it was she was going in her new life.

It had come as a great shock to Samantha to discover, once she had moved in permanently with Piers, that she was not as ecstatically happy as she'd thought she'd be. Although not for one single moment did she ever contemplate going back to Tony. By the time she'd met Piers the marriage had been desperately unhappy for both of them, even if Tony *had* never admitted it. But she had known it, and couldn't wait to shake the dust of Cherry Trees from her feet.

Marriage to Tony had never been fantastic. In fact nothing about marriage had been how she'd thought it would be. Tony had been the first man she'd slept with when stone-cold sober, and she had found it all rather boring. Once she'd been to bed with Piers, however, she'd realized what she was missing out on. It was the sex which had drawn her like a magnet to Piers. With him it was all new and fascinating. Sexual tension had been there from the very first moment they'd met, something which had never been present with Tony.

Now she realized that she had *liked* Tony, but not loved him. He was a sane, solvent, pleasant man with a prestigious job. And, more than that, he had offered her security. She'd grasped that security with both hands, only to find it increasingly claustrophobic until in the end she'd felt imprisoned. Piers did not offer security, nor was she really sure where loving him stopped and lusting after him started. Instead he offered her an indefinable chemistry. For Samantha the chemistry was a chronic attraction which had led her to kick over the traces of her old life and follow him to London.

The chemistry which had sizzled at their first meeting sizzled still. Of course the sex had to be slightly more discreet when the children came to the house for the holidays; all three had a nasty habit of barging into rooms without knocking. At Cherry Trees it hadn't mattered as there was never anything going on between herself and Tony of any consequence. But now it annoyed her, and she knew it infuriated Piers, although he was careful not to say so. But his glacial manner gave him away.

'Angel,' he'd said after one particularly embarrassing intrusion when Samantha had of necessity pretended she was just about to leap into the bath, and a naked Piers had dived for cover under the duvet. 'Angel, they are *your* children, and because I adore you, I adore them. But could you persuade them not to burst in unannounced? It's so terribly antisocial.'

The exasperated tone and the heavily emphasized *your* had not gone unnoticed. Samantha decided that in future the three of them ought to spend more time at Cherry Trees, something she'd been totally opposed to at the beginning. Not because she had desperately wanted the children to stay with her; she had not, and if she was honest she had never really wanted them at all. But because she knew it would annoy Tony, she had said that she did. At the time she'd been furious over the casual manner in which he'd taken her departure. It had reinforced the hopeless emptiness of their relationship, and that, illogical though she knew it to be, had made her angry. So, because she knew he loved them more than her, she had demanded, and her pushy solicitor had got, the children. Now, when she was having one of her more honest moments, she was a little ashamed of her spitefulness, and wished she hadn't insisted. Besides, there was also the added factor that having the children with her cramped her new lifestyle.

Everyone at Oakford, and most of all the children, had been surprised when she and Tony had split up. Of course, Tony wasn't totally surprised, and Venetia not at all.

Venetia, now aged eighty-seven, had said of Tony when Samantha had told her she was to marry him,

'He's not your type. Not your type at all. He's too ordinary. It won't last.'

Samantha had been brought up, very properly and rather austerely, by Venetia. Her own mother had succumbed to cancer at the age of twenty-five, and after her mother's death her father had decided he much preferred sailing around the world to looking after his only daughter. Samantha's last memory of him was watching his sailing ketch disappearing round the bend in the river Thames at Wapping, the small boat gradually becoming obscured by the riverside cranes.

Afterwards postcards occasionally arrived. The last one had said, '*It's frightfully choppy here on the Orinoco*'. Venetia had thrown it on the fire, saying, 'What on earth is he doing on the Orinoco? That's a river, not a sea.'

Samantha had always thought it a pity that she'd thrown that particular postcard away, since it turned out to be the last they ever received, and she assumed her father must have drowned in those self-same choppy waters. She also wondered if it was the lack of loving parenting in her childhood which made her feel so indifferent towards her own offspring.

However, when it came to marrying Tony, Samantha dismissed her grandmother's opinion on the grounds of her snobbery. Venetia was the second child of the Hon. Jeremy Lyttelton-Ross, an impoverished aristocrat. She never let anyone forget it – the aristocratic part, not the impoverished bit; that was skated over in conversation. As a child Venetia had grown up in a large, draughty, crumbling heap on the edge of the Yorkshire moors, and had practically starved in genteel poverty. But, eventually tiring of being poor, she'd married a man socially beneath her who had money. Afterwards she moved to a grand mansion outside Harrogate and lived the life of a lady. Too late did she discover, when he died, that her husband was in hock up to his ears. Almost everything she used, wore, slept in or even drank from belonged to the bank and other various creditors.

But, a survivor to the last drop of her blue blood, she'd upped sticks and moved to London. Partly to get away from the disgrace, and partly to be near the only person she'd every really loved, her daughter Arabella. By then Arabella had a handsome, rather feckless husband, Felix, and a daughter of her own, Samantha. By selling some jewellery which *did* actually belong to her, and using some money from a trust fund which the creditors couldn't touch, Venetia had bought a little house in a then fashionable district of Notting Hill. It had gone downhill since then, but she still lived there, getting on surprisingly well with her Rastafarian neighbours who called her 'Lady England'. A title she was quite happy to accept.

Samantha was a beautiful child, but Venetia didn't believe in spoiling her by letting her know it. In fact, she didn't believe in spoiling her at all. She resented the fact that Felix had swanned off into the sunset after Arabella's death, leaving her to bring up the child on her own, and could never really bring herself to love Samantha, who was too good-looking and took after her father, Felix, and was not all like her beloved daughter, Arabella. But she believed in doing her duty, and, practical down to her little toenails, had sold her last few worthwhile antiques to send Samantha to modelling school, knowing there was no point in considering an academic career. Samantha didn't have that kind of ability. Beauty was the only positive thing she had, and she was obsessed with all things beautiful and inclined to be self-centred. Venetia rightly thought modelling would suit her down to the ground.

After modelling school, through which Samantha glided with the natural confidence of a born coathanger, Venetia badgered the then editors of *Vogue* and *Tatler*, whom she knew through family connections, until Samantha finally made it as a model on to their illustrious pages. Then she sat back while Samantha partied, got drunk, took drugs, starved herself; none of that mattered as long as she was featuring in the pages of the top glossy magazines. Sooner or later, Venetia was sure, a member of the aristocracy, or someone from landed gentry, or at the very least a millionaire would snap Samantha up in marriage. That way, she reckoned, she would ensure a comfortable old age for herself and a life of decorative ease for Samantha. The very last thing she had wanted was for her to settle down with a bourgeois, predictable, middle-class doctor.

But Samantha had thought she was in love. The continual round of drink, drugs and parties was beginning to pall, and it was the predictability of Tony's nature and the security of his job that were an essential part of his attraction. It was only later that her footloose spirit demanded freedom. When she had first met Tony she had needed the rest.

'You'll love Tony as much as I do when you get to know him,' she had said all those years ago. She'd been confident then, because Tony was tall, blond and handsome, with soulful brown eyes. He reminded her of the Labrador puppy she'd once had, whose life had been cut prematurely short by the Notting Hill dustcart on bin day.

'He'll never be rich. In fact, in comparison to most of the men you've been mixing with, he's poor.' There was no greater sin than that, in Venetia's eyes. After spending most of her life trying to make two and two make five, she'd set her heart on Samantha marrying someone with plenty of money.

'I don't care about that.' Samantha had been adamant.

'You will,' replied Venetia ominously. 'You're not cut out for his kind of life. You won't fit in.'

'I shall *make* myself fit,' said Samantha.

They had married while Tony was finishing his training for general practice at St Thomas's in London, and everything was fine. At least, Samantha told herself it was fine. They lived in a poky little flat in the heart of the city, which suited her as there was hardly any housework to do, and she carried on with her modelling. With plenty of money from her fees they were able to eat out most of the time when Tony wasn't working, and when he was, Samantha went to her parties or to the theatre. It was when Tony bought into the practice in Oakford in the New Forest, and Samantha moved with him down to Hampshire and tried to settle down to being a country wife and, later on, a mother, that it all went wrong. It didn't take her long to discover that Venetia had been right. She was not suited to either role. She didn't fit.

Venetia put off visiting, but eventually came down after the twins had been born. Still a tough Yorkshire woman at heart, she hated the lush greenery of the New Forest.

'All these wretched trees,' she complained. 'They get in the way of the view. I like to be able to see for miles and miles.'

'You can't see for miles and miles in Notting Hill,' Tony pointed out.

Venetia did not care for anyone disagreeing with her. 'I can see for *miles* from my top bedroom. Miles and miles of chimneypots. It always reminds me of the Yorkshire moors.'

Tony thought anything less like the moors would be hard to find, and said so. 'Besides,' he added. 'Chimney pots pour out smoke.'

'It's a smokeless zone,' replied Venetia triumphantly.

'Well, fumes, then. Gas and oil pollute even if you can't see it. Trees breathe life into the atmosphere. Our children will be very healthy living down here.'

'What nonsense he talks,' Venetia grumbled later on to Samantha. 'You were always perfectly healthy living in London. And look at me. The picture of health.

Which is more than I can say for you at the moment. You look worn out.'

'I am worn out,' confessed Samantha. 'I've only just finished decorating the bedroom.'

'Yes, I know. I've seen it,' said Venetia, who thoroughly disapproved of Samantha and all this Do It Yourself nonsense. If she'd married the sort of man she, Venetia, had originally had in mind for her, he would have paid someone else to do it.

'Do you like it?' Samantha was desperate for praise. Tony, absorbed in his new work and new family, never seemed to notice when she'd been busy with paint and wallpaper unless she drew it to his attention. As far as he was concerned, the house was there, and as long as it was comfortable he was happy.

'It's aggressively countrified,' said Venetia in damning tones. 'Come to that, so is the rest of the house. I feel as if I'm in one of those twee shops with no carpets on the floor. You know, all stripped pine, dark green and red ribbons, flowery cushions and everything smelling of herbs.'

Samantha was affronted. 'Well, this is a country house, and Tony is a country doctor. Besides, everyone else's house is similar. It's the vogue.' Since giving up modelling Samantha had become reformed where housework was concerned, and now slaved all day to make her home look straight out of *Homes and Gardens*.

'Good God, Samantha,' shrilled Venetia. 'If you're not careful you'll turn into one of those creatures like the Stepford Wives. A dummy programmed to do the housework!' The previous Christmas, Samantha and Tony had bought her a video and now she was an avid film watcher. *The Stepford Wives* had been the last film she'd seen, and all the way through she'd been uncomfortably reminded of Samantha. To Venetia all the wives had been Samantha lookalikes.

'Nonsense,' said Samantha. But all the same, she did feel a faint prick of unease. *A dummy programmed to do the housework* – that was exactly what she felt like.

Venetia peered at her suspiciously. 'I think you've turned into one already. Look, you've even got a flowery print dress on, and I suppose you swap recipes when you meet the other wives around here.'

'Well, yes, I do, but . . .'

Venetia gazed with horror down at her plate. 'And these scones we're eating are ones you've actually *made*. I thought they weren't like the shop-bought ones I always have in London.' Her tone of voice intimated that she thought shop ones were infinitely superior. 'And now I come to think of it, those babies of yours are far too clean and tidy to be normal.'

This was a subject Samantha had been longing to bring up. Venetia was not the most inspiring of confidantes, but she was better than no one else. And there was nobody in Oakford that Samantha felt she could talk to. A model mother, she cared for the twins by the book. For some illogical reason she felt that because she was a doctor's wife she had to be perfect. So she referred to books for everything, from concern over the colour of what was in their potties, to their developmental milestones. But there was nothing in any of the books about how a mother should *feel*. And Samantha was worried sick about her maternal instincts. The problem was, she didn't seem to have any.

'It's not that I don't love my children,' she said to Venetia. The twins were then nearly a year old, and she had a horrible suspicion that she was pregnant again. 'I do love them, but in a very distant kind of way. They don't stir me with emotion as they should. And I feel so terribly tired all the time.'

'There's nothing wrong with you except that you do too much,' said Venetia, who was a firm believer in other people doing things for her, something she usually managed to arrange. 'All this decorating. It's ridiculous.'

'We can't afford to have anyone in. It's far too expensive. And Tony doesn't have the time.' Samantha was near to tears.

Venetia sniffed. 'It's enough to wear any woman to a frazzle,' she said in a slightly kinder tone of voice. 'You're doing your best for the children. That's all any mother can do.' She stopped for a moment, her gaze softening as she looked at Samantha, then she said, 'And another thing. Is it really necessary for you to be on these committees you told me about in your last letter?'

Samantha sighed. Village committees, the bane of her life. A committee for the youth club, another for the summer fête, one for the aged of the district, one for the community bus service; the list was endless. Samantha hadn't even been aware that such things existed before she moved to Oakford.

'Well?' demanded Venetia. 'Is it necessary?'

'Tony says it's part of country life, and I suppose it is. And I do so want to fit in.' As she spoke Samantha heard an echo of Venetia. *You'll never fit in.*

Looking back, Samantha knew that that moment was when she had acknowledged that the rot had set in. It wasn't working. She wasn't happy with her role as a wife or mother. But she said and did nothing, because the following week another pregnancy was confirmed. And after that the years flew by, and she still said nothing. She went through the motions of being a wife but her heart wasn't in it, although Tony didn't seem to notice, at least not at first. All her energy went on the house, garden and children. In that order. Hilary stayed at home and went to day school, but the boys went away to boarding school at seven years old, and Samantha felt guiltily relieved by their absence. But it gave her more time to concentrate on her surroundings, and because she was unhappy she worked on the house and garden until it looked good enough to be used as a film location. Which was the cue for Piers to enter her life.

Tony had met a PR girl for an advertising company at a pharmaceutical company function. 'She's looking for a house to use for location shots for a film,' he told Samantha, 'in the New Forest, with old-world charm and plenty of room, spacious surroundings. I've invited them to come and have a look around here.'

'I don't want a film crew in here, tramping all over the house,' Samantha protested.

Tony was not to be put off. 'Don't be silly. If they

select us we'll have a great fat cheque. It will help with the boys' school fees.'

She was overruled, and eventually the film crew arrived, with Piers as the director.

'Darling,' he'd said, flapping his long, tapering white hands expansively as he inspected everything. 'What a divine house. Absolutely perfect for this promotion. I've been looking everywhere for something which is a cross between Little House on the Prairie and an upmarket bordello.'

'Damned cheek,' snorted Tony, who had disliked Piers on sight, but he was easily soothed by thoughts of the size of the cheque.

As soon as Piers had summed up the decor of the house and garden in that one scathing sentence, Samantha could see where she'd gone wrong. She'd tried to make it cosy and homely, and had gone overboard with the frills, flounces and colours. From that moment on she hated Cherry Trees and every-thing it stood for with a ferocity verging on obsession. But Piers had fascinated her, and before the filming was finished she had gone to bed with him and found that experience even more fascinating.

'Let me take you away from all this,' Piers had said with a delicate shudder. He hadn't said he loved her – in fact, since she'd known him he'd *never* said he loved her – but he *had* taken her away. Now, over a year later, she lived with him in his perfectly exquisite St John's Wood house. Piers liked the minimalist style of furnishing, and after the frills and flounces of the New Forest house Samantha was ripe for conversion. She found the spartan atmosphere both restful and beautiful.

But problems always arose when the children arrived. Then she needed to be permanently on the lookout for dirty coffee cups, Coke bottles, comics, magazines, and surely no other children managed to make so many crumbs or eat cornflakes all the time and slop the milk about? Piers's house was not designed for children.

She knew that the children, used to the comfort of their country home, disliked the clinical atmosphere. But when they complained, she said, 'It's different, darlings. That's all. You'll get used to it.' Half of her believed what she said; the other half knew they would never get used to it.

'But we can't do our bikes here,' grumbled Philip and Peter in unison. Dismantling motorbikes was their current craze, or had been before they'd been transported to London.

'And I can't ride Cotton-Socks in St John's Wood,' said Hilary.

'Those are Cherry Trees things,' replied Samantha. 'Here, in London, there are lots of much more exciting things to do.'

'Such as?' Philip moodily hurled himself into the sofa.

'Piers says you should try to be more intellectual and I agree with him,' said Samantha. 'There are plenty of museums near by.'

What Piers had actually said was, 'Can't those kids get out from under our feet? Send them to the Natural

History Museum. With any luck they might get eaten by a dinosaur.'

Although the children felt out of place in London, Samantha was in her element. She was a different woman. Thanks to the influence of Piers she'd picked up her modelling career again. He'd helped launch her back on the circuit as a mature, glamorous woman, and she revelled in the photo sessions, enjoying being the centre of attention. Piers had by now given up filming and become editor of the very prestigious *London Living* magazine, and Samantha wrote her own small column, under Piers's guidance, on interior decorating. Suddenly she was a person again, not just somebody's wife. A person in her own right, and, what was more, she had her own money to do with what she liked. It was wonderful never having to ask for it, as she had done with Tony after she'd stopped modelling, which had always made her feel wildly extravagant if she bought two pairs of panties at the same time.

Now she had money of her own, and was living with a man she passionately loved. Piers flattered and pampered her, took her to all the smartest restaurants, all the newest and most avant-garde things in the theatre, and introduced her to all his engaging friends. Logically she ought to have been on cloud nine. But she wasn't, and couldn't understand why.

Venetia could, and said so. No beating about the bush where she was concerned. 'You feel guilty,' she said, 'which is exactly the way you should feel. Just because you fancied Piers more than Tony, it doesn't mean to say that you should have gone off with him. You were not free to go anywhere.'

Samantha thought she was being very old-fashioned and said so, adding, 'Our marriage was finished.'

Venetia, however, had fixed ideas about duty and nothing was going to budge them. 'Maybe your marriage was finished, but your family life wasn't. At least, not before you split it asunder. You never gave the children a thought.'

Samantha flushed bright red because it was true. Indeed she hadn't given them a thought, but she'd die rather than admit it to anyone, least of all to Venetia. 'You're being unfair,' she said crossly. 'Lots of people get divorced these days. The children think nothing of it, and what's more they said they wanted to come with me when the judge asked them.'

'I think they chose you because of the *way* they were asked. That smart lawyer of yours put words into their mouths. Personally I think they'd have been better off staying with their father down in the New Forest.'

Samantha gasped at what she perceived to be Venetia's injustice *and* inconsistency. 'But you always said you hated Cherry Trees and the New Forest, and you never liked Tony much either.'

'*My* likes and dislike aren't the point,' said Venetia tartly, regarding her granddaughter through narrowed eyes. A fact which made Samantha extremely nervous. 'The point is, *they* were born there. It's their home. Not that icy palace of a place Piers lives in.'

'Don't tell me you don't like Piers either,' snapped Samantha.

Venetia shrugged. 'He has a certain charm that the upper-class-twit types always have.'

Samantha gazed at her, open-mouthed. If Venetia weren't so old, she thought furiously, I'd hit her! 'I thought you liked the upper classes! You've always gone on and on about them.'

'I don't like twits,' said Venetia acidly. 'Piers is affected. Give me a man with a firm handshake any day.'

Samantha opened her mouth about to mount a further defence on Piers's behalf, but Venetia forestalled her. 'Of course, he won't wear very well, that type of man never does. Hasn't got the right bone-structure. Have you noticed he's got slightly buck teeth? Those are bound to protrude as he gets older.'

Samantha exploded. 'He's a very intelligent, kind and thoughtful man. You always wanted me to marry someone upper-class, but now I've found the right man you don't like him. And what's more he has *not* got buck teeth.'

'And you are *not* married to him,' Venetia pointed out tartly. 'Furthermore, if I'm any judge of character, you never will be. He'll keep his options open.'

'Piers doesn't look at other women,' hissed Samantha in fury.

'How about men?' retorted Venetia.

'Oh!' Samantha shrieked with rage. Never had the desire to strangle Venetia been so strong. She had to clench her hands straight to her side to prevent herself from grabbing her grandmother around the neck. 'The trouble with you,' she shouted, 'is that you will never like any man I love.' Then she burst into tears and rushed out of the house.

Outside she cannoned into Leroy, Venetia's neighbour. 'Hey man!' He grinned, his dreadlocks dancing, and his huge multi-coloured knitted hat glowing like a ray of Caribbean sunshine in the grimy street. 'Where you goin'? Lady England bin upsettin' you?'

Samantha stopped and searched through her handbag for a handkerchief. 'Yes,' she sniffed.

'Sit down, man.' Leroy patted the little garden wall which ran along the whole street in front of the houses and sat down. Samantha had known Leroy for years. Piers wouldn't approve of him, she knew that, and neither did she really. Venetia called him a lazy layabout who managed to live without any visible means of support. And it was true, he never worked, at least didn't do what most people would call work. He was a wheeler-dealer, and always had some money-making enterprise on the go. But he was good-hearted and kind, and both Samantha and Venetia liked him. There was something disarming about his open, laid-back manner. She *had* to talk to someone. She sat down beside him. 'Tell Leroy,' he commanded and, fishing in his pocket, brought out paper and tobacco and began to roll an untidy joint.

'Has Venetia told you that I've left my husband for another man? I'm divorced now and live in London again.'

Leroy rolled his eyes wickedly. 'I know that, man. Venetia don't keep no secrets from me.'

'And now, I find out that Venetia doesn't approve,' said Samantha.

101

'I know that too.' Leroy sighed noisily. 'What is it with you folks? What's the big deal? One man this week, another man the next week. What do it matter, man? As long as everyone love each other, everyone happy!'

'That's the problem, Leroy.' Samantha blew her nose vigorously and wiped her eyes. 'It *does* matter. And I suppose it's because we're not a bit laid-back like you. And, more to the point, we don't all love each other.'

Leroy lit his joint, took a puff then waved it under Samantha's nose. 'Here, take a drag.'

'No,' said Samantha, immediately regretting confiding in Leroy and becoming prim. 'I don't smoke pot.'

'An' butter don't melt in your mouth!' Leroy laughed, a squeaky, infectious giggle. 'Man, don't you come all high an' mighty with me. I can remember when you was modelling an' you lived off pot to keep that stick figure of yours.' He waved the joint at Samantha again. 'Go on, have some. Then everyt'in' look better.'

'It's illegal,' said Samantha.

Leroy blew an uneven smoke ring. 'Got no business to be,' he pronounced solemnly. 'No one ever went looking for a fight after smoking pot. Not like after the beer.'

'It's still illegal.'

'I give it up next week,' said Leroy with an expansive grin. 'Promise.' He crossed his heart, rolled his eyes again, and proffered the joint to Samantha.

'Oh, what the hell,' said Samantha, and took it.

'Inhale, man,' said Leroy. 'Inhale.'

Samantha inhaled once, twice, then several more times before giving the smouldering joint back to Leroy. Smiling now, she relaxed, body sagging on the wall, stretching out her legs before her. The colours of Leroy's hat seemed to fill the whole street. 'You're right, Leroy,' she said slowly. 'What am I worrying about? Everything is OK.' She began to giggle and rose to her feet. 'I love everyone and everyone loves me. I'm going home now.'

Leroy grinned happily back at her. 'See what a little joint can do? Make the whole wide world a better place.'

Samantha set off rather unsteadily in the direction of the main road and a taxi route, then stopped and turned back. 'Do me a favour, Leroy. Get Venetia to take a couple of puffs of that. It might make her more mellow.'

Leroy shook his head vigorously. 'No, *man*! I know that Lady England. She big fierce lady. I show her this,' he flourished the joint, 'and she hit me over the head with that cricket bat she keep in her hall.'

On the way back in the taxi Samantha worried the driver by beaming at him all the way. He slammed the communicating glass shut, and, as Londoners always did should anyone make eye-contact with them, kept his eyes firmly on the road. But, happily ensconced in her own personal little haze, Samantha didn't notice. Eventually she arrived back at St John's Wood still as high as a kite, and gave the children all the money she had in her purse.

'Go out,' she said. 'Enjoy yourselves.'

'Where can we go?' asked Philip suspiciously. None of them was used to their mother being so generous. 'Did Venetia give this to you for us?'

'No. I'm giving it, and you can go anywhere. Wherever you like.' Samantha waved them airily away.

'Let's go to the Hard Rock Café,' said Hilary gleefully, and all three disappeared at the speed of light before Samantha could change her mind.

When Piers came back from his office he found Samantha floating around the house with nothing on but a filmy negligee, and fairly crackling with sexiness. 'I love you,' she said. 'I love everyone.'

'Where are the children?' Piers was permanently worried. Since being caught practically *in flagrante* he was always careful to be absolutely proper in front of them

'Out,' said Samantha. 'I've sent them out. They'll be gone for hours.'

It was only after a very energetic sexual session, when finally Samantha began to flag and fell back sleepily on to the pillows of their enormous bed muttering, 'I love Leroy,' that Piers began to suspect she might have taken something.

Of course, Venetia found out about the pot from Leroy later that evening when he came back from the pub. He called in to make sure she was all right for the night, something he always did, rain or shine, stoned or sober. The combination of beer and pot made him more garrulous than ever, and he happily spilled the beans without even remembering later that he'd done so. Venetia sat rigid with disapproval as he giggled his way through the saga, then she telephoned a very sheepish Samantha the next day. As a result of the ensuing conversation she and Samantha had a row, after which they didn't speak for nearly a month.

CHAPTER 7

By the time Samantha had finally got round to realizing that life never delivers what it appears to be promising, Felicity was also thinking along similar lines. She had been ensconced for two whole months at Cherry Trees as Tony's new wife. Two whole months of seesawing wildly between being blissfully happy, or longing to walk away from everything. But living, she reminded herself, and that of course included marriage, was about getting on with things, making things work even when they seemed to be going wrong. So she did try, despite Annabel being as bloody-minded as she knew how, or when she was being driven mad by all the interruptions of life at Cherry Trees. And sometimes, although she felt terribly disloyal for even allowing herself to think it, when she was being driven mad by Tony himself.

It was so different from when they were lovers. Then they hadn't had a routine. There had been no need. Every moment they had together was their own, and belonged to no one else. In fact it hadn't even occurred to Felicity that Tony was a routine kind of man; he'd always been a spur-of-the-moment lover. But now they were man and wife it was different. Breakfast-time, Felicity discovered to her dismay, was what Tony called his 'quick study time'. No more lingering over the toast and marmalade. Tony ate, it was true, but he read the whole time, usually only raising his head to kiss her goodbye before he went off to the surgery. He read the *BMJ*, *The Lancet*, *Pulse*, *The GP*, *Computing for Medical Practitioners*, *World Medicine*, and always had a mountain of journals by the side of his plate.

Annabel whispered grumpily to her mother. Lately she had taken to whispering as Tony didn't like talking. 'You name it,' she muttered, 'Tony has it delivered and reads it.'

They were both used to the radio going full blast and Irene chattering non-stop at breakfast. And now both were finding the silence rather unnerving. 'And it's not as if it's proper reading,' Felicity had whispered back crossly. 'It's never a novel.' What she didn't say, but thought nonetheless, was that the reason Tony didn't take her work of reading and correcting such things very seriously was because he never read novels. A fact she was finding extremely irksome. Books were her livelihood, but to him they were a frippery of life.

Tony, however, was not so engrossed in his journals that he couldn't listen to their whispered conversation. 'What tosh you do talk sometimes, darling,' he said. 'I read *real* things, not made-up stories.' He pinched her bottom fondly as she passed.

And I *do* wish he wouldn't do things like that in front of Annabel, thought Felicity, who was feeling particularly cross that morning. She was cross because she was exhausted. When Tony was on duty, as he had been the previous night, and the bedside phone rang at regular intervals during the night for him to give advice or heave himself out of bed to go and visit a patient, she felt shattered. It didn't appear to affect him, but it was something Felicity was beginning to think she'd never get used to. So she was bad-tempered, and his pinching her bottom didn't help her mood one iota. Affectionate gestures were appreciated at the right time, but sometimes it seemed to her that Tony could be astonishingly dim-witted. As a doctor, Felicity felt, he ought to have been more tuned in to the psychological machinations of the mind of a teenage girl, and understand that she was going to be very watchful and wary of what went on between her mother and new stepfather. But the evidence was to the contrary, it appeared that Tony never contemplated such a notion.

So she snapped back at him. 'Never underestimate the power of the novel,' she said.

'Power! What power?' scoffed Tony. 'Give me an example.'

'I'll give you two. Steinbeck's *The Grapes of Wrath*, and A.J. Cronin's *The Citadel*. Both those books made people sit up and think.'

'Huh!' was Tony's only response before burying himself deeper in his reading matter. Another of his less endearing habits, as Felicity had discovered, was his inability ever to admit that he was wrong. Or very rarely. But when he did he was usually roaring with unrepentant laughter, and then Felicity found she usually ended up laughing with him, only remembering after he'd gone that *this* time she had intended to stay angry.

Of course she never mentioned any of this to her mother. She had no need, because she knew perfectly well what her comment would be. 'Of course, darling. What do you expect? He is a *man*, after all.' With each passing year Irene seemed to grow more and more impatient with the opposite sex. Several very eligible widowers had tried to court her, but she was having none of that. 'One man was enough to last me a lifetime,' she always said.

Felicity longed to tell her mother about all the down moments as well as the ups. But she didn't. She kept silent and soldiered on trying to run Cherry Trees and do a full day's work for Dickens Books from her makeshift office in the dining room which was never used for dining. The manuscripts piled up, the books for proof-reading piled up, and Felicity panicked.

'We've run out of milk, marmalade, bread and eggs,' Tony announced one Saturday morning. He sat with his pile of reading matter at his aside, and empty plate before him, and a cup of black coffee which Annabel, who was in an unusually sunny mood that morning, had made for him.

'Oh, you'll get used to that,' said Annabel, slurping her own black coffee noisily. 'When Mum gets in a panic about her books she forgets everything else.'

Tony frowned. 'If you know that, why didn't you remind her to go shopping? Or get some food in yourself?'

'I don't care about food,' said Annabel airily. 'I'm on a diet.'

Tony gave a long-suffering sigh. Felicity, who knew exactly what they had been talking about, said, 'What is all this about, then?'

'Felicity, *darling* . . .' *said Tony*.

Felicity wondered if there was another man in the world who could inject such a wealth of long-suffering reproach into just two words. But instead of making her feel guilty as she felt Tony so obviously intended – new wife neglecting her duties as his helpmate etc – it only served to infuriate her.

'Look, Tony, I've been reading solidly for the last two days trying to catch up on my backlog of work, and I've got a great pile of stuff to send back to London today. I just have not had time to go shopping.' She opened the cupboard door, took out an unopened packet of crispbreads, and tossed them on to his plate. 'Here, have one of these. They're supposed to be very good for you.'

'Not when they're past their sell-by date,' muttered Annabel, who'd already looked at them and decided she'd rather starve.

Making a great to do of opening the packet, Tony finally took one out and tried to snap it. It was old and soggy, and refused to snap. Tony sat forlornly holding the crispbread which by now was sagging in the middle, in his fingers. And Annabel had a fit of the giggles and wouldn't stop even though Felicity was shooting her barbed looks which had they been arrows would have pinned her to the wall.

110

'I can't eat this,' said Tony in an aggrieved tone of voice. He gave it to Prudence, who took it, experimentally chomped on it, then spat it out on the floor. 'Look, even the dog won't touch it.'

'Then go down to the garage shop in the village and buy something you *can* eat,' said Felicity.

'No need to shout, darling.'

Felicity took a deep breath. I love him, she reminded herself, although for the life of her she couldn't, at that particular moment, remember why. 'I am *not* shouting,' she said. 'I am speaking in calm and measured tones. *At the moment*! And before you complain about anything else, let me remind you that I have not forgotten the dog food. I have *never* forgotten the dog. So you have three choices: you can either eat dog food, diet, or go to the garage.'

At hearing the word 'dog', Prudence, who had gone back to her basket, leaped into action, lumbering about the kitchen violently wagging her tail. She'd had her breakfast long before but was always hopeful that there might be something else.

'Here comes dustbin dog,' said Annabel affectionately. Prudence was the only thing at Cherry Trees with whom she had formed any real rapport. Prudence turned round and round in excited circles; in the process her tail knocked off the basil plant Felicity was nurturing and had stood on a chair underneath the window in order to take full advantage of the morning sun. Earth and basil leaves flew in all directions, and Prudence jumped in surprise. 'Poor old Prudence,' said Annabel.

'Poor old basil,' said Tony, and suddenly laughed. A small chuckle at first, erupting into a great belly laugh, making Felicity remember why indeed she did love him. 'All right,' he said, scooping up earth and the bedraggled basil plant and stuffing it all back into the pot before passing it over to Felicity, 'I'll nip down to the village now and get something from the "open-all-hours" place. But, darling,' he looked at Felicity, 'we really *will* have to get ourselves more organized.'

Of course, Felicity knew that what he really meant was not *we* but *you* really will have to get yourself more organized. She sighed, feeling rebellious at the injustice of it all. Why should she reorganize? Why couldn't he change a little bit and pull his weight? She thought nostalgically for a moment of life in Primrose Hill with her mother. It was only now that she was living away from her that Felicity appreciated how much her mother had done. Apart from paying her share, Felicity had never even thought about food or other mundane things like toilet rolls and toothpaste. The necessities of life just appeared as if by magic. But only now did she realize that the good fairy in her life had been her mother. She protected me from all the slings and arrows of outrageous fortune, she thought wistfully. But here in Oakford there's no one to protect me. Tony might hold my arm, and walk on my right side whenever we go anywhere, like knights of old protecting their ladies, but that's as far as it goes. A gentlemanly show of chivalry, nothing more, and not in the slightest bit practical.

'Just off,' said Annabel, following Tony out of the

door – it was his weekend for Saturday morning surgery. She pecked Felicity on the cheek. 'Don't worry. You needn't take me, only pick me up later on, I'll catch the bus this morning as my dance class isn't until ten-thirty.' She dragged Prudence across the kitchen floor to Felicity. 'Make a fuss of her. She thinks you're cross with her. It's not her fault about the basil.'

Prudence looked up expectantly, her brown eyes fringed by long lashes reminding Felicity of Tony. She was asking to be made a fuss of and Felicity, like Annabel, couldn't resist her. She long ago had forgotten that her mother had told her she didn't like dogs. She liked this one. Well, most of the time she did. So she sat down and rubbed her ears and Prudence went cross-eyed in ecstasy. The trouble is, thought Felicity absent-mindedly while she fondled the dog's ears, there's always so much to do. Tony seems to have no idea of what's entailed in the running of Cherry Trees. She knew that after Samantha's departure he had hired Mrs Balfour from the village to do the work. But the day Felicity moved in permanently he had got rid of her.

'We don't want her around, darling,' he said. 'She's a compulsive tidier-upper and the most frightful gossip. She'd make your life a misery.'

Felicity had agreed then, but recently had started to doubt the wisdom of the decision. At the moment she felt she could easily cope with being compulsively tidied up, or with the entire village knowing the most intimate details of her private life. What she couldn't cope with were the thousand and one tasks always waiting to be done.

Prudence nudged her hand, reminding her that she hadn't yet had her morning walk. 'Come on, then, you wretch!' she said, but it was an affectionate insult.

Prudence pranced about excitedly wagging her tail, and Felicity hastily moved the re-potted basil on to the table. This was another of the tasks waiting for her at Cherry Trees which she had never even dreamed she'd be doing: feeding and walking the dog. Tony, she had found from the experience of two months, usually had a very good reason why he couldn't walk the dog, so inevitably the task fell to Felicity. Before she'd moved permanently down to Cherry Trees Felicity had always blithely imagined that country dogs took themselves for walks, or galloped companionably along beside you if you felt inclined to take a stroll, to come rushing back if you whistled. But Prudence's upbringing had not included obedience classes; she did come occasionally when Tony called her, but when Felicity was in charge of her she was exuberantly and joyfully stone-deaf. Not only that, she had no road sense whatsoever and expected everything to stop for her, and her homing instinct was non-existent. At least as far as her own home was concerned. She homed in quickly enough other people's houses, where she usually ate everything within reach before she was caught. Felicity, tired of receiving irate phone calls from various parts of the village, had confined Prudence to barracks, only to be taken out on a lead.

As well as walking the dog, there was Annabel to ferry backwards and forwards to dancing classes and often to school. Irene Hobbit had been right: there were no dance teachers in Oakford, the nearest class being in Westhampton. In London Annabel had taken herself to dance classes on the bus which ran every fifteen minutes from the end of the road. But the bus from Oakford to Westhampton only went twice a week, and then at a late hour so that all the pensioners in the village could take the trip to the nearest hypermarket to do their shopping. Living at Cherry Trees necessitated several car trips a day, although recently Felicity had found another mother who did the same thing, and now they were sharing. That helped a little.

But it always seemed that just when Felicity thought she was managing to get on top of things and working out a rota, something else happened. The latest being a small black and white stray cat which had turned up on the doorstep last week, mewing pitifully.

'Go away. Go back home. Shoo!' Felicity had shut the door and tried to ignore it. But it mewed more pitifully than ever, so she let it in and fed it, much to the disapproval of Prudence, fully intending to cart it off to the Cats' Protection League the next day. But by the next morning she, for by now it was indisputably female, had produced three kittens in the airing cupboard.

'She's made her nest in my clean underpants,' complained Tony. He lifted up their back legs and peered closely. 'Two boys and a girl, all fit and healthy,' he announced, tenderly tucking them back into the pile of his pants.

'I thought you wanted them evicted,' said Felicity, watching him. She smiled affectionately, thinking, if he

115

treats his patients the way he's treating those kittens, no wonder they all adore him.

Tony had looked sheepish. 'Well, I don't think it will do them any good to disturb them just yet. We'll leave the little family for the time being, and you can buy me some new pants when you go shopping. Come on, let's leave them in peace.' He shooed Felicity downstairs to the kitchen.

'She's an unmarried mother,' said Felicity, rushing back over to the stove to try and rescue the scrambled egg which she'd forgotten in the excitement. She wasn't entirely thrilled with the thought of yet more additions to the family.

But Annabel had been ecstatic. 'They're adorable, absolutely adorable, all of them. And you *did* say before we came to Oakford that I could have a cat. I shall call the mother Aphrodite.'

Tony grinned. 'Why? Because she's worn the girdle of love?'

'Exactly!' Annabel was pleased Tony had seen the connection. She was doing Classical Civilization for GCSE and to her surprise found she was enjoying it.

'I said one cat, not a hundred,' said Felicity, giving up on the eggs, and feeling once more that events were overtaking and overwhelming her yet again. She threw the scrambled egg saucepan into the sink. 'You'll have to have plain toast today,' she told Tony. 'I've burnt the scrambled eggs, and I'm afraid we've run out of marmalade.'

'Again?' said Tony with a sigh.

The sigh, which Felicity interpreted as being long-suffering, had been like waving a red rag at a bull. She had felt like bursting into tears of exasperation but instead snapped, 'Again!' very aggressively.

'You really ought to go on a course in good house-keeping,' said Annabel tactlessly.

'There's nothing wrong with my housekeeping. It's the system that's wrong,' said Felicity with consider-able force.

'Oh, Felicity. For goodness' sake.' Irritable at being denied his marmalade yet again, Tony picked up a journal to read, only to have it dashed from his hand by an infuriated Felicity.

Having successfully fuelled the flames, Annabel hopped from one foot to another. 'This should be good,' she squeaked. 'I do love arguments.'

'We are not going to argue,' said Felicity. 'And you are not going to stay lounging about there, Annabel. It's Jenny's mother's turn to give you a lift to school, so please take yourself off and stand down by the gate so that she doesn't miss you.'

Because her mother looked extraordinarily fierce even though she wasn't exactly shouting, Annabel for once obeyed instantly and took herself off, shoulders slouched sulkily. 'All right,' was all she said.

Felicity turned her attention back to Tony. 'Now!'

'But darling . . .' Tony was startled but not that surprised. He was beginning to get used to the fact that Felicity was not an acquiescent creature like Samantha, and that her views on life often differed radically from his own. At first he hadn't been sure whether he liked this or not, but on reflection had decided that at least he knew where he stood with Felicity. There would be no dire surprises because she would probably hit him over the head first as a warning shot. Although Felicity denied it fervently, Tony thought she was very like her mother. Once she'd made up her mind she stuck to her guns and didn't give a damn what other people thought.

'But darling, nothing,' said Felicity firmly, sitting down opposite him and helping herself to a sip of his coffee. 'I am a working woman. Just remember that.'

'Yes, but . . .' Tony hesitated, trying to fathom out which direction the conversation was taking.

Felicity jumped into the gap. 'And the fact that I work here in the house and not at an office does *not* mean that I have more time. If anything I have less. I have been working on average sixty to seventy hours a week recently, just trying to catch up, and I just have not got time to cook, clean, shop and launder as well. I know I don't earn a fortune, but you must admit that what I do earn comes in very useful.'

'Yes, I know that.' Tony scuffled his feet about beneath the kitchen table. Like a small naughty boy, thought Felicity, feeling a rush of affection then quickly squashing it. She was *not* going to turn soft. He *must* learn a few facts of life.

For his part, Tony felt guilty. It was true, Felicity did work hard, but try as he might he could never reconcile reading a book with working. He decided to concentrate on facts like money, and forget about the lack of marmalade and burnt scrambled egg. So much easier to think about one concept at a time. 'I know your money is not to be sniffed at,' he said. 'As a matter of fact I was going to ask you if you could help me out with the boys' school fees. They're going up by nearly a thousand quid next term.'

'We'll see,' said Felicity firmly. 'After we've dealt with our other problems.' Personally she considered the boarding school an unnecessary extravagance, and thought that both boys might very well improve somewhat if they went to a normal school and were not cosseted as if they were little angels, which they most definitely were not.

'What other problems?' asked Tony who was always inclined to think all problems were financial ones.

'The housework,' said Felicity.

'Oh, that! Well, housework won't go away,' said Tony dismissively, who thought this was perfectly obvious and was at loss to understand what Felicity was on about. 'It's got to be done.'

'Exactly,' said Felicity triumphantly, 'and if you can't help me out . . .'

Tony was amazed that she should even consider such a thing. 'But, darling, you know I can't help. I haven't got the time. I should be on my way to the surgery now. I'm late as it is.' He stood up, and stuffed the journals into his briefcase, half expecting Felicity to thrust a broom into his hand, her expression was so fierce.

Felicity poured herself a coffee, then discovered it was depressingly cold. Nothing was going right this morning, and to add insult to injury Tony seemed determined not to get the gist of what she was aiming at. Why was everything such a battle? She sighed, 'Of

119

course I didn't really mean *you*. I mean that it can be done by somebody else. I shall advertise in the village newsagent's window. There must be someone in Oakford who would like to earn a few extra pounds a week.'

Never having actually done any housework, Tony had no idea of the hard slog involved. As Irene had observed on her one and only weekend visit so far, he was not one of these *new men* the magazines were always going on about. So now he said without thinking, 'Samantha always did everything herself. *She* managed. I know she didn't work and have a salary like you, but she sat on every committee going, and that took up a lot of time. She always seemed to cope very well. And she never complained.'

'But she did leave you for another man,' Felicity reminded him tartly. It was unkind, she knew it. But she couldn't help saying it.

Tony winced as the remark hit home. 'That was a bit below the belt, darling. I didn't expect that.'

Felicity looked at him, then drew in a deep breath. Extra-sensory perception was definitely not one of Tony's accomplishments. She would have to spell it out for him.

'Sorry, Tony. But if you hold up Samantha to me as an example of wifely perfection again, you'd better expect another slug, and next time I'll aim even lower!'

Now Tony looked and felt even more worried. Were housework and the fact that Samantha had left him connected? He had no idea. And would Felicity do so

120

too? Women! Why were they so difficult to understand? 'You wouldn't think of leaving me for another man, would you?'

Felicity burst out laughing, the idea was so ridiculous. 'Leave you for another man! You must be joking. I'm too tired.'

Tony relaxed and grinned his engaging lop-sided grin. 'Well, thank heavens for that. You had me worried there for a moment.' He leaned forward and kissed the tip of her nose. 'I suppose you can get someone in to help you if that's what you really want.'

'Very kind of you,' said Felicity wryly.

His grin faded. 'But how we shall pay for it I don't know.'

'It's not a question of *we*, it's a question of *me* paying for it,' said Felicity firmly. 'I shall put the advertisement in the newsagent's window on Saturday.'

'Have it your own way, darling,' said Tony, going through into the hall. Felicity followed him and watched him shrug his shoulders into his tweed jacket. 'I really must go now,' he said, 'otherwise I shall be running late the whole day.'

And off he goes, Felicity had thought then, watching him swing the big estate car round in a tight circle on the gravel. Off he goes, and leaves all this behind; never giving another thought to the fact that while he's out in the big wide world dishing out tender loving care to his patients, his dirty washing is whizzing around in the washing machine, dirty plates are being stacked in the dishwasher, beds are being made, and . . . Prudence gave a loud impatient woof. 'And dogs are being walked,' she said severely to Prudence, who wagged her tail and obligingly fetched her lead and laid it at Felicity's feet . . .

Later that Saturday morning black clouds blew in from the west, and Felicity set out for the village, her spirits as low as the rain clouds overhead. Rainy weather in London was bad enough, but she hated it even more in the country. Dank, dark, dripping, and depressing, she thought gloomily. The trees hung overhead, black and menacing, and the road was full of muddy puddles. At least in the city there were shops with bright lights, but here there was nothing to relieve the gloom. To make matters worse the car steamed up, and the windscreen wipers couldn't work fast enough to swish off the rain. She'd done the bare minimum of housework that morning but was already running late. It was all very well airily telling Tony she would get someone in to do it. The point was, who could she get? She had never liked the sound of Mrs Balfour, and anyway sheer cussedness made her want to get someone different. Someone *she* had chosen, not a left-over from Tony's bachelor days. The other worrying factor was, could she truly afford anyone?

Parking her car beside the church on the far side of the village green opposite the post office, she saw the parish ladies, as she had mentally nicknamed them, coming out from their fund-raising coffee morning. Mrs Appleby, the senior partner's wife, was leading the way, easily distinguishable by her violently coloured purple umbrella. Instinctively Felicity ducked, hoping

Alice Appleby wouldn't notice the car, but of course she did. Very little escaped her eagle eye.

'Why, Felicity, my dear,' she heard the voice whooping as the purple umbrella advanced towards the car. 'We were just saying what a pity it was that you haven't been able to join us.'

Felicity sat up, started gathering together her parcels and wound the window down a little, trying to avoid letting in too much rain. 'Hello, Alice,' she said, trying not to sound too rudely unenthusiastic. 'Yes, it is a pity. But as you can see I've got too much work on.' She waved vaguely at the pile of parcels.

Alice peered in through the half-open window, her breath steaming up the outside. Inside, the dampness began misting up the window on the other side and Felicity felt irritable.

'Never mind,' breathed Alice, misting up the window even more, 'I'll be round to see you soon.' She turned to the other women who assembled in a damp little group around the car. 'This,' she said, purple umbrella bobbing self-importantly and gesticulating with her free hand, 'is Dr Hughes's new wife.'

She might just as well have said *second* wife, thought Felicity, bundling up the parcels in two plastic shopping bags and climbing out of the car. Through the hiss of insistent rain she could hear the faint murmur of voices and decided to nip the greetings in the bud before she got completely drowned. 'Nice to meet you all.' She smiled at the semi-circle of pale faces, and had the feeling that they were all mentally comparing this bedraggled stranger with Dr Hughes's previous wife, the glamorous and efficient Samantha. The one who, as Alice Appleby said, had contributed so much to village life. 'I'm terribly sorry, but I can't stop now,' she said firmly. 'I must catch the midday post.' With that she turned tail and squelched across the wet grass of the green towards the post office.

Arriving soaked and breathless, she plonked the parcels on the counter. With any luck Oliver Dickens should have them all by Monday first thing. The thought filled her with relief. At least some of the work was out of the way. The next thing was to place the advertisement for help.

'Good heavens, Mrs Hughes,' said the postmistress when confronted with the mountain of parcels. 'What's this, then? Early Christmas presents?'

'Books,' said Felicity. 'I read them. It's my job.'

'Really!' The postmistress put the parcels on the scales one by one. 'What a lovely easy job. I'd like one like that.'

Felicity bit her lip. Easy! If only she knew. 'How much will that be?'

'Seventeen pounds and ten pence, please.' After the last stamp had been stuck on the postmistress leaned forward so that her lips were level with the narrow gap in the glass shielding her from the customers. 'Of course,' she said confidentially, 'I love reading myself, although I don't get much time to do it. My husband says it's a waste of time.'

'Then tell him he's wrong,' snapped Felicity. 'Books are the manna of life.'

'Oooh! Really!' The postmistress adjusted her spectacles and stared at Felicity.

'Yes, really,' said Felicity loudly, and collected her change and left.

'That new Mrs Hughes is a bit strange, isn't she?' the next customer observed, handing over a pension book.

'Well, she's a Londoner. That accounts for a lot.' The pension book was stamped vigorously.

After the post office Felicity scuttled hastily through the rain to the newsagent's. She'd already written out the advertisement on a postcard and she gave it to the man behind the counter. Today it was Mr Smithson, who worked there part-time and supervized the paper rounds.

He made no attempt to disguise his curiosity and slowly read it out loud, then said, 'Dr Hughes had Mrs Balfour in to do for him when his other wife left.'

'I know. He told me.' Was there anything in this wretched village that everyone didn't know? Felicity got out her purse and held it open ostentatiously. All she wanted to do was pay for the advert and get away.

'Shall I give her a ring and see if she'd do for him again?'

'No, thank you,' said Felicity in what her mother always called her prime-ministerial type voice. 'Whoever comes to work at Cherry Trees will be working for me, not Dr Hughes. And I wish to choose the person myself.'

'Only trying to be of assistance,' said Mr Smithson rather huffily, obviously offended.

'I know, and I'm very grateful. But I'd rather do

things my own way.' Felicity didn't care for Mr Smithson. He'd turned Annabel down when she'd applied for a paper round on the grounds that girls of her age were unreliable.

'He's sexist and ageist,' Annabel had screamed in fury, and Felicity had agreed, although in her heart of hearts she suspected he was probably right. But the upshot of Annabel's inability to get the paper round had necessitated Felicity's digging even deeper in her own pocket for extra pocket money, and that in itself had relegated Mr Smithson into her black book.

She handed a five pound note across, dripping copiously on the counter as she did so. 'I'll pay for two weeks to start with.'

He took the money, took his time in wiping the drips from the counter, then gave her the change. 'I doubt that you'll get any replies. It would be much better if you'd let me ring Mrs Balfour.' A glint in Felicity's blue eyes brought him to a halt. 'Well, you know best, I suppose,' he said, indicating by his tone of voice that he didn't think she did.

Felicity seethed all the way through the pouring rain back to Cherry Trees. By the time she reached there she was in such a bad mood that nothing would have been right. Cherry Trees! A silly name for a house, she thought, glowering at the white sign while driving in through the gate, the wheels splashing violently through the puddles. There's not a cherry tree in sight! Then conscience pricked her. She'd always told Tony that she liked it. And once, a long time ago, there had been cherry trees. She reined in her bad temper, telling herself that she really must keep things in perspective.

The phone was ringing when she opened the front door. Felicity rushed into the kitchen and snatched it up. It was Oliver Dickens, who often went into his office at weekends – it was like a second home to him 'Just to see how you are getting on,' he said. 'Not to complain, my dear.'

'I know I'm behind,' said Felicity wearily.

'Don't worry about it.' Far away in London Oliver sounded calmly disembodied. Which was all right for him, reflected Felicity grumpily; he hadn't just come in out of the rain, wasn't freezing cold and standing with soaking wet feet. 'I was wondering,' he said gently, 'whether you'd had time to do the reports on those four special scripts I sent you last week.'

'I've just sent off all the scripts from the week before, and two of the four specials,' said Felicity. Surely Oliver wasn't going to start getting demanding! She couldn't stand it if he did. 'Not that it was worth it,' she added sharply.

'Really?' Oliver sounded surprised.

'No, it wasn't. The first manuscript was some man's erotic fancies about how it might be if he were beamed up to an alien planet where all the inhabitants were sex-starved women. All naked, all with breasts so big they could knock a man out with a single blow, and all with curly public hair about four inches long.'

'Don't you mean pubic?' said Oliver mildly.

'No, I don't. The horrible man typed "public" all the way through.'

'Oh, dear.' There was a moment's silence while Oliver digested this, then he chuckled and said, 'What about the other one?' He sounded hopeful.

'You mean Melissa Broadbent's manuscript,' said Felicity wearily.

'Yes, I had great hopes of that woman. Don't tell me I've got to write a rejection letter to her as well? She was so sweet.'

Oh, Oliver, Felicity thought, why don't you read some of these manuscripts yourself? But she knew it was hopeless. He would always judge people by their appearance and whether he liked them or not. And as she knew only too well, the nicest people were usually the worst writers. Still, that was his problem, not hers. She read them, he wrote the reject letters; that was the deal. 'A pathetic Aga Saga novel,' she said, deciding that being brutal was probably kinder to Oliver, and possibly to Melissa Broadbent as well. 'The heroine's husband is an MP, who is not only hateful to her and everyone else, but is into insider dealing and a cross-dresser to boot.'

'Sounds interesting,' said Oliver. 'Political scandals are very topical. Why didn't you like it?'

'Because it's *not* interesting. The heroine's reaction to every crisis that arises throughout the entire book is to rush into the kitchen and bake a fresh batch of scones. The only things that were different were the ingredients for the scones. The author should have written a recipe book, not a novel.' One of Aphrodite's kittens swarmed up the curtain in front of Felicity with all the determination of a fluffy Sherpa Tensing. Felicity tried to grab it, but it swarmed even higher and out of reach, and Felicity lost her balance and dropped the phone. 'Whoops, sorry. Are you still there, Oliver? Did you hear what I said?' Felicity retrieved the phone.

'Yes, dear,' said Oliver. There was another long silence, while Felicity anxiously watched the progress of the kitten who was now balancing precariously on the curtain pole and attempting to walk along it, then he said, 'Are there a lot of interruptions in your country life?'

'You could say that.' As if on cue a Land Rover crunched to a halt in front of the house. Felicity peered out from behind the kitchen curtains. It was Alice Appleby. Her heart sank. Why on earth did she have to come *now*? She was always so difficult to get rid of.

'I thought so,' said Oliver, 'because you've always been such a quick reader and now you've slowed down.' Felicity was about to say that it was a marvel she hadn't ground to a complete halt but Oliver continued, happily oblivious of Alice Appleby striding towards the front door of Cherry Trees. 'Why don't you come up to London for two days a week?' he suggested. 'You could stay with your mother, and have your old office back, and apart from Joan bringing you in the occasional cup of coffee you'd have absolute solitude.'

'Sounds blissful.' Felicity watched Alice Appleby's green wellies splashing purposefully through the muddy gravel as she made her way across the drive. The bell rang, long and loudly. She made up her mind. She'd go back to London. She had to get away. That was the answer. 'I'll have to talk it over with Tony, of course, but I'm sure he won't object.' She crossed the fingers on her free hand. 'And there's Annabel to get organized if I'm to be away. But I'll ring you back with an answer. I promise.'

'Good.' Oliver rang off.

The bell rang again. The kitten, halfway along his greasy pole expedition, lost his balance and fell off. Splat! He landed on the floor.

'That's one of *your* nine lives gone,' said Felicity.

Picking him up, she examined the furry bundle, which seemed none the worse for the ordeal and promptly clung to her like an animated burr. He was firmly attached, so she carried the kitten with her towards the hall and the front door. Now, how to get rid of Alice Appleby in double quick time, that was the next item on the agenda.

CHAPTER 8

The rain falling in Oakford fell in London also, and Venetia awoke to the sound of droplets pattering on to her bedroom window. Outside in the street a tin can rattled along the gutter, blown by the wind, and she could hear the teasmade hissing. It was late, gone nine o'clock, but she'd set the alarm late because the last few hours between night and morning were the best sleep she had these days. She moved uncomfortably; her bones ached, as they always did in the morning. Samantha said she ought to buy a new bed, but she couldn't afford it. The only money that was left, apart from her weekly old-age pension, was the money she'd set aside for her funeral, and she wasn't going to spend *that*.

'I want a good send-off,' she had told Samantha. 'Nothing stinted.'

Samantha had sighed impatiently, something she did a lot recently, and said, 'I don't know why you even bother to think about your funeral. It's not as if you're going to be there to see what goes on.'

Venetia hadn't replied. She wanted to say, *You may*

131

not care what people think about me, but I do, and my funeral will be my last appearance on this earth and to me it's important. But if she had said that then almost certainly they would have quarrelled again. It was no good, she had to accept the fact that Samantha, always self-centred, was even more so now. Only concerned, it seemed, with her new life and nothing else. So Venetia had kept silent, about the funeral, her lack of money, and even about the fact that she hardly saw her great-grandchildren these days. Something which distressed her more than she dared admit even to herself. Now, she hobbled across to the teasmade and poured herself a cup of strong tea and took two biscuits from the tin standing at the side of the tray.

Using the teasmade always made her think of Tony and Cherry Trees. In spite of her derogatory remarks about the New Forest she had secretly enjoyed her trips to the country and was now missing them. As old age encroached she found London more and more claustrophobic and began to long for space. Her part of Notting Hill had grown seedy; the back gardens which once flourished with rows of vegetables now sprouted cars in various stages of being repaired, dismantled, or left to rust away. Her own garden was the only one which was green. No vegetables now, all put to lawn, easier to manage, and she could just about afford to pay Leroy from next door to cut the grass once a month in the summer. Although she was lucky if he remembered. He usually needed at least two reminders. In the street at the front, litter from the nearby take-aways blew along and piled up in an unsightly mound by the wall at the end of the road. It hadn't been like that when she had first moved to the area. Then there were proper shops, bakers, greengrocers, butchers, and a lovely grocer's with fresh butter and large lumps of cheese, and huge buckets of soaked dried peas ready to be shovelled up and taken away in brown paper bags. Now there was one newsagent which had stale butter, a few tins of things, and tasteless sliced bread, and take-aways dispensing Italian, Indian and American fast food. Years ago hardly anyone had a car; now they were all three- or four-car families making it almost impossible to find enough space between the parked cars to step off the kerb to cross the street. Venetia could never fathom out why there were bits of cars in all the back gardens, and other cars in the street. She asked Leroy. 'Why do people need so many cars?'

Leroy's answer was, 'Man! If you see a bargain you gotta snap it up.' He had two cars in the street and three rusting hulks in his garden.

Venetia had replied very bad-temperedly, 'Litterbugs, that's what you are. Litterbugs, every one of you.'

But Leroy hadn't been angry. He never was. He just laughed and said, 'That's life, man. That's life.'

And Venetia supposed it was. She was old-fashioned, and not interested in the fast modern world. That was the price of getting old. One always looked back, because the future was uncertain and frighteningly short. She was out of touch, and progressively getting even more out of touch now that she saw so little of the children. The twins and Hilary had kept her more or less up to date with what was happening in their world, the young world, but since Samantha had moved in with Piers she hardly saw them. She wanted to tell Samantha that she missed their company, and ask her to allow them to visit more often, but she was far too proud to say anything.

Instead she kept silent and wondered whether it was because she had spoken her mind to Samantha about moving in with Piers, or whether it was because Piers didn't like her. He knew she disapproved of Samantha's decision, and Venetia had sensed from the moment she'd met him that he was a man who could not tolerate disapproval, unless it was his own of somebody else.

Sitting up in bed, propped up by a mountain of pillows, she fished her dentures out from the glass beside her bed and put them in so that she could crunch the biscuits with the strong sweet tea. Uneasily she moved the bones of her pelvis about, searching for a softer spot on the mattress into which to place her bottom. A new mattress really *was* needed, and Venetia suddenly decided she would have it. Something would have to be sold; that way she could have a mattress. What to sell? That was the problem. The whole house was crammed with large dark furniture she had brought down from Yorkshire. She looked around the bedroom. No, furniture would be too heavy; she needed something portable. Something she could carry herself down to Portobello Road where she could ask the advice of Irene Hobbit. The market was on Saturdays only – often to the bemused dismay of tourists who turned up on other days expecting to see it – but today was Saturday. She made up her mind to visit Irene's stall.

Stimulated by the challenge of decision-making, she sat up higher, her eyes suddenly bright. The day ahead had acquired a purpose.

'Cooee!'

Felicity stifled a groan. Alice Appleby was in Cherry Trees!

'The front door wasn't closed properly so I let myself in,' announced Alice.

'So I see,' Felicity said, forcibly injecting a strong note of disapproval into her voice. Prudence, the traitor, bounced all over Alice in enthusiastic greeting. Wretched dog. What was the point in remembering the dog food if she couldn't do her duty and see off unwelcome visitors?

Felicity's disapproving tone ricocheted, unnoticed, off of Alice Appleby's large bosom. 'Hello, Prudence,' she boomed, 'lovely girl, lovely girl, *down*!' Felicity watched in amazement as Prudence hastily downed and made a mental note to try issuing orders in that tone of voice, although she wasn't certain that she could manage a boom. Alice spied the kitten still tucked under Felicity's arm. 'What a sweet little thing. What's his name?'

'Cat number three,' snapped Felicity. 'I haven't had time to christen them yet because I get so many interruptions.'

'Oh, dear,' said Alice, failing to take the hint and following Felicity through into the kitchen.

The table was littered with the detritus of their spartan breakfast. Amazing, thought Felicity, viewing the scene, how much mess such a little amount can make. Aphrodite, who'd been up on the table licking the butter, skittered away when they entered and Felicity hoped Alice hadn't noticed but suspected that she had. The whole family of cats had taken up permanent residence now. Partly because, although Felicity wouldn't admit it, they were enchanting, and partly because she had never been organized enough to take them to the Cats' Protection League in the first place. And besides, Annabel and Tony were both set very firmly against that.

'They'll miss us,' Annabel had wailed. 'We're the only home they know.'

'We've got plenty of room,' said Tony. 'No need to turn them out.'

So they had stayed, and now Tony's underpants were a complete write-off.

Felicity put cat number three down on the floor. With any luck, she thought, feeling vicious, it might trip up Alice Appleby and she'll break a leg which will put her out of circulation for a while. Shrugging herself out of her wet raincoat, which was clinging to her and dripping all over the floor, she draped it with an ill grace over the back of a chair. Surely Alice would notice how busy she was! But Alice apparently did not. So Felicity walked across to the stripped pine Welsh dresser, which originally she'd hated because of its cosy prettiness but now found useful for accommodating all her clutter, and picked up three manuscripts. They were stacked ready to take into the dining room-cum-office. At the back of her mind was the faint hope that perhaps if she actually went into the dining room and began to work, Alice Appleby might go away.

She turned back towards Alice just in time to see her unwelcome visitor peer into the sink and give a visible shudder at the sight of the burnt saucepan. 'Sorry about the mess,' said Felicity. 'I wish I could wave a magic wand so that it could all be cleared away and everything put back in place.'

'Ah, yes,' replied Alice in a knowing voice, 'I can see now why you're advertising for domestic assistance. But cheer up, you'll soon have someone. Mrs Balfour will come back like a shot, then you'll have masses of spare time. She's a terribly efficient woman. Leaves not a stone unturned.' She nodded at the pile of papers in Felicity's arms. 'She'll soon get rid of that lot for you. Straight down to the recycling centre in the wink of an eye. And this house will be so clean that you'll be able to eat off the floor.'

'I prefer the table,' said Felicity in a glacial tone.

'Only joking,' boomed Alice, totally unabashed.

Felicity raged in silence. The more people mentioned Mrs Balfour, the more antagonistic she felt herself becoming to the unknown woman. 'And this *lot*, as you call it,' she waved the manuscripts, 'is my work for today. Not rubbish. I work for a publishing house and I read this for a living.'

'Really!' Alice Appleby was quite obviously not at all impressed; she was still interested in the muddle all around her. Out of the corner of her eye Felicity saw Aphrodite sneaking past a somnolent Prudence towards the stairs and her lair in the airing cupboard.

Alice saw too and sniffed disapprovingly. 'As I said, Mrs Balfour will have this place sorted out in a jiffy.'

Felicity, who only wanted the house cleaned not sorted out, felt she had to make a stand by making a statement of some sort. 'Of course, I shall interview Mrs Balfour if she applies, but I . . .'

'Interview!' Alice was amazed. 'But everyone does everything on recommendation here in Oakford. We all know the best person to go to for *anything*. There's no need to advertise or interview.'

'Alice,' said Felicity very firmly, 'I *have* advertised, and I *shall* interview. Now what can I do for you?'

Alice sat down heavily on one of the kitchen chairs, and, pushing the remains of the breakfast toast aside, heaved her capacious handbag on to the table and extracted a notebook. 'Well, my dear,' she said brightly. 'Perhaps there is something to be said for advertising, because as soon as I saw it I said to myself, now! Felicity Hughes is going to have some time on her hands in the future, which means she'll be the ideal person to organize our new mothers and toddlers group on Tuesday and Thursday mornings.' Felicity opened her mouth about to object but had no chance as Alice ploughed blithely on. 'Of course, we already have two qualified people to actually stimulate the toddlers, but we need someone to make teas and coffees and to talk to the mothers. Some of whom are very stressed.'

'So am I,' said Felicity.

'Yes, dear.' Alice wasn't listening, she was busy putting little ticks in her notebook. She's a bit like

an out-of-control steamroller, thought Felicity; somebody has set her in motion but nobody can stop her.

'Stressed,' repeated Felicity loudly. 'Me. I'm
stressed.'

'You!' That did it. The steamroller juddered to a
halt. 'Stressed! But how can you be? Life here in
Oakford is so slow, so peaceful, so tranquil. There is
nothing here to cause stress.'

Felicity began to wonder if Samantha had left
because of Alice Appleby and not because of something wrong between herself and Tony. It wouldn't
surprise me, she thought crossly. No wonder Samantha
had been on all the committees that existed; it was
almost impossible to say no. The wretched woman was
so determined, she could probably prise the rock of
Gibraltar from its foothold on Spain.

'If it's so peaceful, why are these mothers you are
talking about so stressed?' she asked. Samantha might
have capitulated; she was determined that she would
not.

'Because *they* are different. They're from a different
social class,' said Alice airily as if that explained everything. She went back to her notebook and the inter-
minable ticks. 'The lower classes always have
problems.'

Felicity nearly exploded with rage. Such outright
snobbishness could not be tolerated. 'Alice, one's social
class does not make the slightest difference to one's
problems in life. Maybe you have none; if so, then
you're lucky. But I have many problems, and the main
one is that I do not find Oakford peaceful or tranquil.

Quite the reverse. I never get anything done because my life is full of interruptions.'

'Really?' said Alice, sounding surprised and obviously missing the point completely.

'That is why,' Felicity continued, determined by now to hammer home her point of view once and for all, 'I intend hiring someone to do all the mundane things like shopping and housework, so that I can go back to London and work during the week.'

'Good heavens!' The chair back creaked ominously as Alice tilted her large frame to get a better view of Felicity. 'What on earth does poor Tony say about all this?'

Poor Tony! The expression infuriated Felicity. Why was sympathy wasted on him? *She* was the one trying to juggle the demands of work, house and home! She glared at Alice Appleby and felt resentful. She, obviously, had never had to juggle anything, which was probably the reason she filled her life with committee work. But saying so was not going to help things, nor was admitting that Tony, as yet, knew nothing about it, so instead she decided to tell a white lie. 'Actually, Tony thinks it's a marvellous idea. He understands that I need my own piece of space in which to work. Nurturing creativity isn't easy.'

'Space! Creativity!' Alice frowned, and Felicity could see that such a thing was an unknown concept.

'Yes,' said Felicity. 'Space is the solitude I need for these.' She put the pile of manuscripts back down on the dresser and tapped them. 'These are works of fiction created by other people who need me to help them.'

'You mean books?' queried Alice doubtfully.

'With any luck some of them will be one day,' said Felicity. 'Now, can I offer you a quick cup of coffee before you go?' She picked up the cafetière and sloshed the cold coffee grouts into the sink on top of the scrambled egg saucepan. 'I'm sure I can find two reasonably clean cups somewhere.'

Alice finally took the hint and, stuffing the notebook back into her handbag, rose her feet. 'No, thank you. I'd better go and leave you in peace.' She got to the door, then paused and said hopefully, 'You're sure you couldn't manage just one toddler and mother group?'

'Positive,' said Felicity firmly.

She watched Alice's departure, the Land Rover bouncing in the holes in the drive as it made its way towards the front gate. Too late she realized that telling Alice Appleby something was the equivalent to hanging a large notice outside the house. By this evening almost everyone in Oakford would know that the new Mrs Hughes intended to return to London to work. She looked at her watch. Twelve noon, almost time for lunch and she had still not read a single word.

At twelve noon precisely Venetia closed the front door of her house, gave the brass knocker a quick polish with her gloved hand, then set off purposefully for Portobello Road. In her arms she clutched a parcel, carefully wrapped, first in brown paper and then in a plastic bag. She hadn't quite made up her mind what she was going to say to Irene Hobbit, and hoped that she would find her alone at her stall. The object of her visit was to persuade Irene to buy the porcelain. A sale was essential if she was to have that new mattress she'd promised herself. She even stopped on the way and looked in a bedding shop called *Beds! Beds! Beds!*

The Asian man who owned it came out. He was small, smaller than Venetia, and anxious to please. 'We have very nice beds,' he said. 'Very, very nice. Please, come in, come in.'

'Not now,' said Venetia. 'I can't afford a bed at the moment.'

'Then you are looking. That is good. We are very cheap, very, very cheap.'

'Maybe later,' said Venetia.

'I promise you these are the best bargains in London. I personally guarantee you to sleep well on my beds. I am not cheating you.'

Venetia looked at him. A small, anxious man, eager to please and even more eager to make a sale. At the back of the shop she could just make out two small children, their liquorice-dark eyes regarding her solemnly, and a young woman dressed in a bright pink sari. A sale would make the day for all of them. She smiled and said, 'I know you are not a cheat, and I *will* come back. But first I must get some money.'

With that she turned and continued on her way to Irene's stall.

The tarpaulin overhead, filled with rainwater, hung like the great curved belly of a whale over the stall. Irene hoped it wouldn't leak. She was sitting on a stool behind the counter table, crammed with the usual selection of bric-à-brac, drinking black coffee and eating a ham sandwich. From her vantage point at the top of the hill she could see Venetia coming. She had recognized her as soon as she had appeared, a tall figure hurrying under her umbrella through the rain, hurrying as much as her age and the hill would allow. She was clad in a flapping raincoat, her thinning grey hair pulled back tightly into an old-fashioned bun, not a single strand allowed to escape. Irene could see, now that she was nearer, that she was clutching a large plastic bag.

She wants to sell me something, she thought, and her heart sank. It would probably be a load of old junk. When people came up to her clutching plastic bags in the way Venetia was now, it usually was. And it was so difficult to say no without offending. Dealers were no problem to Irene; she had no qualms about offending them. It was all part and parcel of business. But ordinary people were another matter. Venetia got nearer. She was not ordinary, but neither was she a dealer. Irene felt uncomfortable when she couldn't categorize someone.

Brushing the crumbs from her lap, she stood up and prepared to meet her visitor. She had only spoken to Venetia a few times, and had come to the conclusion that she didn't much like her. There was something intimidating about Venetia; perhaps it was the aristocratic air she managed to exude in spite of being rather shabby. Whatever it was it had the effect of making Irene feel at a disadvantage, not a sensation she enjoyed or indeed was accustomed to.

'Good afternoon, Mrs Willshire,' she said, a slight edge to her voice because she was feeling defensive.

'Afternoon?' Venetia looked vaguely surprised, then said, 'Yes, I suppose it is. Being so busy, and not having had any lunch, I hadn't really thought about it. And by the way, do call me Venetia, everyone else does.'

Irene remained standing, slightly ill at ease. Should she ask, or would Venetia tell her why she had come? 'Awful weather,' she said at last. 'Would you like a cup of coffee?'

'Yes, please,' puffed Venetia. The hill, though not very high, had drained her of energy and when Irene indicated the stool she'd just vacated she sat down on it gratefully. 'Perhaps it was foolish of me to come out today in this cold and rain, but once I'd made up my mind I wanted to get on with it.'

'Oh?' said Irene, wondering what was coming next, and what was in the plastic bag Venetia was still clutching to her bony chest.

'I know we are only acquainted because the younger members of our family have got their lives entangled with each other,' Venetia began. 'I know I shouldn't, but I still think of Tony as my in-law, even though he's now married to your daughter.'

'I thought Samantha had well and truly disentangled herself from that marriage,' said Irene wryly. 'Didn't she walk away from Tony in the first place?' Obstinately she wanted to make certain that Felicity was not put in the wrong in any way.

Venetia nodded, then said, 'But you can never truly walk away from a marriage, can you? Not if there are

144

children.' She sighed and added, 'But there's nothing I can do about it.'

'No, there isn't.' Irene felt a twinge of pity. The old lady was obviously unhappy about the divorce.

'I do worry so about the children,' said Venetia, reinforcing Irene's views. 'I pray that they'll be happy.' There was a pause, and she said hesitantly, 'Is your daughter kind?'

The twinge turned into a flood of pity that surprised even Irene herself. The explanation was, of course, as she quickly realized, the difference of twenty years or more in age between them. Divorce and family split-up was even more unacceptable to Venetia's generation than it was to her own. The old lady must have taken the break-up of the family very badly. 'Felicity *is* kind,' she said, her voice more gentle than before. 'Once your grandchildren get to know her I'm sure they will get on with her and be happy. Or, at least,' she amended, 'as happy as children from a broken home can be.' She opened her Thermos flask and poured out a cup of coffee which she handed to Venetia.

'I hope so.' Venetia drew in a deep breath, drank some coffee, then shook out the umbrella and unbuttoned the top button of her raincoat. After that she set about unwrapping the plastic bag. From it she extracted a porcelain pot-pourri vase, cover and stand. 'I wondered if you could sell this for me. I'm not sure what it is.'

The words came out in a rush and Irene knew that she was embarrassed. Suddenly Venetia was no longer an intimidating, aristocratic kind of woman, but an old lady who needed some cash. She pulled out the spare stool from beneath the counter and, sitting beside Venetia, took the porcelain from her and on to her own lap. 'It's lovely,' she said, carefully examining the pieces which were all perfect, 'and it is Coalbrookdale, not rare but unusual. What sort of price did you have in mind?'

'I want enough for a new mattress,' said Venetia, 'so I thought about ninety to one hundred pounds.'

Poor old thing, Irene thought, she's probably been selling other stuff to door-to-door dealers, and the price she's got was what she needed at the time. 'This is worth much more than that, at least two hundred and fifty, perhaps more at auction which is where I'd advise you to put it.'

Venetia was disappointed. 'Auction?' she echoed, all her disappointment showing in her voice. 'But if I put it in an auction it will takes months to get the money.'

'And you'd have to pay commission,' said Irene, thinking quickly. She made up her mind. 'Look, I tell you what. I'll give you two hundred and fifty pounds for it now, and I'll put in on my stall in the middle of summer, when all the American tourists come. If I sell it for more than that I'll give you the difference.'

'But that means you won't make any profit for yourself. I don't want charity.'

'It's not charity. I'm not giving you anything, only what belongs to you.'

Venetia was stubborn. 'You won't be making a profit.'

146

'The loss of profit on one item won't kill me,' said Irene robustly, realizing as she said it that this was something she had never done in her life before and thinking that she must be getting senile in her old age. 'Besides, we widows must stick together and you can do me a good turn one day when I need it.'

Venetia smiled slowly. 'Yes, I will,' she said.

'And another thing,' Irene heard herself saying, 'if you ever want to sell anything again bring it here. I'll price it for you and it can go out on the stall. In return you could always mind the stall for me for an hour or so if you have some spare time.' The suggestion about minding the stall was an afterthought so as not to offend Venetia's pride.

Thus it was that an ad hoc arrangement and a firm friendship sprang up. Venetia brought odds and ends to the stall in Portobello Road, but most of all she brought herself, and although Irene dared not leave her for too long, she did give Venetia a list of the bottom-line prices and allowed her to haggle with the tourists. A skill at which she surprisingly proved herself to be something of an expert. Irene always let herself be beaten down quite easily to the bottom line and then wouldn't budge; Venetia rarely let anything go at rock-bottom price.

In fact, as Irene told Venetia, 'I could do with you giving some training to my other assistants. I'd be a millionaire if they were all as efficient as you.'

Venetia bloomed with pride. She felt much happier lately. Life was so much more interesting; she loved the bustle and easy camaraderie of the market once a week when it was so quiet the rest of the time. And she took to wearing a gipsy headscarf which went well with the ambience of Portobello Market, but which sat rather oddly on her tight knot of grey hair.

The afternoon Venetia sold her pot to Irene and bought herself a new mattress Tony came home from his emergency weekend surgery in an emotional turmoil. He had made up his mind to wait until Felicity told him the news in her own good time, but when she didn't say anything except, 'Hello, darling,' and offered her cheek while continuing hastily to peel potatoes for dinner, he decided he couldn't bottle it up any longer.

'What is all this I hear about you going back to work in London?'

Felicity was prepared. Alice Appleby had obviously lost no time in spreading the news. 'Tell me what you've heard, darling,' she said mildly, 'and I'll tell you if it's true.'

'Well,' Tony hunched his shoulders dispiritedly and slumped down in a chair at the kitchen table. 'That's it. You are going back to London to work, which means, I suppose, that I'll be here on my own with your daughter, unless you intend taking her as well. So I might as well be divorced again.' He sighed heavily, was silent a moment, then said, 'You're not really going to leave me, are you?'

Felicity had intended being stern and businesslike, but he looked so apprehensive that she relented. Dropping the potatoes, she flew across the kitchen and put her arms around him. 'I love you,' she said.

'I love you too,' said Tony, 'but you haven't said you're *not* leaving.'

Felicity shook her head in exasperation. 'I'm not leaving you. I want to spend one night a week with my mother so that I can work in London for two days a week. Annabel can stay over at Jenny's for that night, her mother is quite agreeable, so that's one problem solved.'

Tony rested his face in her dark hair. 'But why?' His muffled voice sounded plaintive.

'Because I shall be able to get more work done, and who knows, I might even get a bonus or a rise. I'm going to lean heavily on Oliver Dickens, and I'm sure he'll cough up. He needs me. And just think, I'll be able to help with the boys' school fees.' Felicity winced guiltily as she spoke, and mentally crossed her fingers. It was bribery, sheer and blatant, but as her mother had always told her, there was more than one way to skin a cat, whatever that might mean. 'Anyway,' she added, 'I've no intention of rushing off this week or next. I've got to get the housework and shopping sorted out first.'

'That's all right, then,' said Tony sounding relieved. 'I thought I might have to go back to managing on my own.' Against her better judgement her mother's voice came echoing back once more. *I expect he wants someone to wash his pants and socks!*

But all thoughts of underwear, and indeed the garments themselves, vanished that night as they made what Felicity thought the most perfect love ever. Next morning they both staggered downstairs late, glowing with love and goodwill to all their fellow creatures, to find that Annabel had got up early and made breakfast. Felicity had never found time the previous day to do any shopping, so Annabel had raided the larder and the deep freeze and cooked a breakfast of grilled fish fingers and heated baked beans in tomato sauce.

'There,' she said proudly, waving a dish of fish fingers swimming in a sea of baked beans under Tony's nose, 'what do you think of that?'

Felicity closed her eyes. This morning *had* been a beautiful one. Why was it nothing ever *stayed* right? Surely Annabel knew that Tony only liked strong French coffee, fresh toast and dark chunky marmalade. True, he often went without, but even she, in her most disorganized moment, had never offered him fish fingers and baked beans.

'Super!' she heard Tony say. 'No one's given me fish fingers in years.'

Felicity opened her eyes. From the other side of the table Annabel looked across at her and raised her eyebrows and shrugged as if to say, men are easy to handle if you know how. With a start of surprise Felicity realized that her daughter had started the metamorphosis from awkward teenager into young woman.

'See, even the animals approve,' said Annabel.

Prudence, sitting on Tony's right side, was looking hopeful and dribbling, whilst Aphrodite, unknown to him, had already filched one of the fish fingers and was on the floor sharing it with her kittens.

CHAPTER 9

Noise, a rich variety of smells, and seeming confusion reigned as usual in Portobello Road. The Friday part of the market – fruit and vegetables and some of the cheaper, more touristy, less authentic little bric-à-brac shops – was in full swing. Irene often met Venetia there for a few hours to sort out her wares for the next day. Venetia was engaged busily unwrapping a small biscuit-glazed figurine.

At the back of the small warehouse space just behind where her stall would be, Irene smiled. She was glad Venetia came to help; the old lady had an uncanny knack of persuading people to part with their money. Her sales were always good for Hobbit's enterprises, and not quite so good for the vendees. Still, thought Irene, feeling satisfied, one man's meat is another man's poison. The customer is happy, I'm happy, and most of all Venetia is happy.

Today Venetia was wearing a headscarf of brilliant scarlet. It stood out, a splash of violent colour amongst the myriad items all around her on the makeshift table. She looked up at Irene and her thin, rather severe face was transformed by a wide grin. She certainly puts me in the shade, thought Irene realizing with each passing day how fond she was becoming of Venetia. Although a wrinkled eighty-seven-year-old, when she was flushed with pleasure and excitement as she was now, it was possible to catch a glimpse of what a much younger Venetia must have been like. Probably, mused Irene, I'm the only one now to have an inkling of the attractive young woman she once was. To everyone else she's an old lady. People only ever see the here and now, never the past. Her rambling meditation skidded to a halt with a jolt; good heavens, the same almost certainly applies as far as I'm concerned, she thought. I may be more than twenty years younger than Venetia, but because I'm eligible for a bus pass that puts me in the elderly person bracket. The thought annoyed her, and she tried to convince herself that sixty-five was no different from being twenty-five, apart from the fact that she couldn't hurry quite so fast, and running made her puffed. But it *was* different, and the difference saddened her if she thought about it too much. Away from business, life was not as busy as it once had been. There was no need to rush back to get a husband's meal, or feed children or do the one hundred and one things always waiting to be done when a house had more than one person residing in it. Both Venetia and I are the same, thought Irene. We're both alone. Even our friends are slowly disappearing, as they depart this life, one by one. It was not often she even allowed herself to think that; she was not religious and stubbornly refused to think of death or anything to do with it. While alive, she believed in living life to the full, and because of that she made an impulsive decision.

'Venetia,' she said, 'I've been thinking. We ought to celebrate. We had such a good day on the stall last week that I think we ought to treat ourselves to something. Shall we go out to eat tonight, and perhaps go in to the West End and see a show tomorrow? What do you say? What would you really like to do this weekend?'

Venetia thought for a moment, then said rather slowly, 'What I'd *really* like to do isn't possible.'

'Rubbish. Nothing is impossible. Tell me what it is. I'll fix it.'

'I'd like to visit Cherry Trees again. When the children are there. I used to rather enjoy it.'

'And tell me, pray, why should that be impossible?' demanded Irene.

For all sorts of reasons, thought Venetia, feeling guilty. Not least because I didn't really help the marriage along very much when Samantha was there. I was disparaging, disapproving, and now it's all come back to haunt me. My granddaughter left the children's father for another man. She tore a family in two, and I let her. But Venetia couldn't say all that, because she couldn't really put it into words, it was too much of a muddle. So many emotions jumbled up in her head like so much knitting wool after a kitten has been at it. She hesitated, looked uncomfortable, and said, 'Because I'm not really a relation any more.'

'Of course you are,' said Irene. 'You are still the children's grandmother.'

'*Great*-grandmother,' reminded Venetia.

'Heavens, yes! I always forget. Anyway, you *are* a relation so you *are* entitled to visit. I'll go over to the pub across the road and phone Felicity right now.'

'But what shall you say?' asked Venetia, slightly startled by the rapid turn of events.

'That we're coming down this weekend, and would she please meet the train at Brockenhurst? I'll tell her we're catching the seven-thirty from Waterloo. That will leave us both plenty of time to pack a bag.'

'But you can't,' cried Venetia. 'What about the stall tomorrow? Saturday is the only trading day.'

'No problem,' said Irene airily, determined to let nothing stand in her way. 'I'll get Joe's son from the stall next door to run it for me. He's done it before. Takings will be down a bit, but so what! I told you I've had a good few weeks. I can afford it.' She left the stall and was halfway across the road.

'But – ' shouted Venetia, about to say that it wasn't really fair on Felicity just to suddenly announce their arrival without asking first. But it was too late. Irene had disappeared across the road and into the Bunch of Grapes to make the call.

Friday evening at Cherry Trees and Felicity had somehow managed to get the house up together and reasonably tidy, even to extent of rushing around with a tin of spray polish and giving everything in sight a quick flick. Nothing like the smell of fresh polish for making a house seem clean and welcoming. It had been one of her mother's little tricks, and one which she was happy to emulate. She'd even been shopping, restocking the larder with enough food to last a month, and had prepared an enormous moussaka and salad for their evening meal, half of which she proposed to freeze to eat later the following week.

Of course, all this had been achieved at the expense of her work for Dickens, her *paid* work. Not one single word had she read that day. But she comforted herself with the thought that next week she was interviewing for a home help and then life would change dramatically. She caught a brief glimpse of herself in the small kitchen mirror and paused a moment. Dark hair, plastered to her forehead from the effort of housework. Was there time to wash it before this evening? No, she decided, and fluffed it up a little. She looked exhausted. The one bonus point was that she appeared to have lost weight. Sucking in her cheeks, she peered more closely into the mirror. Definitely thinner. Cheekbones more pronounced. Quite elegant, in fact. For the moment all was well; she felt self-satisfied and slightly virtuous, and the bonus was that Tony would be pleased. The moment she'd thought that, she felt annoyed with herself. What sort of woman had she become, turning herself into a slave to housework in order to please the man in her life? Leaning against the kitchen windowsill, surveying her handiwork, she knew the answer: a wife! That was what she'd become. It was rather frightening.

The sound of the front door slamming announced the arrival of Annabel. Today was the day for Annabel to be picked up and dropped back at Cherry Trees, and she came into the kitchen grumbling about Jenny's mother. 'That woman is always in a rush,' she announced, dropping her haversack on the floor and kicking off her shoes. Prudence lumbered out to meet her, tail wagging. 'Hello, darling,' said Annabel, tearing a handful of grapes from the fruit bowl on the dresser. 'Jenny and I wanted to do our homework together,' she complained through a mouthful of grapes, 'but her mother said there was no time for that and dumped me here before we even had time to talk!'

Felicity raised her eyebrows. A kiss was bestowed on Prudence but not on her, she noticed. 'Like me, Jenny's mother has a lot to do,' she said. 'And pick up that haversack and your shoes and take them to your room.'

'In a minute.' Annabel opened the oven door. 'Great! Moussaka,' she breathed. 'My favourite. Shall I see if it's done?'

Taking a spoon from the drawer, Annabel was about to plunge it into the crunchy topping when Felicity sprang into action. Snatching the spoon from Annabel, she shrieked, 'Don't touch it. You'll spoil the appearance.'

'My word,' said Annabel, 'we are getting fussy. Who are you expecting to supper tonight?'

'No one,' said Felicity. 'Just the three of us as usual, but as I've made a supreme effort and slaved over a hot stove all day,' it hadn't actually been all day but by the time she'd finished it had felt like it, 'I want dinner to be nice and civilized this evening. No hiccups, nothing going wrong, just a peaceful, pleasant evening. The three of us.'

'Yuk! Boring!' said Annabel. 'Why don't we have visitors? Jenny is having her cousins to stay for the weekend, and her aunt and uncle. They're going to have a real party. That's what Mrs Coleman said.'

'You haven't got any cousins,' Felicity pointed out, 'and I thought you didn't like Jenny's mother.'

'I didn't say that. I just said she was always in a rush.'

'And quite understandable if she's entertaining cousins and aunts,' said Felicity. 'Thank heavens we haven't got any family to descend on us this weekend. I don't think I could cope with that.'

'Oh God! Mum, you are *hopeless*!' was Annabel's crushing reply, and, picking up her haversack and shoes, she left the room.

Hopeless! That hurt and was unfair. Annabel was so inconsiderate sometimes. Felicity wondered if she had been as difficult as Annabel when she'd been a teenager. Surely not. She couldn't remember always arguing with her mother. But there was no time to ponder over that; it was time to prepare the kitchen table for dinner if her avowed intention of remaining well-organized for the rest of the Friday evening was to be fulfilled.

At last everything was in place. Felicity glanced at the clock. Just time for a spot of quiet relaxation with a glass of chilled wine. The perfect end to a busy day. A bottle of Chablis was open in the fridge and Felicity poured herself a generous glass then collapsed in a heap into the old wickerwork chair by the window. The telephone rang. Felicity ignored it. Bound to be for Annabel, she reasoned; Jenny was always ringing her.

She could hear Annabel's voice in the hall when she picked up the extension.

'Hi! Oh! Yes . . . well . . . great! I'll get Mum, just a mo.' Annabel came into the kitchen holding out the phone at arm's length. She was grinning broadly. 'How many will that moussaka stretch to?' she said.

Felicity frowned warily and took the phone. 'Who is it?' she hissed, her hand over the mouthpiece.

'It's Gran. She's coming down for the weekend with a friend.'

'What!' squeaked Felicity, sitting bolt upright.

Friday nights were the worst, thought Samantha. On Friday nights she was stretched, pulled in two different directions and always felt in dire danger of being torn in two.

Piers inevitably wanted to go out to dinner, usually with people he considered influential to both their new careers. It was important, Samantha understood that, and she too wanted to dine with Piers' elegant and sophisticated acquaintances. So different from the small social circle in Oakford, dominated by Alice Appleby whom no one could possibly call sophisticated or elegant.

The problem for Samantha was that besides Piers she had the children, and the children meant duty, not pleasure. The boys had taken to coming to St John's Wood every weekend. She wished they would stay at school as indeed they were supposed to, but Brother Tom had telephoned her and specifically stated that in his opinion it would do Peter and Philip good to see more of her, 'during this difficult time of transition', as he had so succinctly put it.

Piers had been furious. 'Interfering old bastard,' he'd said. 'Tell him to get stuffed.'

'I can't stuff a holy father,' said Samantha.

Piers did a double-take. Was she joking? She wasn't. A sense of humour was not one of Samantha's strong points. So the boys came and expected Samantha and Hilary to eat with them every Friday evening while they related everything they'd done during the past week, and then in turn wanted to hear about everything they'd done. It was very wearing and time-consuming and was driving Piers mad with frustration. He hated having his plans thwarted. Sometimes Samantha thought it was as if the three children were trying to prove to themselves that they had done the right thing in opting to stay with her and not their father. This worried her, because her determination to hang on to them in the face of Tony's opposition was something she often puzzled over herself. Was it right? Why did she keep them tied to her when she didn't really want them? Not spite, surely? She'd got over that. Obstinacy? Perhaps. Maternal instinct? No! She didn't have that kind of relationship with them. They weren't really close, the relationship was more of a stand-off thing: the children hung around like ships outside a harbour waiting to be told to come ashore and tie up. But Samantha had no intention of inviting them to tie up.

She was, as Venetia had remarked on one of her rare visits to the St John's Wood house, 'a maternal defective. Or, to put it in PC language, maternally challenged.' Venetia read a lot as well as avidly watching TV, and prided herself on keeping up to date with modern idioms. A trait which Samantha found increasingly irritating.

'I do love them,' Samantha told Piers after Venetia had left. 'In my *own* way.' She felt tense and defensive and swamped by a huge guilt complex.

Piers had recently stepped outside the family side of things. It was, as he quite rightly said, nothing to do with him. For him it was an irritation to be dealt with, nothing more. He kept it all at arm's length, paying it as much attention as he would an annoying bluebottle buzzing around. 'I know you love them, darling,' he said now, in his smooth voice. That was what Samantha loved about him, his smoothness. Very little, except the children, ruffled him. He touched an appreciative hand on her newly cut hair. 'Marcel makes you look a million dollars.'

Samantha leaned against him. With Piers she felt cool and sophisticated. With Piers it didn't seem to matter that by some bizarre arrangement of her hormones she was not equipped for proper motherhood. Thinking about her new hairstyle was much more satisfying than thinking about the children. She turned to face Piers. 'Marcel found three grey hairs.' she said seriously. 'So I let him give me a henna rinse.'

'That accounts for that wonderful mahogany glow.' Piers kissed her. 'It looks stunning, and you deserve to be taken out and shown off just for your hair alone.'

They were back to square one. It was Friday. The worst day of the week.

'I can't,' said Samantha, feeling doubly guilty. 'Not this week. I left them alone last Friday.'

'Of course you can,' said Piers firmly. 'It's about time those kids saw their father. I've already got their train tickets. He can meet the train at Brockenhurst. Ring him now and tell him they'll be on their way soon.'

Samantha felt a sudden surge of relief. Piers was so good at arranging things. She looked at her watch. 'But Tony won't be there yet. He'll still be in his surgery.'

'Then phone Felicity. It's about time she got to know her stepchildren.' When Samantha looked dubious, Piers turned on the charm full blast. 'Look, darling,' he said gently, but very, very firmly, 'this weekend is important for us. We're going to spend it with Hank Haufmann. He's a really important guy in publishing in the States, and he's in the process of setting up a new monthly. A sort of Homes and Gardens USA-style. There's a good chance I'm going to be asked to be editor. And, of course, there'd be a job for you there as well.'

The guilty feeling began to recede slightly. Thoughts of America were much more alluring than worries about the children. 'Would that mean moving, darling?'

'Of course. The Haufmann empire is based in California, and this is why you've *got* to meet him this evening.'

Samantha almost hugged him in glee, then remembered Piers didn't like unduly enthusiastic displays of emotion, unless it was sexual foreplay, so refrained. 'California,' she breathed, immediately thinking of large houses, glamorous golden women, golden beaches, and palm trees. 'How wonderful!'

Piers smiled. 'I knew you'd like the idea. In America life will be a challenge. Once we are free of our shackles we can be ourselves.'

The shackles were the children. She knew that. Piers didn't have to elaborate, and to be truthful that was how she saw them too. But that didn't eradicate the guilt or the worry about what would happen to them.

Piers put her mind at rest in his cool, calculating way. 'Don't worry, and don't breathe a word of this to the children,' he said. 'We'll sort out that little problem when I've got the deal sewn up. Just you go and phone Felicity and say they're on their way, then tell them that they are off to the New Forest this weekend and not to unpack their bags.'

And because Piers was such a wonderful organizer, and because she wanted to be free to develop the woman she had become and not be tied down by motherhood, Samantha didn't worry. Children were resilient; they'd cope. She had nothing to worry about and she was entitled to her own life. She was tired of being a non-person as far as they were concerned. A mother was a non-person, someone who was there just to be, not for any other good reason.

After gathering up her courage to approach Felicity, she phoned, and then closed her ears to Felicity's obvious panic at the thought of three uninvited guests. 'You *are* their stepmother,' she said at one point before putting down the phone. And that is that, she thought, stifling her guilt and telling herself she was just being firm. Stepmotherhood brings certain responsibilities. Felicity will have to face up to them, just as I will face up to telling the children now. Drawing in a deep breath, she went to tell the children that they were being sent away for the weekend. After all their grumbles about London they ought, by rights, to be overjoyed at the prospect. But Samantha knew that was a slim hope indeed.

'I'm sorry, but Piers and I have to go out and we've decided that it's better for you to go down to Oakford this weekend,' she told the trio sitting mutely before her.

They were all overweight. Hilary was particularly enormous and seemed to be growing fatter by the day. Now, she had Hula Hoop snacks on every finger and was slowly pulling each one off and crunching it. Before her on the table lay the bag, half of the contents eaten.

Hilary held up a Hula Hoop, then screwed it into her eye socket like a monocle. A baleful eye stared through at her mother. 'You're *always* out,' she said.

Samantha tried to control her irritation. But the irritation was badly tinged with guilt, her conscience telling her that if she provided proper nutritious meals then maybe they wouldn't continually graze on snacks. It wasn't *all* their fault, an innate sense of fair play made her acknowledge that fact, but nevertheless they did annoy her, all three of them. And yet, as she had told Piers and Venetia, neither of whom really listened, she *did* love them, but it was in her own way.

163

'And we are not going down there while that woman is there,' said Philip, wondering why his mother couldn't see that they were only at the St John's Wood house for *her* sake.

'When Dad leaves her, then we'll go down.' Peter backed Philip up although he was less certain about the tactics they'd embarked upon. Perhaps Brother Tom was right. He usually was.

Brother Tom had said, 'People do wrong and stupid things. But these things cannot always be undone. You have to accept that all human beings are imperfect and take things as you find them and make the best of a bad job.'

Peter wanted to see his father, and he knew Hilary was pining dreadfully for Cherry Trees, her old school, and most of all for Cotton-Socks. She had confided this to him but made him swear not to tell Philip. Philip was the strong one. *He* wasn't going to make the best of a bad job. He'd declared his intention. As far as he was concerned it was war. *He* was going to change things and get everything back to how it was before Piers and Felicity had come along.

'Yes, you can forget the New Forest. We're going to stay here with you for ever and ever.' Hilary avoided looking at her mother, and carefully slid another supply of Hula Hoops on to her fingers.

At this point Piers came into the room to see if Samantha was ready. 'There is no such thing, Hilary, as for ever and ever,' he said sharply, in his precise, clipped voice.

Hilary hated everything about him. His coolness, his

precision, his unflappability, his very essence. 'There is for me,' she said.

Samantha felt an uneasy twinge. No such thing as for ever. She hadn't ever thought about that before. Did Piers mean that *they* weren't for ever? She dared not look at him for fear he should see her nebulous, worrying thoughts.

Piers cleared his throat. Nothing noisy. Just a little, polite, controlled kind of cough. A small sound, but enough to convey his extreme annoyance to all three children. 'You are young,' he said. 'But when you are grown up you will find that everything changes all the time. Now get your things ready; the taxi will be here for you in half an hour.'

Faced with his steely determination the children had no alternative but to comply. Sulkily they slung their belongings together, watched by an increasingly anxious Samantha. Anxious, not because the children were being difficult, but because for the first time since she'd left Tony she no longer felt secure with Piers. *Everything changes all the time*, he'd said. That had to mean their relationship too. Samantha wasn't sure that she could cope with any more changes. Not now. Not after her metamorphosis into the creature she now was. Not now that she'd finally found her own niche in the world.

The children scrambled into the crowded Weymouth-bound train and through energetic pushing found three seats by the window.

'Piers is not bloody right,' said Philip when they'd settled down. 'You can *make* everything stay the same if you want to.' He got out a bag of crisps and, undeterred by the dagger-like glances from the man forced to share the end seat with him, proceeded to crunch them noisily.

Peter stared at his brother. In spite of his forceful tone of voice Peter instinctively knew that Philip was as uncertain as he was himself. 'Perhaps you can *keep* everything the same if you try hard enough at the beginning,' he said diffidently. 'But I think it's difficult putting the pieces back together again once it's broken. It's a bit like a dropped puzzle. It's all a big jumbled heap on the floor, the picture has disappeared, and everything is so mixed up that no one can be bothered to put it together again.' This was another of Brother Tom's little homilies and one which he had been able to relate to.

'Bullshit!' said Philip, and rewarded by another glare from the man beside him.

'Hey, Philip, your language,' said Hilary admiringly. Then she repeated the word experimentally. 'Bullshit! That's what Piers is, a complete bullshitter!'

'Too bloody right,' said Philip.

'Of course,' said Piers, deftly weaving the big black car through London's evening traffic, 'when we go to the States, those children of yours will *have* to toe the line. Hilary can go to boarding school no matter how much she may say she dislikes it, and they'll all have to go back to Hampshire for the holidays.' He turned and flashed Samantha a smile. 'Then, darling, it will be just the two of us.'

166

Samantha smiled back. Why had she ever fought Tony over the custody? Life would have been so much more uncomplicated without the children. Never mind guilt, responsibility and duty, she'd had more than enough of all of that. She'd done her share. 'Tony will be pleased,' she said. 'He always wanted to have them with him.'

Piers parked the car in a square off the Embankment beneath the plane trees. The opaque new green leaves cast a subtle glow across the paving stones, and the evening sunlight slanted through the gaps in the trees on to the first roses of summer in the square gardens. Piers helped Samantha from the car and stood looking at her for a moment, a dark silhouette against the light. 'Don't mention anything to anyone yet,' he said. 'When everything is cut and dried, that's the time to speak. And then you'll need to do a little sweet-talking to that new wife of Tony's.'

Samantha frowned. She had no desire to talk to Felicity any more than necessary. 'Why sweet-talk her?'

'She'll be taking on your children.'

'But they will be at boarding school.' Samantha stopped. She had forgotten about the holidays. 'Oh, heavens,' she said.

'Exactly, darling.' A hint of a smile crossed Piers's smooth features while he carefully checked that the car was locked. 'That's where the sweet-talking comes in. Because what woman in her right mind would want to take on someone else's children?'

CHAPTER 10

Felicity put the phone down. Outside in the garden the rain had stopped falling and a shaft of sunlight shimmered in a curtain of light across the wet grass. New foliage suddenly vibrated with all the energy of early summer and the pink cabbage roses held their faces up towards the sun. All this cheerfulness, however, was unnoticed by Felicity in the house. There the atmosphere was as dreary as it had been all day and Felicity had that horribly familiar feeling of being overwhelmed by events. No matter how hard she tried, it seemed that something always erupted to thwart her plans and aspirations. Samantha's call had come out of the blue, as had her mother's. Coping with Irene and her mysterious (she wouldn't say who she was) friend was one thing, and anyway during the last half-hour she had got used to that idea. But coping with an influx of three children as well was another matter all together.

'*You are their stepmother*,' Samantha had said.

And I am, thought Felicity. Good heavens! I am! Suddenly she realized that the significance of this was not something she had ever given much conscious thought to before. Of course the fact that Tony was a father just as she was a mother was an accepted facet of their life together, but it had never played a major part in their relationship. His children were distant beings living not with them but with Samantha, and when they had declared their hostility towards Felicity it hadn't bothered her unduly. It was Tony's issue to be dealt with, not hers, and the fact that they were not prepared to play any meaningful part in her life had been greeted, if she was honest, by heartfelt relief on Felicity's part. But those four words uttered by Samantha had placed them fairly and squarely into her realm of responsibility. They were part of her life, something, she was now forced to acknowledge, albeit reluctantly, she had picked up along with Tony when she had married him. Like it or not, there was no getting away from that. Felicity could almost hear her mother saying, Well, dear, what did you expect? I'm surprised it's taken you this long to realize it.

Her mother! She looked at her watch. Two and a half hours before she and the children arrived, *and*, it seemed, all arriving on the same train. So much for the quiet, peaceful evening she'd envisaged. Now there were extra beds to be made up, and extra food to be prepared; the moussaka would never stretch for five extra people. Her thoughts galloped along. There were some pizza bases in the deep freeze; Annabel was good at pizzas, she could make up two while the beds were being organized, and they could start with soup from a packet, and thank goodness she'd bought some bread when out shopping earlier, although tomorrow morning she'd have to rush down into the village before breakfast and hope the garage shop had a fresh supply in. But tomorrow was another day; it was tonight she had to get through first.

'Oh, hell,' said Annabel crossly, when she told her, 'I don't want *that* horrible lot of kids coming. I don't mind Gran and her friend, but not them.'

'They *are* Tony's children,' Felicity pointed out, taking care not to show her own resentment. And, remembering Samantha's words, she added for good measure, 'And I am their stepmother.'

'I don't see why you have to be,' sniffed Annabel. 'You're my mother; that's enough, surely?'

Felicity who thought much the same thing herself, reflected that nothing had prepared her for being landed with three extra teenage children. But it was not something she could communicate to Annabel. Instead she threw herself on to Annabel's better nature, and heard herself pleading, 'Don't start being difficult now. I need your help, not antagonism.'

Annabel was silent for a moment or two while she twiddled the gold studs in her ears, a recent acquisition from a visit to Westhampton. Felicity, who didn't have pierced ears, did not really approve but supposed she should count herself lucky. At least it was her ears and not her nose that Annabel had had pierced. She regarded her mother now through screwed-up eyes, her expression abstruse. Then she said in a consolatory tone of voice, 'All right, what do you want me to do?'

'Make two pizzas,' said Felicity. 'That would be an enormous help.'

'OK. But *I'm* not eating pizza, I want some of that moussaka.'

'Of course, dear,' said Felicity and flew upstairs to re-organize the bedrooms. It was cowardly of her, she knew, but she didn't have the strength or time to argue with Annabel at the moment. The time for dividing, and possibly fighting over, the moussaka would come later.

The re-organization involved herself and Tony moving into the boys' old room, so that his three children could share their large bedroom. The boys would sleep in their double bed and Hilary on a camp bed at the far end of the room. Not an ideal arrangement, but with her mother and the unknown friend arriving it was the only solution. The two older women would have to sleep in Hilary's room. She did think for a moment, but it was only a moment, of putting Hilary in with Annabel, but decided discretion was the better part of valour. No point in antagonizing Annabel any more than necessary. Tony's children would be returning to London and their schools after the weekend, but Annabel would remain, for better or worse. So, ignoring the small voice telling her that she was a moral coward, she reasoned it was better to keep on the right side of Annabel.

In the middle of stripping sheets and making up beds she puzzled, wearily trying to find the reason why she felt she was battling against something. What was the intangible something that she was battling against?

There was no satisfactory answer to this question so she continued making the beds.

Tony came in earlier than usual from surgery, and his unrestrained joy when he knew his children were coming for the weekend caused Felicity to be stricken with a double dose of guilt at being less than enthusiastic. She hadn't realized before how much he was missing his children. She felt a responsive surge of sorrow and then was glad that she was having them for the weekend, and didn't allow herself even the smallest glimmer of relief that it *was* only the weekend.

'Well, dear. How does it feel being mother to a whole tribe of children?' Irene sat back on the settee and stretched out her feet, her hands folded peaceably across her full stomach.

It was Sunday afternoon, after an enormous lunch. Struggling to produce a leg of roast lamb, baked potatoes, spring greens, carrots, gravy, mint sauce and an apple pie and custard, all to be ready at the same time, had nearly killed Felicity. Irene and Venetia had offered to h_lp, but, determined to prove that she could manage, Felicity had refused. She had started off on Friday evening vowing to be the perfect stepmother and wife and so far, much to her own amazement, seemed to have managed to please everyone.

The weekend had been a surprising success. Tony's children had been quite subdued and she couldn't criticise their behaviour. A fact which, she was sure, was due in no small measure to the presence of Venetia – one step out of line brought a sharp rebuke to the children which they heeded. Her arrival had been a complete surprise, but after the initial shock of having Samantha's grandmother to stay Felicity found herself warming to the old lady.

'Why on earth didn't you tell me it was Venetia you were bringing?' she'd whispered to her mother.

'Because I didn't want you to say no,' said her mother. Her logic, as always, being perfect. 'If one doesn't know then one can't object.'

'I wouldn't have said no,' Felicity had replied, but she knew that she probably would have done, and was glad that her mother had forestalled her.

'I'm not really their mother,' said Felicity in answer to her mother's question. 'I'm only playing at being one for this weekend.'

Venetia ensconced in the most comfortable chair close to the open fire – although it was early summer there was still a sharp nip in the air to which her old bones were very susceptible – sat up and looked fiercely at Felicity. 'What would you say if you were asked to have them here all the time?' she asked.

Felicity stared at her, trying not to let the panic show. Did Venetia know something she didn't? Was this weekend a trial for the real thing? 'Do you think that's likely?' she said at last.

Venetia subsided into a disappointed heap. 'No,' she said, 'but I think they would be happier here than with Samantha.'

'But Samantha is their mother. She *wanted* custody of the children when she divorced Tony. Surely it's better for children to be with their mother?'

'It doesn't always follow that mothers are good for their children,' was all Venetia would say, and refused to elaborate on that profound statement.

On Sunday evening, after everyone had consumed another enormous meal, salmon sandwiches, crumpets, two complete fruit cakes and gallons of tea and coffee, Tony and Felicity took them in a convoy of two cars to Brockenhurst station to catch the London-bound train.

The train was full of city dwellers returning to London after a weekend in the country, most of them slumped in seats with their eyes closed.

'Poor things,' said Tony. 'They must all be exhausted just thinking of going back to work in London. Thank heavens I don't live there any more. I think anyone who wants to work in London must be mad.'

Felicity recognized it for a dig at her ambitions. But, gritting her teeth and keeping silent, she helped pile Venetia and her mother, plus the children, into the train. She was *not* going to argue with Tony about returning to London. Not now, not in front of the children. In fact, she was not going to argue with him about it. Not ever.

'Mum is going back to work in London,' said Annabel cheerfully to all and sundry.

Irene, who was last into the carriage, and heard both Tony and Annabel, stopped in the doorway. 'Yes, I'm looking forward to having Felicity with me for *one* night a week.' She emphasised the word one. Then she added, 'And by the way, Tony, I'm sure the reason the rest of our fellow passengers look so tired is because they've probably all been rushing around with lawnmowers all the weekend. That's the thing about the country; there's so much to do. At least I never have to mow a lawn.'

Tony's reply, if he had thought of one, was lost in the shouted goodbyes of the children and a series of high-pitched beeps and a swish as the vacuum-controlled doors automatically closed.

'Well, that's that,' said Annabel. 'Can I stop being nice now?'

Felicity said a silent prayer of thanks that the weekend was over, but hoped Tony didn't guess her feelings. 'Went well, didn't it, darling?' she said, slipping her hand into his as the three of them walked back to the two cars in the station yard. She looked thoughtful. Maybe a little confession was in order now. 'I must admit that I feel happier about your children now that they've actually stayed at Cherry Trees. I've always been dreading their first weekend here with me.'

'You'd no need to dread anything,' said Tony. 'You were, *are*, the perfect stepmother.'

Felicity looked at him. 'High praise indeed,' she said lightly. But she felt serious, because Tony's expressive eyes were filled with an infinite sadness.

Tony stopped by the side of his car. 'Yes, it did go well,' he said wistfully. 'But I can't help wishing the children could spend more time here.'

'You've got the summer holidays to look forward to,' said Felicity, and hardened her heart. She loved Tony and desperately wanted to please him. But he was asking too much. True, the children had been well behaved and

175

not too much trouble this time, but she really didn't *want* them at Cherry Trees too often. Tony called her a good stepmother. Not true. She was only pretending. It was no good, she wasn't cut out to be an earth-mother type to hordes of children. Not even if they had all been her own, which they weren't.

Annabel, who'd opted to drive back to Cherry Trees with her mother, slumped in the car seat and let out a long pent-up breath. 'God!' she said. 'I'm *not* looking forward to the summer holidays.'

Neither am I, thought Felicity. But a combination of guilt, loyalty to Tony and a twinge of sympathy for his children who were being dumped around like so many sacks of potatoes kept her silent.

'Thank you, Mrs Balfour. I'm very grateful that you came to see me, and . . .' Felicity tried to end the interview.

'And of course I know the house inside out,' Mrs Balfour interrupted determinedly, glancing once more around the dining room with an all-seeing eye. She sniffed loudly – a great deal could be conveyed by one sniff, Felicity observed. 'There's a lot to be done,' she added ominously.

Felicity seized upon the remark with alacrity. 'Exactly. There is a lot. And if you are too busy, I shall . . .'

'I didn't say I was too busy. I just said there's a lot to be done. Things have gone downhill a bit since I was last here.' She looked pointedly down at the floor where crumbs from Felicity's lunchtime biscuits lay scattered across the carpet.

Felicity would not have been surprised if the stocky woman sitting before her had whipped out a dustpan and brush from her handbag and swept up the crumbs there and then. They obviously bothered her tidy eye, although not nearly as much as Mrs Balfour bothered Felicity. She oozed bossiness. Patently Alice Appleby had not been exaggerating when she'd said Mrs Balfour would not leave a stone unturned.

Only one other person, a Tracy Milligan, had replied to the advertisement, but Mrs Balfour was not to know that and Felicity had no intention of telling her. 'Of course, as I advertised,' she said firmly, 'I feel obliged to see all the other applicants. So I know that you will understand that I cannot give you a definite answer right now.'

Mrs Balfour quite evidently did not understand. 'I come very highly recommended,' she said, an aggressive tone creeping into her voice.

Felicity stood up. Why on earth had Tony ever engaged this woman in the first place? She was an absolute dragon. 'I know. My husband told me. But as *I* advertised I feel . . .'

'Duty-bound, *I* suppose,' said Mrs Balfour, reluctantly taking the hint and also rising. 'Ah, well,' she said, giving one last disapproving look around the cluttered dining room, while Felicity cursed the sun which was beautifully illuminating the thick layer of dust along the window sill, 'I'll wait for your phone call. Don't forget, I can start immediately.'

'I won't.' Felicity ushered her towards the door.

'Who were the others who applied?'

'Oh, I can't remember all the names just now.' said Felicity.

'*All* the names! I wonder there was time for more than one to see that advertisement. I told Mr Smithson to take it down the moment I saw it.'

For a moment Felicity thought she was going to explode with annoyance. No one in Primrose Hill would have ever even thought of getting the newsagent to take down a notice – although on second thoughts not many people there would bother to read it either; they were too busy for it to matter. But this was the country, and in the country people interfered. Something she was beginning to find out. The explosive feeling subsided and Felicity elected to say nothing. There was no point. She was going to run her life in the way it suited her. Her life, and Tony's – mustn't forget Tony. Although there had been days lately when she was so harassed that she had almost forgotten him.

Almost forgotten Tony, who was the reason she'd given up her orderly life in London and moved to Hampshire so that she could be with him all the time. Her mind wandered, and she thought of Annabel, who had not wanted to come, but who seemed to have settled down to the different way of life very well. True, she still disapproved of her mother's relationship with Tony, even after Felicity had attempted to have a long talk with her on how sex and love went hand in hand with a man and woman who had made the commitment of marriage to one another. Annabel had listened in silence, then said, 'You can do it if you like, but I still think, from what I've seen of it, that sex is pretty ghastly.'

Worried, Felicity had told her mother, when she'd arrived for one of her flying visits to Cherry Trees. But Irene's reaction had been a phlegmatic, 'Well, at least you can thank your lucky stars that she's not likely to add to the statistics of teenage unmarried mothers.' At the time they'd been strolling, with Prudence safely on her leash, beside a field full of horses. One large horse, very obviously a stallion, was cornering a not unwilling mare. Irene pointed towards them. 'With sights like that around, it's hardly surprising she's been put off sex!'

'It's natural,' said Felicity defensively, feeling she ought to stick up for the things in her adopted county.

'I'd much prefer it if he wore a fig leaf,' said her mother drily.

Felicity stopped daydreaming and concentrated on Mrs Balfour. 'I'll let you know as soon as possible,' she said, resolutely showing her out of the house. 'I promise.'

Relieved, she watched the sturdy figure cycling away, wobbling slightly every time she hit a pot-hole in the drive.

'Tracy Milligan has got the job,' she told the dog. 'Even if she turns out to be a hundred and one and doesn't know the difference between a dustpan and a dishcloth!' Prudence thumped her tail in agreement, and rolled over so that kittens number two and three could swarm on her silky underbelly, reminding Felicity that someone, probably her, really ought to get around to doing something about the kittens before they became permanent fixtures of Cherry Trees.

However, when facing Tracy Milligan across the dining room table an hour later, Felicity wondered about the wisdom of making a decision in advance.

'Of course, it'll have to be cash in hand,' said Tracy, twiddling the ring in her nose. 'Otherwise they'll stop my benefit. They don't like punks at the benefit office. That lot'll do anything to do me out of my rights.'

'Oh, yes, it will be cash in hand,' Felicity heard herself saying weakly, while she tried not to stare too obviously. Tracy's hair was died fluorescent green and pink at the front and jet black at the back. As well as the nose ring, she had three rings in each ear, wore pale white make-up and had black kohl-ringed eyes, all contriving to make her pinched little face look like that of an anxious bushbaby. She was painfully thin. Looks as if she could do with a good nourishing meal, Felicity found herself thinking. And her clothes: jeans with the mandatory tear at the knees, and a torn black T-shirt. Both threadbare, although clean and obviously carefully washed and ironed, but no match for the sharp easterly wind which was blowing. All this surprised Felicity, but not nearly as much as the fact that she had not come alone. A clean, fat, round, unblinking baby sat gurgling happily on her lap. The baby was well nourished and very well dressed and oozed contentment and happiness. The pair of them sitting before Felicity were a mass of contradictions, and Tracy was quite different from the punks Felicity had seen loitering around the environs of Camden Lock.

'What will you do with . . . er, sorry, don't know its . . . his . . . her name,' Felicity indicated the baby, 'while you are working?'

'Jacob,' said Tracy, kissing the top of his round, downy head. 'Don't worry about that, my friend will have him most times. She's got a baby too. We're both single parents and help each other out.' She gave Felicity a sudden fierce stare. 'Just because I'm a single parent, it doesn't mean that I'm not a good worker. I am. You've no need to worry about that. I *need* the money. Children are very expensive, and I only want the best for Jacob.'

'Five pounds an hour, cash in hand,' said Felicity, offering one pound an hour more than she'd originally intended. 'And I should think two hours a day, preferably mornings, five days a week, would be sufficient.'

Tracy's thin face was transformed by a beaming smile. 'Fifty quid a week,' she said gleefully. 'That'll be great. When can I start?'

Felicity worried. Two hundred pounds a month. Could she really afford it? The answer was, of course, she would *have* to afford it. 'How about tomorrow?' she said.

'Fine.'

Felicity had another thought. 'Is that your own car out there?'

Tracy stiffened and suddenly looked very wary, and

Felicity realized that it took very little to put her hackles up and get her on the defensive. 'So what? It's a rust bucket,' she said gruffly.

'But is it taxed and insured and everything?' asked Felicity.

'Of course.' Tracy was scornful. 'I'm not a fool. I know everyone is out to get me. But it's mine, it goes, and it's just passed its MOT. A car is a luxury, the benefit people say, and I shouldn't have one. But I can tell you this, it isn't a luxury if you live in a village like Oakford.'

'You don't have to tell me that,' replied Felicity with heartfelt sincerity. 'I didn't realize just how inconvenient life could be until I came to live down here. It's a major expedition to buy anything.' She could see Tracy relaxing a little, and guessed that life for her was a continual battle against the disapproval of others. 'I didn't ask just to be nosy,' she said. 'There is a point to my question. If you agree, I'd like you to go shopping at the supermarket for me. The time would count as work, of course, and it would help me enormously. I'd give you a list and some money.'

Tracy relaxed completely and gave another transforming smile. Get rid of those awful rings and make-up and she'd be really pretty, Felicity decided.

'No problem,' said Tracy. 'I can take Jacob with me. He adores riding around in the supermarket trolley.'

Annabel approved of the new arrangement even if Tony was still very uncertain about it. He seemed to think that the fact that Felicity needed to work, and furthermore work in London, reflected on his performance as a husband. Felicity told him that she was too long in the tooth to change and become part of the Happy Hoover brigade, they had no young children to occupy her time and that she needed the intellectual buzz of working. The argument was in vain; Tony stubbornly refused to step into the realms occupied by the New Men of the nineties. He would have much preferred his wife to be waiting at home for him with his slippers warm and his supper ready. Felicity didn't argue, but began to have a sneaking sympathy for Samantha, who'd fled the confines of Oakford for a new life with Piers in London.

Annabel enjoyed staying overnight with Jenny one night a week and they both regarded Tracy with awed eyes. Not only was she not a virgin, because she had a baby to prove it, but she was also a free agent, no parents in sight, and could do as she pleased. However, Annabel was disappointed to learn that Tracy's lifestyle did not match her outrageous appearance.

'Having a baby to look after must be a real drag,' she told Jenny. 'Tracy says she never goes out in the evenings, she's too tired, can't get a baby-sitter and can't afford to go out anyway. I've decided I shall never have children. Which will be easy as I'm never going to have sex.'

'Well . . .' Jenny was not so sure about the no sex bit. 'In all the books I've read it always seems rather nice.'

'What! Having a baby?'

'No. Sex, silly.'

'*You* haven't seen the video I've seen,' said Annabel.

'Anyway,' Jenny moved on to a more interesting subject of gossip. 'My sister was in the same year as Tracy at sixth form college. She says that one of Dr Appleby's sons is the father of that baby. Although Tracy won't say which one. She went out with them both.'

'Maybe she doesn't know. If she slept with them both, how can she tell?'

Jenny shook her head. 'My sister says she does know, but won't tell.'

'I'd tell,' said Annabel fiercely. 'I'd make the rotten sod pay up.' She was developing strong feminist tendencies. 'I wouldn't need to go out cleaning if I had a baby. Which of course I won't. But if I did, then I'd make the father pay. Tony is paying for his children even though they don't live with us.'

'No point in trying to make either Stephen or Sam Appleby pay up,' said Jenny. 'They're both unemployed. Dropouts, the pair of them. They've both disappeared. My mum says that Dr and Mrs Appleby don't even know where they are. But she thinks they're in London somewhere.'

'Fancy!' said Annabel.

'And my mum says,' continued Jenny, 'that's it's all Mrs Appleby's fault. She was always so busy doing good works for everyone else that she never noticed her own sons going off the rails. The Holy Cow, that's what my mother calls her!'

'Fancy!' said Annabel again, digesting this bit of information. This was one feature of country living that she really enjoyed. All the gossip and the fact that everyone knew everything about everyone else. They'd never known anything about their neighbours in London. But Oakford presented a slice of life on a plate.

'Anyway,' said Jenny, 'tell me what Tracy is really like. My mother thought your mother was mad hiring an unmarried mother with green and red hair. She said Tracy wouldn't have a clue about housework and would be work-shy into the bargain.'

'Coloured hair doesn't make any difference. She's good at the job,' Annabel told Jenny. 'In fact she's too efficient sometimes; she's told me off three times about the state of my room. But I don't mind. Mum's much less tense these days, and even old Tony isn't so bad.'

They were sharing a furtive cigarette together in the depths of a laurel bush in Jenny's garden. Jenny's mother had banned smoking, but both girls were determined to try and cultivate the habit as most of their friends smoked and they hated being in the minority.

'I've always thought old Tony, as you call him, is rather gorgeous,' said Jenny, taking a puff, inhaling deeply, and dissolving into a paroxysm of coughing. She passed the cigarette over to Annabel. 'I could never understand,' she said between coughs, 'why Hilary's mother left him. Neither can my mother. She says he's a very sympathetic man. Poor old Hilary,' she added as an afterthought.

'Poor old Hilary nothing,' said Annabel crossly. She thought resentfully of the recent weekend at Cherry Trees. A weekend when she'd been stuck with Hilary

185

whom she'd found boring in the extreme, and her brothers, who, although not so boring, were, in Annabel's opinion, horrible. All they could think about were motorcycle engines. She resented, too, references to Tony's life before she and Felicity had come on the scene. Although she grumbled about him, she now regarded him as her property and didn't wanted to include Hilary and the boys. 'She's fat,' she announced, 'and I don't like her.'

'She didn't used to be fat. She's only got fat since she left here. My mother says she's probably comfort-eating because she's unhappy. And you ought to like her, she's your stepsister.'

Annabel was even more annoyed. 'She's no relation to me whatsoever, nor are those brothers of hers, and you aren't to say they are.' She took a fierce drag on the cigarette, tried to inhale and ended up puce in the face. 'It's no use,' she gasped. 'I'm never going to like these things.'

She handed the cigarette back to Jenny, who stared dubiously at the smouldering stub. 'I'm not keen either,' she admitted. 'Perhaps we should try speed or Ecstasy. I know Maureen Magee can get some.'

'Not this month.' Annabel had gone from puce to pale and was rather wheezy. 'I've almost run out of pocket money.'

'Oh!' Jenny was disappointed. 'I can lend you some money. They we can try it.'

'No, thanks. I don't want to get into debt.' Irene Hobbit's thrifty ways had rubbed off on to Annabel.

She had always told Annabel that it was better to save money and then spend it on a luxury she really enjoyed than to fritter it away without even remembering where it had gone. So Annabel religiously saved half of her pocket money but didn't tell Jenny. Jenny would consider that too *infra dig* – her favourite expression at the moment – for words. Annabel wanted to be with the 'in' crowd, so she kept quiet, nor did she say that she thought smoking and trying drugs really rather stupid and a waste of time.

'Jenny! Annabel! Have you both finished your home-work?' It was Jenny's mother calling them.

'Damn!' said Jenny, then shouted. 'Just coming.'

Annabel was glad of the interruption. It meant they couldn't talk about trying drugs, and that avoided an argument with Jenny.

Much to Felicity's surprise, Tony took to loading the dishwasher each morning after breakfast. She watched him, hair flopping over into his eyes, glasses sliding down his nose, while he loaded the plates carefully. Unlike Felicity, who just slung everything in, Tony believed in utilizing every square inch of space. 'Why don't you leave a great heap on the table like you used to?' she asked. 'I find this new improved version of you slightly unnerving.'

Tony gave an embarrassed laugh, at least it sounded suspiciously like that to Felicity, and pushed his glasses back up his nose. 'Well, to be truthful,' he said, 'I want us to keep our treasure.'

'Treasure?'

'He means Tracy,' said Annabel through a mouthful of toast.

'Right. I don't want her coming into a house that's too untidy. It might put her off.'

Felicity had difficulty in following this particular piece of logic and said, 'What about me? You didn't worry about putting me off by leaving a mess.'

Tony gave her one of his devastating smiles then switched to a serious expression. 'But, darling,' he said, '*I married* you.'

Suddenly Felicity wanted to laugh. So this was what marriage amounted to. She said, 'So that about sums it up does it? I'm worth less than five pounds an hour.'

'And now you know,' said Annabel, grabbing the hessian shopping bag which held her school books and stuffing an apple into her anorak pocket. 'Wives are worth less than cleaning ladies.' She made her exit.

Tony came over and put his arms around Felicity. 'You know that isn't true.'

'All I *do* know is that you're cleaning up for Tracy and calling her a treasure. And this is someone you said we couldn't possibly have doing the housework because she was a punk, and what would the other partners say.'

'That was before I found out how good she was, and what a difference it would make to my life.'

'*My* life,' corrected Felicity.

'No, mine,' said Tony. 'I was beginning to worry that you'd never be enthusiastic in bed again.'

Felicity grinned, and, relaxing, leaned against his comforting, solid bulk. 'So was I,' she admitted. 'I was so tired all the time. Always chasing my tail trying to be the perfect housewife, editor and mother, and failing miserably at all three.'

She thought of Samantha again. Was that how she had felt? Trying to be all things to all men? Perhaps if she'd had a Tracy she would never have run off with Piers. These disturbing thoughts were kept to herself, however. Samantha's loss of Tony was her gain, and she had no intention of allowing *that* to change.

Tony kissed the tip of her nose. 'I wonder,' he said hesitantly, 'if you would mind if I gave her a playpen for Jacob?'

Felicity raised her head and peered up at her husband. 'Of course I don't mind. But why?'

'Well,' Tony looked uncomfortable. 'My motive isn't entirely altruistic. If she has a playpen, a fold-up one, she can bring it and Jacob here whenever her friend can't babysit. Besides, Alan Appleby has given me some money for the child.'

Felicity was intrigued. 'Alan Appleby!' She thought of the rather austere senior partner. Terribly proper, rather pompous in fact. Somehow the thought of him helping punky Tracy didn't fit his image.

Tony looked solemn. 'I've no doubt that you'll hear the gossip eventually so I might as well tell you. Alan is convinced that Jacob is his grandson by his son Sam, although Tracy won't say one way or the other. Anyway, the point is that Alan wants to help a bit with his upbringing but has to do it in secret.'

'Why?' She thought of Tracy in her clean but threadbare clothes, thin as a rake and counting every penny so that Jacob could be a lusciously plump, indulged baby. 'She could certainly do with the extra money. Surely she wouldn't object.'

Tony raised his eyebrows and wrinkled his nose, something he always did when he was thinking. 'That's debatable,' he said. 'There's more to her than meets the eye and she can be prickly. She was on course for a good place at university until she got pregnant.'

'She could have had a termination.' Felicity tried to slot herself into the place of a pregnant teenager. Would she have had a termination?

Tony second-guessed her thoughts. 'Would you?' he asked.

'I honestly don't know.'

'There you are, then,' said Tony. 'Anyway, she made the decision to keep the baby, and that took guts, especially as her family threw her out. Sam Appleby disappeared from the scene, which is about par for the course, and Alan can't offer anything to Tracy openly without causing a terrible family row. Apparently Alice won't admit that Sam might be the father because she's such a terrible snob. Tracy comes from the Warblington council estate. The wrong side of the tracks.' He shook his head. 'So there you have it. Tracy's out in the cold, shunned by both families.'

'Poor girl.' Felicity had always sensed Tracy's bizarre appearance had more to do with a defence mechanism than hippy-type ideology. Now she was certain. 'Alan should tell his wife to take a running jump,' she said crossly. 'It's ridiculous everyone keeping quiet for fear of a row.'

Tony grinned slowly. 'Alan is not a brave man.'

Felicity slipped her hand into Tony's and rubbed her thumb in the dry palm of his hand. 'What a mess some people's lives are,' she said. 'Thank heavens ours is under control.'

Tony was more circumspect. 'Don't tempt fate, darling.' he said. 'You never know what's around the corner.'

'Don't be such a pessimist.' Felicity felt relaxed. Since Tracy had arrived and taken some of the physical burden from her she felt she could cope. Why, she had even coped well and on her own – only on the surface; you didn't enjoy it, her subconscious reminded her – with the visit of Tony's children, her mother and Venetia. Being a second wife wasn't so difficult, it was merely a question of laying down the ground rules and getting on with it. Even the thought of Tony's children living at Cherry Trees for half of the summer holidays wasn't bothering her now. It was only *half* the holidays. A mere three and a *half* weeks. She could handle that. 'Nothing can go wrong for us now,' she said.

CHAPTER 11

'It's Samantha Hughes, for you.' Irene waved the phone. Felicity reached for the receiver and felt slightly apprehensive. What did Samantha want this time? Surely not for her to take the children now! No, that was ridiculous. It was the middle of the week. The boys would be away at boarding school and Hilary should be attending her day school in St John's Wood. 'I have bad vibes,' hissed her mother, shaking her head in a dramatic fashion.

So have I, thought Felicity, but, not wanting to admit it, said, 'The trouble with you, Mother, is that you have an over-active imagination.' She paused a moment, took a deep breath, worried – what *did* Samantha want? – then said, 'Yes, Samantha, what can I do for you?' She used the suitably businesslike tone she'd unconsciously cultivated for speaking to her husband's ex-wife.

In the split-second of silence that followed before Samantha's reply Felicity studied her reflection in her mother's hall mirror and thought enviously of Samantha's svelte slenderness. The small amount of weight she'd lost whilst coping on her own at Cherry Trees had been put back on since she'd resumed working in London. Sitting on one's behind all day reading and nibbling biscuits was not the best figure-forming exercise. The only consolation was that Tony kept telling her that he appreciated her curves.

'I wonder if we could meet for lunch.' Samantha's slightly breathy, girlish voice wafted in her ear. 'How about today? I need to talk to you fairly urgently, and I can't do it over the phone.'

Felicity felt her warning antennae rising and waving briskly. Samantha was a threat. A threat to herself, to her newly reorganized life, and to her marriage. It was a presentiment that had always been there, lurking in the background, but not one to which she'd ever dared give voice for fear that Tony would laugh at her or, worse, think she was jealous and hysterical. In other words, as her mother would have said only too quickly if she'd known what Felicity was thinking, a typical second wife!

'Why?' she asked cautiously. 'Is there a problem with the children?'

At her end of the line Samantha had a momentary twinge of conscience. Was offloading her children a problem? No, she decided, it was not. After all, it was only a *temporary* measure. No one could possibly object to that. But telling Felicity face to face was better, more honest. And Samantha was determined to be honest. In that respect she differed from Piers. He didn't care. Just get rid of them, he'd said, referring to the children.

193

But Samantha couldn't do that; somehow she had to make Felicity understand why.

'No, there's no problem,' she said. 'But I do need to talk to *you*, not Tony.'

And as Felicity also preferred that any talking to be done by Samantha should be to her rather than Tony, that was how she came to be sitting, on a day in June, outside an Italian restaurant under an umbrella with Samantha. The restaurant just off Cambridge Circus, Samantha's choice, was, Felicity thought, considering the location, hideously expensive. They sat in silence, both twiddling the stems of their glasses – Felicity's white wine, Samantha's mineral water – while waiting for their order to appear. It was hot and Felicity could feel the silk of her blouse beginning to stick to her. Soon she'd have dark creases all around her middle, and she began to wish they'd sat inside. Outside had been her choice, and now she was dripping while Samantha looked as cool as the proverbial cucumber. Felicity began to feel irritable as well as hot. When would Samantha say whatever it was she wanted to say? Should she ask outright? Or begin with preliminary small talk? After another sip of wine she opted for the small talk.

'Ridiculous, isn't it?' she said. 'The moment the sun puts in an appearance we British feel that we have to commune with nature and sit outside. Now I'm beginning to feel rather warm.'

'Yes,' said Samantha. The corners of her mouth moved slightly in what Felicity suspected might be a smile, but she couldn't be sure.

The waiter arrived, and with an exaggerated flourish placed two half-moon plates of mixed green salad on their table. Toying with a sprout of rocket leaves, Felicity waited for Samantha to spit it out, as her mother would have said, and watched a man walking past. He was obviously sun-worshipping too, as he was dressed in a T-shirt, long shorts indelicately tight at the crotch, and a pair of sandals. Was he a city gent gone mad with the sun, a tourist up for a day from the provinces or from another country? No, not from another country. Only an Englishman could possibly dress so badly. It was something about the sun that did it, went to their heads, she supposed. She tried to imagine Tony wearing such apparel, but couldn't. At least that was something to be thankful for. By now impatient and bored, she looked back expectantly at Samantha.

The waiter reappeared and put baked cannelloni oozing with cheese and oil in front of Felicity and a small piece of white fish decorated with a few olives in front of Samantha. Still there was silence.

'I can see why you're slim and I am not,' said Felicity, looking at the cannelloni and then at the fish, which didn't appear terribly appetizing to her. 'Are you dieting?'

'No,' said Samantha.

Another silence, and they both watched a mother trying to navigate a double buggy along a broken piece of pavement.

'Poor thing, I wouldn't want to change places with her,' remarked Felicity.

'At least my children are out of nappies,' said Samantha firmly, adding in a breathless-sounding rush, 'It's always sunny like this in California.'

'So I believe.' Felicity was mystified. What on earth had California to do with an overcrowded, hot London street?

'They eat outside like this all the time.'

A van went past belching noxious fumes, and in Cambridge Circus an ambulance siren sounded hysterical as it tried to force a passage through the traffic. Felicity flapped her napkin at the fumes, wiped away some strands of hair which had started off that morning as feathery fronds but which were now plastered to her forehead, and began to feel slightly hysterical herself and in need of a personal respirator. She looked at Samantha, still irritatingly cool and composed, not a bead of perspiration in sight, and still fiddling with her fish but not actually having taken a mouthful yet.

Felicity lost patience. 'Have I come all this way to meet you so that we can talk about the weather in California, or the fact that your children are now out of nappies?' she demanded.

Samantha stopped looking cool and started to look slightly agitated. 'Oh, dear,' she sighed, 'Piers said telling you this wouldn't be easy.'

'Telling me what wouldn't be easy?' demanded Felicity, now feeling distinctly apprehensive. This luncheon was beginning to have an element of Kafka about it, she thought.

'That the children will have to come and live with

you and Tony for a year because Piers and I are moving to California.'

'The children! *Your children*, with me? For a whole year!' The last words she'd said to Tony before she'd left that morning echoed in Felicity's ears. *Nothing can go wrong for us now.*

'You are annoyed.' Samantha sighed, managing to imply that she thought Felicity's reaction totally unreasonable.

Felicity tried to be objective, cool, calm, and above all *reasonable*. She weighed up the pros and cons. Tony would be overjoyed, no doubt about that. Whereas she, herself, was . . . well, what? Overjoyed, certainly not. Flabbergasted and horror-struck would be a more accurate description. She felt a shaft of compassion for the children. How would they feel about losing their mother to America? A year was a long time to young people. Would they settle down with their father and his new wife?

'I didn't say that I was annoyed,' she said carefully.

Samantha shook her head sadly, which *did* annoy Felicity. Illogical though it was, Samantha was making her feel guilty because she hadn't whooped with joy at the prospect of resident stepchildren for a year.

'You didn't have to,' said Samantha. 'No woman in her right senses would want to take on someone else's children. Even if it is only for twelve months. That's what Piers said.'

Felicity was amazed. 'Did he? And yet you still want me to take on yours?'

'Oh, yes, please,' said Samantha earnestly. Then she

heaved a sigh, and delicately picked up a forkful of fish and ate it.

'But how can you do it? How can you just up and leave them?' Felicity looked at Samantha, trying to glean a clue from the elegant woman before her. The woman who had fought for and obtained custody of her children, and who was now proposing to leave them behind for a year. Felicity thought of her turbulent relationship with her own daughter and knew that nothing, no matter how many rows, or how difficult things became, nothing could prise her daughter from her side. Not even Tony. When it came to the bottom line Felicity knew that if the choice had been between Tony and Annabel, the choice would have been her daughter.

Samantha's expression was still earnest, as if she had to convince Felicity of her sincerity. 'I suppose it's because I am what Venetia says I am,' she said slowly, and Felicity thought her voice sounded almost tearful.

'And what is that?' Felicity wondered what new revelations were coming.

'Maternally challenged,' said Samantha.

'Oh, that! Well, aren't we all at some time or another?' It was absurd, she knew, but for some reason Felicity found herself wanting to reassure Samantha. 'But that's no cause for deserting one's children.'

Samantha leaned across the table and looked Felicity straight in the eye. 'It is reason enough for me,' she said, suddenly fierce. 'I need this chance for a new life, for a chance to be really me. It's all right for you. You're different. You can rise to the challenge of fitting in with the children. I can't. I'm a hopeless mother.'

'You were the perfect mother. It's the one thing everyone keeps ramming down my throat,' said Felicity bitterly, adding for good measure, 'including Tony.'

Samantha gave a twisted, slightly wan smile. 'I fooled them all,' she said, 'except Venetia. I did all the right things, but only because it was the *right* thing to do. And all the time I didn't even really *like* my children.' She paused, then said slowly, 'Can you try to understand me? Although I don't like them, I *do* love them, and I do feel responsible, but I know that they would be much better off with you and Tony. This year would mean a lot to them.'

'You mean they'd be better off because you'd be free to do as you please.' Felicity stared back at her through narrowed eyes, damned if she was going to provide an easy sop for Samantha's conscience.

'In a way that's true.' Samantha lowered her eyes and had the grace to look uncomfortable.

'What will you do if I put my foot down and say I don't want them at Cherry Trees for more than the originally agreed time?'

'Piers and I have agreed that they could be fostered during the holidays, and Hilary would have to go to boarding school during term-time.'

Felicity's previous charitable feelings began to dissipate rapidly, and Samantha visibly winced at her outraged expression. 'I know what you're thinking,' she said quickly. 'That I'm a hard bitch. And in a way you're right. But I've burnt my boats behind me now, I've got to go with Piers. I can't go back to Tony.'

On that point they agreed. 'No, you certainly can't,' said Felicity. 'That is most definitely out of the question.'

'Then you'll agree?'

Felicity drained her wine glass and waved to the waiter to bring her another. There really was no way she could see to escape, although she wasn't going to let Samantha know that yet. 'I'll have to talk to Tony,' she said. 'And if they come they will have to behave themselves.'

'They will,' said Samantha fervently. 'I know they will.'

Felicity had her doubts. One weekend under their maternal great-grandmother's eye was one thing. But if past performances were anything to go by they would need to have undergone a radical change of character if they were going to keep that up. Of course Tony would say yes, and she couldn't blame him. But her heart sank at the thought of Cherry Trees overflowing with adolescents for a whole year. It was all right for Samantha to say she could rise to the challenge. For her own part Felicity was not at all certain that she had that ability.

When Samantha got home Piers was in their office working on the computer on a layout for an article on National Trust houses, juggling photographs and columns of print about. 'What did she say?' he asked, not looking up.

Samantha knew he was not really interested, merely anxious to get things sorted out. 'She asked me how I could bear to leave my children for so long.'

200

Piers laughed, touched the keyboard, and juggled a bit more, his eyes still glued to the screen. 'And what did you say?'

Samantha flushed at the memory. Felicity might have thought her composed, but the memory was painful. Admitting her failure as a mother and a woman had been painful, and yet at the same time strangely cathartic. 'I told the truth. I told her that although I love my children, I don't really like them. Therefore it isn't so difficult for me to leave them behind.'

Piers looked up and tutted irritably. 'Did you have to say that? It projects such a negative image.'

Samantha couldn't see how the truth was negative, but didn't argue. 'She agreed to have them,' she said. 'That's the main thing.' This, of course, was not strictly true, she knew, but it was nearly true. She was certain in her own mind that Felicity and Tony *would* have them.

Piers returned to his screen. 'When is the handover?'

'We didn't fix an exact date.'

Piers tutted even more irritably. He liked things 'firmed up' as he always said, at the earliest possible moment. Leaving things was not in his nature. 'No matter,' he said firmly. 'The children will still need to be told as soon as possible. Shall you tell them, or shall I?'

Samantha turned towards Piers and smiled. Smothering a sudden surge of guilt which was threatening to overwhelm her, she said, 'You tell them.'

The departure of Piers and Samantha coincided very neatly with the beginning of the summer holidays for

201

the children. Felicity worked it out and felt a savage anger; it was so that Samantha didn't have to be with them one more day than was absolutely necessary. She was sure of that, although Tony had said it was coincidence. But Tony hadn't seen Samantha's face when she'd admitted that she didn't like her own children, and her confidence was not something that Felicity had betrayed. Tony had picked them up and Hilary, Philip and Peter arrived back at Cherry Trees immediately after seeing their mother off to the States. They were in a sullen, unhappy mood and in spite of not wanting them Felicity found herself feeling sorry for them. They *looked* unwanted, and that, she guessed, was the way they were feeling. They hung back in the drive, as if unwilling to come into the house, and Tony strode on ahead of them.

'God! It was awful at Heathrow,' he whispered, *sotto voce* to Felicity. 'Piers is such a snotty-nosed bastard. He looked at me as if I'd just crawled out from beneath the nearest litter bin.'

Turning her attention to her husband, Felicity had more than an inkling of why Piers had looked at Tony in that particular way. Poor Tony, he'd gone straight from a busy night duty on to Heathrow so that he could be with the children when they saw their mother off. As a result his shirt and trousers were creased, his hair looked uncombed, and Felicity guessed it probably was, and there was half an inch of gingery gold stubble on his chin. On other men this might have looked like designer stubble, but on Tony it merely managed to make him look thoroughly disreputable.

She reached out and briefly touched his arm in a gesture of sympathy, then asked, 'How are they?' She looked out through the door to where they stood in the drive in a little huddle, their most treasured belongings in shabby haversacks on the gravel. They were all, she noted, still unhealthily plump, didn't look terribly clean and were distinctly dishevelled. They looked like the outcasts they were; having no part to play in their mother's new arrangement of her life. And no one, thought Felicity, would ever guess that the glamorous Samantha was their mother.

Tony looked at them as well. 'They're all right, considering. Piers quite obviously couldn't wait to go through into the departure lounge and get rid of them, and Samantha wasn't much better. Although she did manage a few crocodile tears for effect.'

'I'm sure they were real tears,' said Felicity, and found herself hoping that they were. Although whether it was for the children's sake or for Samantha's she couldn't have said. 'After all, they *are* her children, and she *is* going to live in another country. From now on they will be thousands of miles apart.'

'Why are you sticking up for her?' Tony sounded put out. He was tired and in a desperately anti-Samantha mood.

Felicity, on the other hand, was trying her level best to be fair and non judgemental. 'Because she's the children's mother and they must love her, and she them in her way. And remember, she was once your wife and you must have loved her too.'

Tony sighed gustily and Felicity knew he didn't like

203

to be reminded of things he'd prefer to forget. The children started, en masse, towards the front door. 'I just hope this is all going to work out,' he said gloomily.

Felicity stared at him. Why was he gloomy all of a sudden? He'd been looking forward to them coming; she'd been the one who'd been gloomy. Now it seemed the roles were reversed, and she was the one being positive.

'Why shouldn't it work out?' she demanded. 'We're all perfectly normal and civilized. We should be able to function as a family unit.'

But Tony, determined it seemed to look on the black side, merely whispered back, 'There's nothing normal or civilized about the average family unit.'

If the children had been farther away Felicity would have berated him for being defeatist, pessimistic and a complete wet blanket, all the things she had been these last few days. Then she wondered if all these emotions had rubbed off from her on to him. But before she could ask, the children burst, quite literally, in through the front door.

Philip and Peter, attempting to get through at the same time while wearing their haversacks, got themselves jammed. Felicity darted forward, about to say that it would be a good idea if she took one of their bags, when they popped, like two peas from a pod, and exploded into the hall.

'We're going straight up to our room,' announced Philip in a bossy tone of voice which Felicity noted bore an uncannily worrying resemblance to Tony's voice when he was ordering the gardener around. 'I don't suppose it's how we left it, so we shall have quite a lot to do.' He stomped past Felicity looking neither right nor left and Peter started to follow.

Felicity's sympathy withered and died a premature death. 'Your room is exactly as the two of you left it. Nothing has been touched.'

But there was no winning with Philip. 'In that case it'll be filthy. We'll have to spend hours vacuuming and dusting. Come on, Peter.'

Felicity sprang into action. With one bound she leaped three stairs and planted herself in front of a very surprised Philip.

'Darling, you must have a latent kangaroo gene in you somewhere,' said Tony with a laugh which very quickly petered out beneath the combined glowers of Philip, Peter, Hilary and Felicity.

If he was attempting affability he had failed miserably and Felicity was too angry to make any attempt to help him. 'Look here, you lot,' she said, addressing all three children. 'I know you are unhappy, and I'm sorry. But it's not my fault. I'm doing my best, and the least you can do is try to make life for all of us as easy as possible.'

'Why?' Annabel's voice echoed from the top of the landing. She was leaning over the banister rail, as if stationed on guard, staring fiercely down at the assembled company in the hall.

'Because then we can be one big happy family,' said Felicity, echoing what she knew to be Tony's hopes. However, on reflection, it seemed rather an innovative description for what looked like the beginning of full-scale war.

'And pigs might fly!' A scornful Annabel left her on guard position and flung herself back into her own bedroom, slamming the door loudly behind her.

Felicity opened and then closed her mouth. No need to fight with Annabel as well. Not for the moment anyway. 'Go upstairs,' she said firmly. 'You will find your rooms clean and just as you left them. Unpack your things, and when you're ready, come down to the kitchen and have a drink and a piece of cake, then you can go off and do your own thing until dinner time. We eat at seven o'clock this evening in the kitchen.'

'We eat in the kitchen!' Hilary managed to sound horrified, frightfully ladylike and disgusted all at the same time. No mean feat.

'Yes,' said Felicity firmly. 'We eat in the kitchen. The dining room has been turned into my temporary office. I work in there when I'm not in London.'

'I *knew* things wouldn't be the same,' said Philip.

'We are used to dining *properly*,' Hilary announced archly.

Later, when they'd all disappeared into their bedrooms and peace once more reigned, albeit, Felicity thought glumly, temporarily, she asked Tony, 'What's the big deal about eating in the kitchen? Surely you didn't have formal dinner in the dining room every night when Samantha was here?'

'Samantha was quite fussy about that sort of thing,' Tony replied. 'She said the children had to be brought up properly. We used the silver cutlery and had candles most evenings.'

To Felicity's fury he looked slightly smug at the

206

memory. 'No wonder she couldn't wait to get away,' she said acidly.

Tony looked hurt and surprised, which made Felicity long to shake him even more.

'I don't think that had anything to do with her departure,' he said stiffly. 'And I don't mind eating in the kitchen. Not now that I've got used to it,' he added.

'Just as well,' Felicity answered tartly. 'Because if anyone thinks that I'm trudging backwards and forwards with serving dishes and the like they've got another think coming.' She paused and plunged the verbal knife in. 'Poor Samantha. She must have been run off her feet.'

But Tony had a knife of his own. 'Samantha was very efficient. She always got it all ready in the afternoon so that she wasn't rushed in the evening.'

Before she knew it, and without intending to, Felicity heard herself plunging headfirst into a major row. Something she'd been determined that the arrival of the children would *not* precipitate between herself and Tony.

She heard her voice, strident and unpleasant. 'Bully for Samantha! Are you trying to tell me she was perfect, and I'm not?'

Tony, to give him credit, did not shout back. 'Of course not,' he said.

'Good! Because before you tell me about all the other wonderful things she did, let me remind you that she's the one who threw in the towel on this life of rural bliss. And she's the one who has now jetted off to America for a year leaving her children behind. The children I have got to have even though they are *not* mine. Whatever else I might have done, or not done, or do in the future, of one thing you can be certain.' Felicity paused, took a deep breath then said dramatically, 'I shall never desert my child.'

'Well done! That's told *him*!' It was Annabel, leaning over the banisters again.

For the first time Tony began to show signs of temper as well. 'Go back into your room,' he shouted up the stairs, 'and don't butt into other people's conversations.'

'Mum can do with my support. It's me and her against you lot.'

Felicity groaned and shook her head. The last thing she had intended was to alienate Annabel and Tony. 'Don't be silly,' she heard Tony saying very firmly. 'Nobody is against anybody. Your mother and I can have a little argument without it being a war.'

'Tony's right, darling,' said Felicity, feeling suddenly weary. 'Go back into your room. Everything will be all right.'

'Humph!' Annabel's slammed door told them both what she thought.

Going back into the kitchen, Felicity opened the fridge and, taking out an opened bottle of white wine, poured herself a large glass. Out of the corner of her eye she could see Tony's disapproving expression. 'I know it's only the afternoon, but I need this.'

Tony put a gentle arm around her shoulders. 'Why are we fighting?'

For a moment Felicity was tempted to tell him that it was because he'd brought three bolshie kids to Cherry Trees and was a tactless idiot himself. But looking at him and seeing his steady gaze filled with deep affection, she knew she was being unfair. It was not his fault, even if he could perhaps improve on his communication skills where tact was concerned, and it was certainly not the children's fault. They couldn't help being dumped. And they'd been kicked around quite enough without being kicked around by her as well.

She took a gulp of wine, and managed a hesitant grin. 'And why are we fighting about Samantha of all people?'

Tony took a glass from the dresser and poured some wine for himself. 'Let's sit here a moment.' He pulled her over to the window seat and they both collapsed on to it. Leaning his head back against the windowsill, he tightened his arm around Felicity, took a sip of wine, then closed his eyes. 'I am totally exhausted,' he muttered.

Felicity felt guilty. 'Sorry I shouted. I'd forgotten that you'd been up half the night with demanding patients.' She looked at his face; strained lines of tiredness were evident around his mouth and eyes. Lines she should have noticed before, but hadn't. 'And then you come home to an even more demanding family,' she said softly.

'It's all right,' Tony said, hugging her, then he suddenly grinned. 'It was almost worth the ruckus to see you leap up the stairs like that. Gave poor old Philip quite a fright.'

Felicity giggled at the memory. 'Gave me a fright too. If I'd stopped to think about it I would never have dared attempt it.'

'No chance of a repeat performance, then?'

'Not in the immediate future.' Felicity sipped her wine, letting the cool liquid trickle down her throat while she thought back over the events of the previous half-hour. 'Are we really an average family?'

'Absolutely,' said Tony. 'We fit the modern profile. Second marriage. Stepchildren, behavioural difficulties etc. That's us.'

Felicity thought about it. 'All a bit depressing,' she concluded.

Tony sat up and looked at her. 'We mustn't let the children make us fight,' he said. 'Promise me we won't.'

'Promise,' echoed Felicity, thinking that it was a promise likely to be broken, but that she would try. 'We've both got to be careful. All the children are edgy and prickly, and it's not surprising. Apart from laying down the ground rules on a few basic things, I suggest we leave them alone for a couple of weeks and let them settle down. I for one shall count to ten before I answer anyone who annoys me.'

'Including me?' asked Tony, smiling his lopsided smile. Felicity kissed him in answer and Tony kissed her back enthusiastically. Linking his arms around her neck, he rested his forehead against hers. 'Oh,' he groaned. 'We could go to bed if only I weren't so tired.'

Felicity made a face. 'What! With a house full of children. No, thanks.'

'But we *are* married.'

'And this *is* the afternoon.'

Tony drew his head back and looked at her quizzically. 'Since when does that matter?'

'Children can be incredibly prudish,' said Felicity, thinking of Annabel's squeamish view of sex. 'No, darling, you go to bed and sleep. That's what you need. Sleep.'

Once Tony had been packed off upstairs, alone, Felicity got out the large fruitcake Tracy had thoughtfully made for her, brewed a pot of tea and called the children.

Annabel stayed in her room, but the others came down and drank tea and ate the fruitcake in silence, which irritated Felicity tremendously. But, remembering her vow of counting to ten, she said nothing and busied herself about the kitchen, stifling the urge to go into the dining room and finish the manuscript she was halfway through. It was good, and with the right marketing she thought it was a potential best-seller. To get one of her authors into the best-seller list was her ambition.

'Did you make this cake?' Hilary cut herself another slice.

Still thinking about that elusive best-seller, Felicity said, 'Yes,' without thinking. The moment the word was out she knew pride wouldn't allow her to backtrack and tell them Tracy had made it.

'It's very nice,' said Peter quietly.

Felicity glanced at him. What a solemn face he had, and what soulful brown eyes, The same as Tony's. A sad face really. It struck Felicity yet again that life had been unkind to these children. Initially wrangled over by both their parents, then dragged off to London with a mother who didn't really want them and who dumped them when convenient.

'Our mother,' said Philip loudly, 'is a *superb* cook.'

And Philip, Felicity reflected, certainly had an uncanny knack for putting a spoke in the wheel just as she was beginning to feel more kindly towards the three of them. His eyes were not soulful. They were blue, a bright blue, glinting with undisguised hostility.

'*She* had a cordon bleu certificate. Have you?' Felicity noted that Hilary, for all her youth and plumpness, had managed to cultivate a voice which sounded like Lady Thatcher at her most strident.

'I've never had a cookery lesson in my life,' Felicity heard herself saying, a defensive edge to her voice.

'Not even at school?' Philip sounded scornful.

'No. I did Latin instead. And you might as well know it, Tracy made that cake. Not me.'

'Ha!' Hilary lost interest and left the table. 'I'm going to take Cotton-Socks out along the bridle path for some exercise. I don't suppose he's had much recently.'

'None,' said Felicity. 'Neither Annabel nor I rides.'

Hilary left the kitchen muttering, 'Can't cook, can't ride. Huh!'

'And we're going into the old stable to get out our bikes,' said Philip.

'Where will you be going?' Felicity had a nightmare fear of children, bicycles and roads. She'd knocked a child from her bicycle once in London and had never really got over it, even though the child concerned had merely suffered bruising and scratches.

'These are motorbikes. Not ordinary bikes. And we shan't be riding them on the road.' Philip's voice was scornful.

Peter took pity on Felicity, who was looking confused. 'We repair old motorbikes and scooters and sell them for money,' he explained. 'We were in the middle of restoring one when we left.' He smiled hesitantly and started to follow Philip, then came back and said earnestly, 'You didn't have to tell us about the cake.'

Felicity pulled a rueful face. 'I know. But my conscience got the better of me and I thought I'd better be honest.'

Her reward was a big smile. She watched him leave thinking that Peter would be easy to like. Perhaps even to love a little, given time.

Annabel came into the kitchen just after the others had left and cut herself an enormous piece of the fruitcake.

Felicity had an idea. 'Is it still you and me against them?' she asked, smiling.

'You bet.' Annabel's reply was muffled by a mouthful of fruitcake and she looked suspicious.

'Well, then. How about you and me preparing a scrumptious dinner for this evening? Let's surprise them all and make them sit up and think that life back at Cherry Trees isn't going to be so bad after all.'

'I'm not sure *that's* a good idea,' said Annabel. 'I don't want them to stay.'

Felicity made her hands into fists, and, putting them

on the kitchen table, leaned on them and bent her body forward towards her daughter. 'Annabel,' she said gently. 'They have nowhere else to go.'

There was a long silence. Then Annabel said, 'OK.'

CHAPTER 12

One week edged into another, and once the summer holidays were well and truly under way Felicity found she was shattered. She began to look forward eagerly, although didn't mention it to Tony, to her two days in London. They were an oasis of peace and calm where she recharged her batteries in order to face life in the country with the family for another five days.

Her mother had taken to joking that other people escaped to the country but Felicity did it in reverse, escaping to London.

If there is any justice in this world my nerves ought to be visible, Felicity thought one morning when she was feeling particularly jaded and cross. They should be hanging down around me like the fringes on a 1920s flapper's dress. A kitten clawed out at her ankle as she walked past the kitchen table, and Felicity bent down and picked it up. 'Just as well my nerves *aren't* hanging in shreds,' she told it severely. 'If they were, you and your brothers and sisters would be swarming all over me.' She put the kitten down and it dived back under the table to join the others. They were all still at the

215

mountaineering stage, and were spending many happy hours ripping Samantha's flowery-patterned ruched curtains to pieces.

'I never liked them anyway,' Felicity said when Tony complained. Besides the children, the fancy curtains were yet another reminder of Samantha. If they could have afforded it she would have ripped out all reminders of Samantha, all reminders that there'd been another wife before she arrived, but they couldn't, so the house stayed the same. As far as Felicity was concerned the kittens were doing a good job.

Tony's nerves were not frayed, and neither, to give him his due, did Felicity think that it ever crossed his mind that she might be jealous of Samantha's lingering presence. As far as he was concerned, Samantha had gone and that was that. Besides, he was in his element now that the house was full to overflowing. 'This is what I've always wanted,' he told Felicity. 'One great big very happy family.'

Felicity sighed. Sometimes it seemed to her that she and Tony inhabited totally different planets. 'Great and big, I'll grant you,' she said. 'But happy. No!'

Tony swept aside her gloomy tone, being indefatigably brimming with good cheer and bonhomie himself. 'Come on,' he said. 'Cheer up. I never see any squabbles.' He picked up his bag ready to make his getaway to the surgery before the rest of the family surfaced for the mêlée called breakfast. 'Bye, darling,' he kissed Felicity.

Felicity kissed him back. At least they had their breakfast alone together. She supposed she ought to be thankful for small mercies. But she had to put him right over the squabbles. 'You're never here when they fight,' she said.

'None of it means anything. Don't worry about it.' Tony gently pinched the tip of her nose, and kissed her again. 'It's *normal*,' he said.

'Maybe. But I *do* worry. And it *does* mean something. To me, anyway. You rarely see anything important because you're always out dispensing tender loving care to your patients instead of dishing it out here where it's needed most.' She was being unreasonable, she knew. But weariness made for unreasonableness, and Felicity was feeling at the end of her tether.

'Attending to patients is my duty and, what's more, my bread and butter,' Tony said seriously. 'It pays the rent.'

'I know.' Felicity felt doubly guilty knowing she was bad-tempered and a nag.

'Sorry, darling, but I've got to go.' He snatched another brief kiss. 'Bye, darling, bye, Tracy.'

Tracy didn'. answer. She had just arrived that morning, Jacob in tow, and in a very black temper herself if her expression was anything to go by. That's all I need. Felicity felt even more cross. She really couldn't face a morning of treading on eggshells with Tracy because she was in a bad mood as well as having to negotiate the intractable dilemmas posed by burdensome children!

Tracy started clearing away and relaying the breakfast table ready for the next influx. 'If you ask me,' she growled sourly, 'the only really happy families are those printed on a set of playing cards.'

'Got it in one,' agreed Felicity.

The sound of tyres crunching on the gravel drive disturbed them both. Tracy pushed aside a thick mass of trailing honeysuckle which had run riot along one side of the window and looked out. 'Oh, no! It's nosy parker old Ma Appleby.' She plucked Jacob out of his playpen. 'You'll have to finish the kitchen table. I'm off.'

It was not something they ever talked about but Felicity had often wondered what the truth really was. Was Jacob in reality a little Appleby? Was that why she didn't want to see Alice now? She looked at Tracy curiously, but apart from the black expression there were no answers one way or the other to be gained there.

'Why the rush?'

'Ask me no questions and I'll tell you no lies,' came back Tracy's tart answer. With Jacob balanced on one hip she swiftly gathered up together a set of dusters and polish. 'I'll start on the upstairs today. It'll do that lazy lot good to be kicked out of their beds.' She reached the kitchen door just as Alice Appleby sailed in, unannounced, as usual.

'Hello, Felicity. Ah!' She zoomed in on Jacob. 'Hello, Tracy. What a dear little fellow. So intelligent-looking. Can I hold him?'

'No,' said Tracy, and left, slamming the door from the kitchen into the hall.

* * *

218

Tony had a half-day that day, and after lunch settled down to watch cricket on TV. Felicity was feeling slightly more cheerful, having got through that morning without any major confrontations with the children. A rare event.

'I think you're right. There's definitely something between the Applebys and Tracy Milligan.' She related the story of Alice's visit.

'Yes, the something is Jacob.' Tony turned up the volume. 'What did Alice come here for, anyway?'

'Quiche,' shouted Felicity over the sound of the commentator's voice intoning *there it goes round the leg stump, it's a run, no, it isn't, it's a bye*. 'I've agreed to make two for the church fête, or rather Tracy has. Although I didn't think it politic to tell her she was doing Alice Appleby a favour. By the way, Sam Appleby has come back to the village. Do you think he's the one Tracy was involved with?'

'Yes,' said Tony, and Felicity knew from his tone of voice that he was not paying her the slightest bit of attention. His next words proved it. 'This new Hampshire bowler is absolute dynamite. Look at that.'

Felicity looked. All she could see was a man running a short distance and then throwing the ball, after which there was a bit of confusion and all the surrounding men leaped up and shouted something incomprehensible before going back and starting the same thing all over again. It looked very boring, but Tony was riveted. Outside, Philip and Peter were roaring around the gravel drive as usual. Although today they were

219

going extra-fast and riding a much longer distance. The whole way down the drive and into the far end of the paddock and out again in a figure of eight. It looked and sounded hair-raising.

Felicity forgot Tracy and the Applebys and worried out loud. 'Is it legal, boys of fourteen riding motor-bikes?' Tony, his attention still glued to the television, gave an absent-minded grunt. 'Tony! Will you listen to me?' In exasperation, Felicity seized the remote control, turned off the TV and repeated the question.

Tony gave what closely resembled a howl of rage. 'Felicity, how could you? Smithson was just about to bowl again.'

'And I am talking about the safety of your sons. Is it legal for them to ride those bikes like that?'

Tony grabbed the remote control and put the cricket back on. 'Not on the road,' he said, 'but it's OK here. What does that umpire think he's doing? That was never a no ball.'

Desperate to get his attention, Felicity edged in front of the TV a little. 'There's an article in today's paper,' she said conversationally, 'about a new marriage contract in America, which, amongst other things, stipulates that there should be at least half an hour's meaningful conversation a day between spouses.'

'Hmm,' said Tony.

On reflection, though, Felicity realized that Tony would count talk of *no balls and leg byes* as being very meaningful. So she said, 'They drive much too fast, the boys, I mean.'

Tony moved his chair slightly so that he could see

around her. 'Rubbish. Let them get it out of their systems now before they're old enough to ride on the road. Then when they *are* old enough they won't want to. That's my theory.'

'But they're not in control. Only yesterday they nearly ran me down. They roared up the drive and Philip only just managed to skid to a halt by the time he got to me.'

'Proves he knows where the brakes are,' said Tony, ducking the other side of Felicity in order to get a better view of the screen. 'I say, this batsman can really hit the ball. That's his fourth six since the match began. Hampshire had better watch out.'

'I think he did it on purpose.' She had always refrained from criticising too much before, feeling that it was important not to come between Tony and his children. But Tony's studied concentration on the television was infuriating. Like waving a red rag at a bull. Felicity charged. 'In fact,' she continued, 'I'm sure of it.'

'Mmm,' muttered Tony. 'Is there any cold beer in the fridge?'

Felicity bristled. She was tempted to stamp her feet but on reflection thought that was too childish. What did a woman have to do to get her husband's attention. 'Don't you care if your sons try to kill me?'

She had Tony's attention, but only momentarily. 'Don't be so paranoid, darling,' he said mildly. 'I know they're a little difficult at times, but they are not murderers.'

Felicity was not to be placated. Besides, she had serious doubts about the boys' motives. 'Given the chance they would be,' she said crossly. 'And they are much more than a *little* difficult. I feel that I'm in a permanent combat situation.' Why was it Tony couldn't understand how she felt? Tracy could see how difficult the children were, and with children she included Annabel, who was not behaving very much better, alternately belligerent or sulkily silent in turns. Why couldn't Tony *see?*

'That's what I mean about being paranoid, darling,' said Tony, confirming all Felicity's fears. 'Calm down, and be a love and go and get two beers. Then come and sit here with me and watch the cricket.' He patted the upholstered arm of the large armchair.

'I *hate* cricket.'

Felicity flounced out of the room and into the dining room. Ramming her reading glasses on the end of her nose, she attempted to carry on proof-reading. It was hopeless. She couldn't concentrate. As it was a warm day she had the windows wide open. Before the influx of children she had loved being able to do this; to be able to gaze out across the gravel path to the expanse of green lawn which merged into the sun streaked glades of the forest was restful. A huge beech stood right on the edge of their clearing, dipping its boughs majestically over the lawn. All day the busy housemartins skimmed its branches, swooping and diving, forever in search of food for their hungry young ones. The scene had always helped her think, but now Tony's hungry young ones roared up and down with monotonous regularity, throttles fully open, shattering the peace and making any attempt at coherent thought impossible.

I hope they break their silly necks, Felicity thought angrily. That will teach Tony to exert some authority over his children, which is what he should be doing instead of watching TV. There was a crash, then the sound of a madly revving engine. Feeling guilty now for having such wicked stepmother-type thoughts, Felicity leaped up and stuck her head out of the window in time to see a very grimy Philip extricate himself from beneath the bike and give Peter a thumbs-up sign.

'Little toads,' she said, and slammed the windows shut before trying once more to settle down to work.

The door opened and Hilary came in. 'I'm going to ride Cotton-Socks as far as the Brockenhurst water-splash and back, so I'll need a teatime snack.'

'Then get one,' said Felicity sharply. These children expected to be waited on hand and foot; another legacy of Samantha.

'You said I wasn't to take things from the fridge,' Hilary replied in a sanctimonious tone of voice.

Felicity sighed. Hilary was right, of course, and she couldn't allow her own rules to be broken as soon as she'd made them. She'd made that particular rule three days before on finding the fridge practically empty just before the evening meal. She got up. 'I'll come and get you something. Where's Annabel?'

'Gone to see Jenny. Who was one of *my* best friends. So I'm all alone.' Hilary drooped dramatically in the doorway, every surplus inch of her a tragedy queen.

Felicity felt cross with Annabel for being so unkind, but at the same time longed to point out to Hilary that she might get on better with both Annabel and Jenny if she were more pleasant and not permanently truculent. However, deciding discretion was the better part of valour, she remained silent on the issue. 'Spinach and cheese pasty,' she said, taking out one of Tracy's mouthwatering concoctions. Really, she thought, that girl ought to be running a restaurant, not cleaning houses.

'It's always spinach and something lately,' grumbled Hilary.

'A case of waste not, want not,' said Felicity briskly, determined not to get riled. 'We've got masses of spinach in the garden to use up, and it's good for you. Has lots of iron.'

'I don't *want* iron.'

Felicity thought yearningly of the rack, cat o'nine tails, and thumb screws – she was proof-reading a novel set in medieval times – pity all those things had gone out of fashion and were outlawed. She would dearly have loved to use some of them on Hilary at that particular moment.

'The trouble with you, Hilary,' she said, 'is that you never *want* anything.'

'But I *do*. I want things to be how they were. I want my mother here, not you.'

It was a cry, a wail of unhappiness, and the raw, blatant longing in Hilary's voice shocked Felicity. She'd got used to feeling her own anger at the situation, her own resentment, her own very real unhappiness that marriage to Tony had not turned out quite the way she'd thought, or wanted it to be. But now she felt a tide of guilt sweep over her, coupled with another emotion: impotence. Suddenly she desperately wished she could do something positive for the miserable lump of a girl standing before her. But there was nothing. Nothing that she could think of.

'I'm sorry, Hilary,' she said at last. 'But things will never be the way they were before. Your mother will never be here again. But you will be back with her when she returns to London. A month has gone already. Eleven months is not so long to wait.'

'But Dad and you . . . here, together . . .' Hilary floundered, then said, 'You're not *her*.'

There was no answer to that statement. Felicity stood and watched Hilary shuffle unhappily out of the kitchen. The child was near to tears, and she could only guess at the sense of disequilibrium Hilary was feeling. *O what a tangled web we weave* . . . suddenly Sir Walter Scott's words rang around in her head. They seemed very apt.

Irene Hobbit looked at Venetia and worried. As each week passed she found herself becoming more and more fond of the eccentric old lady. Although if anyone had told her the reason was because that she was a mirror image of Venetia, only twenty years younger, she would never have believed them. But she did acknowledge a kindred spirit. Another indomitable fighter, a survivor of her kind, struggling against the changes of the modern world. She knew Venetia worried about Samantha, in spite of her indifferent air, and that she worried even more about the children. At the same time Irene had her worries about Felicity coping with the enlarged family, and about Tony not seeming to take unto himself that, which by rights, she considered to be his problem. She worried too about Annabel's growing hostility to all and sundry. Why was it the young seemed so alien when one reached old age? When did one cross that line which lay between empathy and understanding and total incomprehension at the behaviour of others? These were her worries and those of Venetia as well.

Lately Venetia had looked very tired to Irene's eyes. She had also noticed that the last couple of Saturdays Venetia hadn't even bothered to wear her jaunty, brilliantly coloured headscarf, which made her stand out against all the other stallholders in Portobello. So, after an enormous amount of nagging on Irene's part, Venetia had finally visited the doctor that very morning.

'Well,' Irene demanded now, 'what did the doctor say?' She pulled out a chair for Venetia from under the stall.

Venetia sat down. 'Oh, nothing much,' she said vaguely. 'Took some blood, listened to my heart, took my blood pressure, said something about old age and there being no cure for that.'

'What a cheek!' Irene exploded. 'He'll be old himself one day. I think it's about time they did find a cure. It's something we all suffer from.'

Venetia smiled at her friend's outrage. 'It's natural,' she said. 'Getting old is meant to be.' She rummaged in her large shabby handbag and dragged out a brown paper bag. 'Here, I bought these on the way back from the doctor's. I thought it would make a change from

226

cheese sandwiches for our lunch.' Inside were two steak and kidney pies and a jar of pickled onions.

Irene unpacked the two plates and knives and forks she kept in a box under the stall and the two of them sat side by side, munching. Business was quiet and they were able to enjoy their pies in relative peace.

'What else did he say?'

Venetia carefully cut a large pickled onion into four – she had difficulty with her dentures these days – and said, 'He said I should take it easy. Have more rest.' She sniffed at the idea. 'I've never heard anything so ridiculous in my life. What does he expect me to do, sit around waiting to die?'

'A holiday,' said Irene firmly. 'That's what you need. I shall tell Felicity to invite you to Cherry Trees.' She had a momentary flash of compunction at landing Felicity with yet another problem, but consoled herself with the thought that her daughter was young and strong. Venetia was not a difficult teenager. Just this once wouldn't hurt. 'A week in the country,' she continued, 'being waited on, will do you good. You can also see those great-grandchildren of yours.'

'Felicity will be too busy,' said Venetia, adding, 'and anyway, although I must admit I did enjoy that week-end there, I don't think I want to go again.'

But the last sentence had not been finished before Irene had seen the yearning look. She knew then that Venetia *wanted* to go. So that was that, decided Irene. She would go.

Felicity put down the phone and glared at it; always

the harbinger of bad news, never, ever good! Her mother was crafty, speaking to Tony first, stirring up his conscience over Venetia so that he had said, 'Yes, of course,' thus making it impossible for her to say no.

She looked at Tony. 'OK, so she's coming. But tell me, where on earth is she going to sleep? The boxroom is full of rubbish.'

'No problem.' Tony leaped up and switched off the TV. The cricket had finished, rain stopping play, so now Felicity had all his attention. 'I've been meaning to have that room cleared out and decorated for ages. Now is the time to do it.'

Clearing out! Decorating! All that took time. Felicity panicked. 'But she's coming in four days' time, and I'll be in London for two of those days.'

'Don't you worry, it'll all be done by the time you get back. I'll get Jerry Fox to come in. He's always looking for work and he's not a bad decorator. We can shove the rubbish in the stable loft for the time being and sort it out later when we've got more time.'

When we've got more time! Felicity had her doubts about that day ever coming. How many times had she wished she were a good manager in the house, able to cope with all the interruptions to the routine? She couldn't count. And how many times had she tried and tried to keep calm, and stay organized, and failed? She might tell Tony and the children, when things went wrong, that she didn't care if things were less than perfect, but the sad truth was that she *did* care. It wasn't the perfection itself which was her ultimate goal. Her aim was the elusive peace of mind which she was sure perfection in their daily lives would inevitably lead to.

The room was ready as Tony had said it would be: pale rose-coloured walls and carpet, as it was a north-facing room, with velvet curtains in a deeper crushed strawberry. Felicity went to the nearest auction house at Lymington and managed to pick up a good stripped pine wardrobe and matching chest of drawers, and Jerry Fox put his carpentry skills into action and produced a pine dressing table which fitted into the small alcove of the window perfectly. All was ready for Venetia's arrival in good time.

On the day of her arrival Tony picked her up from the train at Brockenhurst station just before lunch and took her back to Cherry Trees.

The moment she arrived, Felicity understood her mother's anxiety, and insistence that she have a holiday. The old lady looked frail, whereas before she'd always looked fiercely robust. Now her skin had a waxen sheen, and Felicity sensed, rather than saw, a transparency about her being which was difficult to pinpoint but which was there none the less.

'Good of you to have me, dear,' Venetia said to Felicity.

'You are very welcome,' Felicity lied, but at the same time, strangely enough, she knew she meant it. 'The children are looking forward to your visit.' This was absolutely true. She took Venetia's bag and started up the stairs. 'How is Samantha?'

'Well, I should think,' Venetia said, a tart edge to her

voice. 'Judging by the fact that I haven't heard from her lately.' She saw Felicity's startled expression and gave a wry smile. 'I know her very well. She'll be in touch when something goes wrong. Has she been writing regularly to the children?'

Felicity paused, mid-stairs, experiencing the familiar stab of guilt at her own lack of genuine care or even basic instinct where the children were concerned. 'Now that you come to mention it, I don't think I have seen many letters recently.' Then she worried. Maybe that was the reason they'd all been extra-difficult of late. Because their mother hadn't bothered to write. But Tony had said nothing, so surely she was wrong? She tried to persuade herself as well as Venetia. 'Of course, the letters may very well have come on the days when I've been in London.'

Venetia was not persuaded. 'And they may very well have not,' she said shortly.

Venetia was right. Later, by skating around the subject for a delicate half-hour, Felicity finally managed to elicit from Peter that none of them had heard from their mother for more than three weeks.

'Don't tell Dad,' he said.

'Why ever not?'

'I . . . we . . .' Peter hesitated, then said in rush, '. . . we don't want Dad thinking bad things about Mum. I'm sure it's not her fault. Probably that horrible Piers won't *let* her write.'

'Perhaps,' replied Felicity in her most neutral voice. She felt suddenly humble in the face of Peter's obvious loyalty to his mother, and at the same time sad. This is where it starts, she thought, all the self-deceit. Pretending people are different from the way they really are because we can't cope with the reality. Whose fault was it? Those with expectations, or those who should have but did not fulfil them? She didn't know, but she was certain that, in this case, it had very little to do with Piers.

Later that evening, while preparing a enormous lasagne for supper, she did tell Tony, not caring what he thought of Samantha. Although part of herself, a malicious part, she reluctantly admitted, actually *hoped* that it would further damn Samantha in Tony's eyes. Would that destroy the residue of jealousy she nurtured or would it always be there?

'I'll give Samantha a ring,' said Tony. 'Gee her up a bit. How many hours are we ahead of California?'

'Eight or nine, I think. Leave it for a while, then you'll catch her at breakfast.' Felicity carefully laid the final sheets of lasagne over the meat mixture and poured on the bechamel sauce. 'I hope this will be enough.' She eyed the baking dish doubtfully, at the same time wondering whether she'd done the right thing in precipitating a phone call from Tony to Samantha. 'Why do you think she hasn't written?'

'Haven't a clue.'

Tony was cheerfully uncurious and Felicity felt exasperated and yet at the same time faintly relieved that he wasn't thinking too much about her. But she couldn't resist prodding a little further. 'Do you think the children are missing her as much now?'

Tony looked surprised. 'Good heavens, no,' he said

emphatically. 'They've completely settled down. I don't think they miss her at all. And they've taken to you, I can see that.'

Felicity sighed. How could Tony remain so blissfully ignorant of what was going on? 'I can't say I've noticed that they've taken to me much. They still treat me as if I'm leper.'

Tony grinned. 'Perhaps you should go around ringing a bell.' Then he saw Felicity's face. 'Sorry, darling. But I did say that they've taken to you, I didn't mean *like* you. Be realistic, you can't expect them to swoon over you yet. You're still the outsider. It all takes time.'

Still the outsider! If he knew how much that hurt he would never have said it. But why should it hurt? It was true. She *was* the outsider as far as Tony and children were concerned. She and Annabel were not part of their unit. She was the second wife, the stepmother, and Annabel the stepsister.

'I don't want them to swoon over me,' she answered crossly. 'I just want them to *accept* that I'm here to stay, and not always make snide remarks about the way their mother used to do things.'

'They will, darling. They will,' replied Tony, remaining, Felicity thought, infuriatingly calm.

Venetia's five days at Cherry Trees were an unqualified success. Felicity had taken five days' leave, so there were no phone calls from Joan Shrimpton or Oliver to cope with, no deadlines to meet and best of all no manuscripts to wade through. Having thought all her life that she couldn't possibly exist without books and deadlines, Felicity was surprised to find a form of blessed relief in having more than enough time to prepare something for the evening meal, or to meander around the forest in the car with Venetia seeking out an agreeable pub in which to have lunch. Even pushing a wayward trolley around the supermarket was not so daunting when not clock-watching.

On the Saturday Felicity decided to take Venetia and all the children, including a very reluctant Annabel, to Lymington market.

It promised to be another wonderful summer's day; the dew was heavy and a faint mist hung in swathes of grey silk in the hollows hidden from the sun. The broadleaf trees of the forest cast dappled shadows across the landscape, and Felicity felt relaxed and happy. Surprising, she thought, considering the tribe crammed ruthlessly into the back of the Land Rover. They set off early as Felicity knew the market was popular with locals and tourists alike, and in the summer the New Forest was full of holidaymakers.

'Grockles,' said Philip dismissively from the back of the Land Rover. 'They clog up the place.'

'Yes.' Felicity was surprised to hear Annabel agreeing with Philip. 'They are an absolute pest. The New Forest is our *home*.' Felicity was even more surprised. Maybe her daughter was mellowing slightly after all. 'We don't want all these strangers crowding the place out.'

'A very selfish attitude,' snapped Venetia. 'How do you think people living here would work if it weren't for the tourists. They bring the money in.'

'What money?' asked Hilary.

'Think about it,' said Venetia.

There was silence while this was digested.

It's amazing, thought Felicity. She doesn't raise her voice, never *tries* to please them or bribe them as I do, and yet they listen to her, and are not rude and never answer back.

'I suppose,' said Peter slowly, 'you mean the people with hotels and shops. They need the extra tourists.'

'And so do the campsites, and the market people,' added Hilary.

Sitting in the front beside Felicity, Venetia nodded approvingly. 'Exactly! Plenty of people depend on the grockles as you call them. Not everyone lives in a nice house with a pony and motorbikes and everything they want.'

'You make us sound *rich*,' said Philip, sounding grumpy. Felicity smiled; she knew he hated being in the wrong. In that respect he was very like his father.

'You are certainly not poor,' said Venetia quite sharply.

Felicity wondered if she thought the children spoilt. She did herself, although it was not something she had ever, nor would ever, mention to Tony. Insecure in her own relationship with them, she dared not suggest that Tony's was less than perfect. And that his spoiling the children equated with a feeling of guilt, of trying to make up for wrongs done. Did he ever think of it in that way? She had no idea.

It would be an understatement to say that Lymington market was bustling. It was bursting at the seams. It seemed the world and his wife had got up early to browse around the bric-à-brac and antique stalls, to buy from the piles of gleaming vegetables, or to sample the organic cheese and bacon. But the first stop for the Hughes family was the churro van.

'I can't,' said Felicity, trying to close her nostrils to the delicious smell of hot vanilla strips of dough, deep-fried, and dunked in cinnamon. 'I'm too fat as it is.'

'Nonsense,' said Venetia, diving into her enormous handbag, 'you're not fat. You're just right.' She found her purse and waved it. 'My treat. A bag for the whole family?'

'Oh, yes, please, Venetia,' came a chorused reply.

Venetia looked up at Annabel. 'You didn't say. Don't you like them?'

Annabel looked down at her foot. 'Yes, I do, but . . . I'm not . . .'

She didn't finish but Felicity knew exactly what she meant. She didn't really feel part of the family.

'When I said family, I meant you as well. You can't get away from it, my dear. You are part and parcel of this lot, like it or not,' Venetia said quietly, but very, very firmly.

'So there,' said Peter, and gave her a friendly shove.

Annabel grinned and had a bag of churros. The rest of the morning was spent shopping. Peter and Philip offered to do the vegetable shopping and then take it back to the Land Rover, while Venetia and Felicity spent time browsing around the bric-à-brac stalls.

'A busman's holiday,' said Venetia happily.

The two girls decided to go off and sort through the myriad charity shops for clothes. Felicity heard Annabel saying to Hilary, 'You can get some really great gear if you look. I bought a cool sixties miniskirt in a wicked orange colour.'

So that was where that indecent day-glo orange skirt had come from! Felicity worried about her every time she went out in it. It left very little to the imagination, but she did not dare even breathe any disapproval about the colour or length, for fear of upsetting Annabel.

Her mother's view was much more pragmatic than her own. 'Just be thankful that she appears to be emerging from her black phase,' she'd said when she'd seen it.

Venetia finally departed on the Monday. She'd spent five days at Cherry Trees and the change of air seemed to have done her good.

'You do look better,' said Felicity at breakfast on the Monday morning.

'I feel better. Thank you for having me.'

'We've enjoyed having you, all of us.' It was the truth, they had enjoyed her stay. Venetia had a calming influence on the children and even Tony had noticed. 'Tony sent his love, and apologies for having to dash off early.'

'Yes, dear.' Venetia was silent for a moment, looking down at her hands. In the hall the reproduction grandfather clock put there by Samantha chimed nine o'clock. It was as if the clock activated Venetia. She looked up at Felicity and said, 'I want you to know that

I think you're doing a marvellous job with the children. They are happier than I believed possible.'

Felicity moved her chair so that she was opposite Venetia. 'They're not really,' she said. 'I know they still wish their mother were here instead of me.'

'Yes,' agreed Venetia, 'I know they do. But when they are older and look back on this time, they will realize that what they had was a time of stability and security. They'll thank you for it then.'

Felicity wished it could be true, that it would all come right in the end, but she was uncertain. 'I'm not so sure,' she said.

Venetia smiled and said, 'You'd better rouse those children of yours if they're coming to the station with me.'

These children of *mine*, thought Felicity as she went upstairs. The thought was a new one. And, surprisingly, not so unpleasant as once she would have thought. She looked at herself in the mirror landing. A healthily tanned face looked back. In her blue cotton dress and sandals, with tanned arms and legs, she looked the picture of health, and far too young to be the mother of five. She felt good. The few days' holiday had done her good as well.

The stable door was open, letting a pool of sunlight into the dim interior. In the middle of the floor, in the light, sat Peter, wearing an old boiler suit which was much too large for him. He was carefully oiling and cleaning part of a motorbike engine.

'Here, catch!' Philip's shadow momentarily blotted

out the sunlight as he came through the doorway. He threw Peter a bag of crisps.

'Great. Did Felicity give them to you?'

'Nope. I pinched them. I got one for Hilary as well. Where is she?'

'Stole them?' Peter was worried. 'I don't think you ought to.'

'Why not? They're ours by rights. Dad's money buys all the food, doesn't it? We don't *have* to ask Felicity for everything.' Peter and Hilary were making a few tentative steps towards friendship with Felicity, but Philip was still grimly determined not to like her.

'She *is* looking after us.' Peter wanted Philip to be fair.

'Only because she has to. And she only does that because she's soppy about Dad.'

'They're married, so it's not just soppiness,' Peter pointed out. He was a stickler for getting things right. 'Dad married her. So it's permanent.'

'It wasn't permanent with our mother, and *she* was married to him once,' Philip said. 'You can never trust grown-ups.'

Peter thought for a moment then said, 'Well, *I'm* going to trust them.'

'I shouldn't bother,' sneered Philip. 'Look what happened when you prayed! Where did that get us? Nowhere.'

'Shut up.' Unknown to Philip, Peter still prayed. Only now he didn't have anywhere of his own to pray he did it in the bathroom. There he could lock the door and know that he wasn't going to be interrupted. Brother

Tom said that it didn't matter to God where you were as long as you did it and meant what you were saying. Leaning on the side of the bath was perfectly acceptable. But Brother Tom had also said that it was no good just asking God for something. You had to work for it yourself as well. In his own way Peter was trying to do this, trying to turn his dream of a united and permanent family into a reality. He put his bag of crisps on one side. 'I'm not going to eat these. I'm going to put them back in the cupboard.'

'Smarmy bastard,' Philip sneered angrily.

It was Peter's turn to get angry. 'I am *not*.' He flung down the oily piece of engine, and dived at Philip's legs, bringing him down in a rugby tackle.

Philip fought back, and the pair of them rolled across the dusty stable floor, grunting, squeaking, kicking and punching.

Hilary and Annabel were making their way across to the paddock. The two girls had not exactly become the best of friends, but they were beginning to tolerate each other. Hilary was teaching Annabel to ride, and in return to Annabel giving her guitar lessons. They heard the ruction in the old stable from the far end of the yard.

'Wretched boys!' said Hilary. 'They're fighting.' She raced across the yard to the stable. 'Stop it, stop it,' she shouted from the doorway.

Annabel, standing close behind her, stared in amazement.

'Crumbs, some fight,' said Annabel. Not having any brothers or sister, she'd never been involved in, or seen

239

anyone fight before. She watched them biting, kicking, rolling across the floor. 'Just like on the television,' she added on an admiring note.

Hilary was not impressed. She'd seen it all before. 'Stupid boys,' she said, aiming kicks at both of them. 'What are you fighting about?'

Hilary's kicks had the desired effect. The boys disentangled themselves and sat up looking sulky.

'Nothing,' they both said at once, neither willing to tell on the other.

'I've got you some crisps.' Philip crawled across the floor, retrieved a flattened bag of crisps.

'No, thanks. I'm on a diet,' said Hilary.

'What for? There's nothing wrong with you.' They were all fat, and Philip knew it, although he refused to admit it.

'I'm dieting because I'm too heavy for Cotton-Socks. He's started complaining if I ride him for too long,' said Hilary.

'Get a bigger horse, then,' said Philip nastily. 'Send Cotton-Socks to the knacker's yard. That's all he's good for anyway. To be made into glue.'

Hilary gasped in horror at the idea, and Annabel shouted, 'You horrible, horrible boy. We love that pony. He's wonderful to ride.'

'And you shouldn't let *her* ride him,' said Philip to Hilary, jerking his head in Annabel's direction. 'She's only Felicity's daughter, and they're both only here temporarily.'

'Sometimes, Philip, I think you are really, really stupid,' said Annabel angrily. 'I get fed up with you running my mother down. She's doing her best for all of us. She's trying to make us into a proper family.'

'Well, she needn't bother. I know what a proper family is, and it's not one with *your* mother in it.' He emptied the remains of the crisp crumbs into his hand then swallowed them.

Annabel darted forward and snatched at the packet. 'Where did you get these from?' Philip made a rude face and Annabel glared at him. 'Don't bother to tell me. I know. You got them from the back of the larder. Mum says that crisps and biscuits are always disappearing, and now I know why. You're stealing them.'

'None of your business, you nosy parker,' muttered Philip, feeling guilty, and at the same time uncertain about everything. The feeling of uncertainty made him even more angry.

All this time Peter had been sitting silently, his head between his hands resting on his knees. Now he raised an oily, tear-stained face. 'Yes, he's stealing them,' he said.

It was the final straw. A betrayal. Philip exploded. 'You bastard!!' His fist shot out, caught Peter on the side of the head and sent him over with one blow. There was a sickening thud. Peter fell, his head hitting the discarded piece of engine.

For a split second nobody spoke. The silence hung like a palpable presence in the dimness of the old stable block. A bird ran along the corrugated roof, its feet clonk, clonk, clonking. Like a bird with hobnail boots.

Peter didn't move, but a thin trickle of blood oozed from the corner of his mouth.

'You've killed him,' whispered Hilary.

Philip said nothing. He just screamed, and screamed and screamed.

Felicity looked at her watch. Only a quarter of an hour, but it seemed hours and hours that they'd been waiting outside Casualty while the doctors had Peter in the cubicle. She wished Tony would arrive.

'Dad will be arriving soon,' she said, trying to appear calm. The truth was, she didn't know when he would be arriving. The one day when she really needed to get him on his mobile, and he had the damned thing turned off.

Philip began to cry. 'Will he die?'

'Of course not.' Felicity held out her arm and Philip squeezed in beside her on the chair. His hair smelt oily and dirty. 'Perhaps you'd better tell me what happened?'

'We were fighting.'

'It wasn't Philip's fault. He didn't do it on purpose,' interrupted Hilary.

'Yes, Mum, It's true.' Annabel said. 'It wasn't on purpose. It was only a little punch, and Peter fell and hit his head on a piece of old engine.'

'But what on earth were you fighting about?' Felicity had the vague notion that it might help if they started at the beginning.

'You,' said Philip in a very small voice.

'Me?'

'Yes. Peter was sticking up for you, and I said that I didn't want you as a stepmother, and then Peter said he would tell about the crisps. So I hit him.'

'The crisps?' The stepmother bit made sense, but not the crisps.

Philip hung his head and said in muffled tones, 'The ones I've been stealing from the larder. Now you know where they went to.'

Felicity smiled down at the tousled, grimy head. 'I've always known that, Philip,' she said gently. 'I've been waiting for you to grow out of the habit.'

'Then it wouldn't have mattered if Peter had told you?'

'No.'

'Then I needn't have hit him.'

'No.' Felicity tightened her hold on him. 'But there's no point in even thinking about it. Just remember next time you argue with anyone, not just Peter, anyone, count to ten before you say or do anything. Because whatever you do cannot be undone.'

'If Peter gets better I'll never argue with anyone ever again.'

'He *will* get better,' said Felicity firmly, and yet she despaired at the same time. But it was an anguish she had to keep to herself. Why didn't someone come in and tell her what was going on? It wasn't easy playing the confident, comforting mother role, when she didn't feel in the least bit confident about anything.

At this moment the door burst open and Tony strode in. 'What's all this, then?'

'How is Peter?' The four in the waiting room asked in unison.

'Right as ninepence. Well, maybe not ninepence, but definitely eightpence. He's sitting up in bed rabbiting on about it not being Philip's fault, and that he started the fight anyway.' He looked sternly at Philip. 'So you two were fighting.'

Philip hung his head down even lower. 'Yes,' he sniffed, and wiped his eyes on the back of his oily hand.

Tony still looked stern. 'What were you fighting about?'

Felicity glanced at Philip's grimy, guilt-ridden face; he had enough to contend with without a fight with his father as well. 'We don't want to go into all that now,' she said quickly. 'It isn't important. Boys always fight. The most important thing is, when can we take Peter home?'

Tony looked from one to another. Philip holding on to Felicity as if his life depended on it, and Felicity herself, her arm clasped protectively around him. 'Not tonight,' he said more gently. 'Peter's had enough excitement for one day. He's going to stay in overnight for a little peace and quiet.'

'But, Dad.' Philip was near to tears. 'I've *got* to see him. To say I'm sorry.'

'And I argued too,' said Hilary.

'Me too.' Annabel was determined not to be left out.

'Not tonight,' said Tony firmly.

'I'll tell Peter that you are all sorry,' said Felicity. Tony opened his mouth and she glared at him. 'And don't tell me *I'm* not allowed. After all, I *am* his stepmother.'

'Wouldn't dream of it,' said Tony and, disenga-

244

ging her from Philip, took her hand. 'Wait here, you lot, until we get back.' Outside the room he stopped. 'Is it my imagination, or has the atmosphere between you and the kids suddenly taken a turn for the better.'

'I thought that you never noticed my battles with them.'

'Of course I did,' said Tony comfortably. 'But I saw no point in making a mountain out of a molehill.' He paused and turned towards her. 'Well,' he demanded. 'Is it suddenly better?'

Felicity smiled, thinking of the way Philip had clung to her. True, it was an emergency, but the fact that he had turned to her in a crisis gave her a warm feeling inside. She must be doing something right. 'It's not your imagination,' she said. 'There are probably many battles ahead, but somehow I think we've crossed the Rubicon.'

Tony smiled back at her. 'Don't worry about the battles,' he said. 'Battling families are healthy. It's the silent ones you need to worry about.'

By the time they got back from the hospital it was late. Way past dinnertime. The oven was still on. In her panic to get to the hospital Felicity had forgotten to turn it off when they left. The breasts of chicken meant to simmer in cream and chives were burnt to a cinder.

'Oh, dear.' She looked at the shrivelled brown biscuity things which were all that was left of the chicken breasts. 'I'll have to think of something

245

else.' Everyone inspected the brown biscuits, tutted sympathetically, then left to do their own thing. All except Philip. He stayed at Felicity's side.

'We could go and get some fish and chips,' he said. Then added, 'I want to say thank you properly.'

Felicity wondered what was coming next. 'What for?'

'For letting Dad think it was an accident with me and Peter.'

'Stop worrying about it. I'm sure that's what Peter would want.'

Philip smiled shyly, and Felicity felt her heart give a ridiculous skip because it was the first time he had ever smiled directly at her. It changed his face completely. 'I'll go down to the chip shop on my bike if you like,' he said. Felicity handed over some money and Philip went outside to get his bike, but he was back in less than three minutes. 'I've just remembered something awful. It's Monday, and the chip shop doesn't open on Mondays.'

Felicity groaned. 'I'll see what I can dig out of the deep-freeze.' Dig being the operative word, she hadn't defrosted it for months.

'Or we could have pasta and salad. We've got loads of salad stuff, and I could do my tomato and cheese pasta,' said Philip.

Another surprise. 'You?' she queried.

'Yes. I love cooking. I'm going to be a cook when I leave school.' This was the first Felicity had heard of it, and wondered what Tony would say. 'I know the cheese and tomato recipe off by heart. I cooked it

nearly every day when Peter and I went camping with
the school last year.'

'You're on,' said Felicity. 'I'll watch. If it's as easy as
you say, even I might be able to learn the recipe.'

A big grin spread across Philip's face. 'It's easy-
peasy,' he said. 'Just lead me to the tinned tomatoes.'

A beginning, thought Felicity, allowing herself a
small moment of triumph. It's a beginning.

CHAPTER 13

Summer began to slip away. Already the redolence of autumn lingered in the forest, a pungent smell of leaf mould. And Prudence took longer to walk, spending much more time sniffily investigating interesting scents.

'Pity that dog can't be trained to sniff out truffles,' said Tony, on one of the rare occasions he accompanied Felicity walking the dog. 'There are plenty here in the forest if you know where to look.' He sighed. 'We could sell them to London restaurants and make a fortune.'

It was one of Felicity's contented days and she didn't want to think about money, something of which there never seemed to be enough. Financial matters, as far as she was concerned, were a supremely uncomfortable subject. Whenever they looked at their joint finances they always came close to arguing; expenditure, nine times out of ten, exceeding income. Felicity blamed the boys' school fees but Tony was adamant that *they* were absolutely sacrosanct and not up for discussion. On the other hand he, ridiculously in Felicity's opinion, had other ideas of where to save money in the general housekeeping budget, none of which she ever agreed with. 'Don't let's talk money again,' she said.

Tony sighed again, then recompensed with a smile. 'Sorry,' he said, then added, 'but I can't help it; trouble is I'm always thinking about it.'

They came to a steep bank and Tony reached out, Felicity slipped her hand into his so that he could pull her up the bank. She scrambled up, dislodging deep mounds of leaves on the way, and arrived at the top breathlessly reflecting that life was a bit like the bank. A struggle, often difficult and through mounds of detritus, not leaves but the extraneous matter of other people's lives. But in life they never seemed to reach the top. The slope went on and upwards with varying degrees of difficulty. However, today she was not going to let that put her off. '*Don't* think about it, Tony,' she said firmly. 'We're not *that* poor.'

Tony was determinedly gloomy, and was not to be lifted from the slough of despond. 'We're not rich either. I pay the bills, remember.'

Felicity stopped dead in her tracks. Ahead of them Prudence lumbered on, following a scent which took her right through the middle of an enormous clump of rhododendrons. Half of her watched Prudence happily rummaging through the sun-soaked forest, the epitome of joyous contentment, while the other half slipped down in a depression somewhere near to Tony's as she felt the twinge, which was becoming uncomfortably familiar. No matter how serene she felt these days, even when everything *seemed* harmonious, it would appear. A small cold contrapuntal note of discord, not complementary to but at variance with life in general. It made her despair that she'd ever get *everything* right. Although exactly what right was she had never fathomed out, and because of this had never mentioned the feeling to Tony. Now she felt exasperated and angry with him for letting in the demon again.

Against her better judgement she heard herself saying, 'Sometimes, Tony, I think you have a character defect somewhere. All this obsession with money.' Not only should she have not said it, but she knew her voice was much too sharp. '*And* I do help pay the bills,' she added.

Tony kicked at a piles of leaves, sending them flying high into the air, the swishing noise causing Prudence to think it a game and to come galloping back. 'I know you do, and I wish you didn't have to. I *hate* you having to help me. It isn't fair that you should be my wife and yet I can only offer you a measly twenty per cent of my income because all the rest goes on the remains of my other marriage.'

Felicity was immediately stricken with remorse. She had wronged him, he *did* think about it. It wasn't his fault, well, not *all* his fault, that, because of the divorce, he was saddled with a second mortgage. It was Samantha's fault for being greedy. She felt a second wife's righteous surge of indignation against Samantha, and a corresponding surge of affection for Tony. She said softly, 'I knew that when I married you. And the children aren't remainders, they are still very much part of you.'

'I still feel bad that you should have so much

responsibility to shoulder.' Tony hunched his shoulders, and Felicity recognized he was having one of his soul-searching days.

She too often felt that she was shouldering too much responsibility, but had reluctantly adopted her mother's attitude, which was, if you can't change it, get on with it. Tony should do the same. She tugged at his arm, trying to lift his mood. 'Surely it doesn't matter who pays what, so long as the bills get paid?'

Tony looked at her sideways out of the corner of his eye, something Felicity knew he did whenever he'd upset the equilibrium. 'I suppose not.'

'The most important thing is that we're happy. And we *are* happy. Aren't we?'

'Yes, we are happy.' Tony suddenly shook the hair out of his eyes, rather like a shaggy dog coming out of water, thought Felicity, and gave a proper, deep-seated smile. 'You're right. It *is* an obsession.' He whistled to Prudence then threw a stick for her and laughed. 'Maybe I should get some counselling. It's all the rage these days.'

His laughter helped Felicity climb back on to her platform of contentment. Everything would be all right. *Was* all right. So what was she worrying about? What were either of them worrying about? 'Alice Appleby is starting a counselling course,' she told Tony. 'She told me when she came round the other day. At Westhampton College, two evenings a week.'

'That woman couldn't counsel a sausage,' said Tony. 'Race you up the hill.'

Laughing like a couple of children, they ran up the

sharp incline, leaving a trail of leaves flying behind them. Prudence thought it wonderful, and ran snapping at their heels.

The air now had a distinctive nip to it. Philip and Peter, with the help of Felicity and Tracy, were gradually gathering together their clothes ready for school. The new term started the following week. Tracy was a dab hand at sewing on name-tapes, which was just as well as Felicity was hopeless and her fingers were sore from where she pricked them so many times on the needle. From the gardens in Oakford village acrid blue bonfire smoke permeated the air. The garden at Cherry Trees was no exception; the bonfire the boys had lit was going great guns. Felicity stopped loading the tumble-dryer, a never-ending task these days with the rush to get every item of clothing clean, and looked out of the kitchen window to where Philip and Peter were leaping about like a couple of gremlins, happily torching the skeletal remains of the runner beans. Philip had his baseball cap on back to front, a sure sign that he was feeling happy. Opening the kitchen window, she leaned out and took a deep breath. 'Doesn't it smell gorgeous? I love the smell of bonfires.'

'No accounting for taste,' said Tracy, who'd just arrived for the day. She had baby Jacob with her and, after unfolding and securing the playpen, plopped him in it. She was obviously in a mood. Not a particular aggressive one this morning, more a determined one, as if she had made up her mind about something.

Felicity looked at her, and wondered if her mood had anything to do with Sam Appleby. She'd seen Sam for herself recently. He had been out running and had said good morning to her as he'd passed by. Felicity thought he looked rather nice. He had a lovely, boyish smile, and was tall, lean and bronzed, and obviously physically very fit. Definitely Jacob's father, she had decided; there was no denying the likeness. There was talk in the village that Sam had been seen hanging around with Tracy and Jacob. And had even visited the flat Tracy rented. Felicity had always prided herself on not being part of the gossip, on being an outsider, and therefore above that sort of thing. But even she found it impossible *not* to hear, and lately, though she hated admitting it, she'd found herself listening to other people's conversation when in the post office or the Open All Hours garage shop. Now, she decided to chance mentioning what she'd heard. 'I hear Sam Appleby has been seeing you.'

'*Trying* to,' said Tracy gruffly.

'I saw him myself. He seems rather a nice young man.'

'He might be when he grows up,' was the acerbic reply.

'What *do* you mean?'

Tracy stood, feet apart, arms akimbo, and looked straight at Felicity. She looked defensive. 'I hope you're not going to try and get me hitched to Sam Appleby as well,' she said.

'Wouldn't dream of it,' Felicity hastened to reassure.

Tracy jutted out her lower lip in an expression of

grim determination. 'It's not just old Ma Appleby I've got to contend with, it's my own mother as well ever since Sam came back. She thinks it's a chance to make me respectable.' Tracy sniffed scornfully. 'It's the only thing she *will* speak to me about, though! Never says anything useful, like here's a fiver to help you out.'

Felicity thought hard, then said cautiously, 'It isn't only respectability that a partnership offers, it's financial security as well.'

Tracy gave a scornful laugh. 'Sam Appleby, offer financial security! The only security he has is the social security. He's never earned any *real* money in his life.' She paused and then said bitterly, 'Despite the fact that he's got a degree. *He* didn't have to give up his university place. He got it, but then he wasted it.'

Felicity busied herself sorting out another pile of vest and pants by the side of the tumble dryer. So Tracy *did* care about not going on to university. No degree for her, but a baby instead. Whereas Sam had gone on with his life as planned. Or had he? She remembered Annabel telling her that the Applebys' son was a dropout even though he'd got a university degree. She wondered why. Could Tracy be the reason? 'Surely he could get a job?' she said carefully. 'He has qualifications of some sort.'

Tracy sniffed. 'A degree in psychology, but he'll never use it. He's too lazy to apply himself. The only thing Sam is interested in, besides sex, is training.'

'Training? What for?'

Tracy bent down and gave a finger rusk to Jacob who took it, waved it triumphantly, then chomped on it, showing a wide expanse of pink gum. 'He's a keep-fit fanatic,' she said. 'He'd rather keep fit than work. So long as he has biceps the size of a leg of pork he's happy, no matter that his brain is shrivelling by the day.' She looked up from Jacob to Felicity, her gaze defiant. 'Me, I'm different,' she said fiercely. 'I've got Jacob to think about. I'm not going to waste my life. I'm going to work hard and provide well for my son. I don't want him growing up like his father. I'm better off without him, and so is Jacob. We don't want or need him.'

'Ever thought that he might need you?' said Felicity.

Tracy stopped, a pile of dusters and a can of polish poised mid-air. 'No,' she said.

'Well, think about it,' said Felicity, and wondered whether she ought to be interfering.

There was silence for a moment, then Tracy said, 'If he had needed or loved me he wouldn't have just gone off when I was pregnant. He would have stayed.'

'Yes and no,' said Felicity.

Tracy looked indignant. 'What is that supposed to mean?'

'Just that men don't always react in a very mature sort of way when they're presented with problems. Quite often they run away. Pretend their problems don't even exist.'

'I don't want a man like that.' Tracy was adamant. 'As I said before, I can manage on my own.'

'I'm sure you can.' Felicity's admiration for Tracy grew although she felt sad to think of her battling on alone. But she had no doubt that Tracy would provide well for her son. Whatever it took, Tracy would rise to the occasion. Felicity felt humbled and little ashamed at her own, often negative, attitude to life's problems. Compared to Tracy she had no problems at all.

'Now,' said Tracy firmly, unequivocally dismissing the subject, 'having got that off my chest, where shall I start on the domestics today?'

'Wherever you like.' Felicity turned back to the tumble-dryer then suddenly stopped and straightened up as a nauseous feeling swept over her. She closed her eyes and willed the feeling to go away. She was *not* going to succumb to the threatening stomach bug which was rumbling away inside her; there was much too much to do. Besides, tomorrow she was starting her two-day London stint.

'You all right?' Tracy came over and peered at her. 'You look a bit green about the gills.'

'Bit off-colour, that's all.' Felicity took another deep breath and felt the feeling receding.

'Not pregnant, are you? I thought I was a bit off colour,' said Tracy, 'then he came along.' She pointed at Jacob.

The nauseous feeling gone, Felicity switched her mind into another gear. 'Of course I'm not pregnant,' she said briskly. 'Out of the question. I'm very careful about that sort of thing.'

'So was I,' said Tracy.

Felicity opened her mouth to say that she'd obviously not been careful enough, then thought better of it. She looked at Jacob sitting happily in his playpen, still chomping on his rusk. A stream of dribble hung in a blob on the end of his chin. She couldn't remember

256

Annabel being so dribbly, but supposed she must have been. It was all such a long time ago she'd forgotten what it was like, and she was not maternally inclined enough to want to find out again now. Babies were definitely not for her; she was too old. Besides, she and Tony had both agreed that they couldn't possibly afford more children.

That night they did their bi-monthly accounts together which confirmed they couldn't afford the children they had, let alone any more.

Tony sat before his computer, 'trying to make two and two make five,' he said.

Felicity, leaning companiably on his shoulder, peered at the complicated spreadsheet he had on the screen. She did her sums on pieces of paper, whereas Tony preferred to click his mouse, import, edit, and select options on his screen. They both usually came up with the same answers, more or less. She looked quizzically at the figures on the screen. 'Heavens! It's not *that* bad, is it?'

'It's that bad,' said Tony. 'Everything has gone up this month. School fees, the mortgage since that last damned interest hike. And now you tell me that the children need new school uniforms. How can they? They've all lost weight. I can see that for myself.'

The weight factor had been another of the successful aspects of the children moving back to Cherry Trees. Felicity had embarked upon a healthy-eating, lose-weight plan. The first four pounds had been difficult for them all. Felicity had stopped buying crisps and biscuits, locked the larder door and kept a strict eye on their high-energy, low-fat diets. But once four pounds had disappeared there was no stopping the ensuing enthusiasm. They'd all become figure-conscious, watching not only their own figures but everyone else's as well. Felicity encouraged this, in the vague belief that it was a team effort, after reading an article in one of Tony's magazines called 'The Psychology of Family Therapy'.

'Claptrap,' Tony had said, and flung it down.

But Felicity had tried to follow the advice, albeit in a rather haphazard manner. Although watching each other did have its disadvantages. She could cheerfully have strangled Peter that morning when he'd said, 'Hey, Felicity, that skirt of yours is a bit tight isn't it?' and then whipped away her breakfast cornflakes, weighed them, and announced, 'You've got an ounce too many.'

Tony had laughed. 'That's telling you,' he'd said, then whispered, 'Family therapy has a nasty habit of bouncing back!'

He was the only one in the family who had not taken happily to calorie-counting, firmly believing that his figure was perfection itself. Choosing to ignore the fact that the slight bulge over the top of his belt was not muscle, as he fondly imagined, but excess flesh.

But diets had nothing to do with the need for new clothes. Felicity drew up a chair and sat down beside Tony. 'You'd better add in another four hundred for new clothes,' she said. 'Size has nothing to do with it. They do wear out as well, you know.'

'Mine don't.' Tony was obstinate. 'I'm still wearing the jacket I had at medical school.'

'Children are rougher on their clothes,' said Felicity, resisting the temptation to tell him that the jacket in question was hardly fit for gardening and was, in fact, on her list of things to be sent to the tip as in her opinion it was even past the Salvation Army stage.

Tony sighed heavily and hit a few keys on the keyboard. The page jiggled and reset itself. 'There you are,' he said. 'I shall be hopelessly in the red.' He turned a face furrowed with worry towards Felicity. 'I think I'll have to take the boys away from St Boniface. I've been thinking about it for some weeks. It's the only way to make ends meet.'

Felicity looked at the furrows and anger fizzed up inside her at the unfairness of life. He worked hard, they both did, so why should their lives be blighted by this never-ending shortage of money? People who thought one could live without money were wrong. Money had the power to make or break you, the power over misery or happiness. If the boys were taken away from St Boniface they'd be upset and angry. It would mean starting all over, winning their confidence again. She didn't want to lose the hard-won progress they'd made as a family unit. 'We'll have to use some of my money,' she heard herself saying, and this was something she'd promised her mother she'd never do. 'I've got a few thousand put away. We'll use that for now, and by next year I'll have a rise and that will help.'

Tony looked even more worried. 'I can't expect you

to pay for my children. Besides, I thought you didn't approve of them going to such an expensive school.'

Felicity thought for a moment. Who was she trying to please? Tony or the children? But then she realized that she couldn't really separate the two. It was their overall happiness that mattered, all of them, herself included. 'I didn't approve, initially,' she said. 'But they're happy and settled there. We've achieved such a lot together, as a family, these last few weeks, that I don't want to let anything upset the applecart now.'

Tony was thoughtful. 'And when Samantha takes them back next year, as she is bound to want to, she'll have to meet the expense of the day-to-day living from the money she already has from me.'

'Do you want them to go back to her?' Felicity was puzzled. She had begun to get used to the idea of them all being together all the time, and was now uncertain of the future. Did she or did she not want them to leave again?

'No, I don't *want* it. But you must admit that it will be a help, financially.'

'Yes, but . . .'

'I don't want you to always have to work so hard all the time. I'd like you to be able to stay at home if you wanted to.'

Felicity laughed. 'Things really are looking up,' she teased. 'Fancy you admitting that I do work hard. No more thinking that reading manuscripts is not a proper job!'

Tony grinned sheepishly, and, leaving the keyboard, put his arms around Felicity. 'I was a selfish brute when you first married me. How did you put up with me?'

Felicity looked at him, every contour of his beloved face etched indelibly in her mind. No matter how much they might quarrel, no matter how many problems there were, she knew she would always love him. No one else. Only him. 'By loving you a lot,' she said, kissing him. 'But not forgetting to tell you that you *were* selfish sometimes.' Tony grinned slowly. 'Come on,' said Felicity, 'Let's do the sums again, and add in my money this time.'

The spreadsheet, finally finished, showed a break-even point and Tony printed out the accounts and switched off the computer. 'The annoying thing,' he said, looking at the rows of figures, 'is that everyone thinks doctors and their families are rolling in money.'

'Hum!' Felicity put on her reading glasses and squinted at the printout. 'At this rate we'll both have to work until we're tottering around on Zimmer frames just to keep our heads above water.'

'And definitely no more children,' said Tony. 'They're far too expensive.' Then the worried look returned. 'Darling, I'm being selfish again. You might *want* babies.'

'I've had one, Annabel,' said Felicity, 'and I like my life just as it is. Anyway, I've a decidedly unmaternal streak in me.'

'Rubbish,' said Tony. 'You're heaps more maternal than Samantha ever was, and the kids recognize it in you. That's why you've been such a success with them. And me,' he added with a grin.

Felicity hugged him. 'I've got all I need. You and the tribe. I don't need babies.'

And I don't, she thought the following morning, watching Jacob being plopped in his playpen yet again; Tracy's babysitter friend was away staying with her own mother for a few days so Jacob was coming in with Tracy. He howled for the rusk he knew to be coming, pink starfish hands beating at the air. No, definitely no babies, they were much too demanding.

Tracy leaned on the side of the playpen, dangling the rusk down to Jacob. 'It must be nice,' she said, looking enviously at Felicity's smart city clothes, 'having a really exciting job, and working with all those glamorous and interesting people.'

Felicity stopped her mad rush around gathering together her bits and pieces and thought for a moment. Glamorous and interesting! To Tracy, stuck in Oakford doing someone else's housework, it must seem that way. 'Most of the staff at Dickens are very ordinary,' she said. 'Like you and me, except that they live in London and have to fight their way to work each day on the bus and tube. My boss, Oliver is sweet. He is interesting, but he's very elderly, and Joan Shrimpton, his personal assistant, is not exactly a barrel of laughs.'

Tracy gave a little shriek of excitement. 'There you are. You know Joan Shrimpton. I've seen a picture of her in one of my mother's old magazines. She was a model.'

'That was Jean, not Joan. The nearest Joan Shrimpton has ever got to modelling is trying on a crimplene two-piece in Littlewoods.' Grabbing her handbag and the large canvas bag full of manuscripts she was taking back to London, Felicity made for the door. 'Now I've really got to dash, Tracy, otherwise I'll never get a place in the station car park. There's a chicken pie I bought from Plested's in the fridge for lunch today. Could you bung it in the oven before you leave? Philip is going to do the potatoes and vegetables to go with it. Thanks.'

She fled from the house, mind switching into work mode, thinking now of nothing but the report she had in her bag for Oliver. Her spirits lifted at the thought of it. It felt wonderful, finding a really good book lurking amongst the slush pile of unsolicited manuscripts; this particular one she'd only stuffed into her bag as an afterthought on the way out of the office last week. It was disloyal, she knew, but for a few moments after finishing reading it she'd wished she were an agent. Then she would not have given it to Dickens, with their small print-runs and hardback-only editions; she would have auctioned it amongst the bigger publishing houses, and let the one who'd be most likely to do it justice have it. But, resigned to the fact that nothing was perfect in this world, she knew she couldn't do Oliver out of a good book, and prayed that the rights department would get their concerted finger out and get the author a good paperback deal.

'What are they supposed to eat for dinner tonight, and tomorrow lunchtime?' Tracy leaned out of the kitchen window and hollered after her.

'Don't worry about it,' Felicity called back. 'Philip is

doing the cooking. It's pasta and pasta, probably. I've left it up to him.' The pink and green coxcomb of hair bobbed up and down, indicating disapproval, and Felicity smiled. Tracy was incredibly old-fashioned in some senses. She knew just what she was going to say, and she did.

'I don't approve of boys in the kitchen. It's not right.'

'He's going to be a chef one day.'

Felicity reached the car and wrestled with the key stuck in the lock, wishing that Tony had found time to oil it as he'd promised he would. He never got around to doing any of the little jobs in the house and garden he was always promising to do, the surgery and his patients taking up an ever-increasing amount of his time. But then, she reminded herself, as the key grudgingly turned, he *had* got stuck into the accounts last night. Although the net result of that was the conclusion that she would be working full-time until her dotage.

Tracy was still leaning out of the window. 'Huh!' she sniffed. 'I only hope he doesn't mess up the kitchen too much.'

'If he does, you have my permission to tell him off. See you the day after tomorrow. Bye.' Felicity roared down the gravel drive towards Brockenhurst, the station, and London.

Oliver Dickens stared at the manuscript Felicity had just put in front of him. 'You're sure?' he asked.

'Positive. This is a spellbinding thriller, set on the dark edges of the medical world. It is absolutely convincingly shocking. You don't know for sure what will happen until you get to the last couple of pages.'

'Hum!' said Oliver, making the fingers of his two hands into a steeple.

'So take it, make it the lead title for the month, and for goodness' sake put a bomb under the rights department so that they're motivated into making a good paperback sale.'

Oliver smiled. 'You sound disapproving of them.'

'I'm not, I'm . . .'

'Don't worry. I don't mind. It's good to see you so enthusiastic about a book. Joan and I were beginning to think that affairs at Oakford had taken precedence over affairs here at Dickens Books. Joan says that you are always tired, that you . . .'

'Joan says too much,' said Felicity sharply. It unnerved her to think that they had noticed her packed routine was getting her down. She prided herself now, since the advent of Tracy, on coping very well. 'I admit that sometimes I get tired, but I enjoy working here. I should hate just to be a housewife. In fact I don't think I could just stay at home. I'd go mad with boredom.'

Oliver beamed. 'Good,' he said, and pulled the manuscript towards him. 'I promise I'll do my level best to do justice to this author.'

'Thanks, Oliver.' Felicity stood up, well pleased. 'I'd better see what this week's mail has in store for me.'

On leaving the office she immediately cannoned straight into Joan Shrimpton who hissed conspiratorially into her ear.

'I thought you might be here. I was looking for you.

There's a phone call from the ex.' Miss Shrimpton's rather narrow lips were even more narrow than usual.

'The ex?'

'Your husband's ex-wife,' said Miss Shrimpton, closing the door behind Felicity so that Oliver Dickens shouldn't hear. 'She says it's important that she speak to you. Of course I told her that you were very busy, but she wouldn't take no for an answer.' The older woman bristled with indignation and self-importance.

Irritated by the phone call which she didn't want, and Joan Shrimpton's officious air of secrecy, Felicity nevertheless managed to conceal her feelings and smile gracefully. 'Thank you, Joan. I'll take the call now in my office.' Alone in her office, a puzzled Felicity picked up the phone. Samantha hardly ever phoned the children from the States, let alone her, their step-mother. No doubt she'd find out in a moment what she wanted. It was bound to be a request. Couldn't be anything else. 'Felicity Hughes here,' she said.

Samantha sat in the St John's Wood house looking out on to the paved garden. It was as perfectly manicured as ever. Piers had made arrangements for the gardener to continue while they were in California. Every dead leaf or flower that had dared spoil the perfection had been picked off and tidied away. The potted plants had been watered and mulched, and the paving slabs hosed down. For a few moments Samantha let her thoughts dwell on the garden at Cherry Trees and gave a mental shudder. This time of year, the autumn, had always given her nightmares. She'd fought a never-ending battle to cope with the falling leaves, and maintain some semblance of order in the flower and vegetable garden. But the reality of nature had always defeated her in the end, and the garden at Cherry Trees had always finished up looking like all the other gardens in Oakford: unkempt and wild, with thistles popping their tufted heads up amongst the dahlias and sprouts, and fluffy old man's beard running riot in the hedges. She smiled briefly. Here, in St John's Wood, nature was under control, which was how she and Piers liked it.

Control. That was the key to everything. But for the moment her grip on it had slipped a little, and she'd come back to England to regain it.

Samantha gripped the phone tightly. So tightly that her knuckles shone white under the skin. Control, she reminded herself. Control was the key. She dialled Venetia's number, then slammed the receiver down the moment she answered. Now she found herself dialling Felicity's office number. Why Felicity? The honest answer was that she didn't really know. All she *did* know was that she had to talk to someone, and somewhere at the back of her mind was the vague notion that Felicity was more likely to sympathize and not condemn as Venetia almost certainly would.

'You know what you have to do,' Piers had said when he'd seen her off at Los Angeles airport. 'It won't take long. The sooner the better.'

Samantha had said, 'Yes, of course, darling,' because she knew that was what he wanted her to say, and anyway it was what she wanted as well. It was all quite straightforward. But that was in Los Angeles.

Here, in London, nothing seemed quite as simple as it had done there. Now, she had doubts. They were put there by the receptionist at the clinic this morning, and then the nurse, and then later the doctor. They had all said, 'Now, you are *quite* sure, Mrs Hughes?' with so much emphasis that she had begun to doubt her own mind. She *had* been sure. But now she wasn't. And it was all their fault; other people had put the doubts in her mind. But still, she had to ask someone else. Get their opinion. The reason she had put the phone down on Venetia was because she instinctively knew what *she* would say.

She would say, 'No, my dear. You can't possibly do that. Some things are right and some things are wrong. And that is wrong.' Venetia always set such a store by doing the *right* thing.

Felicity was bound to be different. She was younger, more relaxed and modern about these things. At least, Samantha hoped so. She just needed someone here, in London, to give her the green light and she would go ahead. Felicity was the only woman she knew who hadn't previously been a friend of Piers, and Piers had forbidden her to contact any of their friends and acquaintances.

'We don't want anyone knowing that we've been careless, do we, darling?' he'd said. 'It's too utterly boring for words. The whole thing is so infra dig it makes me want to cringe.'

Samantha agreed. It certainly did nothing for the cool, sophisticated image they'd both projected so successfully. Felicity was different. She was not a friend, she was a different sort of acquaintance, and not a person who mixed with any of Piers' crowd.

At long last, after battling with the touchtone telephone obstacle course which was all the rage now, and subsequently biting off the head of the woman who eventually answered, she got through to Felicity and heard her say, 'Felicity Hughes here.'

For a split second Samantha was tongue-tied, as she always was in Felicity's presence. What could she say to this woman? This clever woman who edited books, was married to her ex-husband and who, according to Venetia's letters, was making a much better job of bringing up her children than she had ever done. But her need was greater than her nervousness, and she recovered herself and said breathlessly, 'Can we meet somewhere? Anywhere, you choose.'

On hearing the breathy, little girlish voice, Felicity experienced the familiar pang of envy and jealousy. She knew the jealousy was ridiculous, but knowing didn't help. She would never stop being jealous of the time Samantha had spent with Tony before she knew him. Because of her she would always be the second wife. And the envy – Felicity glanced at herself in the small mirror on the other side of her office – there was no point in that either. Nature had never intended her to be an elegant clothes-horse, but that didn't stop her wishing that she were.

'Meet?' she said. 'Well, yes, if you wish. How about some time next week? I take it that you're in London?'

'Yes, but I can't wait that long.'

'But . . .' Felicity was about to protest that she was busy, and only in London for one night a week.

'Please,' said Samantha. The anxiety in her voice reached Felicity.

'I could manage this evening,' she said reluctantly, thinking of all the other things she had planned to catch up with.

'Thank you.' The perfect garden became blurred and untidily out of focus as tears filled Samantha's eyes, although why she was crying she wasn't sure. After all, she *was* going to do as she wanted. Wasn't she? Felicity would approve. Of everything. She *had* to. 'Where shall we meet?'

'Vincenzo's, at eight o'clock. We both know where that is.' It was the place they'd had lunch when Samantha had told Felicity she was leaving the children behind for a year.

Samantha swallowed hard; she mustn't let Felicity know she was crying. She'd despise her. 'Yes, eight o'clock,' she said huskily.

Felicity put the phone down slowly, irritated by and yet wishing she could cultivate a low, sexy-sounding voice like Samantha's instead of her own briskly efficient one. Then she dismissed the idea as ridiculous. She was stuck with her own voice, just as she was stuck with everything else. But the call had disturbed her; she couldn't concentrate and stared with unseeing eyes at the pile of typewritten pages on her desk. What catastrophe was about to land in her lap now? Samantha wouldn't have rung unless it was something important. Why was life such a roller-coaster? Why couldn't it continue on a smooth and even path? But, on reflection, she realized that nothing had been smooth and even since she'd married Tony. *It's not easy being a second wife.* She remembered her mother's words. It was true, she thought, feeling cross. All their problems stemmed from Tony's first marriage.

Suddenly she felt sick again, and remembered that she'd had nothing to eat or drink since she'd left Oakford that morning. She buzzed down to the post room and asked if someone could bring her up a coffee and a biscuit, and waited for the nausea to pass.

A knock on the door and Joan Shrimpton entered. 'I was down there getting my own coffee,' she said, 'so I brought yours as well.' She stopped, put the tray down on the desk and leaned forward like a small, beady-eyed bird. 'Oh, dear,' she said, 'I wondered why you buzzed down for coffee instead of coming to collect it. You do look pale. Are you all right?'

'A bit off-colour. A tummy bug, I think.' Felicity took the coffee and sipped it gratefully. She eyed the tray; the biscuits were chocolate creams, and the mere sight of them made her feel sick. 'I think I'll give them a miss –' she indicated the biscuits '– they look a bit rich.'

Miss Shrimpton darted outside and came back in a instant carrying a packet of cream crackers. 'Here, have some of these,' she said, then added timidly, 'You're not . . .' she hesitated, blushed bright pink, swallowed hard and said in a rush, 'You're not expecting a baby, are you?'

'No, I am not,' said Felicity loudly, then immediately felt sorry when Joan took a nervous step backwards.

'Sorry, Joan, didn't mean to bite your head off. But I'm not, I'm just overworked and a little under the weather.'

'Yes. Of course,' said Miss Shrimpton, and beat a hasty retreat.

Left on her own, Felicity bit viciously into a dry biscuit. Everyone had one-track minds. Just because she was married, it didn't mean she was pregnant. She certainly was not. Why, only last week she'd had a period. It had arrived on the dot, as usual. She ate another biscuit and the nausea began to recede. Hunger, a bug, something, anything, but not pregnancy was causing her to feel ghastly. But whatever it was, it was very inconvenient.

Pulling the typewritten pages towards her, she began to read, and in no time at all she was soon immersed in another world. The world of fiction, where everything could be manipulated towards the end the writer wanted to achieve. Where everything was under control. Unlike the real world.

CHAPTER 14

While Felicity was meeting Samantha in London, Tony found himself in the role of father confessor and advisor to Tracy and Sam. They had turned up on the kitchen doorstep of Cherry Trees, Tracy looking hot and bothered and Sam looking slightly mulish but determined. 'I want your advice, please, Tony,' said Tracy. 'And I want Sam to listen.'

But Sam wasn't in a listening mood, more of a talking one. 'Well, you see. It's like this,' he said. 'I want to take responsibility for Tracy and Jacob. After all, I am his father.'

'Haven't you left it a little late?' said Tony mildly. He could see that Tracy was not over-enthusiastic about the idea. 'And how are you going to take responsibility, as you put it? You haven't got a job, have you?'

'Exactly right. On both counts,' said Tracy. 'I've told him that I can manage without him. Anyway,' she added defensively, 'I don't know why he's so worried. He doesn't know for sure that he is Jacob's father.'

'Well, who else were you sleeping with? Were you

273

two-timing me?' Sam stood up and looked as if he was about to hit Tracy.

Tony jumped out of his seat and pushed Sam back down into his. 'We'll open a bottle of wine and discuss this in a civilized manner,' he said. He got a good bottle of Chianti from the cupboard they called their cellar. For a moment he looked ruefully at the label; a Montepulciano, a bottle which he'd been saving for a himself and Felicity when they were on their own. But now, he decided, was a more pressing need. He opened the bottle; pity there wasn't more time to let it breathe, but hopefully the wine would mellow them both. There was nothing so calming as discussing matters over a bottle of wine while nibbling something savoury. He got out a tin containing biscuits which Tracy had cooked that very morning.

The three of them sat round the kitchen table in Cherry Trees, eating biscuits and sipping the strong red wine. Sam ate one biscuit and took another. 'These are good,' he said. 'I've never tasted anything like it before.'

Tracy preened slightly. 'I made them,' she said. 'Very easy; I put pesto and sundried tomatoes on the tops.'

'Yes, Tracy could easily earn her living as a cook,' said Tony. 'She has natural flair. Which brings us back to the subject of work. How do you propose to earn money, Sam?'

Sam looked suddenly stubborn. 'I'm not so sure that I *do* want to support her and Jacob,' he said sullenly. 'Not if I'm not the father.'

Like everyone else, Tony was absolutely certain that Sam was Jacob's father, but it was something Tracy had to admit herself. He leaned across towards her, his expression serious. 'Were you sleeping with anyone else when you and Sam were together?' he asked quietly. 'I think you owe it to Sam to be absolutely honest.'

Tracy stopped looking defensive and looked down into her glass. In a split-second she changed from an aggressive punk young woman into a vulnerable girl. 'No,' she said at last in a small, quiet voice. 'I wasn't, and I haven't. I've never slept with anyone except Sam.'

Sam heaved a sigh of relief. 'And I've never slept with anyone except you,' he said.

Tony looked from one to the other. Two young people with everything to gain and nothing to lose by putting their lives in order. He refilled their glasses. 'Look,' he said gently, 'I'm not going to tell you what I think you ought to do. But I am going to tell you both to think long and hard before you accept or reject any options. Ask yourself the following questions. Are you fond of each other? Do you want the best for Jacob? Are you willing to compromise? And last of all,' he turned to Sam, 'are you willing to give up the footloose life and settle down to work?' He shrugged his shoulders and grinned at them both. 'At the risk of sounding an old fashioned fuddy-duddy I'd say that if you don't work you don't have any money, and if you don't have any money, life can be very difficult. Believe me, nobody needs a lot of money to be happy, but you *do* need enough.' And nobody knows that better than me, he thought, watching their faces.

Sam spoke first. 'I've got myself lined up to start a gardening business,' he said. 'Mum and Dad aren't keen, because it's not using my degree. But to tell you the truth I've never really been an academic. I only went to university to please Dad. The exams were murder; I'm not a natural scholar.'

'Gardening is all right, as long as you're fit,' said Tony, hating himself for having to pour cold water on Sam's idea, but knowing he had to point out the pitfalls. 'But if for any reason you can't work, then you've got no income.'

'The sensible thing to do would be to run a gardening agency,' said Tracy. 'Employ other people on a part-time basis, spread your net far and wide. That way it wouldn't matter if you couldn't do the physical work yourself, because you could always do the administration.'

Sam looked at her. 'I'd need a good organizer,' he said, 'to sort me out.'

'You're looking at one,' said Tracy.

Tony opened another bottle of wine. One by one the children popped their heads through the kitchen door to say goodnight, and still the three of them were closeted together, by now poring over sheets of paper with calculations scribbled everywhere.

When they eventually left Tony could hear Tracy expounding on her idea to have not only a gardening agency, but also a home cooking agency as well. The plan was that she would fill people's freezers with her home cooking which they could then pass off as their own. He stood at the kitchen door as their figures faded away into the darkness of the autumn night. There was a chill nip in the air, and the ground was crisp underfoot with a hint of a frost to come, but Tony had a warm glow inside. Of course, it was early days yet, but he had high hopes that Sam and Tracy would sort themselves out, and that the outcome would be a happy ending. He almost hugged himself with glee. He couldn't wait to tell Felicity.

'Well, dear. Do tell. What on earth was this assignation with Samantha all about?' Irene sat in her comfortable old armchair, feet up on a stool, the ever-present schooner of sherry in her hand, and a half-empty bottle on the tray beside her.

'I thought you'd be in bed.' Felicity dropped wearily into a chair opposite her mother.

'I'm not. I'm waiting.'

'So I see.' Felicity's mind was whirling with thoughts. Some pleasant, some unpleasant, some rather worrying. What she really wanted to do was to sit down quietly and tiptoe around them, sort them out and then decide what to do. Although, even after a brief reflection she realized listlessly that she had little choice. Decision-making was a luxury life had not afforded her recently; her lot seemed to be merely to get on with it.

'Well?' her mother was getting impatient. 'Do I get to hear? Or are you going to keep it a secret? Come on, the suspense is killing me.' She sat up, grunted with the effort, and reached for the sherry bottle. 'I need another drink.'

Felicity smiled. 'That's what will kill you.' She nodded towards the bottle. 'Not suspense.'

'Rubbish. It's terribly weak, and anyway at my age one is entitled to live a little dangerously. There's a good bottle of Chablis in the fridge if you feel in need of a little something yourself.'

Felicity heaved herself from the chair and went through into the kitchen. 'I'm not sure I should tell you anything before I've talked to Tony,' she called back. 'Samantha told me some things in confidence. She used me as her confessor really.'

'And did you absolve her, and send her away feeling better?'

Felicity sat down carefully opposite her mother again and took a slow sip of Chablis, savouring the taste and letting the cool wine trickle down her throat. What should she tell? All or part of it?

'I don't think I made her feel better,' she said. 'I'm hopeless at giving advice, and anyway, she had already made up her mind. I think she just wanted approval. Not mine necessarily, it could have been anyone. I happened to be available.'

'Good heavens,' said Irene. 'You make it sound intriguing.'

'One thing does affect me, and that is she wants Tony and me to have the three children permanently. She and Piers have decided to stay on in the States for the foreseeable future. The children are not part of their plans.'

Irene looked at her daughter curiously. 'How do you feel about that?'

Felicity took another sip of wine. Let her thoughts skitter about and then settle down. 'It may surprise you to hear that I don't actually mind. In fact, if I'm honest, I'm quite glad. For several reasons. One of them, of course, is Tony. There's no doubt he adores his children and loves having them around, and I'd think much less of him if he didn't. It's natural to have affection for one's children.'

'And the other reasons?' asked her mother quietly, but with, Felicity thought, an approving note to her voice.

'For the children's sake as well. I think they will be happier all together and permanently back at Cherry Trees. It must be very unsettling to be shunted around from one home to another, and to live with their mother and Piers, a man who, from everything Samantha has said about him, quite obviously dislikes children.'

'And you?' Irene probed. 'Do you *like* them?'

Felicity was honest. 'Not entirely, but I'm getting to like them, and I know they are beginning to like me. However, I'm not saying that it's easy, or that there haven't been problems, or even that there won't be difficulties ahead.' She thought of the expenses Tony was counting on going away when the children went back to Samantha. *That* was a problem. Her nest-egg wouldn't stand being dipped into too often; the cupboard would soon be bare. But money was not something she could discuss with her mother. That was something she and Tony had to sort out on their own.

She turned to her mother and smiled. 'We'll manage,' she said.

'I'm sure you will,' said Irene, adding comfortably, 'and at least Tony's relatively well-heeled. I mean, he *is* a doctor. You'll never have to worry about money.'

Felicity nearly laughed out loud, but managed to bottle it in and gave nothing more away than a wry smile. It was as Tony had said; everyone thought doctors were well off. Although to be honest she had to admit that Tony would be financially secure if he had not had to underpin Samantha's future as well as everyone else's. There was no justice in this world.

'And what were the other things she said?' Irene's voice interrupted her thoughts. 'The "in confidence" things. The things she wanted approval for.'

'She's having a termination.'

'You mean an abortion.'

'Nowadays it's called a termination,' said Felicity.

Irene snorted disapprovingly. 'Only because it sounds tidier. Less offensive. But it's still an abortion whatever it's called. I'm old-fashioned.'

'I know.' Felicity got up and went into the kitchen to get herself another glass of wine. 'That's why I probably shouldn't be telling you this. Promise you won't breathe a word. Not even to Tony.'

'Of course not.' Irene settled herself more comfortably in the armchair and waited for Felicity to return. When she came back she said, 'Well, tell me.'

'Not much to tell really. Samantha is pregnant and doesn't want to be.'

'I assume that Piers,' her mother pulled a face, 'a

280

ridiculous name if ever I heard one, implanted the seed of life.'

Felicity began to laugh. Whatever the situation, her mother could be relied upon either to make her laugh or get angry. 'What a quaint way of putting it.'

'It's the way I taught Annabel.'

Felicity raised her eyebrows. '*You* taught Annabel?'

'Well, somebody had to put her straight after the school made such a frightful mess of it. I didn't want her to go through the rest of her life being anti-sex and anti-men.'

Felicity digested this piece of information, then said, 'So that's why Annabel has become more amenable towards myself and Tony sharing the bedroom. I must say it is a great relief not having her say "Yuk!" every time she passes the bedroom door.' She raised her wine glass. 'Thanks, Mum. You certainly made a better job of it than I did. Although I'm slightly surprised. I've always thought you were inclined to be anti-men yourself.'

'Nonsense. Your father and I were very happy. But now I'm on my own I'm also very happy. But come on, tell me more about Samantha.'

'There's not much to tell,' said Felicity, thinking of her meal with Samantha, and how she'd been struck by a sense of the other woman's vulnerability. There was something unfinished about Samantha, as if she were a beautiful child waiting, just waiting to grow up. Somehow the Samantha she saw didn't fit in with the Samantha she knew. The woman who left her children and husband to live in another country with another man, and who was getting rid of a baby because it was inconvenient. 'No, not much to tell,' she continued, 'except that she's pregnant. And yes, it is Piers', *and* he most certainly doesn't want it, and neither does she. But . . .'

'She's finding it difficult to actually bring herself to get rid of it.'

'Something like that,' said Felicity, remembering how that despite the vulnerability Samantha still had a deep thread of steel running through her. Like a child who'd set her heart on something, she was determined that nothing should stand in the way of what she perceived to be her happiness with Piers. 'She's made up her mind, and yet she still needed approval. I suppose you're right about the absolution bit. That was what she wanted me to give. Absolution.'

'And did you?'

Felicity was silent for a moment, then said slowly, 'How could I, when I'm not sure that I approve of terminations merely because the arrival of a baby is inopportune?' She stopped, then said, 'Although perhaps in Samantha's case it is a good idea. She has already abandoned three children; no point in bringing another child in the world to abandon sooner or later.'

'So what *did* you say?'

'I said that everyone is different. That she must do what she thinks is right for her. I didn't go into details, there seemed no point. She seemed satisfied with my reply, and is going into the clinic tomorrow. She wants the children to stay with her at the St John's Wood house next weekend, before they go back to school.'

'So that she can tell them that she doesn't intend to see them again, I suppose,' Irene muttered.

'No,' said Felicity sharply. 'I've told her *not* to say anything. I'm sure that Tony will agree with me when I see him tomorrow. I think that it will be much better all round not to drop that piece of information like a bombshell. They're bound to be upset at first, so it's better that they're introduced to the idea gradually. They must never think never as far as their mother is concerned. It would be too cruel.'

Irene put the empty sherry glass back on the sideboard with a loud clink. 'You aren't by any chance leaving yourself an escape route, are you, should things go disastrously wrong?'

Felicity bristled, but it was a weary bristle. The thought had crossed her mind, true. But at the same time she knew it was hopeless. No matter what happened, Samantha had no intention of *ever* having them back. From now on she was mother to one and stepmother of three. 'No, that is *not* the reason, and it's very unfair of you to even suggest it. I do genuinely care that the children are not hurt any more than necessary. It must be terrible to be a child and know your mother doesn't want you. And quite apart from that, I don't honestly think they'd believe it. Despite everything; they're intensely loyal towards Samantha.'

And I am jealous. But of course Felicity only thought that, she didn't tell her mother. It was an emotion of which she was ashamed. But try as she might she could not expunge it. Sometimes she wondered vaguely if moving might be the answer, as the ghost of Samantha *did* still haunt Cherry Trees just as her mother had forecast. There was no escaping old books with her name on, tidy piles of linen she'd left in cupboards – easily distinguishable from Felicity's piles, which were anything but tidy – lists of things to do ticked off but still to be found in the drawers of the Welsh dresser.

Whenever Felicity found one she tore it up in a rage, usually because the things on it which had been neatly ticked were all the things she ought to have done but had not.

'Tony doesn't think about her, you know.' Irene Hobbit looked quizzically at her daughter.

Felicity drained her wine glass and pulled a face. There was no fooling her mother. She knew her weaknesses and skewered them with deadly accuracy.

'He has to sometimes,' she said. 'Even if it is just for financial reasons.' Then without meaning to she said, 'Samantha left him very poor.'

'Oh.' Irene took a moment to digest this, then said, 'So you're not well off.'

'The understatement of the year,' replied Felicity.

'Huh!' Her mother snorted. 'Samantha is the type of woman who will leave any man poor. But Piers, I think, is probably a different cup of tea. Samantha has probably got the right man. They suit each other well. A couple of cold fish, the pair of them. Although whether or not that relationship will last is anybody's guess. Personally, from what Venetia's told me, I think not.'

Felicity smiled. 'Strange. Samantha more or less said the same thing.'

'But money or not, you and Tony are happy. Aren't you?'

Felicity got up and collected her mother's sherry glass and took it together with her own into the kitchen. 'Yes, we *are* happy. So don't start worrying. And as for money, we'll manage. We're not exactly on the breadline.'

Irene suddenly looked serious. 'But what would you do?' she asked. 'What would *you* do if you became pregnant?'

Felicity sighed. She felt exhausted. It had been a long, long day at the office, the whole morning spent on the phone with an over-excited author, who couldn't believe the advance she was offering, but who also couldn't believe that she actually wanted some editorial changes to his precious manuscript. It had got to the point when she'd felt like slamming down the phone and telling him that, good though his book was, he was not in the Booker league and never likely to be. But she'd bitten her tongue, tried the softly, softly approach, and it had eventually worked. The rest of the day had been beset with problems, deadlines not met by authors, covers wrong, printers behind with the schedules, and then to cap it all dinner with a jittery, neurotic Samantha. The whole day had left her feeling totally drained. Now she was tired and wanted to sleep, and the last thing she needed to be bothered with was hypothetical questions. Yawning loudly, she said, 'Goodnight, Mum. See you in the morning.'

'You won't. I shall be gone long before you're up. I'm doing the stall in Brick Lane myself tomorrow, and

I've got to start setting it up by seven o'clock. So I want you to answer me now. What *would* you do?'

Felicity took a deep breath, and gave her mother a tired impatient smile. 'Getting pregnant is not part of my plan,' she said. 'Nor Tony's. We both agree that four children between us is quite enough.'

'Very sensible,' said her mother. But Felicity thought she sounded a little disappointed.

Venetia regarded the three children, overflowing with exuberant youthfulness until her tiny sitting room seemed as if it was about to burst asunder, with a mixture of affection, exasperation, and most of all an overwhelming feeling of helplessness. Was it because she was at the opposite end of life's spectrum to them that she found them exhausting?

Samantha stood behind them, smiling in an anxious and yet determined way, and Venetia felt a surge of irritation. She thinks I don't know she wants to offload them on to me for the day, she thought crossly.

'So why have you all descended on me without notice?' she asked, determined not to make it easy.

'I didn't realize that you needed or wanted notice,' said Samantha. 'I thought you'd be pleased to see them.'

'At my age I need notice of everything,' snapped Venetia. 'Gone are the days when I could knock up a meal in five minutes like I used to. They'll be lucky to get a microwaved potato; there's not much in the fridge.'

'We've come to see *you*,' said Philip with a wide grin.

He had his barometer baseball hat on back to front, and Venetia supposed she should be grateful for small mercies. From past experience she dreaded the days when it was facing the right way round.

'Mum is going shopping,' said Hilary.

'I didn't want to leave them behind in Piers's house in case they messed it up. I've only got a cleaner coming in once a week.' Samantha looked pointedly at her watch. She had a hair appointment at eleven. She was surprised and hurt at Venetia's reaction. For someone who was always grumbling that she didn't get to see the children often enough, her attitude today was very strange. Why was she objecting? Why was she saying she couldn't cope? She always had done in the past. Venetia was one of life's copers, unlike me, thought Samantha, who was still feeling slightly weak from the termination and longing to confess it to Venetia but not daring to. She looked more closely at Venetia, but her eyes did not see a tired old woman. She saw the same organizing, dominating Venetia of her childhood. The woman she'd always been a little afraid of, but whom she'd always admired for her sheer guts.

'So you've brought them to mess up mine,' said Venetia grumpily. 'And I haven't got a cleaner at all,' she added for good measure.

'Oh, Gran,' said Peter. 'Don't be bad-tempered. We don't see you very often nowadays.'

Venetia relented. Peter was her favourite, and she thought perhaps he looked a little peaky. As if he'd been crying. She held out her hand and took his and looked carefully at all three. They looked well, she decided, and the three of them had lost their previous podgy look. As well as being slimmer, she was pleased to see they all were tanned a nice nut-brown colour. Life back at Cherry Trees with Felicity and Tony was obviously suiting them. But there was something else, a polite sort of self-containment. A kind of loneliness, and now she looked more closely she thought that Peter had not been the only who'd been crying. Their clothes were shabby, and Hilary's skirt, where she'd shot up during the summer, now scraped her behind in what Venetia considered a most unseemly way.

'Sorry,' she said. 'But when one gets to eighty-seven and a bit one is allowed to be bad-tempered sometimes. I have my bad-tempered days.'

Peter smiled sadly. 'Could you have it another day when we're not here?' he asked seriously.

Venetia promised she would try. 'I thought you'd like to see them, Venetia.' Samantha hovered by the doorway. 'They're not up in London very often now.'

'That is because *you* are in America,' Venetia replied sharply.

Philip quite suddenly switched the baseball cap on his head round to face the right way, and both Venetia and Samantha's hearts sank. 'And *that*,' he said loudly, 'is where she's going to be *all* the time from now, isn't it, Mum?'

Venetia jerked her head towards Samantha, who looked very uncomfortable. She had not followed Felicity's advice and had decided to tell the children.

'Not *all* the time,' she said. She edged nearer to the

door without meeting Venetia's eyes. 'I've just explained to them that I'm not coming back permanently to the UK and that Piers and I can't possibly have them with us in the States.'

'She's ditching us,' said Hilary.

'No, no, I'm not. I've already explained it once, Venetia. I shall be coming back regularly, and I shall have them with me. But it's just not possible to have them all the time.'

'Anything is possible if you want it,' said Venetia.

Samantha rounded on her. 'How can you say that? You know it's not true. And anyway, you told me yourself that you thought they'd be better back at Cherry Trees with Tony and Felicity. A more stable relationship, I think you said.'

'True,' Venetia snapped back. 'But that wasn't giving you carte blanche to throw the towel in.'

'I . . . oh, you are impossible.' She turned and rushed to the door. 'I'll collect them after supper.'

Venetia and the three children watched her hurry towards the narrow front door at the end of the long thin hall. So she's not hearing what she doesn't want to hear, as usual, thought Venetia. She knew she shouldn't have been surprised or disappointed, but she was, and felt too that Samantha's failure as a mother was partly her failure as well. 'Why the rush?' she said.

'I'm going to the hairdressers at eleven, and then I'm going to Bond Street. There's a new boutique opened there which I'm doing an article on. All designer clothes. I shall probably buy some.'

'Your children could do with some new clothes.' Venetia followed her to the door.

'Venetia! Designer clothes are different,' Samantha said irritably. Hurrying through the door she nearly fell over a pot of dead geraniums standing outside on the step. 'Why don't you move this thing?'

'Because I'm old and tired and because I can't afford to have people in to help me.'

Samantha paused, conscience pricking her. She never asked about Venetia's finances, partly because she didn't want the worry of knowing if she was short of money, and partly because she was pretty certain Venetia would never tell her anyway. Thoughts, the guilty, unpleasant, worrying kind that threatened to push her into doing something positive to find out, were quickly squashed. Venetia could manage. She always had. But the feeling lingered and she made a suggestion. 'What about the social services? I believe they provide home helps at very reasonable prices.'

'How dare you suggest I take charity?' growled Venetia, her small frame jerking upright with indignation. 'I *give* charity, I don't take it.'

'I didn't mean . . . I only meant . . .' Samantha petered out before Venetia's fierce stare.

'Let's get back to clothes,' snapped Venetia. 'You tell me you are looking at designer clothes when your own children *need* new ones. Why don't you use the money for them?'

'Because it's money that Piers has given me,' said Samantha glad to be on what she thought was safer ground. 'He wouldn't like it if I spent it on the children. After all, they're not his responsibility.'

'No, they're yours.' Suddenly all the anger drained out of Venetia. She longed to shake some sense into Samantha, make her see where her own responsibilities lay, but realized regretfully that it was something that she should have done years ago when she was a child. Now it was too late, and anyway she didn't have the energy.

'I'm having an early dinner with the editor of the magazine Piers used to edit in London, but you needn't worry about cooking anything for the children this evening,' Samantha was saying. 'I've given Philip some money. You can send them out for a take-away. I noticed there's a Kentucky Fried Chicken place near the tube, or there's a McDonald's further along the road.'

'Ugh!' Philip had followed them into the hall and up to the front door. 'Why do you always try and fill us up with rubbish?'

'But you've always liked chicken, chips and hamburgers.' Samantha was amazed that he hadn't jumped at the idea of Kentucky Fried.

'Only because you always gave them to us,' said Philip, his voice suddenly very clear and piercing and making Samantha feel uncomfortable. 'You stuffed us full of high-fat rubbish because it was easy, then you went out with Piers and ate properly at posh restaurants.'

Samantha took a step backwards and nearly fell over the geranium pot again. She opened, then closed her mouth, because for the moment she could think of nothing to say, and glared at Philip. Naughty and difficult children were one thing, but having the truth flung at her was quite another. She didn't like it.

Venetia smiled grimly. 'Out of the mouth of babes and sucklings,' she quoted.

Samantha's short supply of patience ran out. She couldn't wait to get away. Away from difficult, too perceptive children, and away from Venetia who, in her opinion, was being particularly difficult today. 'Give them whatever they want to eat,' she said, mentally dumping the whole burdensome lot. She flung the words over her shoulder as she hurried down the ribbon of concrete which led through Venetia's tiny front garden to the gate. 'I just haven't got time to waste in arguing now.'

Leroy was sitting on the wall in front of his house as usual, wearing the ever-present multi-coloured knitted hat. 'Hey, man,' he called as Samantha swooped past him on her way to the tube. 'Why the hurry? Life aint goin' to run away. There's no need to rush, man. No need at all.'

Samantha didn't answer. Leroy merely served to increase her irritation, and besides he reminded her uncomfortably of the not-so-distant past, something she was determined to put firmly behind her. One never saw a black face where she and Piers lived now, apart from the maids and the chauffeur. But they were servants, not neighbours. She decided she hated everything about Notting Hill and wished Venetia wouldn't continue to live amongst such a hotchpotch

of people. She couldn't possibly bring Piers here.
Piers didn't like blacks, as he called them. He didn't
believe in mincing his words where that sort of thing
was concerned and was proud *not* to be politically
correct. She knew what he would say about Venetia's
house in what the council said was officially a multi-
cultural area. He would say that was PC-speak for a
slum. And in this case it was true.

Philip ran down the path and joined Leroy on the
wall. He sat swinging his legs and didn't wave as
Samantha looked back on turning the corner. As soon
as she was out of sight he heaved a sigh and turned his
baseball cap back to front. 'I was rude to Mum,' he told
Leroy.

'Man!' Leroy shook his dreadlocks so that they
danced a wild dance beneath his knitted hat. 'You
shouldn't do a thing like that. A mother is a woman
to be cherished. Yes, sir! Cherished.'

'Not mine,' said Philip. He sighed heavily, and
scuffed the back of his heels along the wall, idly
watching the ancient cement pointing fall out. Then
he scraped it into a little heap with his feet. 'Do you
know what?' he said.

Leroy waited and fished out a packet of cigarette
papers and a pouch of tobacco from his jacket. He
looked at Philip, waiting for him to continue, and
when he didn't said, 'What, man. What?'

'Sometimes,' said Philip, very slowly, 'I think I
prefer my stepmother to my own *real* mother. Do
you think that's bad?'

Leroy laughed, a squeaky giggle of a laugh. 'There

you are, then. You got a woman you can cherish. Stepmother, mother! It make no difference. You got someone you like, who is kind to you. That the main thing.'

Philip hunched his shoulders thoughtfully and looked at Leroy. 'Why can't everyone be like you?' he said. 'Always happy. Never bothered about anything.'

Peter came down the path and joined them, waiting while Leroy moved over on the wall and made room for him. Leroy leaned forward and solemnly wagged a finger at both boys. 'Cause they don't know the secret, man.'

'What secret?' asked Peter.

'The secret of life, man,' said Leroy, carefully measuring out a pinch of straggly tobacco. 'The secret of life.'

'What is the secret?' said Philip.

'Have no hassle in your life. Just take it all as it come, and make the best of it. That way you is never disappointed.'

Peter looked at Philip, slightly disappointed. He'd been hoping for a grand revelation he could put to some practical use. 'That means you never have any ambition,' he said.

'Ambition!' Leroy laughed squeakily again and lit up his cigarette. The boys waited while he took a long slow draw, and then let the smoke slowly drift out of his mouth. 'Man,' he said eventually, 'you get ambition, you got an ulcer. Me, I got no ambition, and I'm a healthy man. Don't never see the doctor. Don't never need to. I love everybody, everybody love me.'

Peter doubted it was as simple as that. He *had* ambitions and was sure that if he could achieve them he'd be happy. Philip was a bit dubious too. 'I'm not sure that life is that easy, Leroy,' he said.

''Tis for me,' grinned Leroy.

'Leroy.' Venetia called from the doorway. 'Don't forget my wheelie bin. The dustmen come this afternoon.'

Leroy jumped off the wall and, turning, bowed towards Venetia, pulling his black plaited hair in a mock salute. 'Lady England,' he said, 'do I ever forget your bin?'

'Yes. You forgot it last week. Veronica came and did it for me.'

Leroy giggled unrepentantly and nudged Philip. 'She is speakin' the truth. But I was drunk last week. I forgets everything when I is drunk. But today I'm sober, so let's get the wheelie bin.'

Jumping off the wall, he led the way up the path to where Venetia stood, Philip and Peter following closely behind.

'They're staying to supper,' Venetia said wearily when Leroy was level with her.

Where has my pride and independence gone? she wondered. Why do I feel that everything is such an effort lately? What would I do if I couldn't rely on Leroy and his woman Veronica? Even Portobello Road and Irene's stall no longer held the thrall it once had, and this week she'd made an excuse not to go, and had stayed in just sitting in the chair doing nothing. Nothing at all. She looked at the two boys following

Leroy down the passage towards the back garden and the wretched wheelie bin. I love them, she thought, and yet I can't be bothered. It was all so ridiculous. Writing to all three of them every single week, always feeling she didn't see nearly enough of them these days, but now they were here she felt too tired to do anything about it.

'You tired, Lady?' asked Leroy bringing the bin out through to the front garden. He stopped for a moment and put a long arm around her hunched shoulders.

'Yes,' admitted Venetia. 'I don't know what on earth to cook them for supper.'

Leroy didn't pause for thought but said with an ear-splitting grin, 'No problem, Lady. Why don't you cook them my favourite dish?'

'What's that?' Hilary joined Venetia. She'd always been a little in awe of Leroy with his bright woolly hats, plaited black hair and intrinsic bounciness. But with a momentary flash of insight which sometimes happens in the young, she suddenly realized that Venetia depended on Leroy far more than she would ever have admitted. And she could also see that Leroy was genuinely fond of the woman he mockingly called 'Lady England'.

'It's called sausage jambalaya, man,' said Leroy, including Hilary in his expansive grin.

'Haven't a clue what it is,' Venetia said very grumpily, 'and it sounds very complicated to me.'

'We could do it,' said Philip. 'I'd like to cook something different.'

'Philip is going to be a cook when he leaves school,' Hilary told Venetia.

'That may be so. But I haven't got any sausages for whatever Leroy said.' Venetia looked at the expectant children and felt an immense sadness. She wanted them here and yet she didn't want them. She was letting them down, not loving them enough. But she couldn't help it, she was too weary to help. Then in spite of her weariness she felt a rage boil up. Rage against old age, because it must be that which was making her feel so incapable; and then a rage against her life in general. Never easy, always a struggle, and, apart from her own childhood which was not particularly pleasant, always having children around her. First her own, then her granddaughter and now great-grandchildren. All children were demanding and she had nothing more to give. Over the years she'd been bled dry and now she was an empty husk. All she wanted to do today was to sit down quietly, not fiddle about with soup and sandwiches for lunch and attempt to cook some exotic thing for supper.

Leroy's voice dragged her back to the present and the narrow hallway of her house. 'Don't be awkward, Lady,' he was saying.

'I'm not being awkward. I only keep in what I need. Baked beans, tomatoes, a bit of bread and cheese. I don't need much. And I certainly don't have the ingredients for a . . .'

'Jambalaya?' prompted Leroy.

'We'll go shopping,' said Philip, taking charge. He took a twenty pound note from his pocket. 'Mum gave me this to spend on food.' He waved it at Leroy. 'Will it be enough?'

Leroy practically jumped with glee. 'I'll come with you to Mr Patel's mini-market. He have everything you need there. Then we come back and we make the best jambalaya this side of the Atlantic. A Leroy special.' He gave an exuberant wave of his woolly hat.

Venetia sat in her easy chair by the window and watched them go off down the street. Three blond heads bobbing along side Leroy's rainbow hat. Off they went, past the little houses occupied by the City yuppies with their hanging baskets and wooden tubs outside the front doors, filled with neatly planted red and blue flowers. Past the houses owned by the West Indian and Asian families, easily distinguishable by the brightly coloured doors and windows, mostly painted in fluorescent pinks and yellows. The rest of the houses in the street were owned by elderly residents like herself. Most of them needed painting, the paint peeling off in feathery strips, and many of the sash windows hung crookedly, letting in the London dust and draughts. At least my windows are straight, she thought, looking at her own frames, although she would have loved to have been able to afford to give them a coat of paint. She had dropped hints to Samantha at Christmas-time, but Samantha always gave her expensive perfume, which she rarely used. Venetia sighed. How she would have loved a pot of paint, preferably with a man and a paintbrush attached. But it was too much to hope that Samantha would see what she really needed. Samantha had never been able to see what other people needed, forever immersed in her own needs. My fault, thought Venetia pensively. It must be. I encouraged her to place too much emphasis on material things, to want money, to be successful. And then when she married I didn't encourage her to be successful as a wife and mother, even though I could see she was trying very hard at the beginning. I should have spurred her on to find out about her own children and husband, to develop deeper relationships. I should have told that it's the people in life who matter, not things. But I didn't. I scorned her efforts because they didn't fit in with my ideals. I thought she would see what I meant, but she didn't. She never did and never will. My fault. Somewhere in the past, our lines of communication got hopelessly tangled and we've never been able to get in touch with each other since that day.

Venetia lay back in the chair and pulled a knitted blanket over her knees. Although it was a sunny day, warm for autumn, she felt cold. A slow, bone-numbing coldness which made her feel even more tired.

I am so tired. Thoughts blundered like heavy moths through her head. The past and present all jumbled together. All this heart-searching is wearing me out, but it's too late now. Too late to change anything. She closed her eyes. The light from the window filtered through her eyelids, pink at first, then gradually darkening. Too late. The thought came from somewhere far away. Too late.

CHAPTER 15

The day of Venetia's funeral crept in on a bank of dank, grey drizzle. Felicity knew this because she'd been awake for hours and had seen the dawn reluctantly struggling to shake off the shades of night. The miserable dull light now spilling through the open curtains and filling the bedroom matched her mood perfectly. Venetia might not have been her relative, but now she knew she was never going to see her again Felicity was conscious of an empty space where once she had been. More than that, it reminded her of her own mother's mortality, and a sudden deepening gloom swept over her at the thought of what life would be like without her mother to complain to or quarrel with.

Beside her Tony lay still, dead asleep. She slid out of bed silently, not wanting to disturb him until it was absolutely necessary. He'd been on duty all night and had had numerous patients to visit in the small hours. Now he was exhausted. Tenderly, Felicity pulled the duvet cover back over his bare shoulder; a pity he'd had to be on duty last night of all nights, but it was the only way he could get a day off for Venetia's funeral at such short notice.

Once out of the bedroom she padded downstairs in her bare feet to be greeted by much tail-thumping from Prudence, who then demanded to be let out into the garden. There was also much mewing and rushing about from Aphrodite and her kittens, who all thought breakfast should be served immediately. Felicity shooed the cats outside after giving them a few dry biscuits, let Prudence back in, and made herself a cafetière of coffee. She sat at the table taking cautious sips – her wretched stomach was still playing up and she could never be certain these days whether or not what she swallowed would stay down – and thought about Venetia.

She wished that she had invited her down to Cherry Trees more often. She had told Tony this, and Tony had said he couldn't understand why she was tussling with her conscience on that score. She had nothing to reproach herself for. After all, Venetia was Samantha's relative, not hers. But Felicity still wished it, and blamed herself for not appreciating that Venetia was old and ill. She had noticed her frailty that last time she'd come to visit, but once Venetia had been put on the train for London she had forgotten all about it. She should have realized, they all should have done, that at eighty-seven Venetia's days were drawing to a close. The children ought to have seen as much of her as possible in the time she'd had left, and there was no one but her to arrange such things. True, she was the children's stepmother and it was Samantha's responsibility really. But Samantha hadn't been in England to be able to do it. And mother or stepmother, it made no difference. The mothers of this world were the people who did the arranging, and she should have done something, but had not. She wondered what Samantha was thinking now. How was *her* conscience?

Then, without wanting to but unable to avoid it, her mind went back to the traumatic day just a week ago when the children, in London for the day, had come back from shopping to find Venetia dead in her armchair. Samantha had seemed quite unable to cope. It had been left to Felicity, who'd driven up to London as soon as she'd received the news, to try and do what comforting was possible. Annabel had come along with her. At first Felicity had tried to put her off, but she had insisted, and once they'd reached the little house in Notting Hill Felicity was glad that she had come. Annabel arrived with the uncomplicated mind of youth and viewed things as a friend not a relative. She had liked Venetia but because she wasn't related she had no hang-ups, no guilt, nothing to be sorry for other than the fact that a rather nice old lady was no more.

'Why couldn't she have died in hospital like everyone else?' Hilary had sobbed hysterically.

'Not everyone dies in hospital. Your father visits lots of people who die in their own homes.' Annabel was kind but very matter-of-fact. She surprised Felicity with her mature composure. 'And Venetia was *very* old,' she added.

Philip and Peter were not hysterical but were very subdued. Samantha was even more subdued, and, in

Felicity's opinion, looked positively ill. Although she was as elegantly dressed as usual Felicity noticed she had a strange, unhealthy pallor; beneath her make-up she was as pale as death. Felicity asked if she was all right.

'Yes,' said Samantha, adding so that only Felicity could hear, 'I'm just feeling very, very tired. I expect it's because I've only recently been in the clinic, don't you?'

'Probably,' said Felicity, who was feeling very tired herself and slightly nauseous from an empty feeling in her stomach. She couldn't go for long these days without having something to nibble. 'I'm going to make some sandwiches, I'm ravenous, and you look as if you could do with something yourself.'

The sandwiches, cheese and tomato, the only thing Felicity could find in the fridge, were eaten in the kitchen. As soon as she had eaten something Felicity felt better again and perked up immediately, but Samantha, although she appeared to have quite a hearty appetite and ate at least three substantial sandwiches and drank two cups of coffee, looked as ghastly when she'd finished as when she'd begun. Shock, Felicity decided. It must be. Shock and a guilty conscience.

'I was going back to the States the day after tomorrow,' said Samantha in a quavery voice. 'But now I'll have to stay for the funeral. I've phoned Piers and told him. He wasn't very happy.'

'You needn't stay if you don't want to,' said Philip, his young voice high with angry hostility.

'Philip!' said Felicity sharply. She looked across

uncomfortably at Samantha, but she seemed serenely unembarrassed, as if she hadn't heard. 'There's nothing more I can do here now,' she said. 'So I think I'd better take everyone back to Hampshire. Out of your way.'

'Yes.'

Felicity looked about the tiny little kitchen. It was filled with Venetia's bits and pieces, as if she had just popped out and would soon be back to deal with everything. There were reminders scribbled on pieces of paper stuck on a hook on the dresser, a bag of sweets and small, sealed brown envelopes marked 'Milkman', 'Newsagent', 'Electricity' and 'Gas'. Felicity could see that Venetia was meticulous with her money, the way that the elderly often were, and knew down to the last penny what she owed and to whom. A world away from her own chaotic method of housekeeping. She looked back at Samantha. 'Are you sure you'll be all right?'

'I expect so.'

Samantha seemed so vague that Felicity felt uneasy. Was she all right to be left alone? She hustled the children off to collect their things with instructions to put *everything* in the Land Rover. 'I put you in charge,' she told Annabel. 'Make certain they leave nothing behind.'

'Don't worry, Mum, I will,' she said, pleased to be put in command. She collected the other three children to her like a mother hen gathering together her chicks.

Felicity turned back to Samantha. 'What about the funeral? Is there anything I can do to help with the arrangements?'

Samantha shook her head, and drew out a long, slim brown envelope from her handbag. 'It's all here,' she said. 'I found it in the dresser. Top drawer. Detailed arrangements. Even down to the caterers. Venetia left nothing to chance.' There was silence for a moment, and then she said bitterly, 'I suppose she didn't trust me to do it properly, or thought I wouldn't bother, because she stipulates that I am not to be involved. She has left instructions for her solicitors to do it.'

Felicity found herself reaching out a tentative hand towards Samantha. She could sense the encroaching feeling of desolation in the other woman, and vaguely wanted to comfort her and searched for appropriate words. 'I'm sure it's only because she knew how busy you are,' she said at last. 'She wanted to spare you all the extra work.'

'She never really liked me,' said Samantha. 'We could never talk to each other and be absolutely honest. My children don't like me much either; same problem, I can't talk to them, can't reach them. And sometimes I think even Piers has got tired of me. I'm sure he's seeing someone else.' She stopped and put her hand over her mouth. 'Oh, dear, I didn't mean to tell you that. It's probably my imagination.'

'You're overwrought,' said Felicity hastily, worried at the direction the conversation was taking and not wanting to get involved with any more of Samantha's problems. 'Go back to St John's Wood and take a sleeping pill tonight. Get a good night's rest. It will all seem better in the morning.' Not the most comforting of suggestions but the only one she could think of.

Felicity told Tony about Samantha's comments concerning Venetia and the children later that evening when they were alone, although she kept silent where Piers's real or imaginary infidelity was concerned.

'Perhaps she's being honest with herself for the first time in her life,' he said slowly. 'Now I come to think of it, I suppose I could never talk to her properly either. In a way I feel sorry for her.' He looked swiftly at Felicity. 'You don't mind me saying that, do you? You're not jealous?'

Felicity thought of the Samantha-inspired shards of jealousy which had regularly fragmented her life with Tony and suddenly realized that they were no longer so sharply defined. 'I think I feel sorry for her too,' she said. It was a revelation, and one which left her feeling contented with her own lot. Not smug, she told herself, I mustn't be that. But I'm pleased I'm me, even if I am the second wife. That fact, ridiculous though it was, still jarred, but then, she supposed it probably always would.

Now, on the morning of Venetia's funeral, she could hear the cats scratching, a synchronized chorus, at the kitchen door, and by her side Prudence's soulful brown eyes were beseechingly saying, breakfast, breakfast. She finished the coffee and looked at her watch. Just time to feed the animals before raising the rest of the family.

She heard Tony's mobile phone ring and he came downstairs sleepily clutching it and saying, 'Yes, Nurse Henderson. Yes, I'll come and see her. Yes, now. Yes, I know all about Mrs Merryweather's problems. Now don't you worry, I'll be there in about twenty minutes. No, no problem at all.'

Felicity looked at her watch. 'What do you mean, no problem? It will be a problem if you're late back. Don't forget you've got to pick up the minibus.' They had decided that it would be easier to hire a minibus for the day to transport the whole family and Irene back and forth to the funeral. 'Can't you pass this patient on to whoever's next on call?'

Tony poured himself the remains of the coffee. 'No,' he said. 'She's my patient. And I ought to be there for her. But don't worry, I won't be late and I won't forget anything.'

Felicity began the ritual of opening dog and cat food tins, and spooning it into bowls. 'What's wrong with this Mrs Merryweather anyway?'

'Old age,' said Tony looking in the fridge for something quick to eat and finding a piece of cheese which he took. 'Poor old thing is a piece of crumble hanging on to life by her fingernails.' He started to go back up the stairs gnawing on the cheese as he went. 'Nothing I can cure; I think she's tired of this earth and wants to go now, so I'd better be there as she has asked for me.' He blew Felicity a kiss. 'Don't worry, I promise I'll be back in time. Just make sure the kids are ready and make them wear their glad rags. We've got to give Venetia a good send-off.'

The animals fed, and Tony departed for Mrs Merryweather, it was time to arouse the rest of the house. Felicity knocked on doors, eliciting sleepy responses, and then went into the bathroom before the rush started. Once there, she started feeling sick again and sat down on the edge of the bath and worried. Period on time or no, she was reluctantly beginning to wonder about pregnancy herself. Surely not? But, she told herself grimly, it is necessary to face up to the possibility, and the best thing to do is to find out for certain. So the purchase of a pregnancy testing kit was the next item on the agenda. Then what? She would have to tell Tony, of course. But tell him what? The fact of the matter was that either she was pregnant, or there was something rather unpleasant wrong with her. Neither option had her feeling like leaping about with joy. She bent over the lavatory bowl and retched. She couldn't possibly have leapt anywhere at that moment, feeling as wretched as she did.

When she finally came out of the bathroom Peter was waiting outside. 'Do you think Venetia died happy?' he asked in a conversational tone of voice. 'And do you think she wanted to die?' Then he looked very serious. 'And do you know what dying is really like?'

Felicity hung on to the door jamb, gulped and tried to clear her muzzy head. Never had she felt less like answering questions on the deeper meaning of life and death. Why hadn't she read any books on how to answer impossible questions? She wondered if everyone else struggled along in a mist of hopeless incomprehension about life in general, always feeling inadequately prepared. In the past she'd read books on potty-training, sex and drugs, none of which had been particularly useful or relevant, but she hadn't even glimpsed anything about the imponderables of life. This is where God and religion would come in very handy, she reflected, but as she had chosen to have access to neither it was no help. This last week, since Venetia's death, she'd wished that she had thought more seriously about religion. But now was not the moment. And even Tony, who'd been trained in psychology, was useless. If anyone asked a difficult question he always said, 'Ask Felicity. She reads a lot.' As if that somehow made her the fount of all human knowledge. Something Peter obviously thought now, judging by his expectant expression.

Felicity decided that Tony's opinion would be better than nothing. 'Dad back?' she asked hopefully.

Peter shook his head. 'He called while you were in the bathroom.'

Philip joined his brother. 'His exact words were, "The crumble is needing a lot of attention. Tell Mum I'll be some time".'

'Oh, dear,' said Felicity.

Hilary stalked past wrapped in a bath towel. 'Out of the way, everyone,' she said haughtily. 'I want a bath and I'm going to wash my hair.'

'That's all she cares about these days, washing her silly hair,' said Philip, tugging at the towel as she passed.

'Go away, you disgusting little boy,' shrieked Hilary. 'I don't want you looking at my boobs.'

'You haven't got any,' mocked Philip. 'That's why you're covering them up.'

'I have. So there. And you're not seeing them.' A well

aimed kick caught Philip on the back of the shins and he howled.

'Shut up and stop fighting.' Felicity tried to sound authoritative in spite of feeling sick again.

'Yes. What would Venetia say? We ought to have respect.' Bless Peter, he was always so thoughtful.

'What exactly did Dad mean about the crumble needing a lot of attention?' asked Philip.

'I think he means the old lady he has gone to visit is dying,' said Felicity.

Hilary gave an ear-splitting howl, burst into tears, and dived into the bathroom. 'Don't talk about dying,' she sobbed noisily. 'Isn't it bad enough that we're going to Venetia's funeral today, without somebody else dying?'

'I expect someone somewhere is dying every second of the day,' said Peter slowly. 'But until it happens in your own family you don't think about it.'

'I don't suppose Venetia thought about it,' said Philip. 'Not when she sat down in her chair. She was probably only thinking about the supper I was going to cook. She didn't actually *plan* to die.'

'Nobody does plan it,' Felicity said.

'Suicides do,' shouted a tearful Hilary from behind the locked bathroom door. 'Perhaps Venetia committed suicide. It was very sudden.'

'Nonsense.' Felicity was very firm. 'Her death was natural causes. Old age. Her heart just stopped beating and that was that.'

They were back full circle. 'That's what I want to know,' said Peter earnestly. 'Do you think she was happy? Did she want to die like that?'

Felicity remembered Tony's words about Mrs Merryweather being tired of life and said, 'I don't think she minded at all. She was eighty-seven, and that's pretty old. You told me yourselves she was tired. I think that is what it was. She was tired, and she was glad to go to sleep and wake up somewhere else.'

'Where else?' said Philip. 'Why doesn't anyone ever say?'

'They do say.' Felicity could see from his expression that Peter had no doubts on that score, only on Venetia's willingness to leave this earth. 'We go to heaven.'

'I don't believe in heaven,' scoffed Philip. 'It's a made-up place. No one has ever been and come back.'

'That's because it's the celestial abode of immortal beings,' said Peter seriously. 'If you don't believe me, look it up in the dictionary. Once people reach there they don't *want* to come back.'

'How do you *know* if no one alive has ever been there?'

'Brother Tom says,' said Peter, 'that the reason for that is because we always have to make the important journeys on our own. We arrive in this world quite alone and we leave it alone. But there is always someone waiting to meet you either end.'

'Who?' said Philip.

'Your mother is waiting for you when you arrive,' said Felicity with a flash of inspiration, and hoping to put an end to the conversation before it all became hopelessly complicated. She felt out of her depth as it was. 'And God is there when you leave.'

'And all the other immortal beings,' said Peter. 'Don't forget them.'

'Only if you believe. And you,' Philip turned to his brother, 'make heaven sound horribly crowded.' Felicity noticed, not for the first time, that Philip seemed to have the world's share of cynicism on his young shoulders.

'I'm sure Venetia believed, and that now she is happy and at peace,' she said decisively, hoping that she sounded as if she knew what she was talking about. Her own beliefs lay somewhere between the realm of Philip's total cynicism and Peter's unwavering belief. Normally a comfortable area where one believed that if you didn't do anything too awful you were all right. Although what you were all right *for* she had never been very certain. Peter's probing questions had opened up an uncomfortable gap in her unassuming faith, if that was what it could be called, leaving it open to the cold draughts of doubt.

'And she's definitely gone to heaven and is sitting up there right now?' called out Hilary from the bathroom. It sounded as if she had stopped crying, Felicity noted thankfully, and her voice was accompanied by the sound of sloshing water.

'Yes,' said Peter.

'Bollocks!' said Philip.

'And she's happy,' said Felicity loudly, glaring at Philip and making shut-up signs with her eyebrows. There was no point in letting the children know about her own doubts. They'd probably have their own in later life, and have to sort them out as best they could

like everyone else. 'Now, hurry up both of you,' she said
to the boys. 'As Hilary's still in the bathroom, come
down and have breakfast now. Then you can wash and
get ready later. One in the bathroom, the other in the
downstairs cloakroom. We haven't got time to waste.
It's a long way to go to the funeral.'

'She *was* happy waiting for her sausage jambalaya,'
muttered Philip as they clattered down the stairs to the
kitchen. 'But she didn't get it. I bet she's cross about
that. Leroy kept all those sausages and things I bought.'

'Food isn't that important, and you're a stingy
bastard,' said Peter. 'All you ever think about is your
stomach and money.'

'I am *not* a stingy bastard.'

Philip raised his fist to hit Peter and Felicity watching from over the banisters shouted, 'Stop that!' and
Philip guiltily lowered his fist, then looked up and gave
her a seraphic smile.

The nauseous feeling overwhelmed her again, and
Felicity wondered wearily why everything had to be
such a battle.

Hilary came out of the bathroom, her head wrapped
in a towel, another clean towel wrapped around her. Yet
another item to contribute to the mountain of laundry,
thought Felicity wearily. She looked at her. In the space
of a few weeks, and without her really noticing it before,
Hilary had changed from a roly-poly teenager into a
leggy young woman who seemed disturbingly grown-
up. And even more disturbingly, from Felicity's point
of view, like her mother in appearance.

'Ghastly, aren't they? The boys,' Hilary said with an

313

air of 'we are all women together and understand and suffer these things'. 'I'm not surprised my mother walked off into the sunset.'

'She didn't walk off into the sunset. She flew to California,' against her better judgement Felicity heard herself snapping. She felt like adding *and left me with her children to try and sort out,* but didn't. It wasn't Hilary's fault, it wasn't any of their faults, and she must remember that when the going got tough. Like now. Except that it wasn't really tough. It just felt tough because she was feeling so ghastly.

'She went west. Same thing,' said Hilary airily with indisputable logic. Then she gathered the towel around her more tightly and swayed her hips sexily as she walked away down the corridor.

Felicity didn't feel up to arguing and stood watching Hilary walk away. She really had lost a lot of weight very quickly and Felicity felt a quick pang of worry. She tried to remember if Hilary had been starving herself, but no, in fact, if memory served her well she'd been eating quite normally. Certainly just as much as Annabel and the boys. But something had happened, because now her figure was probably better and more slender than Annabel's. Maybe I should try whatever she's doing, thought Felicity. For despite all the vomiting she'd been doing recently she hadn't lost weight. She went back in to the bathroom and looked at herself in the mirror, carefully turning around so that she could view her figure from all angles, and it seemed to her anxious eyes that there was a definite thickening around her waist. 'Oh, please God,' she prayed out loud to the unknown improbable Deity of her non-belief, 'don't let me be pregnant. It would be a disaster. I couldn't cope, and we can't possibly afford a baby.' But there was no time to stand and ponder on either Hilary's weight loss, or her own weight gain. She felt very, very sick and promptly threw up again.

'Back, darling,' Tony called up the stairs. 'You'll be glad to hear that Mrs Merryweather has rallied yet again, and I left her in the tender loving care of Nurse Henderson.'

'Poor old thing,' muttered Felicity, holding her stomach and closing her eyes. She'd met Nurse Henderson, the community nurse, a few times, although once would have been enough. She was large, well-upholstered woman, grey-haired and imposing, and had told Felicity, who fervently believed it, that she stood no nonsense from anyone. If Nurse Henderson had decided that Mrs Merryweather was not to die, then she had no doubt that even the Lord God Almighty would not be able to get his hands on her. 'Poor old thing,' she said again.

'I'm ravenous,' yelled Tony. 'Is breakfast ready?'

'No. I'm having a bath,' Felicity lied, quickly running the water to make it almost true. She *would* have a quick bath, it was sure to make her feel better. 'Get something for yourself. There's not much time.'

Five seconds later a voice floated up the stairs. 'Darling, I can't find the chunky marmalade, and there doesn't seem to be any of my favourite butter.'

'They are both in the usual place,' Felicity called back through gritted teeth, recalling that her mother had always maintained that men were programmed at birth never to know where anything in the house was kept. After nine months of marriage to Tony she was beginning to believe her, and wished that Tracy had been able to come in earlier this morning to help get them off. But immediately reprimanded herself for even thinking it. Poor Tracy, how could she be expected to come in even earlier? She had a baby to tend to. And now, if rumours were to be believed, and it was true that Sam had moved in with her and Jacob, then she had additional work. A man about the house always made work. Anyway, true or not, and Tracy had not said, the fact remained that everyone in Cherry Trees was perfectly capable of doing things for themselves. At least, in theory they were.

'And there's only *thin* sliced bread.'

Why did he make it sound so *important*? Thin bread, thick bread, it was bread, wasn't it? 'Stick two pieces together and put them in the toaster at the same time.'

She heard Tony laugh good-naturedly. 'That's what I love about you, darling. You're so original.'

She heard the door slam and assumed he'd gone back into the kitchen to sort out the thickness of his bread. After sloshing an extravagant amount of bath oil into the water, Felicity sat and looked at her ten pink-varnished toenails sticking up through the scented water at the end of the bath. She wiggled them, and felt better, more cheerful, and definitely less pregnant, she decided. She was being stupid even thinking that because she almost certainly wasn't. Anyone could get a stomach bug which could linger for weeks. She really had to go to the doctor. It was silly to leave it. But no need to mention it to Tony. It would only worry him unnecessarily.

Tony knocked on the bathroom door, interrupting her musing, and then came in. 'Just checking that you hadn't got drowned,' he said, 'and to remind you that we've got to make a start for London and the funeral.'

Felicity sat up. 'Now that you're here you can scrub my back.' Tony obliged briskly with the loofah. 'I wonder what we'll be like when we're old,' she said, thinking of Venetia who'd departed and poor old Mrs Merryweather hanging on to life by her finger-nails.

'Well, for one thing one gets stiff. So it's unlikely that you'll have the luxury of sitting in a bath,' said Tony. 'Not unless we can afford one of those hoists.'

Felicity threw the sponge at him. 'Get out. I don't want to think of creaking limbs and all the other horrible things that go with them.'

'Old age comes to us all.'

'I know. But I want a dignified old age, I want to enjoy myself and then be snuffed out quick, like a candle. Like Venetia. By the way, why didn't you do the decent thing and let your old lady slip away this morning?'

'I'm not God, I can't make the decisions. Besides, the old lady's granddaughter turned up as well as Nurse Henderson, and they breathed new life into her.'

'Poor old thing,' said Felicity again thinking of Nurse Henderson battling with the powers that be.

Tony paused in the bathroom doorway. 'Actually,

317

you know, I came away thinking that the old duck was happier now than she has been for a very long time. When I left, Nurse Henderson was arranging to get her some knitting wool. White and fluffy, if I remember Mrs Merryweather's instructions correctly.' Felicity looked puzzled and Tony grinned happily. 'There's another great-grandchild on the way and now she knows about it Mrs M. has decided to stay around and wait until it's born. Nothing like a new baby to keep things going in families.'

The funeral service was held in an ugly grey stone chapel at the side of the crematorium. To get to it the funeral cars had to drive through the cemetery. A depressing place; serried ranks of soot-grimed, black-ened headstones. Neat tarmac paths ran in between the headstones and not a tree was in sight. Even the few flowers that were there looked cowed, as if they felt their presence an intrusion into this monochrome landscape of the dead. A wizened privet hedge divided the cemetery from the crematorium grounds, and at the back of the crematorium chapel stood a gloomy edifice of black and grey marble. A huge wall into which, if paid for, the names were carved of those who'd been cremated and had their ashes scattered in the rose garden. *The Garden of Remembrance*, said the signpost pointing towards an area which didn't look in the least like a garden. The roses appeared to have almost given up the unequal struggle to survive against pollution and neglect and the ever-encroaching tarmac. The whole place had a desolate air, as if the gardener had also been cremated, and the officials who administered the place were just waiting for the last petal to drop, so they could swoop in and neatly tarmac the garden over as well.

'Those roses aren't doing very well,' said Irene, peering out of the car widow. 'What on earth possessed Venetia to choose this place for her funeral?'

'Nearest place, I suppose,' said Tony. 'She didn't have a church. Never went inside one as far I know.'

'And quite right too,' said Irene.

But Felicity thought she didn't sound quite as vehement or as positive as she usually did. She wondered if her mother was perhaps wishing that Venetia had got the comfort of a God.

At the entrance to the crematorium part of the cemetery they got out of the cars, leaving them in the car park next door to the Garden of Remembrance, and followed the lead car towards the chapel. Venetia's mortal remains lay beneath a mass of flowers in a shiny mahogany coffin. Samantha and the three children walked first, followed by Tony, Felicity, Annabel and Irene.

'Veneer, if ever I saw it,' said Irene with a knowing nod towards the coffin in the hearse. 'Nothing solid about *that*. And I bet Venetia paid for solid wood.'

'I don't suppose she cares now,' said Felicity. It made her sad and yet amused her at the same time to see her mother so incensed over the fact that Venetia might have been cheated.

The hearse stopped at the entrance to the chapel.

'Looks like an extermination hut from a concentration camp,' muttered Irene.

'Gran!' hissed Annabel, who was looking suitably funereal and devout. She was wearing a very long black dress and a black velvet hat with the brim turned backwards. No doubt a bargain she'd snapped up from one of Lymington Market's second-hand stalls.

'Yes, shut up,' said Felicity. But she was right. It did look like that. Grey, forbidding, and dirty. Nothing looked alive, even the weather was grey. She suddenly thought of the churchyard in Oakford and wished Venetia were being buried there. Even on a misty October morning like this morning, colour abounded there. Headstones, tilting at crazy angles, glowed with age old lichen, and the grass was sweet and short, since the vicar had introduced two sheep to keep it down, and there were no tarmacadamed paths, only a moss-covered gravel path with ancient yews dipping their branches in silent homage. There was a different atmosphere altogether. It was a place of quiet repose, a place of sleep, not death. Quite different from this clinical, controlled, soulless place.

The pall-bearers lifted the coffin and they all walked the mandatory measured pace behind it into the chapel. The first sight which met their eyes was Leroy's brightly knitted hat. He was sitting in the front pew, and beside him sat Veronica, his woman, wearing a silk coat covered in lurid purple flowers and an enormous black dustbin lid of a hat.

Samantha gave a sigh. She knew of course that

Leroy and Veronica would come, Venetia had wanted him to, but she couldn't help wishing they had sat at the back and not worn such bright colours. Beside her Hilary snuffled, and searched in vain for a handkerchief. Without looking at her Samantha passed over hers. She too felt near to tears, but for different reasons. Too late now to rebuild bridges between herself and Venetia; any chance of the companionship which had eluded both of them all their lives was now gone for ever. She saw a fleeting image of them both standing in cages of their own making, and even now she knew she was reinforcing the bars of her own cage where the children were concerned. Why? Was it because she was afraid of being found wanting in a loving relationship? Or was it because she now valued the small degree of self-sufficiency she'd achieved beyond everything else? She didn't know. All she did know was that she longed to get away from the disturbing atmosphere of grief around her. It was claustrophobic, threatened to seep too deeply into her psyche and ruffle the depths she had no wish to unsettle. She thought longingly of Piers, of his cool, groomed good looks. She thought too of the cool, sunlit, air-conditioned house they shared overlooking the Pacific ocean in Malibu, and wished she were there, in the world she felt comfortable in. Even though the affair between herself and Piers had now matured and had taken on an altogether more distant tone, she still felt comfortable. They still made love, although not so often, and sometimes Samantha thought Piers might have someone else, but most of the time it didn't seem to matter. She had decided she felt happy without passion. It was their chosen way and their chosen world and no one from outside imposed their ideals of love, hate or any form of moral judgement on them.

Felicity watching her wondered what Samantha was thinking. In her opinion she still looked ill, although today her pallor was skilfully camouflaged with make-up. They stood there, the four of them, Samantha and her three children behind the coffin which had now been laid on a shiny slab at the end of the chapel.

'One press of the button and it's curtains,' whispered Irene irreverently.

'Mum!'

'Well, one has to joke, otherwise there might be tears. When you get to my age you know it won't be so long before it's you up there waiting to be electronically activated into the unknown.'

Felicity turned to reprimand her mother again and saw that her eyes were full of tears, although her chin was jutting out defiantly. Annabel put her arm around her and gave her a little hug, and once again Felicity was forcibly struck by the fact that her daughter was metamorphosing before her eyes into a thoughtful and caring young woman. She was pleased, but it made her feel unsettled and old.

The priest, an elderly man with a snowy white surplice which matched his shock of snowy white hair, entered and stood behind the small wooden pulpit, opened his prayer book and ostentatiously cleared his throat. The organ played a few more notes then stuttered into silence.

'Thank God, we're about to start,' said Irene.

After a stern look in her direction the priest began, and Venetia's final journey commenced.

CHAPTER 16

The solicitors of Venetia's choosing, Paris, Smith and Pugh, had, on her instructions, arranged a small reception after the funeral. It was held at Venetia's Notting Hill house. The whole thing had been arranged by their representative, a formidable young woman called Ms – she insisted on that – Wylie. Dressed in funereal black from head to toe, with stark white make-up, kohled eyes and a red slash for a mouth, she oozed cold efficiency and obviously had every intention of getting the whole thing over and done with as soon as possible.

'I don't think this should be rushed,' muttered Irene rebelliously, angry at having a drink thrust into her hand and not being offered a chair. Ms Wylie had whipped all modes of seating away, obviously on the premise that if people couldn't sit, they wouldn't stay long. 'I think Venetia would have wanted us to enjoy ourselves.'

Peter and Philip looked at her doubtfully, and Hilary put their thoughts into words. 'Do you think so? It seems wrong to be happy. After all, it is only just after her funeral.'

'Of course she wanted us to enjoy ourselves. Why else did she arrange all this before she died? She did it because she knew you'd all be here. It's her way of saying goodbye, have a party on me before you go on your way.'

Samantha overheard Irene, and silently fumed. She would have much preferred not to have a reception of any kind, and heartily concurred with Ms Wylie that the whole affair should be brought to a close as soon as was decently possible.

'Do you think so, Mum?' asked Peter.

'Venetia was old-fashioned,' Samantha was forced to admit. 'And she arranged this because it was the thing to do in her day. I suppose she wanted it done today in the same way as she'd always known it.'

'Exactly,' said Irene. 'She wanted a hoolee.'

'Not at all,' Samantha snapped. 'I think she wanted a dignified and brief reception.'

'Nonsense,' Irene came back firmly. 'If she had wanted it to be brief she wouldn't have spent all this money.'

Philip caught Irene's eye and suddenly grinned. 'Then it's all right,' he said. 'She *did* want us to have a party.' He looked at the buffet spread out on Venetia's front room table with curiosity and a potential chef's professional interest, making a mental note of everything. There were smoked salmon rolls with asparagus, canapés of every shape, size and description, sandwiches, meringues, eclairs, and petits fours. The table practically groaned out loud. 'The food looks delicious,' he said. 'I can't wait to try it.'

'It is from Fortnum and Mason's,' said Ms Wylie sharply, 'so it ought to be good.' Personally she had thought it the height of extravagance but was bound by her deceased client's instructions. 'And this is *not* a party.' She looked daggers at Irene, who, knowing she'd won the battle, smiled serenely back. 'This is a small reception.'

Samantha shot her a look of grateful thanks, and pinned her hopes on Ms Wylie's keeping order. Outside in the street Leroy's car was drawing to a halt. Today he was using his bright yellow Chevrolet, and the chromed vestigal tail wings seemed to fill the whole street. She shuddered slightly; the vulgarity was appalling. 'I suppose he's got to come,' she muttered to Ms Wylie. 'And he'll bring that woman in with him who's not even his wife.'

'You're not Piers's wife,' said Philip loudly. Peter coloured with embarrassment. It was not something he liked to think about, let alone say. But Philip had no such inhibitions.

'Anyway he's invited,' said Hilary, 'and he *is* coming.'

Watching on the sidelines Felicity saw Samantha stiffen with annoyance. She, Tony and Annabel, with a plate of sandwiches and a glass of wine each, stood to one side. This was Samantha and the children's reception, and as non-family they felt slightly isolated. Unlike Irene, who was determined to enjoy herself in the way she thought Venetia had intended, and had thrown herself into the proceedings with a gusto Ms Wylie thought positively indecent. She was already on her third glass of wine.

'I shall not encourage him to stay for long,' Samantha said, helping herself to a dainty smoked salmon and asparagus roll.

'You won't be nasty, will you, Mum?' asked Peter anxiously. 'Venetia did like Leroy, and he *was* good to her. So was Veronica. She often cooked dinner for Venetia when she was tired.' His voice trailed away in disappointment as Samantha moved across the room to speak to some old friends of Venetia who'd made the long journey down from Yorkshire. Why couldn't his mother understand that Venetia's friends were important?

But although elegant and composed on the surface, Samantha hardly heard Peter. She seethed inside. Philip's nasty barbed jibe about herself and Piers had struck home painfully. It reminded her, once again, that this was not a situation with which she was entirely happy herself. Piers could scoff at marriage as much as he liked, telling her that they need not succumb to such peasant instincts as the desire to marry, but it had never really changed her mind. She still wanted to be married, still wanted the security of a piece of paper that proclaimed they belonged together, even though she knew it to be an insubstantial form of security. And marriage offered a form of shape and structure which, although she didn't allow herself to think of it often, she nevertheless knew was missing from her life. But I am happy, I *am* happy, she reminded herself now, and immediately longed for

Piers and California. She looked around the small room in the front of Venetia's London house, crammed with the porcelain and silver, inherited or collected by Venetia over the years. It crowded in on her, the place and all the memories. But she didn't belong here, didn't want to belong here, not any more. She didn't *want* to be tied down by this claustrophobic world of people and possessions; the sudden fears of insecurity and life with Piers were dismissed as nonsense. Once she was away from the children and London she'd be all right. The children, particularly, always unsettled her.

Ms Wylie came across to her. 'Some more guests have arrived,' she said in a very disapproving tone of voice.

Samantha turned and looked at Leroy. His knitted hat seemed to have a life of its own, bobbing violently as he shook her hand and introduced Veronica to the assembled company. 'My, but I'm glad to be here,' he said, smiling broadly. 'Uncle Ignatius, he'll be coming in just a minute. He just gone home to get his drums and banjo.'

Ms Wylie looked as if she needed some smelling salts, her pale face turning ashen at the words 'drums' and 'banjo', and Samantha's heart sank. She vaguely remembered Uncle Ignatius from the past, and prayed that it wasn't the same one. But then reminded herself that Leroy *had* been good to Venetia. She must remember that. So she said to Leroy very firmly, and in her most dignified voice, 'Uncle Ignatius is welcome.'

'But not the drums and banjo,' muttered Ms Wylie.

But Leroy wasn't listening. He and Veronica plunged into the canapés with gleeful enthusiasm.

'This reception is *not* going to turn into a party,' said Ms Wylie. But her voice lacked conviction.

'Some party!' said Tony, as he drove the minibus, filled to overflowing with the family, back to Primrose Hill to drop off Irene.

'It was great,' said Philip. 'Venetia would have really enjoyed it.'

'You've had too much sherry.' Annabel giggled from the rear.

'You all did from what I could see of things.' Felicity rubbed her stomach. She was feeling slightly queasy again, and tried to remember if she had felt the same way when she was pregnant with Annabel, then dismissed the thought abruptly. She was *not* pregnant, and it was stupid to keep thinking about it. But it was no good, no amount of denial could alter the fact that the nagging doubt was gaining momentum.

'I'm glad in a way Venetia died *before* we went back to school,' said Peter. 'Because if we'd been away perhaps we shouldn't have been allowed to go to the funeral.'

'Of course you would have been allowed, dear,' said Irene. 'You're at boarding school, not prison.'

'Feels like a prison sometimes,' said Philip. 'Can't do this, can't do that. Orders, orders, orders, that's all you get.'

In the front Felicity looked across at Tony, whose face was now registering intense annoyance, and wished that Philip would shut up. Although of course he was not to know that his father was almost bankrupting himself in order to send him to a school he was now professing to dislike.

'The education is marvellous,' said Tony. 'That's why you go there.'

'We started ancient Greek last term,' Philip told Irene. 'I can't even read the alphabet. It's backwards.'

'So what?' taunted Hilary. 'You're the backward one. You can't even read the English alphabet.' She ducked as Philip aimed a punch at her over the back of his seat.

'Of course, school won't be the same without Brother Tom,' chimed in Peter mournfully. 'I shall miss him now that he's gone on retreat.'

'Gone on retreat? Where has he retreated to?'

Annabel's curiosity uncomfortably reminded Felicity that she had totally failed her as well where religion was concerned. It had not featured at all in her education, either at school or at home. Although why she should start worrying about it now she wasn't sure. Maybe it was because they had just come away from a funeral, and funerals did tend to turn one's mind on to a higher plane, and make one think of the whys and wherefores of life. But in Felicity's experience the effect usually only lasted for a short time.

'He's gone off to pray,' said Peter.

'Don't look so pious about it,' said Hilary, who also, having gone to a state school for most of her life, was totally irreligious, apart from some very muddled thoughts about Hinduism and Buddhism. 'He's not going to pray for you.'

'He is too. He promised,' shouted Peter. Nothing

330

irked him so much as criticism of his beloved Brother Tom.

'Stop shouting,' said Felicity. 'It distracts the driver.' She looked at Tony and knew he was thinking about the wretched school fees. Her black shoes were tight, so she kicked off her shoes and looked down. Heavens, her ankles had flowed down into her feet! Swollen feet? Was that a sign of pregnancy? The worries crowded in. If she had a baby, would Oliver let her go back to working from home again, and still pay her the same salary? They needed her salary; after all, she had promised Tony she would help with the boys' school fees. They couldn't stay at St Boniface's without her money. Oliver would *have* to be persuaded. Then she thought of Samantha. Like her, there was always the choice of a termination if necessary. Neat and tidy, over and done with in a few hours. That was one way out of the dilemma and no one but herself need ever know. But no, Felicity gave an inward shudder; whatever the consequences she knew that if life did exist within her, then she couldn't possibly extinguish it. The decision was not based on logic, conscience, religion or anything else she could put a name to. It was sheer gut instinct.

'I wish you had interesting friends like Venetia had, Gran.' Annabel's voice dragged Felicity back to the present, and the continuous and increasing tumult in the car.

'Venetia was quite a lot older than me. She had more time to accumulate them,' said Irene. 'But I'm working on it, and anyway I am interesting in my own way.'

'Yes, but you haven't got a West Indian one-man band as a friend.'

'If I had, I'd make sure he could play more than one tune,' replied Irene, a touch acidly. 'I could have strangled that "Yellow Bird High up in Banana Tree" by the time he'd finished.'

Tony laughed. 'Leroy and his relations certainly added a distinctive flavour to the proceedings.'

'But not quite the flavour that Samantha or Ms Sourpuss Wylie had in mind,' said Irene, as the children burst into a ragged rendition of 'Yellow Bird'.

'Shut up,' said Tony and Felicity in unison.

'Yes, it was a good send-off,' continued Tony in a musing voice, negotiating the traffic roaring around Regent's Park, before turning off towards Primrose Hill. 'For all her eccentricity Venetia was very methodical. Fancy leaving envelopes all carefully marked out to be given to the milkman, and binmen, *and* one for Mr Patel at the mini-market. I'll bet they'll be surprised.'

There was a moment's silence, broken only by the constant hum of the traffic outside the minibus, while they all thought about it. Then Irene said. 'Perhaps not as surprised as you think. The age of graciousness has not entirely disappeared. It lingers on in most of the old folk whether they live in a city or in the country. Showing that you are grateful still means something to them.'

'Do you think that's why she said we could all take something from the house?' asked Hilary. 'Because she was grateful to us?'

'Yes, but not just grateful, mostly because she loved

you,' said Felicity, wondering at the same time why Venetia hadn't left the three children a share of the house. That money, if put in trust, would have come in very useful for their futures. But it was not to be; Samantha had the house and contents, and they were all told to take whatever they wanted from the house.

And, not having reached an age where they could evaluate material possessions, none of them had wanted very much. The boys had chosen an ancient stamp album, and Hilary took a porcelain figure of a horse, and at her instigation, Annabel, who Samantha said could also choose something, had taken the matching figure. For her own part Felicity, feeling embarrassed at looking over Venetia's belongings – being taken from room to room by Samantha and Ms Wylie, she felt as if she were being party to a very personal kind of boot sale – wanted nothing. But Samantha had insisted on giving her a pair of antique silver and amethyst drop earrings.

'Take them,' she'd said, when Felicity had protested. 'They will only be sold along with the rest of the stuff. They're not me. I shall never wear them.'

'But I can't,' said Felicity. 'Venetia wasn't my relation.'

'Don't be such a fool,' Irene hissed, *sotto voce*. 'They are beautiful and worth a mint.'

'Please,' said Samantha. 'Venetia would have wanted you to have something good. She always liked you.' She looked straight at Felicity, and once again Felicity was struck by her ashen complexion. Samantha, in her opinion, looked ill. 'I think,' said Samantha, 'that she approved of you far more than she ever did of me. I have the feeling that recently she was always wishing I'd turned out to be the kind of woman you are.'

'Rubbish,' said Felicity. 'Venetia loved you.'

'Love, yes. But she didn't really like me, that's the difference. A bit like me with the children really. Loving and liking don't necessarily go hand in hand, although everyone seems to think it should.'

So Felicity had taken them and felt sad, suspecting that Samantha didn't really like herself very much either. But there was nothing she could do about it. She wondered if perhaps everyone was born with their basic nature already formed, an underlying life-force which ticked along and was fixed in everyone. A kind of inner core which no power on earth could alter. She found it a depressing thought.

Tony chose an ancient mahogany shaving mirror complete with a little mahogany tray with a Royal Doulton shaving mug and a brush holder.

'I do hope you're not going to let him actually use that thing,' said Irene. 'Those old badger hair brushes get frightfully smelly.' Then she pounced, after Samantha invited her to also take whatever she wanted, on something she'd coveted ever since she had known Venetia. A sewing box on tall spindly legs, with a quilted inside full of little pockets for cottons, needles, scissors etc.

'Mum!' Felicity was scandalized. She'd seen similar ones in auction and they had gone for a thousand pounds or more. 'That's much too valuable.'

'Samantha said anything,' Irene was stubbornly insistent.

'Venetia would be happy for you to have it,' said Samantha, and then went on to ask Leroy to choose something as well. He went off happily clutching an old gramophone and a pile of 78rpm records.

'What will happen to Venetia's dear little house?' asked Philip, when they finally left, their accumulation of Venetia's belongings piled on to the back seats between themselves and Irene and the girls. The sewing box was a problem, and eventually Felicity ended up having it wedged over her knees.

'I assume your mother will sell it,' said Tony, and sighed.

'Yes, and then she's going pay for us to go to America,' said Hilary.

'I'm not sure that you should count on that,' Tony told her.

'But she promised,' said Hilary stubbornly. '"When I've got Venetia's money you can come and visit me in America. We'll make a date for this Christmas." Those were her exact words.'

'Hmm!' said Tony.

Felicity couldn't help but think about the money again, and how useful it would have been if Venetia had left even part of it to the children. If that had happened, then she would not have had to solve the problem of how to juggle her inherited ready-made family, a job and the baby which was probably on the way. It was difficult enough paying Tracy at the moment, let alone a child-minder as well, so she'd *have* to work from home. She sat up straight, or as straight as she could with the sewing box wedged over her knees, and firmly applied brakes to her runaway thoughts. Of course, she didn't know for *sure* whether or not she was pregnant. All her worries were merely hypothetical.

'That money would have come in useful,' said Tony under his breath, echoing her own thoughts. Then he turned towards her briefly and smiled. 'But never mind, that rise old Oliver Dickens gave you last month will come in very useful, and I can always do an extra couple of sessions a month at the hospital if any unexpected expenses come along.'

'Are you hard-up, then?' Philip leaned over the gap between the two front seats.

'No,' said Tony.

'Yes,' said Felicity at the same time, thinking it would be no bad thing if the children realized that money had to be earned and didn't just miraculously appear from nowhere.

Irene, who didn't approve of talking finance in front of anybody, said sharply, 'Sit back, Philip, and fasten your seat-belt properly, and don't listen to other people's conversations. It's rude.'

'But, Gran, you do it all the time,' said Annabel.

'That's because I'm older than you.' Felicity smiled at her mother's illogical logic. 'And keep still, you two, or you'll fall out of the back.'

'I don't understand it,' whispered Peter to Philip. 'Why is it rude to listen if you're young, but OK when you're older?' He caught a glimpse from Irene's beady eye and lapsed into silence.

Philip, however, was not to be silenced until he'd had his say. 'I tell you one thing,' he said loudly. 'I don't care how hard-up we are. *We* are not going to sell our stamp album.'

'No one would dream of asking you to,' said Felicity with some asperity, wishing that Tony had been more circumspect and not mentioned money.

Tony found a parking space a few yards from Irene's house.

'Are you coming in for a cup of tea?' she asked, clambering out. 'You might as well, you've got to bring in my sewing box.'

'Yes.' The boys were out of their seats and off towards the mews house before either Tony or Felicity could utter a word. They loved the tiny house crammed full of bric-à-brac, and were fascinated by the 'antiques attic', always making a bee-line for it the moment they arrived on a visit.

'Don't you touch anything up there,' Irene shrieked after them as they clattered up the stairs.

'Of course not,' they chorused back.

'They will,' said Hilary. 'They always do.'

'Of course they will. They're boys,' said Irene, picking up the evening paper from the mat and leading the way through to the kitchen. 'Boys are always into everything, then once they become men they forget most things, latch on to one single thing and quickly develop tramline mentalities.'

'Don't you like men?' asked Hilary curiously.

'Of course I do, dear.' She threw the evening paper down on top of the sideboard. 'I like them in small doses.'

'What about your husband? The one who's dead. Was he a small enough dose?'

Irene smiled at Hilary and considered for a moment while she filled the kettle. 'Yes,' she said firmly, 'he was just about right.'

'Aren't you glad you've only got me as a grandchild?' asked Annabel, who was not at all sure that she approved of what she perceived to be the pally relationship developing between Hilary and her grandmother. Before Venetia's death she had always separated the family into two parts. Hilary and the boys had Venetia, and she had Irene for herself alone. But now it looked as if Hilary expected to muscle in on to something she had always considered her own private property.

Irene smiled and said, 'Get out the best set of bone china, the one with the roses on.' She watched Annabel, who although as tall as Hilary and just as thin somehow managed to look more stocky. There's a lot of her mother in her, Irene thought fondly, and they are both looking a little worried at the moment. She thought she knew the reason for Annabel's anxiety. The green-eyed god of jealousy, pure and simple; and that could be dealt without too much bother. But Felicity was another matter. What was worrying her?

'You didn't answer me, Gran,' said Annabel, piling the tea service on to a tray and looking very glum.

'No,' said Irene wondering how to tackle it, then deciding honesty was the best policy. 'Because I think you know the answer. I haven't just got you. Just as you have merged in with Tony's family to make one whole unit, so you must let me merge in a little as well.'

'But you are *my* grandmother, not theirs.'

'We shan't take her away,' said Hilary. 'We only want a little share.'

'Very sensible, young lady.' Hilary blushed with pride at the compliment and Annabel looked even more glum. Irene beckoned to Annabel. 'Come here.' Annabel put the tray of china down on the table and went across to her grandmother. 'Annabel,' said Irene kindly, 'there is one thing you must learn and never forget, and that is there is no limit to love and affection. It's the one thing in the world which isn't rationed. It can stretch, and stretch, and stretch, and there will still be enough to go around.'

'I don't think everyone thinks that,' said Annabel doubtfully.

Hilary agreed. 'You might be able to stretch yours,' she said. 'But others can't. Look at my own mother. Once Piers arrived, there wasn't enough love left over for us.'

That was a difficult one and for a moment Irene was floored into silence. Then she said slowly, 'Perhaps some people are disabled in love in the same way other people are disabled in body. There is nothing you can do about it, and I don't think it means that your mother doesn't love you. I think she does, but in a slightly different way.' She wasn't at all sure that Tony would approve of her telling his children that his ex-wife and their mother was emotionally disabled, but it was the best she could do on the spur of the moment without being hurtful. She hoped the explanation would do. Hilary looked sceptical but she didn't argue.

Then Annabel laughed and flung her arms around Irene's neck. 'You are special,' was her verdict.

So that was all right, then. 'I know,' said Irene, allowing herself to feel a little smug. 'Now, if you stop strangling me I'll get on and make the tea. And take a fruitcake out of the tin, will you, please, Hilary? It's in the sideboard, yes, in the door beneath this evening's paper. I dare say Philip and Peter will have room for a piece.'

Felicity and Tony came into the kitchen just as the phone rang. It was Oliver Dickens for Felicity. 'My dear,' he said, 'sorry to bother you on a day like this, but I wanted to tell you before you read it in the papers.'

'Good heavens, it sounds exciting,' said Felicity. 'What on earth is it?' She waved at Tony to pick up the paper from the sideboard.

'I'm afraid it's not exciting. Dickens Books have been taken over by Warbler International.' Oliver sounded very weary.

Felicity sat down suddenly. 'Warbler International! But the stuff they publish is porn, or near as dammit.'

'I know. But that has nothing to do with it. They wanted to expand into another market and picked on us. I can't tell you how sorry I am. I didn't want this to happen.'

'Then why let it?' Felicity cried. 'It's your firm. You don't have to sell.'

'Felicity, what I am trying to tell you, very badly,' said Oliver, 'is that you and Joan, as well as most of the other staff, are out of a job, as I am myself. You will get some redundancy money, of course, but I'm afraid Warblers are not known for their generosity.'

Felicity couldn't assimilate Oliver's words. Out of a job? Unthinkable! What would she do? Where would she go? 'But I don't understand, Oliver,' she said. 'Is this what you want?'

'No, it isn't. But there is nothing I can do about it. The whole matter is out of my hands.'

'Why?' Felicity understood even less. 'It is *your* company, Oliver. You can do as you like.'

Oliver heaved a sigh. 'No, my dear, that is the problem. It is not my company. It belongs to my elder brother. It always has. I've just run it. I own a quarter of the stock and he owns three-quarters. He says he can't refuse the offer and is cashing in his stock. And of course he is legally entitled to do that.'

Felicity thought she could see a shred of hope. 'Can't you hold on to your quarter? You don't have to sell. You could stay and fight. Keep your toe in the door?'

'These big business boys would snap my toe off in two seconds.' Oliver's voice sounded wobbly, as if he was near to tears, which in fact was the case. 'You know I'm not in that league, my dear. Never have been, and I'm much to old to learn how to be an aggressive player now, and anyway that's not how I want to be. No, I shall take retirement. Joan Shrimpton will get the pension she's paid in for, and when she's sixty next year the state pension as well, so she won't be too badly off. But I'm afraid of all my little group it is you who will be hit the hardest. You must come in tomorrow and get the financial settlement sorted out.' Oliver heaved another gargantuan sigh, and the tiny shred of hope Felicity was nurturing dissipated as the sigh evaporated. Then

Oliver said, sounding a little brighter, 'But at least I know I don't have to worry too much about you. You've married again, so thank goodness you are financially secure.'

'Yes, Oliver,' said Felicity in a small voice. There was no point in saying more. She couldn't possibly burden him with any more problems; besides, the financial arrangements of the Hughes family were nothing to do with him.

'You'll come in tomorrow, then? And we'll sort things out as best we can.'

'Yes. I'll do that.' Felicity put the phone down.

'Was that about what I think it was?' asked Tony. He spread the *Evening Standard* out on the table, and pointed to a headline. '*Tiddler Swallowed by Whale*'.

Felicity read it. 'Yes,' she said, 'and I've lost my job.'

'Never mind, dear,' said Irene brightly. 'You know what they say; as one door closes, another opens, or something like that.' She began pouring the tea. 'Get the milk out of the fridge, please, Hilary.' She passed a cup of tea to Felicity. 'No need to look so miserable. Now you can move to another firm with better prospects. A whole new exciting future awaits you.'

'No it doesn't,' said Felicity, and burst into tears. 'I can't go to another firm. No one will want me, because I think I'm pregnant.'

'Darling!' shouted Tony.

'Oh!' said Annabel and Irene in unison.

'What?' shrieked Hilary.

'Does that mean . . . ?' Peter blushed bright scarlet.

'Yes, she's having a baby, stupid,' said Philip.

Peter suddenly did a little jog. 'A brother for us,' he squeaked.

'Or a sister,' said Philip.

'I'm not sure,' said Felicity. 'I only think. I haven't had it confirmed.'

'I've been thinking lately that you've put on a little weight,' said Tony, beaming from ear to ear.

Felicity fished in her handbag for a handkerchief, found one, and started mopping her eyes. 'What on earth are you crying about?' asked Irene, cutting a large wedge of fruitcake and passing it to Felicity. 'Here, you'd better have this now that you are eating for two.'

'But Tony and I can't afford a baby.' There, she'd said it. Told the truth. Finances just wouldn't stretch to a baby.

'Of course we can.' Tony put his arms around her and hugged until Felicity thought she'd break in two. 'We can afford anything if we put our minds to it.'

'Anyway,' said Philip, 'you'll have to afford it, because it's on its way now, and that's that.'

'It won't be easy,' sniffed Felicity, still wiping away the stray tear.

'Nothing of any worth ever is,' said Irene. 'But where there's a will, there's a way.'

'Mum, I do wish you'd stop talking in clichés. Anyway, I only *think* I might be expecting. I could be wrong,' said Felicity hopefully. Then she noticed the sea of faces around her all registering intense disappointment.

They want it, she realized in surprise. They really want it.

CHAPTER 17

Felicity left Dickens Books for the final time the day after Venetia's funeral. The train journey to London had seemed the same as usual, and yet unreal. It was difficult to absorb the fact that this was going to be her last day. Yet at the same time she felt a nonentity, a nobody without a purpose in life. She looked about her and wondered about all the other people on the train; most were familiar faces but there was nobody there that she could actually say she *knew*, nobody she could tell how she was feeling. She looked around more carefully, trying to glean some information from her fellow passengers' faces. Some were reading, others doing the crosswords in the morning paper, and some, mostly eager young men with horn-rimmed glasses, were tapping busily away on their laptops. Nothing in their demeanour gave anything away. But of course they were all going in to work today *and* tomorrow. This wasn't the last day for them. How would *they* feel if it were? How would they feel if they were going in to be formally sacked? 'Made redundant, darling,' said her mother. 'Sounds so much better than saying sacked.' Sacked, redundant, what difference did it make? The end result was the same: you were out of a job. Everything seemed so unreal that morning that she didn't feel even in the slightest bit pregnant, and began to wonder whether she had dreamed the whole thing including Venetia's funeral the day before.

When she arrived at Dickens the lack of reality persisted to the point where everything seemed insubstantial. Joan Shrimpton bid her a tearful farewell. Overcome by emotion, she kissed Felicity warmly, something she'd never done before. Then she became completely flustered and blushed a magenta shade of pink. 'Oh, my dear,' she said weepily. 'I never thought I'd live to see this day. I can't put into words what I feel.'

Felicity supposed she was feeling much the same way as she was herself. Shocked into a kind of numbness because their working world was coming to an end. But for Joan Shrimpton Felicity knew it was much more than that. It wasn't just a job she was losing. For her, it was the end of the world as she knew it. Her entire life, since she had left secretarial college, had revolved around Dickens Books. Felicity wanted to commiserate with her, but, apart from kissing her back, and muttering something about yes how awful it all was, she dared not for fear of denting the armour of fierce pride with which Miss Shrimpton had surrounded herself. She didn't think she could cope with her in floods of tears. As it was, one tiny trickle, down her carefully powdered cheek, was quite unnerving enough. And yet, strangely, it was Joan Shrimpton's distress which began to help her put things into their proper perspective.

Oliver Dickens was managing a stiff upper lip, but Felicity knew one wrong word would bring his defences tumbling down as well. So she was very careful, aware of that though she was losing her job, which was bad enough, he, like Joan Shrimpton, was losing a lifetime's work.

The whole of the building oozed melancholy. Some staff had already gone, others, like Felicity, were clearing their desks, and those who were staying on looked tense. Fear of what could be on the horizon with the new management was almost palpable, and Felicity was glad to make her escape to the train, Hampshire, and home. Home! For the first time since she had married Tony, Felicity realized that she was thinking of Cherry Trees as home. Not Tony's house, not Samantha's old home, but her own. Surging along with the crowds making their way from the Bakerloo Line towards Waterloo, Felicity found herself smiling. Perhaps she had finally laid the ghost of Samantha to rest. Cherry Trees was hers. Hers, to share with her jigsaw puzzle of a family, and the baby who, she was now certain, was on his way – she had forgotten now about the morning when pregnancy had seemed a surreal dream. Also, illogical although it was, and without medical confirmation – that would be awaiting her when she arrived back as Tony had insisted on her giving him a urine sample this morning which he'd borne off to the laboratory, not trusting the over the counter kits one could buy and do yourself – she was sure not only that she was pregnant, but that it was a boy, and she had already named him Jonathan.

On Waterloo concourse an unfriendly autumn wind swept across, tugging at the coats of her fellow travellers, a reminder that winter was on the way even though it was still only the beginning of October. Pulling her coat collar up around her ears, Felicity hurried towards the platform to catch the three-thirty train with all the other commuters making an early getaway from London. They all had jobs, and she did not. For a moment the indignity of it all swept over her again and she mentally clutched her wounded pride and the redundancy cheque closer to her. She had refused an offer of dinner with her mother. 'To celebrate your new direction,' Irene had said that morning. But at the time, as Felicity didn't feel she was going in any direction except down, and there was nothing to celebrate about that, she had said no. Ridiculous, she now told herself. Redundancy happens to many others. Every day in the newspapers there were articles stating that in the modern world there was no such thing as job security; big companies swallowed up smaller companies, then downsized themselves, making staff redundant, before proceeding to outsource their labour. All of which Felicity knew was a euphemistic way of saying that it was every man jack for himself.

'Look on it as downshifting,' her mother had said. She had also been reading articles. 'Now you will be free to work from home. Be a freelance. You must do as Oliver says, become an agent. You know enough about publishing, what is good and what is not, plus you have all the necessary connections. You could do it.'

All this, of course, was completely true. But on the day she left Dickens for good Felicity didn't feel positive about anything to do with publishing. Working from home hadn't seemed wildly attractive even when she was making the choice herself, but working from home because there was no alternative seemed even less so. Besides she wasn't sure whether she could, or even wanted to cope with dozens of neurotic authors with inflated egos, all convinced that they had written the greatest book since *Gone With The Wind*. As an editor she'd been able to distance herself from the really pushy authors, but an agent had to have some sort of ongoing relationship. Not something that she relished. Being realistic, Felicity recognized that if she was to earn any money at all, she would have to broaden her horizons, and look outside the realm of publishing. It was all very depressing and wearisome.

Sitting on the train, however, the weariness and depression gradually vanished, and Felicity's thoughts drifted on to the future. So many things to think of. Life was changing yet again. More pieces of the jigsaw to be fitted together. She began to look forward with some trepidation to whatever the future held in store. That they would be happy she had no doubt, but the unease about money would always be there, especially now that there would be another member of the family arriving soon. Then she found herself wondering about Samantha. What did the future hold for her? She was flying back to America, to her new life with Piers. And a simple one in comparison to life at Cherry Trees, no family matters to complicate anything, and no money problems. Piers was wealthy enough in his own right, and Samantha had her own monthly column in a prestigious magazine, plus a weekly syndicated column on *The English Country Home and Garden*. For Samantha all would be smooth plain sailing, and Felicity couldn't help but feel a small twinge of envy. For Samantha, everything was certain and planned down to the last detail. Whereas the only certainty she herself faced was the daily balancing act of juggling the needs of the family, plus now the urgent need to seriously balance the family budget. Without a monthly salary cheque there could be no more topping up when things ran short, no more dashing into the nearest supermarket and buying a packet of convenience food at a grossly inflated price. That thought was so depressing that Felicity stopped thinking and, leaning her head back against the head-rest, closed her eyes. Tomorrow she'd face all that. Not today. The train trundled through the suburbs of London into the open country, and Felicity dozed fitfully.

On arrival at Cherry Trees, she found the place bustling with a cheerful activity which was quite at variance with how she felt it ought to be. She'd just arrived from London, and was now one of the millions of unemployed. Didn't they realize that? Why didn't they come rushing out to commiserate?

She could see Hilary and Annabel with Cotton-Socks in the paddock, trying, not very successfully from the look of it, to make a reluctant, much too fat pony go over the jumps. She stood and watched for a moment as Hilary galloped up to the first hurdle, a low affair of a pole strung between two old oil drums. Cotton-Socks galloped happily enough but within two feet of the hurdle did a sudden sharp right turn, bolted across the paddock to the far side and proceeded to eat the hedge, ignoring all Hilary's efforts to get him to move.

The revving noise from the old stables told Felicity that the boys were there with their motorbikes. Tony was energetically raking leaves and waved a cheery hello but didn't come to meet her. Feeling neglected, Felicity went into the kitchen and found Tracy still there.

'You should have gone hours ago,' she said, mentally totting up the overtime she must, by now, be owing Tracy.

'I know.' Tracy's brightly coloured coxcomb of hair bobbed, an exotic plume, quite out of place in the decor of the English cosiness of the kitchen. 'But Tony asked me to stay.'

'Did he?' Felicity was surprised. Surely Tony hadn't forgotten that *she* paid Tracy, and that the source of supply was now at an end.

'There's been a family pow-wow,' said Tracy in a confidential voice, adding happily, 'and they included me in on it at the end.'

'That's nice.' Felicity kicked her shoes from her aching feet. London pavements and pregnancy did not go together.

'Now, sit down and put your feet up,' said Tracy in

an officious and motherly tone, 'and I'll make you a nice cup of tea. You don't want to tire yourself out now, do you?'

Felicity found herself pushed down into the battered arm chair by the window in the kitchen, and kitten number two – the numbers had stuck as names – seeing an empty lap, immediately jumped up and began purring like a small steam engine while at the same time energetically kneading her skirt to make his bed.

'Tracy,' said Felicity, feeling that Tracy's mothering of her was faintly ridiculous and totally unnecessary, 'I'm pregnant, or *might* be, not an invalid.' She also wanted to say, and it's no use rushing around making yourself indispensable, because I'm going to have to tell you that I can't afford you any more. But she said nothing because she couldn't cross the difficult bridge of hurting and disappointing Tracy, right at that particular moment. Perhaps tomorrow she'd know how to do it. Leaving Dickens and her colleagues of years was quite enough for today. Losing Tracy would have to be tackled tomorrow.

'Of course you're pregnant,' said Tracy, beaming beneath her pink and green sprouts of hair, and dropping teabags into the teapot before pouring hot water in. 'It's as plain as the nose on my face. Anyway, Tony has told everyone. The result was positive.'

'He might have told me,' observed Felicity, feeling slightly disgruntled. 'No such thing as privacy in this place.'

'Nope!' Tracy cheerfully agreed. She put the teapot on a tray together with some cups and saucers and taking a plate of golden brown scones from the cupboard and put the whole lot on the kitchen table. 'I made these cheese scones at lunchtime; I know they're everyone's favourite.'

The scones were the final straw. Felicity burst into tears. 'Tracy,' she said, between sniffs and feverishly searching for her handkerchief. 'You know I shan't be able to keep you. I can't afford it any more, not now that I've lost my job.'

To her amazement Tracy laughed. 'What do you think the family pow-wow was about?' she asked, buttering scones before pouring out the tea. Opening the kitchen window she leaned out and shrieked, 'Tea!' in Tony's direction, then closed the window and passed Felicity a cup.

Felicity sipped her tea and idly pulled the kitten's tiny pointy ears, a procedure he thoroughly approved of, rolling over on his back and presenting her with a round fat stomach. 'A family pow-wow can't manufacture money,' she said.

The back door opened and Tony came in just in time to hear Felicity's gloomy pronouncement. 'No,' he said, 'but resources can be redistributed. I believe that's the current managerial jargon.' He took two scones and a cup of tea and, pulling up a chair, sat down by Felicity.

'I'll leave you two together,' said Tracy. 'I've left Jacob with Melanie for quite long enough.' She skipped gleefully out of the room, and a few seconds later Felicity heard her ancient car stutter into life and rumble off down the drive.

She looked at Tony. 'How on earth can you redistribute anything?' she asked. 'Every last penny is accounted for.'

'Was,' said Tony. 'Not now.' He passed her a scone, saw her opening her mouth to object and said, 'Now shut up and listen.' He then proceeded to tell her that the boys had offered to leave St Boniface's and change to Westhampton Comprehensive, thus injecting a considerable amount of money into the family coffer each year. 'With the boys at a state school our financial problems are over,' said Tony. 'We can even afford to keep Tracy.'

'I'll be here all the time now, and I can do the housework,' said Felicity. 'So I don't really *need* her. At least, not all the time.'

'Which brings me to another matter,' said Tony, smiling. 'It's something that Tracy has been worrying about. She hasn't known how to break it you.'

Felicity frowned. What was the problem now? 'Break what to me? Isn't she happy. Am I not paying her enough?'

Tony shook his head. 'You are not the only one whose life is changing. Tracy's life is changing direction as well.' He took another scone and buttered it. 'As you've probably already heard,' he said, through a mouthful of crumbs, 'Sam Appleby has moved in with Tracy.'

Felicity nodded. 'I know, but . . .'

'Listen,' said Tony. 'Sam has got himself a job working in Holliers Garden Centre. He plans to go into business on his own later, do garden maintenance, but for the time being is learning the ropes at Holliers. He's intelligent, and he likes gardening. I think he'll be successful.'

'But what has that got to do with Tracy working here?' Felicity thought of Tracy's fiercely independent stance. 'I can't imagine her wanting to rely on Sam's income.'

'She doesn't,' admitted Tony. 'But I have to confess that I'm guilty in that respect. I've persuaded Tracy that if she wants the relationship to stand a chance she has to let Sam feel that he really is contributing something worthwhile to their lives. That his job is for all of them. So, she has agreed to come in here just twice a week. The rest of the time she'll stay at home, look after the three of them, and start up her home-cooking service.'

'What home-cooking service?' Felicity hadn't heard of this before, and was beginning to feel that things were racing out of control yet again.

Tony explained the idea and how it had come about. 'So you see,' he finished, 'in a way, your losing your job, Sam's picking up the reins, etc . . . it's all slotted in together very nicely.'

Felicity was silent for a moment while she digested it all. Then she said, 'But where is Tracy getting the money from to start up this cooking business? She'll need pots and pans, food containers, not to mention having to pay in advance for all the ingredients.' Tony blushed bright red. 'You!' said Felicity, pointing at him.

'Yes,' Tony admitted. 'I've given her four hundred

pounds to get started. It's important she doesn't have to worry about cash-flow to begin with.'

'You are a soft touch,' said Felicity, but she was smiling.

Tony grinned slightly shamefacedly. 'I know. But I want them both to have a good chance of making a go of their life together. It's not only for their sakes, but for Jacob as well. They've all had a bad start, and now they've got the chance to begin again.'

Felicity leaned back comfortably in the old armchair. 'And do you think they will? Make a go of it, I mean.'

'Who knows?' Tony shrugged his shoulders expressively. 'In the end it's up to them. All we can do is hope, and give them a little push in the right direction.'

Felicity laughed. 'Sounds to me as if you've given them a huge great shove,' she said.

Tony grinned and said, 'Now, let's get back to you. Once you've got over the shock of redundancy, you can do as Oliver and your mother both suggested: work freelance from home.'

'I don't know about work. I'll have a baby to look after,' said Felicity, feeling gloomy again, thinking of nappies, broken nights, and if her memory served her right the mountain of equipment she would need to service and maintain in order to sterilize and replenish bottles. 'By the way, you might have told me first that the test was positive.'

'Sorry, I thought you'd want everyone to know. But anyway,' Tony, was not to be deterred, 'with a baby in tow you can do as much or as little as you can manage.' He looked at Felicity's gloomy face and said, 'Darling, I

355

do know you by now. You'll go mad with frustration without something cerebral to get your teeth into.'

Felicity suddenly had a ravishing vision of sitting back for days on end and doing absolutely nothing. Nothing to think about, nothing to do, and not going mad with frustration at all, but sinking into a blissful pillow of restful oblivion. But now, just when Tony was waxing so enthusiastic about the possibility of a new career for her, hardly seemed the moment to mention such thoughts.

Tony continued, 'But the important thing to remember is that you won't be desperately scrabbling around working like mad to make money. You can do something you enjoy and any money you make will be a bonus. And you can bank your redundancy cheque, or do whatever you like with it. Keep it for a rainy day.'

Felicity remained silent for a moment, then said, 'It seems unfair that the boys have to make this sacrifice for me.' This was the truth. She *was* worried about that. Changing schools could ruin the progress they'd all made in their stepchild/stepmother relationship. They would perhaps hate her for causing their lives to be turned topsy-turvy, for taking them away from the place they knew so well. 'Are you sure it's what they wanted?' she asked doubtfully.

'Quite sure. And it won't change anything between you,' said Tony gently, second-guessing her thoughts. 'If anything, I think it will make us all closer as a family, because they will be here every day, instead of going away for weeks at a time.'

It would have been too ungrateful to say that she

wasn't sure that she could cope with having them all at home *all* the time, so Felicity remained silent. Her future was spreading itself before her, and yet again it was not the one she had visualized.

Hilary and Annabel sat on the bed in Hilary's bedroom munching apples. The two boys sprawled on the floor trying to see who could flip their apple pips the farthest – they had already finished their apples. The CD player was going full blast, belting out a song by an elderly pop star about not cutting down trees and saving the world for all the poor people.

'It's all right for him to save the whole world,' said Philip bad-temperedly, 'he's a millionaire.'

'Probably forgotten what it's like to be poor and doesn't even know what a tree looks like,' said Annabel loftily. 'After all, he *is* only a pop singer.' She had recently discovered the classics and was heavily into Mahler.

'I'm sure he means well,' said Peter, as usual trying to look on the bright side.

'Yeah! Like you did just now. I don't know why you had to volunteer for us to leave St Boniface.' Philip rolled over on to his back and spat a pip as high as he could into the air.

'You *said* you wanted to leave.'

'I know. But I didn't expect you to tell Dad that. I meant we could *think* about leaving, but you had to open your big mouth and now here we are, ex St Boniface boys, soon to be rotten Westhampton boys.'

'Westhampton pupils,' corrected Hilary. 'Don't forget it's co-ed.'

'Damned girls to contend with as well as all the other local nerds.'

'Nerd yourself.' Hilary threw her apple core at him. She jumped off the bed. 'I'm going to get a book.'

'Didn't know you could read,' sneered Philip.

Hilary exploded. 'Yes, I can,' she screamed, and slammed the door so that whole house shook.

'What's going on up there?' Tony called up the stairs.

'Nothing,' Peter shouted back hastily, signalling to Philip to be quiet.

'It's a very noisy nothing.'

Tony's interruption calmed the boys down, although Annabel thought the general feeling of gloom persisted.

Hilary came back into the bedroom, cheerful as if nothing had happened, and waved a travel magazine. 'Of course,' she said, 'we've all got something to look forward to at the end of this year.'

'What's that?' asked Annabel.

'How can you have forgotten? It's our holiday in America this Christmas. Mum promised at Venetia's funeral, and she included you, Annabel, remember? She's going to use some of the money from the sale of Venetia's house to pay for it. And we'll travel around with her but without Piers because it will be her money, not his.'

The corner of Peter's mouth crept up into a smile, and even Philip looked almost cheerful. 'It will be the last big holiday before we start our exam work,' he said.

Philip suddenly decided he *was* cheerful. 'Whoopee!'

he yelled. 'And we'll get away from all the talk of the new brat, thank heavens.'

'I think you're absolutely horrible,' said Peter feeling cross again. 'It won't be a brat. It will be a lovely little baby.'

'Yuk!' said Annabel and Hilary together, and then burst out laughing.

'Only teasing,' said Annabel. 'I'm sure it will be quite nice as babies go. But America, now that's really something to look forward to.'

'Yes,' said Philip thoughtfully, 'and Mum said we could make out our own itinerary, so we could start doing that now. There's a Cybercafé opened in Westhampton; we could go there and get on the Internet, and find out all the interesting places to go to.' He sat up and hugged his knees to his chest. 'It'll be great to see Mum without that ghastly Piers in tow.'

'I wonder what America is really like,' said Hilary.

'California *in* America,' corrected Peter, who liked to get things right.

The girls weren't so keen on the Internet idea, but were interested enough to find an old atlas loitering amongst the school books on Hilary's bookshelf. It was pulled out, and all four children spent the rest of the afternoon squabbling over what was or was not the most exciting place in California.

Having found a luggage trolley and pushed it across the concourse, Samantha then struggled to heave her heavy suitcase from the carousel at Los Angeles airport. Piers hadn't contacted her in England before her flight but she was sure he'd be in the Arrivals lounge to greet her. She hoped so, because the fatigue which had been plaguing her ever since she'd had the termination was in danger of overwhelming her. It needed all the concentration she had to put one foot in front of the other, and the thought of tackling the journey to the house at Malibu on her own was daunting.

Once through customs and immigration she looked eagerly around for Piers and saw him almost immediately. A familiar, elegant, slim figure in a light-coloured summer suit. He was standing talking to a much younger man, dark, Hispanic-looking, and very – Samantha searched for the right word but could only come up with one – pretty. Yes, that was it. The young man was pretty. And besides that, he was obviously wealthy. One glance was enough to see that the designer clothes in which he was dressed must have cost a fortune.

She waved and Piers lifted a languid hand in brief recognition, and then went back to his animated conversation with the pretty young man before coming over to assist her with the luggage trolley.

'Meet Rick,' he said, introducing the dark young man.

Rick smiled. A big expansive, self-confident smile that didn't reach his eyes and made Samantha feel nervous. 'Great to meet you,' he said. 'From what Piers has told me I'm sure we'll get along just fine.'

Samantha wondered why it was necessary to get along with him at all, and wished Piers had come to meet her alone. She wanted it to be just the two of them.

'I'm terribly tired,' she said to Piers, pointedly ignoring Rick and hoping that he'd take the hint and go away. 'Jet-lag, I suppose. I can't wait to get home and have a sleep.'

'No one I know gets jet-lagged flying in from the UK. What is it with you?' said Rick rudely. 'And I wouldn't count on getting too much sleep, we're having a party tonight.'

'Soirée,' corrected Piers, turning towards him with an indulgent smile. 'An evening of cultural entertainment and pleasure.'

'Gee, you Europeans and your fancy words. Here in the States a party is a party.'

The airport noise crowded in on her, and Samantha felt as if her head would explode. She also had the strangest feeling; as if she was standing in some place a long way off watching a woman, whom she knew to be herself, standing with two men, both of whom, Piers included, were complete strangers.

Piers took her bag and led the way through the milling crowds; holidaymakers, fat women in Bermuda shorts, elderly men also in shorts and wearing panama hats, mixing in with the chic international travellers, of whom Samantha was one. She longed to ask who Rick was, and what did he mean, *we're* having a party? But Piers strode on ahead and gave her no opportunity to talk. Once through the glass sliding doors leading out from the airport lounge, Piers led the way towards a cream stretch limousine and a uniformed chauffeur leaped out and opened the doors for them. 'This is Rick's car,' said

Piers, and gave her luggage to the chauffeur who put it in the boot.

'Oh,' said Samantha, and then was silent. There was nothing more she could say as Rick climbed in with them and sprawled across the seat opposite herself and Piers. It was very inhibiting, at least she thought so, although she noticed Piers seemed very happy.

'Some chariot, eh?' Rick grinned, and pressing a button opened a cocktail cabinet. 'What do you fancy? A Manhattan, a Martini or just plain Scotch on the rocks?'

'Nothing,' said Samantha. She felt ill, tired and most of all confused. 'All I want is to get home, Piers. It's been a long and exhausting trip one way and another.' She looked at him, willing some kind of loving, knowing response. Surely he hadn't forgotten the termination, the sole reason for her trip to London, and then Venetia's sudden death, which was why she was late back? Leaning forward slightly, she looked into his face. His eyes met hers and then he looked quickly away. There was silence and an awful sense of disquiet settled over Samantha.

The chauffeur nosed the limousine out from the airport confines on to the freeway. The heat from the day had settled into the usual layer of smog over Los Angeles and the setting sun was nothing more than a cataractous eye, a reddish smear in the sky. Samantha closed her eyes. At Malibu the air was clear and sea breezes swept right up into the Santa Monica mountains. She would feel better there, and would talk to Piers when they arrived, and got rid of this man Rick.

Although from what he'd said she'd have to wait until after the wretched party which had been arranged. Something to do with Piers' magazine, she supposed.

Through half-closed eyes Samantha watched Rick pour himself a whisky. The light glinted on his huge gold watch. How common he is, she thought, not the type of person Piers is usually friendly with. The ice clinked in the glass. That was the only sound, the clink clunk of ice, until he suddenly said, 'Gee! Piers, we can't pussyfoot around like this for ever. You've got to goddamn tell her.'

Samantha opened her eyes properly. His words fell like a pebble into the car, although she couldn't understand the ripples it made. 'Tell me what?' she asked quietly.

Piers looked straight at her then, and after a moment's hesitation, said, 'Tell you that I've fallen in love with Rick. He and I are living together now, and I am leaving you.'

'But you're welcome to share the house with us until we find somewhere else,' said Rick, leaning forward and smiling cosily at her. 'If you were a different kind of chick I'd suggest a threesome. Might be fun for a while. But you don't look the type.'

'I am not,' said Samantha icily.

Rick poured himself another slug of whisky before topping up the glass with more ice. 'We'll be moving out of the Malibu house soon. I've got my eye on a swell mansion in Beverley Hills, used to belong to an old movie star. The whole place is full of Art Nouveau stuff imported from Paris. It'll suit Piers down to the ground.'

There was another silence. A long silence while Samantha tried to think and quell the rising tide of revulsion gradually sweeping over her. She stared at Piers. This was the man who had made love to her, made her feel special, made her feel the ultimate in femininity. This was the man for whom she had left her husband and family, with whom she had thought to spend the rest of her life. This was the man who had made her come *alive*, helped her find her true self. And now he was telling her he was not the man she'd thought him to be at all. He didn't want her. Now, he was making love to someone else. Not another woman, that would have been bad enough, but a man. A man! A man!

She began to feel sick, and then quite suddenly, without warning, she was angry. Angry! Angry! So angry she was consumed with anger. Piers had made a nonsense of everything, and she hated him for that. Why couldn't he have fallen for another woman? At least that would have been normal. She could have coped with that. But not this. Not with this leering, pretty young man sitting opposite her. Leaning forward, she rapped loudly, sharply and viciously on the darkened glass screen which separated them from the chauffeur, the blows increasing in intensity and speed until she found herself hammering hysterically at the glass.

'For God's sake! What are you doing?' said Piers. 'Control yourself. Be dignified.'

Samantha's rage boiled over, a seething, roaring mass over which she had no control. 'Dignified!' She heard her own voice screaming as if from far, far away. 'Don't you talk to me about dignity. Is sleeping with a man dignified? I can't even bear to think of it. And to think I ever let you touch me. You are disgusting. *Disgusting*.' She flung herself away from Piers, unwilling to even let herself brush against him.

'You, dear lady,' drawled Rick, 'are homophobic. You need educating.'

'Don't tell me what I need,' screamed Samantha. 'I can think what I like. And I think it's unnatural, and disgusting, absolutely disgusting.'

'So you keep saying,' said Piers, his voice frigid. 'So I take it that you don't want to stay with us, not even temporarily.'

'Too damned right,' said Samantha. 'Just let me get out of this car.'

Rick picked up the intercom phone piece and dangled it by its flex across to Samantha, who snatched it from him and pressed the speak button.

'Yes, sir.' The driver's voice, quiet, and normal, echoed into the car. It helped to calm Samantha.

'Please stop the car at the first good hotel you pass in Malibu,' she said, fighting to keep the tremble from her voice.

'I'll pay your hotel bill,' said Piers. 'For the first month, until you find somewhere to rent.'

'Get lost!' hissed Samantha, the venom in her voice amazing even herself. 'I'd die sooner than take one single penny from you.'

'You may regret turning my offer down,' said Piers, his distant, cold voice, which once she had loved, now making Samantha feel as if she was curling at the edges. 'America, especially California, is a very expensive country.'

'Some things have too high a price,' said Samantha. 'My pride is not for sale.'

Venetia would have been proud of her.

CHAPTER 18

Standing in the checkout queue on a cold day at the end of November, Felicity smiled at the baby sitting in the trolley in front of her. It smiled back, a damp, dribbly smile, and surveyed her inquisitively with a bright and beady stare. It was a very round baby. Everything about it was round. A round head, plump round dimpled hands protruding from a round little body wrapped up like a cocoon against the cold. It had kicked off one of its shoes and, aware now that there was an audience, slowly, and, with much effort, triumphantly pulled off the sock, then spraddled its toes against the rungs of the trolley. The sock was then solemnly offered to Felicity, who took it, smiled, and then handed it to the baby's grateful mother.

'Thanks.' She stuffed the sock into her pocket and retrieved the shoe from the bottom of the trolley. 'He's always doing this. Only eleven months, and already he's a right handful.'

The mother moved on; it was her turn to have her goods whizzed through the scanner. The girl doing the scanning looked as if she'd been bar-coded brain-dead;

367

she threw bread, potatoes and tins together so that the fresh bread was flattened, and potatoes spilled out of the plastic bag. The young mother had to move fast to retrieve the quickly growing mountain of jars, bottles and packets from the other end of the conveyor belt and transfer them into bags.

Felicity turned her attention back to the baby and watched as he busily tried to prise off the other shoe and wondered whether her baby would be a *right handful* by the time he reached eleven months. As if to give her an answer, she felt a tiny butterfly-like flutter in her stomach and knew that Jonathan was moving. Tony had told her not to be so certain it was a boy, but she was sure it was and always thought of it now as him, or, more often than not, Jonathan. She looked around at the garish gold and red Christmas decorations strung along the shopping aisles, and let the Christmas muzak wash over her. Once she would have hated this crowded rush. But now she felt quite relaxed and surprisingly happy standing in the midst of the store crammed with Christmas shoppers. A whole month now since she'd left Dickens and metamorphosed into a full-time wife and mother, and so far she'd not been bored for one single day.

'It won't last,' her mother had said, determined to be gloomy, when she'd been down to stay at Cherry Trees the previous weekend. 'I was very bored when I was pregnant. I went to see every show and play in London. Most of them several times.'

Felicity laughed. 'I'm not you,' she pointed out. 'Neither do I now live in London, and besides, I have a family to look after. You didn't. You were just waiting for me to arrive.'

'Yes, but they're not *your* family,' said Irene tactlessly, and even more gloomily. She was bad-tempered because she was missing Venetia more than she cared to admit either to herself or to anyone else. But it was not only Venetia's company that she missed. There was something else. The truth was that Venetia's death had sharply reminded her of her own mortality. Not a subject she cared to think about. 'Samantha's family. Not yours,' she affirmed.

It was one of those moments when Felicity wanted to strangle her mother, but guessing part of the reason for her unusually subdued and depressed mood over the weekend she held her tongue in check. 'Wrong again, Mum,' she replied mildly. 'They *are* mine. For better or for worse I've picked up the pieces. Samantha has given me carte blanche.'

Now, in the supermarket, mulling over that conversation with her mother while she stacked her own shopping on the end of the conveyor belt, Felicity suddenly realized that Samantha hadn't written. Christmas was getting very near, and there had been no word about flight arrangements for the children's visit to California. Perhaps a letter had got lost in the post. She made a mental note to ring her once she got home.

But a telephone call was not necessary. At Cherry Trees, lying on the table, a late delivery by the postman, was a long white envelope with blue airmail stickers across the top and USA stamps.

'Can we have those stamps for our album?' asked Peter. 'When you've finished reading the letter, of course,' he added politely. Felicity smiled at him. Peter was very easy to like. He wasn't smarmy, as Philip often called him; he didn't consciously *try* to please. He just had an in-built sense of courtesy and an innate goodness. She often thought that if he chose to follow his father into the medical profession he would make a very good doctor.

'No need,' said Philip airily. 'We can buy loads of stamps when we're over there. That'll be the letter from Mum giving the dates and everything, I expect.' Philip, although much easier to get on with now, could still be extremely prickly and hostile at times. And Felicity, suspecting that he was still feeling very insecure, did her best to make allowances. Something which she did not always find easy.

'I should think so.' Felicity picked the letter up and put it on the Welsh dresser, then dumped the shopping on the kitchen floor. 'I'll read it as soon as I've sorted this lot out. In the meantime you'd better get on with your homework. Try and finish some of it before supper.'

'But I thought franked stamps were supposed to be more valuable,' Peter said to Philip as they disappeared upstairs towards their bedrooms and their homework.

'Not American ones. They're two a penny.'

Felicity eyed the envelope, decided there'd be nothing in there that couldn't wait, and that the shopping had a higher priority. She began to stack the groceries away carefully, another task she had discovered she rather enjoyed. She was quite proud of how tidy the larder looked these days. Lately, Tracy had taken to always reeling back in mock horror at the neatness, and Felicity continually amazed herself by actually finding the thing she was looking for. What was more, she had stopped discovering half a dozen packets of one item and none of whatever it was she actually needed. Once, before the tidy days, when she was making a salad dressing, she had discovered seven bottles of wine vinegar and no oil.

The stacking finished, and the door closed on shelves full of tightly packed jars and packets, she made herself a cup of tea and finally settled down, in the comfortable armchair by the kitchen window, to read Samantha's letter at leisure.

Felicity read the letter through twice, then took her reading glasses off, folded the letter and put it in her lap. She sat, swinging the glasses by the earpiece, and gazed into the distance. Samantha's letter was not long, but its contents were a bombshell. Felicity felt irritated that, yet again, someone else's problem had landed in her lap. But the letter was addressed to her. Not to Tony. Not to the children. Samantha expected her to tell the children. The problem was how and when.

The how and when was solved almost immediately. Peter and Philip erupted into the kitchen.

'We're starving,' announced Philip, 'aren't we?' In the background Peter nodded confirmation. 'Is there something we can have to keep us going until suppertime.' He didn't wait for Felicity's reply, but opened the fridge door and looked in. 'Great! There are some spare roast chicken drumsticks left over from lunchtime. Can we have those?'

'They're not exactly spare,' Felicity protested. 'I was planning to do something with them.'

Philip gave the plate closer inspection, peering intently under the cling film covering the drumsticks. 'Only six, not enough to do anything worthwhile with,' he said. 'But just enough for two each for me and Peter and one each for the girls.'

Felicity capitulated. No need to be strict, not now of all times, when she had to give them bad news. 'All right. Call the girls down. I've got something to say to you all.'

Peter looked at the letter on Felicity's lap. 'It's about our American trip, isn't it?' he said happily.

'Yes,' said Felicity, wondering where she was going to find the courage to say what was necessary. But it wasn't really a matter of courage. It was a matter of necessity, and although the nub of the message was not of her making, the manner of its imparting would be hers. And that, she resolved, would be done with care and compassion, no matter how difficult the following scenario might be.

The girls came into the kitchen, and Philip passed the drumsticks and some bread rolls around. There was a moment's silence while they all began munching hungrily.

'Are you going to tell us what is in Mum's letter?' said Hilary.

'Yes,' said Felicity, and unfolded it and put her

glasses back on. 'I'll read it to you.' She started, carefully controlling her voice so that it was level and even. Each word clearly enunciated so that there should be no misunderstanding.

> "'Dear Felicity. I am writing to you because what I have to say is very difficult, and I cannot write directly to the children. The fact of the matter is, I am not able to have them this Christmas as I promised. There are many reasons, but the main one is that Piers has left me for someone else, and I am now on my own. I have had to move into a smaller apartment, and everything is at sixes and sevens, as there is so much to sort out financially and otherwise. I know they will be very disappointed and I am sorry. But everything that has happened is beyond my control. There is nothing else I can do. Please give them my love, and tell them they will hear from me soon. Yours, Samantha.'"

Felicity folded the letter, took off her glasses and waited for the storm to break. But it didn't. There was silence, then Philip said gruffly, 'I expect America is overrated anyway. We've got plenty to do here.'

'At least she's not still with that horrible Piers,' said Peter, adding in a voice which Felicity knew was perilously close to tears, 'I hope she's all right. It can't be very nice being on your own in another country.'

'I'm sure she's all right,' said Felicity. 'She just needs to get everything sorted out.'

'She could come back to England,' said Hilary. 'But I bet she doesn't.'

'It's early days yet,' said Felicity. 'I don't suppose she's decided what she'll do. Maybe she's expecting you to go over later, and this is only a postponement. We'll have to check with her.'

'We'll never go to America,' said Philip in a flat voice. 'Come on, Peter. Let's go and do our bikes for half an hour.' Both boys got up and left the kitchen.

'I haven't quite finished my homework,' said Hilary in a wobbly voice. 'I'm going upstairs.'

Felicity didn't reply. What could she say?

Annabel hung back. 'Do you think she is just postponing the visit?' she asked.

Felicity looked at the letter again and sighed wearily. 'I don't know, Annabel. I just don't know.'

Annabel came over to where she was sitting. 'They *are* terribly disappointed really,' she said. 'Even though they're trying hard not to show it.'

'I know.' Felicity shook her head, despairing of Samantha and her fickle ways. 'Believe me, I do know.'

Annabel leaned over and, reaching out, put a tentative hand on Felicity's shoulder. 'I'm glad I've got you for a mother,' she said softly, then hurriedly left the kitchen and followed Hilary upstairs.

A miasma of despondency, thick and treacly, hung over the whole kitchen during supper. Felicity imagined that if she leaned forward she would actually be able to stir it. No one spoke for at least ten minutes, except to say things like 'pass the salt, please', or, 'can I have

374

another piece of bread?' Felicity noticed that Hilary and Annabel only picked at everything and ate very little. The boys' appetite appeared unchanged, and they munched their way stolidly through everything as usual. The only difference being that there was none of the usual lively badinage which normally accompanied every meal. Sometimes the noise gave Felicity a headache, but tonight, in the oppressive silence, she found herself yearning for it.

The moment supper was over the children left silently en masse. Tony looked at Felicity, signalling with his eyebrows to say nothing until the room was empty, and when it was he exploded with, 'You would have thought she could have had the decency to tell us before now. Putting off the kids' visit at such short notice is just not on.'

Felicity leaned across to the Welsh dresser and retrieved Samantha's letter. 'Don't blame her too much,' she said. 'It can't be easy being dumped.'

'She dumped me,' said Tony.

Felicity looked up from the letter and frowned. 'Surely you're not *still* bitter about that? If you are, that doesn't reflect very well on me and my capacity to make you happy.'

Tony was silent for a moment, then gave a shame-faced smile. 'I haven't been really bitter since the day I met you,' he said. 'And if I'm honest, Samantha did me a favour when she left. But I still find it difficult to feel sorry for her just because Piers has found someone else. And I *do* think she could have told us sooner.'

'She's in a different country, with all the problems

that go with that,' Felicity reminded him. 'No wonder she hasn't written before. Getting herself sorted out with a house, a job, and, more importantly, financially, can't have been easy.'

'But a quick phone call, just to tell the kids that the plans were off. She could have made that.'

'Yes, she could,' agreed Felicity, and wondered why she hadn't.

She read the letter again but there were no clues as to why she had remained silent for so long. Just the bald statement that Piers had left her for someone else, but no mention of the woman's name. Although, on second thoughts, Felicity thought she was unlikely to pass on the name of her rival. But there was no mention either of Samantha's new work, and she must be needing to work if Piers was no longer supporting her. The only information was that vaguely worded sentence about there being so much to sort out financially and other-wise. And on reading the letter yet again Felicity realized that although she and Tony had assumed that Samantha meant she had found herself work, she had not actually said that. In fact, apart from saying that Piers had left her and the children could not come, the only other concrete piece of information was her new address at the top of the letter.

The following morning Felicity watched Tracy flying up the drive on her bicycle. That meant that Sam was at home, and probably taking baby Jacob shopping. When he did that, Tracy always cycled. Felicity smiled. That had been Tony's good deed for the year. It seemed all was well between Tracy and Sam. Of course, it was early days yet, plenty of time for them to argue. But hopefully by the time they did, they'd both be mature enough to sort themselves out. Or, more likely, Tracy would sort it out. She had, Felicity and Tony had both noticed, become much more bossy since Sam had moved in. She had a new-found confidence. And Sam, to give him credit, didn't seem to mind being bossed at all.

'It's because he's been bossed by his mother all his life,' said Tony. 'He's merely substituted Tracy for Mrs A.'

'Go away and take your homespun psychology with you,' Felicity had laughed.

'It's in the books,' said Tony seriously.

And Felicity guessed that it probably was. Now she watched Tracy. She did look much more healthy these days, and she had started letting the lurid pink and green grow out of her hair, and the nose ring had disappeared. In fact, although Felicity wouldn't have dreamed of mentioning it, in case it provoked a reverse reaction, Tracy was beginning to look like quite a normal young mother. And now she was at home and not in London, she looked forward to her visits, because besides doing the housework they always had a good gossip.

'Of course,' said Tracy when she came in and heard the news that morning, 'I know that type. I bet *he's* gone off with another you know what! I always thought that Piers bloke was a poofter.'

'Poofter! Tracy! What an old-fashioned expression.'

But her words started Felicity's mind off along a track she hadn't explored before.

'I'm an old-fashioned girl where things like that are concerned,' said Tracy primly, an expression which did not tally with the multicoloured coxcomb of her hair.

Felicity couldn't help smiling at her outraged expression, then said thoughtfully, 'Do you know, that never occurred to me before. Nor to Tony.' Then she dismissed the idea. 'I can't believe he's gone off with . . .'

'Another man? Believe me, I'm sure. I knew as soon as I saw him that he was AC–DC. It wasn't only Samantha he was after when he was down here filming. You should have seen him fluttering his eyelashes at the cameraman in the pub most evenings. I was a part-time barmaid down there at the time. You see a lot when you're working behind a bar.'

Felicity shook her head. 'So it seems. But even so, Tracy. I can't believe it. It's too far-fetched.'

'Betcha I'm right. Why don't you ring her? It'll be evening there now, won't it? She'll probably be at home.'

Felicity was tempted. Tracy egged her on in between squirting the oven with energetic bursts of Mr Muscle, and eventually Felicity's curiosity got the better of her. 'All right. But, of course, I won't actually ask her outright.'

'Why not?'

'Well, I can't, can I? It's not the sort of thing one asks.'

'*I'd* ask,' said Tracy, reminding Felicity of her

mother. Some days she sounded just like a smaller, younger Irene Hobbit.

'Well, I can't. But I'll ask her how she's managing, and if she's means the trip is off completely, or just postponed? And I do genuinely need to know that as she didn't actually say. Maybe she intends them to go at Easter.'

'And maybe she doesn't.' Tracy's cryptic comment was accompanied by a long blast of the oven cleaner.

In the airy apartment she'd rented on the outskirts of Malibu Samantha sat, exhausted. The air-conditioning was playing up and it was stiflingly hot. In fact the only good thing about the whole apartment today was the view. From the main window she could see the Pacific ocean rolling in across the golden sands. Usually it was blue, but today it was grey, and the waves were spitting and frothing angrily. It reminded her of the seas around England and she felt homesick; something she'd felt often lately. As always it was a sudden, gut-wrenching feeling that made her almost physically sick. How she longed to return to England. And the longing was made worse because she knew there could be no going back. Not now, especially not now. The decision to stay had been made, and she would stick by it, until the very end. Now that the sale of Venetia's house had been completed, all her ties with England were broken. The children, whom she'd once thought would be tied to her for ever, were gone. She'd handed them over, without regrets, or so she had thought. Of course, at the time she had thought that it would be possible to maintain a tenuous holiday relationship with them, a link which, in her honest moments, she knew she had planned more to suit herself than them. But life played strange tricks, and now even occasional meetings were no longer possible. Samantha sighed, and gazed with unseeing eyes at the ocean spread before her window. It seemed that her own plans had counted for nothing in the great game-plan of life.

She leaned her head back on the large sofa, and let the tiredness, which afflicted her all the time these days, rain down upon her; small debilitating blows, each one knocking a little more life from her body. Strange, she mused, once I thought I wanted to be completely alone. But now it's an accomplished fact it turns out to be like so many other things in my life, a totally empty achievement.

She felt despair, dark, lonely and all enveloping, wrap its mantle of misery around her.

The cheque from the sale of Venetia's house was lying on the table beside her and she picked it up and looked at it again. It was for eighty thousand pounds. A lot of money in England, but very little here in America. She worked it out roughly eighty thousand pounds was approximately one hundred and twenty thousand US dollars. Just enough to pay the medical bills she'd run up, and the rent on the apartment for the next six months. That should be just about enough. After that there would be no more bills to pay.

She wondered if her letter had arrived at Cherry Trees, and thought again with regret, of how bitterly disappointed the children would be. I promised, she thought, but like many other promises in my life I've broken it. Closing her eyes she could see the familiar outline of Cherry Trees standing amidst the green lawns, which were always such a problem to keep smooth and green in the summer. She could see the great tall trees of the New Forest, sunlight filtering through the branches to dapple the green of the leaves. Then she remembered it would be cold there now. The end of November often saw the first sharp frosts sending the last of the leaves, left clinging on to the trees, scuttering down to the forest floor.

When the telephone rang and she answered it and found Felicity on the other end of the line she was not surprised. Because she was thinking of the family at Cherry Trees it seemed right that Felicity should ring. 'You've got my letter?' she asked.

'Yes,' said Felicity. There was a faint echo on the line, giving Samantha's voice an ethereal sound. She wondered if her own voice sounded the same. 'I rang to say that I understand. The children are very disappointed, of course, but they'll get over that. Maybe we can organize something for Easter instead. You'll be more settled then.'

'No,' said Samantha.

'Oh.'

Outside the kitchen window at Cherry Trees two magpies were tussling over a piece of bacon rind on the bird table. One of the kittens was sitting beneath the bird table, and, hopeful of either catching a bird or a piece of bacon, began, with great difficulty, to try and climb up. Felicity watched the antics of the birds and cat absent-mindedly while she tried to think of what to say next in view of Samantha's uncompromisingly negative reply.

Samantha guessed that her monosyllabic reply had confused Felicity. 'I won't be here at Easter,' she said. 'I'm not just being bloody-minded.'

Still not knowing what to say, Felicity said 'But . . .' and tailed off as she heard Samantha draw a deep breath.

'I might as well tell you, then you and Tony can decide how and when you tell the children,' said Samantha, the steadiness of her voice surprising herself. 'I've got acute myeloid leukaemia. I've had all the chemotherapy I can take and it hasn't worked properly. I'm in a brief period of remission now, but the doctors tell me it won't last for long. If I could, I would have the children over now for a short time, but I'm afraid I haven't got the energy or the money. The money, practically all of it, has gone on the treatment, as my insurance didn't cover it, and everything else is a bit of an effort.'

Felicity sat, stunned into silence. What could she say? What could anyone say? In the end she said what everyone said when they couldn't think of anything else. 'I'm so sorry.'

'Don't be,' said Samantha calmly. 'I've come to terms with it now. More or less. One has to when there isn't any alternative. And anyway I'm too tired to fight it.'

'But how are you managing?'

'I'm managing.' In Malibu Samantha glanced

around her luxurious apartment, consoling herself with the thought that at least she was going to make her exit in style. 'Of course, as I've just said, I've spent practically all my money, on treatment and on the rent for my apartment. Even the money from the sale of Venetia's house has gone, or it will do as soon as I put the cheque into my bank account.'

Sitting as she was in the warm, comfortable kitchen of Cherry Trees, Felicity felt a chill strike at her. She couldn't imagine anything worse than to be ill, alone and penniless. But words of comfort were difficult to find, and anyway words alone were not a lot of use, but she had nothing else. So she said lamely, 'I'm so sorry that Piers has left you at a time like this.'

Samantha laughed, the familiar low husky sound that Felicity had always envied because she thought it sexy. 'That seems an aeon ago even though it's not that long. What's more, it doesn't seem at all important now. By the way, he left me for another man. Tell Tony, he can have the last laugh.'

Felicity almost gasped out loud. So Tracy *was* right about Piers. 'You know he won't,' she said slowly. 'He's far from perfect, but he *is* compassionate.'

'True. He has his faults, but basically he is a good man,' Samantha agreed.

'And it doesn't matter who Piers left you for,' continued Felicity; 'the fact that he left you alone at a time like this is the thing that matters. A hateful thing to do.'

'He didn't know about my illness,' replied Samantha. 'I hadn't been diagnosed then, and I haven't told him since because it doesn't change anything. The last thing I want, or need, is charity.'

Felicity was silent for a moment, forgetting even the money and minutes ticking away on the transatlantic call. This was a different Samantha. Not the elegant clothes-horse she had always appeared to be, not the cool sophisticated woman whose life was easy and uncomplicated, but a woman totally alone, preparing to face her death. It took a lot of courage to face that knowledge alone. Felicity mentally saluted Samantha's courage.

'You said you don't need charity, Samantha,' she said, feeling her way with uncertainty, not really sure of what to say next. 'But is there anything you *do* need. Is there anything we can do? Is there anything you *really* want?'

Back in Malibu, Samantha smiled. It was strange how their relationship had subtly developed over the past eight months. From that first meeting when she'd regarded Felicity with something akin to awe and envy, to later on when she viewed her almost as an enemy, to now, when she felt she was the one person in the world whom she could really tell her innermost thoughts; although she could not analyze why. She made up her mind. There was nothing to be lost.

'Yes,' she said, 'there is something I would like. But before I ask you I must tell you that I shan't be offended if you say no. And if you *do* say no, I will understand your reasons, because if I were in your place I'd probably say no.'

'Ask me,' said Felicity.

Samantha took a deep breath. 'I should like to come back to Cherry Trees for Christmas. To see the children for one last time.'

'I think you must be suffering from a touch of the sun,' said Irene Hobbit, standing in the kitchen of Cherry Trees, feet apart and arms akimbo.

'I agree,' said Tracy, 'except that it's December and we haven't had any sun for a week.'

'I think perhaps I am mad.' Felicity was stirring the Christmas pudding mix. She dared not tell her mother how many hundreds of worrying thoughts she'd had since making her impulsive gesture of kindness. She held out the spoon coated in the rich, sticky brown mixture to her mother. 'Stir and make a wish,' she said.

Irene seized the spoon and stirred vigorously. 'I wish that Samantha weren't coming here for Christmas,' she said.

Felicity took the spoon back and began stirring again. 'That wish is not granted, because she *is* coming, and I shall make her welcome, and so will Tony. And if you are going to be difficult, then it is *you* who will have to stay away.'

Irene glowered mutinously. 'I won't be difficult,' she muttered. 'But I wish I could understand you.'

Felicity stopped stirring and leaned on the spoon. A warm feeling of happiness spread through her as she felt baby Jonathan give a hefty kick, as if to say, Go on, Mum, tell her.

385

'It will only be *this* Christmas,' she said. 'She won't be coming again.' She and Tony had agreed not to mention Samantha's illness to anyone. They would discuss that subject with Samantha when she arrived, and when they saw how well, or otherwise, she was.

'You might not be able to get rid of her,' said her mother. 'She might decide to stay now there isn't a man in her life.'

'Crumbs!' Tracy leaned across the kitchen table, the upstairs dusting and polishing forgotten. 'You don't think she will, do you? Make a play for Tony, I mean.'

'It's a possibility,' warned Irene.

'That'll give Oakford something to talk about. Dr Hughes living at Cherry Trees with both of his wives.' Tracy hugged the polish tin to her front, gleefully anticipating all the gossip.

Felicity smiled at her mother's and Tracy's over-developed sense of melodrama. 'That won't happen,' she said quietly. 'Just wait and see. And please remember that Christmas is a time of peace and goodwill, and about giving to others. And we,' she eyed both of them sternly, 'will give Samantha a happy Christmas.' She thought of the future. Maybe they ought to be fore-warned a little, just as the children would need to be. 'And whatever happens after Christmas we shall deal with as it comes.' That was as much as she could say. For now, anyway.

'I suppose you know what you're doing,' said her mother.

'I do, Mum, believe me, I do.'

Suddenly the doubts disappeared. She *did* know. She had been right to persuade a reluctant Tony to agree to have Samantha to stay over Christmas. Now she was never more certain. She no longer felt alarmed at the thought of Samantha, no longer regarded her as a threat. She, Felicity, was Tony's wife now, and she was the main perpetrator of whatever happened within the family, not a helpless bystander. Together, she and Tony would cope. They would cope with all the latest problems, whatever they were. They would cope with Samantha's illness and help her as much as possible, if that was what she wanted. All were merely hurdles to get over, another part, for good or bad, of the total fabric of their lives. And Samantha was an integral part of that fabric as well. There was no denying that. Only now, nearly a year after marrying Tony, did Felicity realize that a second marriage could never dispel the remnants of the first. And that fact in itself was nothing to worry about. It was only bad when that element was allowed to be disturbing and provocative, and allowed to undermine the foundations of a new relationship. Samantha's physical presence couldn't do that. Not now. True, her imaginary presence had caused harm in the past, but Felicity knew she had well and truly laid that ghost. Now, Samantha was a woman who needed the sanctuary which was within her power to give.

Felicity knew she couldn't possibly explain all the complicated reasons to others. All she knew was that it was right that Samantha should come. Other people might think her foolish or naïve to offer shelter to Samantha, but that was not how she felt.

Sometimes, Felicity reflected, one had to swim with the tide, not against it, and now was one of those times.

Sometimes, just to *do* something was far more important than understanding the reason why.

 # THE EXCITING NEW NAME IN WOMEN'S FICTION!

PLEASE HELP ME TO HELP YOU!

Dear *Scarlet* Reader,

As Editor of *Scarlet* Books I want to make sure that the books I offer you every month are up to the high standards *Scarlet* readers expect. And to do that I need to know a little more about you and your reading likes and dislikes. So please spare a few minutes to fill in the short questionnaire on the following pages and send it to me.

Looking forward to hearing from you,

Sally Cooper

Editor-in-Chief, *Scarlet*

QUESTIONNAIRE

Please tick the appropriate boxes to indicate your answers

1 Where did you get this Scarlet title?
Bought in supermarket ☐
Bought at my local bookstore ☐ Bought at chain bookstore ☐
Bought at book exchange or used bookstore ☐
Borrowed from a friend ☐
Other (please indicate) _____

2 Did you enjoy reading it?
A lot ☐   A little ☐   Not at all ☐

3 What did you particularly like about this book?
Believable characters ☐   Easy to read ☐
Good value for money ☐   Enjoyable locations ☐
Interesting story ☐   Modern setting ☐
Other _____

4 What did you particularly dislike about this book?
_____

5 Would you buy another Scarlet book?
Yes ☐   No ☐

6 What other kinds of book do you enjoy reading?
Horror ☐   Puzzle books ☐   Historical fiction ☐
General fiction ☐ Crime/Detective ☐ Cookery ☐
Other (please indicate) _____

7 Which magazines do you enjoy reading?
  1. _____
  2. _____
  3. _____

And now a little about you –
8 How old are you?
   Under 25 ☐   25–34 ☐   35–44 ☐
   45–54 ☐   55–64 ☐   over 65 ☐

cont.

9 What is your marital status?
   Single ☐   Married/living with partner ☐
   Widowed ☐   Separated/divorced ☐

10 What is your current occupation?
   Employed full-time ☐   Employed part-time ☐
   Student ☐   Housewife full-time ☐
   Unemployed ☐   Retired ☐

11 Do you have children? If so, how many and how old are they?
   _____
   _____

12 What is your annual household income?
   under $15,000   ☐   or   £10,000   ☐
   $15–25,000   ☐   or   £10–20,000   ☐
   $25–35,000   ☐   or   £20–30,000   ☐
   $35–50,000   ☐   or   £30–40,000   ☐
   over $50,000   ☐   or   £40,000   ☐

Miss/Mrs/Ms _____

Address _____
_____
_____

Thank you for completing this questionnaire. Now tear it out – put
it in an envelope and send it, before 30 June 1998, to:

Sally Cooper, Editor-in-Chief

USA/Can. address	*UK address/No stamp required*
SCARLET c/o London Bridge	SCARLET
85 River Rock Drive	FREEPOST LON 3335
Suite 202	LONDON W8 4BR
Buffalo	*Please use block capitals for*
NY 14207	*address*
USA	

Scarlet titles coming next month:

MARRIAGE DANCE   Jillian James
Anni Ross is totally committed to her career in dance. She's
positive that she's got no time to spare for falling in love! But
attractive lawyer Steve Hunter has other plans for Anni's
future . . .

SLOW DANCING   Elizabeth Smith
Hallie Prescott is plunged into the world of glitter and
glamour when she accompanies her screenwriter husband
to Hollywood. But it's not long before the dream goes sour.
Can Grant Keeler help Hallie rebuild her life?

THAT CINDERELLA FEELING   Anne Styles
Out of work actress Casey Taylor will take any job she can
find. Which is how she ends up delivering a kissagram to the
offices of Alex Havilland, a businessman who has no time
for frivolity and who is definitely *not* amused!

A DARKER SHADOW   Patricia Wilson
Amy Scott can handle any problem that the world of
computers throws at her. But when it comes to coping
with sudden and frightening events in her private life, she
doesn't know where to turn. Until her arrogant and disapproving boss Luc Martell decides to intervene . . .